MY BEAUTIFUL DANGEROUS

LAILA AMLANI

Print ISBN 979-8-9853233-0-6

Edited by John Hudspith
Cover design by Jodi L. Cobb of Dark City Designs

www.lailaamlani.com

Thank you for reading my debut novel.

My Beautiful Dangerous is a romantic suspense blended with tragedy, plot twists, and humor.

It contains dark themes, adult language, and explicit sex scenes. It is intended for readers 18+.

Possible Triggers: Sibling bullying/humiliation, mentions of physical and sexual abuse.

To my sister, Rosy, who has an opinion on everything and is usually (and annoyingly) right. She believes in me with an unwavering certainty, even on the occasions when I stop believing in myself. Without her encouragement and loving badgering, My Beautiful Dangerous would still be a work in progress.

There is no greater wisdom
than your own heart.
That can be a disturbing thought
if you have lost faith in your heart.
It can seem like a pronouncement
that if you cannot yet remember
that you are an Angel,
you will be forever entombed
in human dissatisfaction.
-Emmanuel

PROLOGUE

"She's trying to take it from me." Helena's voice rose to a whine, her pale blue eyes glittering with fake tears.

I glared at my older sister while she circled our small kitchen, honing in like the predator she was. Helena attacked like a shark. Just the faintest inkling of blood and she'd swoop in for the kill. And all too often, I was free-floating chum.

A lengthy breath did nothing to slow my heart rate while I followed her movements. I'd learned early on not to turn my back on her. So why hadn't I considered that before tearing out of my room to confront her? I knew better than to be so careless.

Show no weakness.

I had returned home from school to find my bedroom ransacked. Same old scene—scattered clothing, drawers upended, bed tossed. My initial concern had been for my computer, but after confirming its safety at the bottom of a box filled with graphic novels, I relaxed. Thank goodness Helena had no inclination for physical labor and even less for touching a book. Few things were safe from my older sister.

But my relief died when I realized what she had taken.

"You know that's a lie," I said. "*You* took it from *me*."

"Did not," she countered like an eight-year-old child. Even at age fourteen, I surpassed her in the maturity department. "You're always stealing my clothes and jewelry."

I gestured to her outfit. "Right... Because I love looking like a third-rate hooker."

She slapped me hard across the face. "One of these days, that smart mouth of yours is really going to piss me off."

I rubbed my burning cheek. That Helena recognized anything smart was a miracle, but I kept that thought to myself. There's a fine line between showing no weakness and being suicidal. My rebellious nature frequently resulted in bruises.

"Fine," I said. "Keep it. I don't care anymore."

"You're pathetic," Helena sneered. "You know you still want it. Admit that you want it, or you'll never see it again."

It had been worth a shot. While Helena's academic repertoire extended no further than lip gloss flavors, her street smarts—more like streetwalking smarts—weren't falling for my reverse psychology.

"Okay. I want it back."

She crossed her arms. "What's the magic word?"

I gritted my teeth. "Please."

She paused as if considering my request. "I have a better idea." She faced the doorway and called out, "Daddy! She did it again!"

Her well-rehearsed tone carried the perfect balance of victim and martyr and from the approaching footsteps, it had the desired effect. Not seconds later, his gigantic frame appeared in the cramped kitchen, swallowing up the confined space and rendering escape impossible.

I was trapped.

"What the hell did you do now?" my father belted out in a

voice graveled from years of smoking. His fingers curled around a bottle of Jim Beam, a sight as common as Lady Liberty holding her torch.

All fake sniffles and indignation, Helena raised her hand to point a red lacquer-tipped finger at me. "She's been stealing from me again."

He narrowed his blurry eyes. "You live in my house, eat my food, sleep under my roof, and this is how you repay me? By disrespecting this family?"

"I didn't do anything." I tried to explain, but from his unsteady gait and slurred speech, he'd hit the bottle early, which meant no reprieve. Even when he was sober, I never stood a chance.

"Look, Daddy." Helena pushed back her long blonde hair to reveal a lily-shaped pin fastened to her clingy angora sweater. *My* pin. Stolen from *my* room. Its silver and purple petals sparkled with merriment despite her ominous presence. "It's the only thing I have left from Mom," she whined. "She only wants it because she's jealous that Mom loved me and not her. She hates that Mom left it for me." Her eyes connected with mine from behind my father's broad shoulders, and her pout shifted into a smirk.

With no warning, he flung the bottle. I squealed and lunged to the side as it shattered against the cupboard, sending broken glass and cheap whiskey flying everywhere. My heart raced as I gripped the counter, watching for his next move.

Even the slightest reference to my mother ignited an uncontrollable rage in him. A fact Helena knew all too well, and her satisfied expression confirmed it.

Great, now he would blame me for destroying his booze, a crime worse than anything Helena pinned on me. As if on cue, he looked down at his empty hand and then at the mess on the floor.

I shot forward to zip past him, but with surprising reflexes for a drunk, he flung me back against the counter. Though my father had yet to lift anything heavier than a bottle in recent years, he somehow retained his athletic physique with no loss of strength. Strength he frequently targeted at me.

"You little ingrate," he spat. "This is all your fault."

I assumed he was referring to the bottle, but as the poster child for scapegoat-ism, I carried an extensive list of sins. His next statement clarified his grievance. "If it weren't for you, she'd still be here with me." He stepped forward and, reacting on instinct, I shuffled back and cried out when my bare foot stepped on a shard of glass. Helena laughed.

"You are the worst thing that ever happened to this family!" he boomed. "I can't stand the sight of you!"

I cast my eyes down as would an animal deferring to its alpha. After fourteen years, I'd learned a thing or two about taking a hit —physical and verbal. I burrowed inside myself, pushing to a plane of dissociation I'd perfected. A place where nothing could reach me because nothing mattered.

He leaned in and I braced for a blow. It didn't come. Instead, his warm breath brushed against my cheek. "Lucky for you, I'm giving you another chance to redeem yourself." Even with the heavy scent of alcohol in the air, my nose twitched at the stench of booze on him. "I have another job for you."

The statement made my guts wrench.

Of course, he wouldn't hurt me. Not when he needed me. Drunk and washed-up, his hard-core criminal days were over. But now that he'd discovered my gift, he would exploit it until his recklessness left me to face the consequences. He'd use me, break me, and cast me aside.

Just like he did our mother.

Satisfied, he turned and stalked out of the kitchen. No doubt in search of a replacement bottle.

It's time, my instincts interrupted. *An encore performance will destroy you. Do it. NOW!*

But I was a coward.

I pushed away the conflicting thoughts. I couldn't focus on that now. Not with my foot throbbing. I hopped on the counter to attend to my immediate need and winced at the embedded shard. At least I wouldn't need disinfectant.

A sharp chuckle interrupted, and I looked up to find Helena watching me.

Lovely on the outside with flawless skin and exquisite bone structure, my older sister appeared almost angelic. Until you dug deeper and discovered the adorable face belied a twisted darkness, a curse that flowed through our family blood.

"Why are you still here?" I asked. "You got your entertainment."

"If that were true, you'd be out on your ass by now," she said. "You're only here because Daddy feels sorry for you. He doesn't want you around. Nobody does. Not even your own mother wanted you."

I pretended the words glanced off me like pebbles when in fact, they hovered with the crushing weight of a boulder, always looming above me. No matter how many times I heard it, the abandonment stung.

Show no weakness.

"Leave me alone," I mumbled.

"How could anyone want you when there's nothing special about you except how annoying you are?" Helena continued, as if reciting indisputable facts from an encyclopedia, though she had never opened one in her life. "The sooner you pull your head out of your ass and get it, the easier all our lives will be." She sighed as if burdened by my ignorance.

I pretended to ignore her. Anything to make her go away.

Until she unfastened the lily pin.

A sliver of hope ran through me. With the show over, would she return it?

She held it away from her like it was contagious. Too bad it wasn't. Though, with the company she kept, it wouldn't be her first rash.

"I don't know why you keep this hideous piece of shit anyway," she sneered as she dangled the trinket in front of me. "It's been nine years since she left. For Christ's sake, get a clue. Even an idiot like you can figure out she never wanted you. Keeping junk around to remind you of her is just stupid. I'm doing you a favor."

She wedged it into the pocket of her skin-tight jeans.

My heart sank.

Nine long years since Mom had bailed and Dad had responded by crawling into a bottle. Nine slow, painful years filled with restless nights spent wondering what I'd done to drive her away. Nights spent praying for her to return—or for the bastard to drink himself into the grave and straight on to hell—but neither happened.

"So be a good girl." Helena walked towards me, careful to keep her stripper heels clean. "And say thank you."

I remained silent. For such an insolent bitch, she was big on 'pleases' and 'thank yous'.

She backhanded me. *Ouch.* Same side as before.

She raised her hand again and I quickly blurted, "Thank you."

Never pick a fight you can't win.

She turned away. "Now clean up your mess."

I entered my broom closet of a room and groaned at the wreckage. With barely enough space for my few splintered pieces of furniture, Helena's destruction somehow managed to outweigh that restriction. Hurricane Helena loved to do maximum damage.

What could a kid be hoarding that she wanted anyway?

The answer was simple. Anything that meant something to me.

Once, on one of my feistier and stupider days, I had installed a cheap drugstore lock. Not only had she smashed it to bits, but she also extended the violence to my face. Lesson learned. Helena could do whatever she damn well pleased around here. Even if that included ransacking my room then calling me a thief. The worst part? She was right. How else would a kid get her hands on an expensive laptop? Deep down, I was no better than the rest of them.

I heard the front door open followed by the click of slutty heels. Helena. Within the next hour, she'd be lying under some sweaty oaf, also known as her latest victim. She'd offer him her body and the poor sap would leap at the chance, unaware she'd take him for everything he had.

It ran in the family.

My dad's silence indicated he'd located more booze and was well into his nightly stupor. A virtual legend prior to taking up residence in a bottle, it was pathetic to see him now, but since conning clients out of their hard-earned savings required a clear and sober head, my dad was officially retired. One of the greats, defeated by a pedestrian vice and now reduced to petty cons on a good day.

Which is why he needed me to get it all back.

Helena was wrong about one thing. Daddy didn't let me stay out of pity. I earned my keep and the minute I stopped, I'd receive worse than a one-way ticket out on my ass.

Because even on his best days, he'd never come close to my talent—something I shouldn't take so much pride in.

His requests had started out small and when my compliance had led to a reduced number of bruises, my self-preservation rationalized it as harmless. But nothing stayed benign around here for long and what began as protection for my body eventually demanded payment from my soul.

That explained the sick, hollow feeling in the pit of my stomach at the mention of another job. What now? Use my skills to steal from another innocent who had the misfortune of getting on my father's bad side?

It's time. You can't do it again. Not for him.

I sighed. Either enact my plan or... what was the alternative? Stay until I died in this hellmouth? If Helena had her way, that would be sooner rather than later. How sad if I perished with nothing but the memories of a sadistic monster and his sadistic-monster-in-training sidekick.

That sobering thought had me digging in the box for my computer.

I may not deserve it, but I wanted more.

I almost backed down, much like the previous hundred times, but my options were dwindling. Now that he had an inkling of what I could do, the crimes were escalating. I'd already inflicted more damage and pain than I could atone for, but all that would be child's play if he ever learned the true depths of my capabilities.

I wasn't naïve enough to think I could survive in the world without committing more crimes—it was in my blood, and I was too damn good at it—but at least if I got the hell out of here, I'd dictate the terms. That accounted for something.

I focused on the screen but instead of words, images bounced across like characters in a video game. *Focus.* I shook my head.

So much for the information that's supposed to set me free.

I cast the computer aside and laid on my bed, shifting to accommodate a protruding spring. After years of sleeping on my sagging mattress, my body had conformed to the divots so well, it almost felt comfortable. I stayed in that position, well into the night, waiting until I heard nothing more than the sounds of a neglected house in the throes of collapse. Then I sprang—more like a weak shuffle—into action.

Like a well-researched intruder, I crept into Helena's bedroom, careful to avoid each creaking floorboard committed to memory. I halted at the bed and watched her sleep, mouth open, salivating. She mumbled something—which I assumed was evil—and rolled into her drool puddle.

If all the boys could see her now.

When I reached the dresser, I ignored the scattered condoms and inched open the ballerina jewelry box—*my* jewelry box. At one time, the tiny dancer twirled to Tchaikovsky's Nutcracker Suite, but the plastic doll had long since broken like everything else around here.

When my fingers brushed against the daintiest piece of jewelry amongst Helena's garish collection, I clutched it in a death grip. Confident, I sneaked back to my room and smiled at the lily pin, twinkling as if happy to be reunited with its rightful owner.

As much as I hated to agree with anything that bitch said, Helena had a point. Given the resentment I harbored for my mother, why did I keep it? Yet, in a rare show of sentiment, I coveted the cheap gift. It reminded me of a day in my childhood when innocence blinded me to the genuine nature of those around me. Before I learned I could only count on one person. Me.

Which meant if I didn't save myself now, nobody would.

I stuffed the pin in my pocket and returned to my laptop. This time, instead of gibberish, the concise information on the screen validated my decision. After playing this scenario multiple times in my mind, the execution seemed like a case of hard-core déjà vu.

I finished typing and paused, my hand trembling above the Send key. One more click and our lives would be irrevocably altered. Would it be for the best? Could it get any worse? I came close to mumbling a prayer but stopped before committing hypocrisy. God and I were not besties. What had He ever done for me?

CLICK

No going back now.

I packed my computer and swung my duffle bag over my shoulder. With as much stealth as my clumsiness allowed, I edged toward the living room. A cold sweat broke out when I saw him sprawled on the recliner, bombed out of his mind. If he woke, he would end me.

Unless I got to him first.

So many choices: smother, bludgeon, or plunge a knife into his black heart.

But none of them compared to what lay in store for him. He would pay. I'd make sure of it.

In the longest twenty seconds of what could be a stunted life, I tiptoed past my tormenter. When my hand gripped the doorknob, I fought the impulse to bolt.

The door squeaked open.

Shit.

I crouched down in the shadows and held my breath.

For all my planning, how hard would it have been to apply a little WD-40 in advance?

He didn't move.

In heart-pounding slow motion, I crawled slowly through the doorway. Once clear, I flung my bag over the rickety railing then followed, cursing when my shoulder hit the unforgiving ground.

With freedom only ten feet away, I belly crawled through the camouflage of neglected weeds—much like my avatar in Medal of

Honor. I emerged on the sidewalk and spun around, relieved to see nothing but the shadows of a decaying house.

My dilapidated childhood prison looked even worse from here. Sagging with age and rot, its shoulders hunched as if defeated by a weight too heavy to bear. I sympathized with it.

But no longer.

Because today was the last day I'd ever lay eyes on that godforsaken eyesore. Today marked a turning point—the day I seized my destiny, reinvented myself, and said goodbye to the girl I would never be again.

1

Sixteen years later...

I pushed open the door and stilled at the sounds—moaning, panting. *What the hell? Is James watching porn?*

A smile crept across my face. Why not? A little pre-dinner excursion sounded appealing. In fact, since our relationship amounted to nothing more than good sex, who cared if he started without me? I removed my heels and left them, along with my purse, in James' tiled foyer. With a seductive expression and a sway to my hips, I sneaked around the corner.

And froze.

James wasn't watching an X-rated movie, he was starring in one. A trail of clothing littered the living room's plush white carpet, ultimately leading to my pseudo-boyfriend, James, who lay sprawled naked on his back, his impressive body on display. A Hispanic bimbo, her face alive with pleasure, was sitting astride his face, gyrating her hips and bobbing to an unknown rhythm while some Asian chick, in a lacy red thong, devoured his erection like a popsicle on a scorching summer day.

"What the fuck is going on?" I shouted.

The participants jumped as one, and the Hispanic beauty rolled off my boyfriend's face. "Hey, Jaime. You didn't say you were married." She scowled, more annoyed with the interruption than the idea of a spouse.

James wobbled to his feet and attempted to take a step, but he stumbled and fell to his knees, giggling like a schoolboy. His spiked hair protruded in multiple directions and his handsome face glistened with the Hispanic woman's arousal. He blinked several times through blurry eyes—no doubt trying to determine which of the many versions in front of him was me. The idiot chose incorrectly and addressed the lamp. "Hey, Jasmine baby," he slurred and raised an arm. "Come on in. There's room for one more."

Am I being punked? Is my half-ass excuse for a boyfriend asking me to join his rendition of *Girls Gone Slutty*? I waited for a camera crew to leap out and yell "Gotcha!" but nothing happened. Instead, the Asian and Hispanic beauties knelt to the floor, their lips meeting in a long, lingering kiss.

At least he's an equal opportunity cheater.

They toppled over in a tangled pile of sweaty limbs, bare thighs, arms, and breasts. The scene burned hot and even bordered on erotic, if not for the envy that surged at the sight of their flawless, unmarred skin. That, and the unrepentant douchebag in the mix. James had propped his back against the couch to hold up his drunk ass, his bloodshot eyes fixated on the spectacle. A string of drool hung from his open mouth.

With a derisive snort, I marched back towards the exit and scooped up my bag and shoes. The moaning started up again before the door slammed behind me.

I emerged on the street and shuddered from the unexpected burst of frigid air. After sixteen years, you'd think I'd have acclimated to New York weather, but as much as I loved the seasons, my California blood still rebelled at the icy temperatures. Where I came from, we had two seasons—hot and not so hot.

At times like this, I missed the Pacific Ocean. As a kid, few things soothed me like the sound of waves crashing onto the shore, the palpable taste of salt with every inhale, and the feel of cold sand squished between my toes. I briefly debated heading towards the beach but quashed the thought. To try and recreate one of my few pleasant childhood memories would only bring disappointment.

Instead, I robotically joined the faceless throngs of pedestrians in their ant-march formation. A young guy deviated from the fray and jostled my shoulder. "Hey, lady, watch it," he snapped, not bothering with eye contact.

"Watch yourself, jackass," I shot back.

That Manhattan trait I'd embraced far quicker.

Loud laughter drifted from a small bar on the corner. From the looks of it, the occupants' ages on their fake IDs exceeded their IQs. Not surprising since James lived in a sought-after neighborhood near the university. He insisted the location boasted culture, but from the age of those slutty girls in his apartment, more likely it provided willing coeds.

I considered stopping for a drink. Wasn't that the normal response to finding your boyfriend cheating? Waltz through the doors, sidle up to the bar, and order a shot of indignation with a chaser of self-pity?

But James was nothing more than a distraction. And an expendable one. I expected this behavior. After all, he was a man. They lied, cheated, and screwed everything not nailed down. Hell, my father's mistresses could have been collectibles the way he displayed them. In fact, I was convinced scientists would someday discover the Y chromosome carried an infidelity gene. Men only wanted one thing—a sexual diversion. On the plus side, the sex made for a temporary respite from the prevailing numbness inside of me.

With all the secrets I held, allowing any man to infiltrate my world would be as stupid as trusting one. Any woman gullible enough to believe in a man only had herself to blame when it all came crashing down.

It's that kind of awareness that saved me from getting sloppy drunk in a random bar during the afternoon.

Besides, I preferred solitude.

Given my secrets, I required it.

Given my actions, I deserved it.

I approached a patch of grass New Yorkers laughingly called a park and raised my arm. Within seconds, a taxi came to my rescue. Too much exercise was bad for the brain. I gave the driver my address, settled back, and spent the drive home checking emails.

The apartment building stood tall against the East River backdrop, nice enough to rent for a small fortune, but not nice enough to provide an attendant. I pulled open the heavy glass door then paused when I spotted Mr. Atherton at the mailbox, his beautiful Golden Retriever obediently at his feet. When the dog noticed me, her tail whooshed in windmill circles with excitement. Mr. Atherton shuffled over, a smile on his craggy face. "Barbara and I appreciate you watching Ginger last week." He gestured towards the dog, now blanketing my legs with a thick layer of golden fur.

"My pleasure." I hunkered down to scratch behind her ears. An enormous pink tongue whipped out followed by a full-face slobber. Laughing, I hugged her close.

A shame humans aren't wired for this type of unconditional love.

"Barbara baked you a surprise. She dropped it off with—" His brows furrowed. "Are you okay, dear? You look out of sorts."

"My sorts have never been more in," I assured him and rose.

With a last pat on Ginger's head, I stepped into the elevator. "Thank you for the treats."

I entered my apartment and inhaled the delicious aromas of chocolate, coffee, and oranges. Having one of New York's top chefs as a roommate wreaked hell on the waistline but came with undeniable perks.

"Hey, Jas, did you hack that junior chef's records for me?" Nicki emerged from the kitchen, wiping her hands on her favorite apron. The one that had *If you want to kiss the cook, you can kiss my kiester* scrawled across the chest in red letters. "France, my ass. Everything she sautés makes Ginger's food look appetizing. Once I get the truth, I'm gonna take her lies and shove them up her—" Her baby blues narrowed. "Wait, didn't you have a date tonight?"

I nodded.

"Let me guess. You found that ass-hat in bed with someone."

I plopped on the overstuffed couch and kicked my heels across the scarred wood floor. Nicki had crafted an oasis in the middle of Manhattan. Sheer white curtains framed tall windows that filled the spacious room with sunlight. The polished honey-colored furniture gleamed which explained the citrus scent in the air. A smattering of blooming plants added to the nature illusion while Nicki's colorful artwork—from every phase imaginable—brightened the walls. I dug my toes into the plush rug and felt my muscles unwind.

I held up two fingers.

"A threesome?" she shrieked, her crazy blonde curls vibrating with outrage. "That dick-wielding, slutty jackhole. We'll tag that two-timing—no, three-timing punk ass's car, tell everyone he's impotent, break into his mailbox and steal his Netflix movies."

Did I dare tell her everyone was streaming nowadays? Nah. What she lacked in revenge skills, she more than made up for with loyalty.

"Before you break any federal laws on my behalf, I've got it covered." I scanned the immaculate room. "Where's my computer?" She had this annoying habit of putting everything in its place. And not just objects.

"You can add him to the NSA's watchlist later. I'd rather talk about you." She tilted her head and scrutinized my face. "You seem okay but... I'm not going to wake up in the middle of the night to find you mumbling nonsense while swimming in a vat of Swiss Almond Vanilla ice cream, am I?"

That sounded good regardless of the circumstances.

I waved her off. "I don't care about him. I'm a little pissed at being disrespected, but it's not a big deal."

"I never liked him much," Nicki muttered. "Not that you would have known since I make it a point to not butt into your love life."

I let out a sharp laugh. She was about as subtle as that insane mop of hair on her head. "Doesn't matter now. Moving on. He's history." Which is what I hoped this conversation would become. "Are we done here?"

"No, because I'm worried about you," she sighed. "Look, Jas, I realize you need more than one person for an intervention, but since I'm your only friend, it falls on me. Why do you go for such losers when there are better men out there? I don't get it." Nicki shook her head and her curls bounced long after she stopped. I swear, they looked as confused as she did.

"Because people suck." Once you accepted basic human nature as a cesspool of greed and power, it lost its ability to hurt you. A brilliant strategy for surviving this life, one which I highly recommended.

"Then what about me?" she asked. "If people are so bad, explain how amazingly awesome I am."

No lack of self-esteem there. "Yes. You're one in a billion," I said while a twinge in my gut reminded me that she knew nothing about the real me. If she learned about my past, she'd hightail her amazingly awesome self out of here so fast, her curls would be the slowest moving part of her. And then I would be relegated to doing what I did best. Being alone.

"Damn right," Nicki said, "So if there's a female one in a billion, why can't there be a male version out there?"

I sank further into the couch and closed my eyes. "In theory, you have a point, however, based on your own math, the odds are better for winning the lottery, getting struck by lightning, and Ed McMahon knocking on my door holding a comically huge cardboard Publishers Clearinghouse check—all on the same day." I opened one eye. "Did I mention Ed McMahon died in 2009?" I reached out to tug a blonde spiral. *Boing.*

She slapped my hand away. She hated when I messed with her curls, but I couldn't resist. While my thick, dark hair hung down my back and garnered many compliments, her zany golden coils mesmerized me with their unruly wildness. They reminded me of curly fries.

"Stop worrying. I'm fine. I like being promiscuous. We both know I'm not an attachment type of girl. Hell, I barely tolerate people. I'm happy being alone." Or maybe I just accepted it. Was there even a difference?

"Then why are you with me?"

"Because you gave me no choice." For some bizarre reason, the moment Nicki had focused her large blue eyes on me, her bizarre brain destined us to be friends and, similar to a puppy that follows you home, her relentless attachment eventually wore me down. When she added a rational argument regarding Manhattan's exorbitant rents, poof... I gained my first roommate and friend. As it turned out, she proved better company than my demons.

Except for this moment. Right now, she was annoying the hell out of me.

"And I was right back then, which means I'm right now," she insisted. "What kind of friend would I be if I let you go on this way?"

"The best kind that minds her own business?"

"Geez, you're even surlier than usual." She shot me a scowl. "Maybe we can counteract that bitterness with something sweet. Don't move." She sprang to her feet and disappeared into the kitchen to retrieve whatever culinary cure her chef's mind assumed would solve the world's problems.

I debated running but propped my feet on the table instead. She'd only follow. Ironic that, after a lifetime of no one giving a damn about me, I wound up with a mother hen roommate. Her concern was almost laughable, yet mildly touching. But it was too little, too late. I was beyond saving. Now, if I could only convince her of that.

Nicki returned carrying a plate piled high with chocolate brownies—also known as diabetes on a platter—and a bag of Cheetos. She tossed the latter at me. "Here. These always improve your mood." She settled beside me, grabbed a chocolate square, and critiqued it as if judging *Top Chef.* She nibbled a corner and I hoped, for Mrs. Atherton's sake, it passed muster. "Eh." She shrugged and then gobbled half the brownie, a zealous response for such a lukewarm review. Crumbs spewed from her mouth as she talked. "You know what your problem is?"

"I hope that's a rhetorical question, or we'll be here awhile."

"You need to learn to dream bigger, girl."

One of the most dangerous phrases in the English language.

I ripped the bag open and popped a Cheeto in my mouth. Unlike her, I waited until I'd swallowed before speaking. "Since when did you convert to hopeless idealism?"

"Are you insinuating lesbians can't be romantics?" She devoured another bite, and the air danced with crumbs.

I lifted a corner of her apron to dust my face. I had long ceased wondering how she kept the place OCD pristine. "No. I'm stating that *you* can't be. Not when all your girlfriends require a high tolerance for abuse."

She kicked me and my feet slipped off the smooth surface to land on the floor with a thud. They smelled like lemon now. "Although, you may have the right idea about the whole lesbian thing," I mused. "Life would be better without men." Except for sex. Dammit. Why did I like sex so much?

For all her disinterest in the male race, Nicki attracted her fair share of them. With her heart-shaped face, wild mane, and all that padding in the right places, it was comedic bearing witness to guys tripping over themselves to get her attention. They had no clue. And no chance.

Compared to her, I considered my willowy frame more stick-figure chic. Not that I suffered any neglect. Men mistook the haunted shadows and defiance in my cobalt eyes for broody.

Dumbasses.

"This is your fault," Nicki explained as she returned her half-eaten brownie to the plate. She licked each finger clean. "You attract that which you expect."

"Confucius?"

"Fortune cookie," she flashed me a toothy smile covered in brownie goo. "Start believing you deserve more and see what happens."

Although I lived in a state of lies, that one was even too tall for me to swallow. "Has anyone ever explained that low expectations are the key to happiness?"

"If yours were any lower, you'd need a backhoe." She wagged a finger in my face, making my eyes cross. "Doesn't it bother you that your entire dating life reads like a cautionary tale?"

"Nope, because it's not dating. It's sex." And self-absorbed men didn't care enough to ask questions.

"Come on, Jas. Relearn what you think you know, adopt a new paradigm, embrace the world."

I resisted the urge to leap up and yell "Hallelujah!" Instead, I pointed at the television. "Now that you're on dinner shift, you're addicted to Oprah again, aren't you?"

"That's irrelevant." Nicki wiped her hands on her apron and sat up straight. "There is more out there, and I will prove it to you. We will crack through that wall of cynicism by finding you a decent man."

"And how do you propose to do that? Take a dog catcher net to the street?" *Here, Perfect Man that doesn't exist. Here, Perfect Man that doesn't exist...*

A gleam entered Nicki's eyes and my blood pressure jumped. That expression often preceded some cockamamie idea that usually ended with regret, embarrassment, and on one occasion, bail. I still received Christmas cards from my former jail acquaintance, a lovely woman named Snake.

"You're going to play the opposite game," she began. "When you're tempted to act on your natural tendencies..." She shot me a pointed look. "Don't."

"You mean like how I'm pretending to listen right now?"

She rolled her eyes. "Left with your own judgment, you'll tumble into bed with the first unscrupulous jerk-off who flashes his ding-dong at you and when he fucks around, you'll thank him for validating your misguided theories. As of today, your options are nice men and vibrators. Preference on the former."

I made a mental note to buy more batteries. "Give me some credit. It's not like I'd hop into a van over a six pack of abs."

"Of course not. Your supercomputer brain analyzes the pros and cons of getting out of bed every morning."

I couldn't fathom an alternate way of life, because I never had the freedom of choice. Probably because my actions always carried dire consequences. Sometimes I caught myself wishing for a taste of the liberty Nicki enjoyed, but the difference between wishes and wrenches was one of them had a use. The world did not succumb to your wants. You played with the hand dealt and if they rigged the game, you folded and lived to play another round. My life demanded restraint. A fate I accepted.

So why did that thought suffocate my insides like a veil of cursed smoke I couldn't exhale? I blew out a sharp breath. "Nicki, just leave things alone."

"I get why you're nervous. It's new. Just have a little faith."

Faith. Hopes. Dreams. The language equivalent to carnival milk bottles. Prop them up and an endless stream of people will line up to knock them down. Only a fool would continually rebuild them.

And for all my vices, I was not a fool.

"As much as I'd love to sit around and justify my life choices, I have things to do."

"For God sakes, Jasmine. Stop deflecting. You may be the genius here, but even I can see that you're being unreasonable. Don't you get that I care about you? I just want you to be happy."

The sincere tone in her perpetually joking voice stopped me. She wanted more for me than I did for myself and unchecked, that sentiment cut deep. I wanted to explain how happiness didn't exist for people like me, people who came from where I did. Trust was dangerous and trusting someone like me even more so. I shut the urge down. The last thing I wanted to do was drag someone as good-hearted as Nicki into my world. Besides, I couldn't bear to see condemnation replace the friendship in her eyes.

Misinterpreting my guilt for acquiescence, she played her

trump card. "Promise me or you will never see a Better Than Sex Chocolate Cake again." She grinned. She knew she had me.

"You wouldn't." My eyes widened in mock horror. Nicki baked a sinful concoction so incredible, I swear it caused an orgasm. "That's low. Even for you."

"I'll up the ante. All your favorite desserts." She pointed at Barbara's generous attempt. "I'll bake the crap out of that. Your dentist will hate me."

I sighed. Nicki's persistence rivaled a dog with a bacon-wrapped cat, which meant my chance of escape ranked almost as high as my hand-delivered check from Ed McMahon.

"Fine," I grumbled. "But only long enough to prove *you* wrong. I am not abstaining forever from the only thing men are good for."

She draped an arm around me. "Awww. Stop sulking like you've been sentenced to the gallows. Good guys know how to fuck too. Maybe not like the bad ones, but missionary is a classic for a reason."

I pitied the women she'd lure in—or bash on the head and duct tape.

"Just do everything I tell you," she said.

"Cause a lesbian knows so much about men," I mumbled.

"I can't do worse." With a satisfied nod, she rose and darted into the kitchen again. I heard a cupboard slam before she returned, holding up a bottle of cheap tequila and two glasses. "To no more screw-ups. Drink up, girlie."

Ugh! Why do construction crews work so damn early? I buried my head in the pillow and sputtered at the mouthful of carpet fibers. My eyes flew open, and I blinked a few times before the living room ceiling came into view. The jackhammer wasn't outside, it was drilling into my skull. I rolled to my side while the room plotted against me and tilted in the other direction. A sliver of sunlight reflected against an object, and I squinted until the outline of the tequila bottle sharpened. It mocked me with its smug face—er, label. "Shut up." I kicked it across the room.

I thought about lying and calling in sick, but since I worked for myself, that idea fell beyond idiotic. That's the price of owning your own business—no time, no sanity, no money, and if you're smarter than I am... no tequila. I dragged myself up and teetered to the bathroom.

Why couldn't James keep it in his pants until the weekend? Inconsiderate prick.

I chose my favorite outfit, a black pencil skirt paired with a red silk blouse. I pulled my hair back, applied makeup, and fastened the lily pin. I evaluated the finished product. *Whoa!* Whoever said dressing well elevated the spirit had never succumbed to the evil pleasures of Mexican liquor. My splotchy face, red-rimmed dark blue eyes, and rug patterns etched in my skin added a whole new visual to the word 'hungover'.

Nicki entered to find me tugging sections of hair over my face. "What are you doing?"

"Going for the Cousin It look," I said from behind a thick curtain of tangles.

"Come on. You're more beautiful half-drunk than most women on a normal day." She snatched the hairbrush from my hand. "I'll fix it."

"It's beyond resuscitation." I stepped away and secured it in a messy bun. "I'll just be working on the Lyndham bid anyway." With the potential for my biggest contract looming, I planned on sequestering myself all day to work on my proposal.

I reached down for my sandals and stumbled as the room hopped to the left. "I meant to do that."

"That account is a big deal. You sure you want to touch it when putting on shoes requires a balancing act?"

Maybe not the smartest endeavor in my current state, but when it came to writing code, I could spare a few brain cells. I slipped on a pair of less complicated flats. "No problem. I'm on it like lipstick on the collar of one of my ex-boyfriends."

"Funny," she said. "But not anymore. Not after your promise last night."

I groaned. I was hoping the liquor had killed her memories of that nonsense. My frown deepened as I noticed her white shorts, pink tank top, and glowing complexion. "How can you be so perky after last night?"

She grinned. "Genetics. Now move over and let me fix your makeup. You look like a raccoon coming off a bender."

She was only half wrong.

I decided to walk the six blocks to my office, trusting the fresh air would do my head some good. My plan worked and like the bolt of lightning that shocked Frankenstein's monster, the familiar frequency crackling through the city air sparked my tequila-soaked brain to life. Maybe Nicki's suspicions were correct, and I was more machine than human. A thought that should have bothered me more.

When I reached the sleek glass building, I wasted no time taking the elevator up to the suite I rented.

Monroe Security Software Consulting.

It never got old.

I entered to a vacant reception area, thankful I'd given my assistant, Sue, the week off to party at a punk rock concert in Florida. When I entered my office, I laughed at the bag of Flaming Hot Cheetos propped on my desk, stuck to an orange Post-It.

Some brain food while you get cracking on Lyndham. I want a bonus.
-Sue

Five hours of programming later and my muscles groaned, threatening to go on strike without a well-deserved stretch. I obliged by standing and reaching for the ceiling. I loved my work and could go on for days, but sometimes my body protested my methods.

The moment I'd touched my first computer, something in the world finally made sense. Almost like a kindred spirit, we forged a bond rooted in logic and predictability, traits no human possessed. And when I finally worked up the nerve to leave the hellhole I called home, my natural talent afforded me an income—maybe not a legal one, but it beat sleeping on the streets. My computer had been my lifesaver.

I had just sat back down when the outer door chirped. I ignored it. Most likely a solicitor. Without Sue at the front desk, they would leave.

Not this one.

Footsteps grew closer. "Not interested," I said as I looked up. "Don't care what you're selling, I'm—"

My mouth fell open as I stared at the doorway.

My sister, Helena, stared back.

2

I'm still drunk. I rattled my head hard enough to dislodge brain matter, but my ailment remained standing in front of me. Its eyes raked me over, and the confidence I'd cultivated through the years vanished in a puff of insecurity. Her eyes narrowed at the lily pin.

Show no weakness.

"Nice digs," she said, and I cringed at the voice I hoped never to hear again. "Pretty color on the walls."

Show no—

"Huh?" After sixteen years, my recurring nightmare strolls in and... *comments on my decorating?*

A wave of hysteria threatened to erupt. Barely a few words from her and I was already losing it. I glanced behind her. Maybe I could I make it to the door before—?

Show no weakness.

The ease in which my childhood mantra resurfaced pissed me off.

For fuck's sake, stop it. You are not a child anymore. Act like it.

But the tequila-soaked brownies churning in my stomach disagreed.

She cocked her head. "My how you've grown, *Ms. Monroe.* I barely recognized you."

But she had. Which means somewhere along the way, I screwed up. But how? I'd executed my plan with flawless precision. Or so I thought.

"How did you find me?" I asked.

"Who cares?" She settled in a leather chair and crossed her legs. "I'm here now."

I returned her scrutiny and begrudged that the years had been generous. Her tight jeans, leather high-heeled boots, and snug sweater mimicked her attire as a teen, except now they boasted designer labels. She wore her pale blonde hair shorter with the ends skimming her shoulders, and her makeup a tad more professional, but her eyes remained the same—capable of freezing you from the inside. Still beautiful. Still cold.

"Relax," she said, no doubt referring to the horror plastered on my face. "Can't I reconnect with my little sister?"

Was she for real? *Hi sis, never mind all the cruel things I did to you as a child. Let's be BFFs now.*

She was out of her fucking mind.

My body tensed, ready for a fight. "I've built a new life, so if you're here to cause problems, get on with it."

"Don't be so dramatic." She settled deeper into the chair as if hunkering down for a lengthy visit. "But I am curious. Where did you go?"

"Who cares? I'm here now." Her eyebrows shot up at my response. "How did you think this would go?" I continued. "You show up and I welcome you with arms wide?"

"What else do you want?"

An apology for starters, maybe some groveling, a little

remorse, a dash of repentance.

Instead, she spoke as if bestowing a gift. "I'm giving you the chance to start afresh." Her smile made the hairs on the back of my neck prickle. A pseudo-pleasant Helena rattled more than a vindictive one.

"No." I shook my head. "You're not that good an actress."

Her face twisted. "For Christ's sake, it's been years. Quit being a bitch and get over it already."

Ah, there she is.

"Why are you here?" I repeated though I expected zero truth. Helena liked to keep you guessing. At one time, I misconstrued her tactic as erratic but after numerous strikes, I discovered her strategy. How do you prepare for an attack you can't predict?

"I'm getting married this summer," she announced, "and you're going to be there as a bridesmaid."

I blinked. Of all the words I imagined spewing from her vituperative mouth, that fell between "I know I'm an evil bitch" and "I will stab myself with a sword in shame." I waited for a cackle, but her face remained stoic.

Holy shit! She's serious. And insane.

"You can't think...?" I trailed off. "Why in the name of all that is holy would you want that?"

"I need family support and I have no one but Gabriella."

"You're still in contact with that idiot?" Vapid, superficial, and slutty, Helena's childhood best friend had always trailed after her like a dog, though not as smart or trainable.

"At least she stuck around when everything went to shit," Helena shot back. "You weren't there when the cops came banging on our door. You didn't hear the whispers or see the finger pointing every time I went out in public. You don't know anything because you had a tantrum and ran off like a baby. As usual, you had it easy while I lost everything."

Bile crept up my throat and I pushed it down, but like my past, it wouldn't stay there. "You managed fine." I gestured to her outfit. Her handbag alone cost more than half my closet.

"I did what I had to, to make it out of Riverside."

Knowing her, she did *who* she had to. "Even if I wanted to help, which I don't, I'm not going anywhere near that city again."

"God, no." Her slim shoulders shuddered. "You couldn't pay me enough to go back there."

I blinked in surprise. Her memories of home must be tarnished. It took a lot for Helena to decline a buck. I pried open my mind to allow for the possibility that what she endured had changed her. Maybe she was here to put the past behind us.

Ouch! My brain snapped shut.

Never let your guard down.

"I live in San Diego now with my fiancé, Phil. He's perfect—tall, gorgeous, athletic." Helena's face brightened and, in that moment, she almost resembled a human. "And his family is fucking loaded."

And the moment ended.

She extended her left hand to display a diamond capable of feeding a third world country for a year. "His large and extremely loaded family will be at the wedding. If Phil and I have any chance at that inheritance, I must meet their asinine requirements. Number one being family. I need to appear stable."

"Why waste your time with me? You need a miracle worker."

Helena's eyes chilled another degree. "I see your smart mouth hasn't changed."

I shrank back. Always pushing boundaries.

"I need family there," she continued. "And with everyone else gone, you're it."

The request confused me, but one thing remained clear. My need to get away from her. "No. It's a horrible idea."

"It's *my* idea," she said as if that made it better.

"It will never work."

"Why? Because you're a terrible actress?" She waved her hand around. "All this proves otherwise."

"That's not it." I was an exceptional liar. A fact I never disputed. Although if I did, you would believe me. That's how good I was.

"Then what?" She leaned forward, eyes zeroed in, waiting to shoot down any excuse.

"Because... er..." I couldn't think with her looking at me like that. Like she wanted to leap over the desk and smack me for old times' sake. But I was bigger now. Could I take her in a physical altercation?

What the hell are you thinking? Planning a street brawl with your sister?

How many times did I have to remind myself I was an adult now?

I reached for the first excuse. "Because Jasmine Monroe has no siblings."

"I see your smart mouth isn't the only thing that hasn't changed. You're still as dense as ever. I don't want you there as my *sister*," she said the word as if swallowing something bitter. "She disappeared years ago." The sharp glint in her eyes vanished, and I watched with fascination as grief softened her features, the quivering lower lip a nice touch. If there was a formula for distress, she had perfected it.

Hell, if I hadn't known better, I may have offered my condolences.

Before I could blink, she morphed back to her bitchy self. "Why would I want my missing sister returned when I haven't come close to exhausting the sympathy mileage your little stunt bought me? I can play that card for years."

No surprise there. Grifting was our second language.

"If my absence set you up so well, why do you want me back?"

"Don't be delusional. No one *wants* you in their life, but there is a role you were born to play."

Victim.

I pushed the word out of my head. Not now. Not again.

"And what is that?"

"Whatever I say it is," she answered with a smirk. "You will come as my cousin, someone who grew up with me. You can confirm what a delightful child I was, and how my loyalty to family never wavered even after they betrayed me." She gave me a pointed look. "They will eat that shit up."

"Why not ask Gabby?"

"She's the best friend/maid of honor. Phil's family judges people on familial ties, not friendships. And Gabby's too unpredictable to play anything but herself."

Finally, something we agreed on, though I preferred the word 'psycho'.

"So hire someone."

"You're missing the point, little sis. Any idiot can take the job for a buck, but only a person with something to lose brings commitment. The greater the cost, the better the puppet." She perused my office again, this time with excruciating slowness. "I can't imagine Fed scrutiny would be good for your quaint little business. A shame if the truth came out, *Jasmine Monroe*... interesting choice of names, by the way." She smiled, revealing pointy shark teeth. In reality, they were probably normal, but I never saw them any other way. "Are you willing to give all this up over a silly grudge? Even you can't be that petty."

She may not have been tossing my room anymore, but the message remained the same. 'I can do whatever the fuck I want to you whenever I damn well feel like it'. A bead of sweat trickled down my back.

She uncrossed her legs and leaned forward. "Stop being so damn selfish. You owe me. You bailed like a chicken-shit just before everything hit the fan. We lost everything while you were off creating this make-believe bullshit fairy tale that you don't deserve. Consider yourself lucky that I'm letting you keep it."

I gripped my desk to keep from recoiling. God help me if she ever found out why she lost it all. What I had done.

Never pick a fight you can't win.

But something was off this time. Helena's sadistic plots usually yielded instant gratification. She never played the long game. Being that she possessed no virtues, patience was not one of her traits, which meant there was more going on. If she wanted a dancing monkey, she'd be cranking up the music. She needed me for something more.

The memory of the last time someone used me for personal gain flashed in my mind. My father forcing me to hurt people. It had nearly broken me. That was never supposed to happen again.

The thought of him chilled me, but I shook it off. He wasn't here. But his little protégé was and she rolled her wicked eyes. "I don't know why you're making this so complicated. Do what I say, and I'll keep your secret."

"Gabby too?"

"She'll do what I say. Bitch can't get dressed without me."

That explains the Wonder Twins slut outfits they wore.

"How do I know you'll keep your word?"

"Trust me."

The skepticism must have shown on my face.

She sneered. "I'll have the life I deserve, and you'll still be nothing. Why would I give a shit about you after that?"

After years of drifting, I had accomplished the impossible and created a life for myself as Jasmine Monroe, a woman no longer ruled by fear and emotions. It was time to put her to the test. I quieted my mind and processed the options like a supercomputer.

Declining meant blowing up my world around me. Not the best choice.

Go through with the farce and maybe she'd leave me be. Unlikely.

Figure out what she wasn't saying and somehow use it against her. Possibly.

Or in the likely event she screwed me, start over again. I'd already done it once as a kid. Doing it now would be much easier. I already had a contingency plan in place.

I wasn't helpless anymore.

God, I hated that I had to keep reminding myself of that.

But I was about to prove it. "Fine." I lifted my chin. "Let's do this."

"I have a few hours before my flight." She glanced at her Cartier watch. "Let's go to your place. I'm dying to see how Jasmine Monroe lives."

Something told me she already knew.

I raced back into the apartment to answer the ringing phone and winced at the caller ID. Helena had sent instructions about the bridesmaid's dress a week ago, but with the Lyndham presentation looming, I'd skimmed a few words and remembered even less. Plus, I suffered from the added disadvantage of not giving a damn.

"Hi, Helena." I visualized her pacing the floor, dressed in an outfit from this month's designer tramp catalog.

Helena's voice crackled. "Why haven't you picked up your dress? Are you trying to screw things up for me?"

Right. Because I commit all my actions with the sole purpose of inconveniencing you.

"I've been busy with work. I'll swing by the dress shop later."

"Don't bother," she said. "I figured you'd be difficult, so I shipped the dress to your office. You'll get it today. I would have sent it to your home, but I don't trust your homo roommate."

I rolled my eyes. Nicki and Helena had taken to each other like Jell-O and mustard. Nicki expressed no inhibitions in her contempt for Helena's bitchiness, and homophobic Helena returned the favor.

"Are you listening?" Helena snapped.

No.

"If it needs alterations, take it in today."

"No need," I said. "Nicki is a whiz with clothing. She can handle a few stitches."

I imagined Helena's face pinched and waited for her objection, but she moved on.

"What's your date wearing? I don't want him clashing with the dress. If he's with you, he obviously has poor taste."

"I'm going solo."

"Of course you are," she retorted. "Who would put up with you? Normal people have no problem getting a date, but you're a special kind of loser. If it were me, I'd have men fighting each other for the chance. In fact, when Phil and I met..."

I groaned. Here we go again. I'd heard enough of this saga at our previous meeting. "Helena," I attempted to cut her off. "I know someone I can ask." No one sprang to mind but anything to shut her up.

But she was on a roll. "...and then Phil asked me to..."

I walked into the kitchen.

"...so I told him..."

I opened the cupboard.

"...and no man would dare..."

I grabbed the aluminum foil.

"...because they worship..."

I ripped off a sheet.

"...because I am so..."

Crackle, crackle.

"Helena, I'm losing you."

Crackle, crackle.

"I'm going through a tunnel," I said.

"But I called your home phone."

I hung up on my bitch of a sister.

As promised, the box arrived at my office late morning. I treated the package as if it contained anthrax and left it on the floor where I swear it emitted ominous pulses. By lunchtime, I couldn't postpone the inevitable any longer.

How bad could it be?

I ripped open the package as if tearing off a Band-Aid and gasped at the dark purple lace and taffeta.

Bad! Very bad!

I stood in the bathroom down the hall from my office and stared at my reflection in horror.

Did Helena purchase this thing out of a demented fairy tale catalog?

Its short sleeves puffed out from the shoulders, ending at the elbows in a cinched band of stiff lace that clawed into my skin. The smooth, high, square-cut bodice clutched my chest so tightly, I expected an oxygen mask accessory. It would make a porn star look flat chested. And the skirt. Dear Lord, where to begin? The English language didn't have enough synonyms for 'hideous'. It fell to the floor in an abundance of spiky, sharp, lacy tiers that looked like a Christmas tree with anger issues.

You can dangle ornaments off me.

I debated which was worse—the pain in my arms, my

constricted chest, or the burning in my eyes from that which could never be unseen.

No reason to panic. Maybe if I smooth down these ruffles, push my boobs up, fluff a little here and... Holy hell! Either I shifted to a fun-house mirror or I made Satan's prom dress look worse—a feat a mere mortal would deem impossible. The taffeta tiers now shot straight out as if the dress had stuck a lacy appendage in a light socket.

I conceded defeat. Round one went to the eggplant-colored dress.

I poked my head out and swiveled as if preparing to cross a major highway. A couple steps and I tripped over the hem and slammed into the wall. Damn dress was programmed to cause maximum damage. With relief, I reached my door and attacked it like a lifeline.

It didn't open.

Oh no. This can't be happening.

Jasmine Monroe, genius computer security expert, just locked herself out of her own fucking office. The irony would have made me laugh if not for the lack of air in my lungs.

I retraced my steps and closed the bathroom door. The only spare keys to my office belonged to Nicki and the building maintenance officer. With my phone still on my desk—next to my normal clothes—that left the latter, twenty-five floors below.

I weighed the options. Venture downstairs either wearing the eggplant dress or not wearing it. Dress or underwear? A tough decision, but ultimately, I chose the one with no jail time. Unless the fashion police showed up. Then we were looking at life with no parole.

In an imitation of the Frogger video game, I confirmed an empty hallway, darted out, and toppled over the basketball player-length hem. I considered the stairwell, but with the high risk of hyperventilating or a nasty tumble, I eliminated that option. Neither ailment bothered me so much as being found unconscious wrapped in the eggplant.

I scurried towards the elevator and pressed the button.

Come on! Come on!

I shuffled from one foot to the other then smacked the plastic circle until my thumb hurt.

Slowest goddamn elevator in Manhattan.

I tried everything—cursing, scowling, even a kick—but the elevator remained impervious to my dilemma.

Patience. Deep breath.

Nope. Lungs smashed. Stop breathing.

That's when I heard voices.

Please be another personality in my head.

I strained to listen. Dammit! People. And they were getting louder.

Please don't be a client.

Additional voices mingled in.

A group?

Shit! Open, open, open.

Laughter. More talking. Moving closer.

Come on. Open.

I could make out their conversations now. Around five, maybe six people, laughing over a joke.

One last corner and they'd have a new joke to laugh at.

My reputation would be toast.

Ding.

Woo-hoo! I sprang between the opening doors and plastered myself against the wall. With closed eyes, I offered a mental congratulatory high five.

"Why do I suddenly feel underdressed?" a deep voice spoke.

Fucking hell. I wasn't alone.

3

I jumped, stumbled over the hem, and landed hard… on my ass. A tanned, muscled arm appeared, and I accepted the lifeline which effortlessly hauled me to my feet. “Floor?” the voice asked.

“Um, two, please,” I mumbled and smoothed down the dress for no apparent reason other than to avoid eye contact until my embarrassment subsided. Realizing that may not happen for months, I gave up and glanced at my fellow occupant.

And did a double take at the gorgeous specimen of a man. At five-foot ten, I wasn’t a short woman, yet he bested me by at least six inches. His thick, jet-black hair hung slightly longer than conventional and curled around the nape of his neck. A few strands flopped over his face in a charmingly boyish fashion, although, given the raw masculinity he emanated, no one would dare associate the word ‘boyish’ with him. His white T-shirt allowed a view of defined arms while displaying an ornate tattoo that swirled above his right elbow, heading to an unknown destination beneath his sleeve.

Oh, a bad boy.

I experienced an insane urge to trace the intricate curves and find out where they led. Enthralled, I continued my heated appraisal and slid my gaze down his body. Tight, well-worn jeans hung low on his hips and boldly advertised long legs and muscular thighs. All leading to a well-defined, impressive bulge nestled in between.

Holy Shit! I'm staring at his package.

Mortified, my eyes flew up, but my disconcertment transformed to shock as I stared into breathtaking jewel-green eyes. Breathtaking jewel-green eyes that were watching me with open amusement. I could almost read his mind. *Do you like what you see?*

I should have let Nicki do my hair.

Right, 'cause that would make the dress so much better.

"Casual day at the office?" he drawled while his eyes mimicked my perusal. Something told me this man did not miss much.

"Didn't you get the memo?" I applauded my calm voice. "It's dress as your favorite fairy princess day." I imagined the spectacle from his perspective and sighed. "Or dress like your vegetable of choice day. Either way, it's awful." He responded with a deep laugh that made my body tighten.

"Princess, with your looks, I wouldn't worry about pulling it off."

A rush of hot pleasure swept through me.

Then reality struck it down like a hammer blow.

This dress couldn't make a supermodel attractive, which meant these were nothing more than cheesy platitudes. Beneath the angelic face and sexy exterior loitered the heart of a typical, opportunistic man.

"Just stop. I'm not interested." I blamed my mental lapse on suffocation. Who designed the eggplant? A boa constrictor? I resisted the urge to tug at the neckline. "I gotta get this damn thing off," I muttered to myself.

With one stride, he stood in front of me. Surprised, I tilted my head to see his face. *Christ, he's even more beautiful up close.* His dark mane framed a firm jaw, sculpted cheekbones, and a sensuous, full mouth that initiated sinful urges. His wicked smile did nothing to quell my wayward thoughts. "I'd be happy to offer assistance." His gaze drifted down my body.

I mentally slapped myself for considering the offer and took as deep a breath as possible—more like a sniff. I instantly realized my mistake. He smelled amazing—an intoxicating combination of pine, earth, mint, but mostly... man.

"Er, um, I..." Were these ridiculous sounds coming from me? I never lost my composure around a man. *Get a grip!* "Do you make a habit of trying to undress random women in elevators?"

His face broke out in a mischievous smile that made me question the merit of my inquiry. Most of the Manhattan female population would drop their drawers for this man, the remainder being lesbians.

"Just aiding a damsel in distress."

"My freaking knight in shining armor," I mumbled and attempted to take a step back, but instead of putting much needed distance between us, I fumbled and caught the rail.

His brows drew in. "Careful, Princess, that dress is dangerous."

Danger lurked in the elevator but not in the shape of a garment. In fact, he made the eggplant seem like footy pajamas. *He's just a man.* I closed my eyes against the vision that proved otherwise, but my body refused to cooperate. Probably payback for dressing it in ugly taffeta and lace.

This really is the slowest goddamn elevator in Manhattan.

As if refuting my complaint, the elevator dinged and the doors slid open. I charged out.

Rippppp...

The sound came seconds before I pitched forward. I careened towards the rising floor and braced myself for an inevitable face plant. It didn't come. Instead, powerful arms circled my waist, hoisted me up, and when my feet touched the floor, I found myself back in the elevator, my chest pressed into Tall, Dark, and Dangerous.

Maybe he is a knight in sexy armor.

He chuckled, "I don't think a woman's fallen for me that quickly before."

I waited until my heart slowed. "Thanks." I spoke against a solid wall of muscle. "I thought the most lethal part of the dress was turning humans to stone. Now we know it has other ways of killing us off."

His chest rumbled with laughter and against my brain's wishes, I raised my face. Colossal mistake. His eyes locked with mine and the amused expression disappeared. The jewel-green depths darkened infinitesimally and my chest pounded out a drum solo that ended in a heart-stopping crescendo.

Why isn't he letting me go?

Why am I not pulling away?

I needed to focus elsewhere but I couldn't. My head buzzed as if a swarm of bees had taken residence, and my mouth went dry. I licked my lips. His eyes dropped.

What would his lips feel like?

What the hell are you thinking?

I'm not.

But you never lose control.

Don't care. Go away and let me have this.

My eyes communicated my offer, and I warmed at his answering expression. When his arms gathered me closer, I could no longer blame my ragged breathing on the dress. He dipped his head towards mine, and I pushed high on my tiptoes. That hypnotic mouth inched closer. Soft breath lingered on my parted lips. I closed my eyes.

And soared a foot in the air as two men and a woman barreled into the elevator. Their conversation halted at the sight of us.

I came to my senses with a jerk, but Dangerous' arms remained secure. I shot him a 'not on your life' expression. Annoyance flashed across his face before he dropped his arms but kept a steady hand on my back.

The awkwardness grew palpable as the woman openly ogled Dangerous, while the men tried to avoid sniggering at my dress. I concentrated on the display panel but from the corner of my eye, saw Dangerous. He was lounging against the wall, focused on nothing.

This time, I confirmed the floor number before I hitched up my skirt and bolted down the hallway. I chanced a peek over my shoulder and glimpsed Dangerous, watching me with a bemused expression.

"This is a gag, right?" Nicki hooked the hanger over the door and poked at the eggplant. She bobbed as if expecting it to punch back while her curls rebounded with matching anticipation. "It's a slap in the face. No—a roundhouse kick."

I perched on the edge of my bed and nodded. "Can you shorten it? It's about a foot too long."

She gawked at me as if I'd left my mind at the office, though I'm sure I had lost it eons ago at an undisclosed location. "Wait. You're telling me that when you look at this dress, the one thing you notice... *is the length?* Are you crazy? It's like a gruesome car wreck. I want to look away, but I can't."

"Can you fix it or not?"

She cocked her head to the right. "Nope." She tilted her head to the left. "Nope." She straightened and squeezed her eyes shut. "There. That's better."

"Not an option."

"I don't get it. This cousin of yours slithers back into your life and asks you for a favor."

I nodded.

"Because nothing says thank you like the humiliation of wearing a McDonald's Grimace costume?"

"That's typical for Helena," I explained. "If you knew her, you'd understand." *If you knew her, you'd duck for cover.*

"You're right. I know nothing about her." She frowned and planted her hands on her hips. "And why haven't I heard of her before?"

"Because I try to think of her as little as possible." According to public records, Jasmine Monroe was the only child of deceased parents. A lie created from wishful thinking. "She basically tortured me as a kid."

"Shocking," she said with a heaping dose of sarcasm. "So why help her now?"

"We're grown up. She wants a fresh start."

"And you're buying her 'let's make up and bury the hatchet' routine?"

"Heck no."

"Good, 'cause it'll end up in your spine. That woman is warped."

"You know the old adage, keep your friends close and your evil family members under surveillance." I'd hacked into every digital piece on Helena and besides questionable life choices, found nothing to explain what was going on.

“Screw her,” Nicki declared. “If she causes you any grief, you have my full support to add her to a most wanted list.”

I responded with a smile, but the thought of lashing out left me cold. Full blown war was suicide. Helena tortured for fun then aimed for the kill with an accuracy that a sniper would envy. After countless losses against her, I had long relinquished any notion of victory. A fresh beginning was safer than gambling on my recurring history.

And on the off chance I survived, what price would I pay? Become like them by tapping into the same darkness that lived dormant in my DNA? Unleash something that terrified me? I’d already experienced a propensity for deviant behavior. Did I have it in me to come back, or would I turn into a full-fledged monster?

Nicki’s sigh reminded me of the issue at hand. “Here’s the plan.” She stared the dress down like a worthy adversary. “Contain the damage. Minimal contact. In and out of the wedding. No wandering. No public. You could burn someone’s eyes out and we don’t need a lawsuit.”

“Too late,” I mumbled.

“Oh no. Have we been served?”

I recounted an abbreviated version of my elevator fiasco, minus my crazy responses. Few things shocked more than the eggplant, my earlier behavior amongst them.

“No kinky anonymous elevator nooky for you,” Nicki lectured. “You’re reformed now. Though it does sound fun. I saw that in a porno once.”

Probably in James’ building.

4

I laid on my office couch and tossed my stress ball high in the air. I caught it then glanced at the clock. *Two hours to go.* I chucked the ball up again and caught it. *Up, down, up, down.* The rhythm soothed my nerves and tempered the adrenaline rush that preceded every presentation.

"Jasmine," Sue blared and the ball landed squarely on my face. "I have the copies you wanted."

"Thanks for harshing on my Zen," I mumbled as I strode out of my office. My assistant was standing at her desk, her slender frame clad in a short red and black plaid skirt, purple leggings, and a white sleeveless top. Violet streaked through her bobbed black hair. On anyone else, her bizarre ensemble would appear ridiculous, but Sue made quirky look amazing.

I accepted the samples. "It's a shame I can't show my best stuff."

"We're trying to win a contract, not land you in prison," Sue said. "I know you're pressed for time. Do you want me to grab you lunch?"

“God no,” I quickly answered. Sue grinned at the fear in my eyes. As an organic, vegan health nut, Sue’s idea of a meal consisted of anything green, slimy, or recently liberated from the ground. Against my better judgment, I had capitulated once and allowed her to feed me. I could still taste the grass and dirt flavored mush on my tongue. “I’d rather gnaw on my stress ball.”

“How about some tea instead?”

My brows rose. “Now I know you’re worried.”

After working her way through college as a barista, Sue detested serving beverages. She was also terrible at it. Although she’d screwed up my order multiple times, something about her drew me in. When the time came to launch my business, she jumped at the chance to help and a year later, after graduating with honors, shocked me by staying and accepting the meager salary I could afford. Many times, she believed in me more than I did.

I smoothed my long ponytail and straightened my suit. “You look fabulous as usual,” Sue said, “but if you want my advice, hike that skirt up a couple inches. Your legs will have them signing before you open your mouth.”

“And set the feminist movement back a hundred years.” I stepped through the door.

As I waited for the slow elevator, an image of Dangerous popped in my mind. Would he be around?

Right. Because he has nothing better to do than ride around in elevators all day, trolling for women in ugly dresses.

It arrived devoid of any occupants and, with disappointment—no—relief, I stepped inside.

I exited the cab in front of a brick structure with LYNDHAM INCORPORATED lettered across the front. As I waited in the lobby, I noticed a picture of a nice-looking, older man with a killer smile. I read the accompanying article. *‘Lyndham Inc., a leader in financial software. Founded and owned by Erik Lyndham, a CPA whose disappointment with market resources spurred him to design an integrated finance, accounting, and tax solution...' blah, blah, blah.* I knew this from preparation.

Would I be pitching to the big kahuna himself?

My answer came when the receptionist escorted me to a conference room furnished with a heavy table and matching sideboard. I declined her offer of a beverage. The butterflies in my stomach consumed too much real estate to consider anything else.

The table accommodated twenty, but only five gentlemen occupied the surrounding leather chairs, none of them resembling the older man in the picture. They stood in unison, as if competing in a synchronized Olympic event, and a man with sly gray eyes and slicked-back brown hair approached.

Somewhere, there's a used car dealership missing a salesman.

He drew himself up to his full height and attempted to peer down his nose at me, which proved comical since I towered over the shrimp.

"Leonard Bryce, Director of Software Technology." His handshake started out bone-crunching then softened, lingering too long for comfort.

"Wayne Parker, Vice-President of Development." An attractive blond man stepped forward. His soft brown eyes crinkled at the corners when he smiled, reminding me of Ginger. Handsome but nothing like—an image of black hair and green eyes flashed in my mind.

NOT NOW!

Wayne gestured for me to begin and I froze. After multiple presentations, I should have been a pro, but I still wrestled with any situation that forced me into the spotlight. In my experience, attention preceded horrible things, which is why I preferred living in shadows, away from scrutiny. I unclenched my hands, leaving nail indentations in my palms.

The men waited.

I pictured the group in their underwear. Wayne's lean form did well beneath his expensive suit. Then my eyes fell on Leonard.

Blech! Terrible idea. Abort.

Pull it together.

It always began the same, with my childhood insecurities and grown-up paranoia. But I always pulled it off. Why? Because I was not that helpless child anymore.

I am Jasmine-fucking-Monroe. A successful, adult businesswoman who kicks ass.

I inhaled a deep breath and began. A few phrases in and my audience became irrelevant. While people made little sense with their irrational and emotional tendencies, data never disappointed. Once my analytic mind slid into gear, I lost myself to the sophisticated encryption algorithm I'd created to ensure the security of Lyndham's client data. I ended with references, credentials, and a list of my *noncriminal* projects.

Nailed it! I punched a mental fist in the air while I waited for questions.

Wayne spoke first. "Are you familiar with a product under development called Wolfe?"

Wolfe was an anticipated security software created exclusively to protect business interests. Originally developed by a small software shop, the company had since been acquired by Predator Industries, a gaming company branching out into other platforms.

Anticipating this question, the answer rolled off my tongue. "While I don't doubt Predator's claims that Wolfe will revolutionize security, it's still a packaged system. Your data requires a dedicated and adaptable approach, otherwise I wouldn't be here."

"Excellent." Wayne seemed pleased.

Nailed it again!

The men concluded with a few more questions, then Wayne escorted me to the lobby.

I shook his hand. "Thank you for the opportunity."

"The pleasure is all ours."

Oh, this is good.

"Very competitive proposal," he continued.

Even better.

"I'm eager to discuss your ideas further," he added.

Bordering on awesome.

"Let's continue this conversation at the Software Association banquet tonight."

Noooo!

"I've spent my entire career avoiding these events. How the hell did I get railroaded into this one?" I logged into my computer and pulled up the Software Developer Association website. One lousy day. If I had met with Lyndham one lousy day later, I would have avoided this. For all my faults, why couldn't procrastination be one of them? I hacked into the list and winced at the long list of attendees.

Nicki rifled through my closet as if it were a Rolodex. "It's called socializing, and did you know paranoia is a form of narcissism?"

I added my name and made a mental note to send payment. "Just because you're paranoid, doesn't mean they're not out to get you."

"They should bow down and crown you their geek queen. I don't know why you can't see how amazing you are."

My father's idea of 'amazing' boomed in my head. *"Better hope you turn out to be a looker, because that's the only way any man will tolerate you."* I could almost feel the backhand that followed.

Ever since Helena's arrival, family highlights had been rolling through my mind like a greatest hits reel.

Nicki held up a red pantsuit and made a face. "The seventies called. They want this back." She threw it on a pile. "Go schmooze. Learn how to socialize."

My blood pressure rose at the thought. "It's a group of drunk nerds embellishing their accomplishments. The only thing missing is the measuring tape for their joysticks."

"So take a ruler and have some fun," Nicki retorted. "Practice our new strategy. Find a nice guy, flirt, but no one-night stands."

"These guys will be lucky if they ever kiss a female outside of the robots they build."

"That's even better. Gratitude is a powerful tool." She tugged a pair of overalls from a hanger and threw them on the growing reject mound. I groaned. Those were comfortable.

"Eureka!" she yelled and held up a short, slinky blue dress I don't remember buying. I accepted it from her and darted into the bathroom. She rolled her eyes. "You're such a prude."

While I allowed Nicki to assume I was shy, a fact she loved to mock, I preferred her teasing to the alternative—explaining the scars on my body. The fewer questions, the more likely our relationship continued. Men were simpler. With a guarantee of getting laid and minimal blood flow to their brains, they were oblivious.

Fifteen minutes later, I stepped into silver sandals and walked towards my full-length mirror. *Holy shit!* My blue eyes, now sultry from Nicki's hand, widened. The dress hugged my subtle curves and ended mid-thigh, making my long legs appear to go on for miles. The halter fastened behind my neck, and with my hair piled high, accentuated my bare neck and shoulders. Never argue with Nicki on matters of design, cooking, or style.

My fairy godmother.

She twirled a finger in the air and whistled as I spun. "Damn, I wish I had your legs."

"Genetics," I said.

"I hope those geeks bring their inhalers, or they won't be able to handle those genetics of yours."

I paused at the entrance. All hope that a computer virus would attack, rallying nerds to don superhero costumes and save the day, vanished when I saw the throngs of well-dressed people mingling and dancing.

I'm at a nerd prom.

A few eyes turned my way. Last chance to bolt.

Disgusted by my cowardice, I set my jaw and marched forward. A lanky man smiled, and I decided to give small talk a shot. I joined his group and politely listened while they discussed the well-worn topic of Star Wars versus Star Trek. I didn't care enough to get involved. Not even when someone misquoted Yoda.

I tuned out the rest while I followed a cute guy's ass. Not bad for a nerd-fest. Maybe I could hit him up later for a—someone said my name and I returned to the discussion. Time travel. Too bad it wasn't possible, or I'd go back and never come here.

If I gain any business tonight, it'll be a miracle.

As the evening progressed, I acclimated to the schmoozing game. It seemed to consist of feigning interest while people droned on about themselves. Easy enough. Thankfully, not everyone bored me. The man with the nice ass turned out to be a software architect who dabbled in the occasional risky endeavor. Although too young for me in the bedroom, I yearned to compare notes but resisted. No consorting with like-minded criminals. Rookie mistake.

This night was getting depressing.

I was scooting away from a technical writer droning in perpetuity about his six cats and ferret when I heard my name.

My relief died when I saw Leonard Bryce, the car salesman—I mean Director of Technology—bearing down on me. His expensive blue suit did nothing to conceal his stocky frame, and I marveled at how not one stiff strand of hair shifted with each movement. I wrinkled my nose as he grew close. Ugh! Did he marinate in his cologne?

"Miss Monroe, what a pleasure." His eyes gleamed as they darted down my dress.

"Mr. Bryce, nice to see you," I lied.

His brow creased. "I reviewed your proposal, and I'm afraid I have some concerns."

"Oh." I tried to conceal my disappointment. "Anything I can address?"

"I hope so." He gestured for me to follow. "If you would be so kind as to indulge me."

"Of course," I murmured. I was too close to this contract to screw it up now.

He led me through wide glass doors and into the famous hotel gardens where four cobblestone paths wound in various directions. Leonard chose the path furthest to the right, and in merely a few seconds, the surroundings transformed into a Thomas Kinkade painting. Manicured shrubs sloped through hills of ongoing lush lawns with vibrant flowers scattered between. Rustic lanterns hung from old-fashioned posts, blanketing the night sky in a soft warm glow. I swept my gaze, expecting to find a chocolate-box cottage on the horizon.

We crossed an olde-worlde bridge and veered into a hairpin

turn. I heard running water seconds before a magnificent stone fountain came in to view. Neptune, God of the Sea, towered above, his triton extended toward the sky in a declaration of battle.

Someone cleared his throat, and I remembered my unsavory companion. I stretched my neck to gauge our location but frowned when I saw nothing but foliage. How long had we been walking?

"Mr. Leonard, we should return."

"Nonsense." He gestured to the edge of the fountain. "Please sit and we can discuss your proposal."

I shivered when the backs of my legs touched icy stone. "You mentioned you had questions?" The sooner we addressed them, the sooner I could get away from this creeper.

"Yes." He sat close. "Your pitch was impressive."

"Thank you."

"Though not as impressive as you."

What?

"You're an exquisite woman, Jasmine." He rested his hand on my knee. "May I call you 'Jasmine'?"

Groping my thigh is okay, but using my first name crosses the line?

"No." I nudged his hand away.

"Now, Jasmine." His hand found my leg again. "We both know how this business works."

Apparently, Sue's not alone in trying to set the women's movement back.

"Mr. Bryce, if I've done anything to give you the impression I'm interested in more than software, I'm sorry." Why was I apologizing? He's the one who couldn't get a clue through that shellacked helmet he called hair.

Because he held the decision for the biggest contract I may ever get in his hands.

Hands that were steadily creeping up my leg.

"No need to be stubborn." When his fingers reached the hem

of my dress, they slipped beneath. "I'm sure we can come to an *understanding.*" The emphasis on the word made my skin crawl.

I scrambled to get to my feet, but he grabbed my shoulder and slammed me down. His fingers painfully dug into my flesh.

"Don't be naïve." His squinty rodent eyes hardened. "You're competing for something I can give you. All you have to do is give me something first."

I struggled against him. "Let me go."

"You're in the big leagues now," he snarled and released a hand to position it behind my head. "If you don't understand how to play the game, you'll learn soon enough." He leaned in and the pungent smell of snake oil singed my nostrils.

I shoved hard against his chest, but he didn't budge.

"Hold still, you little bitch." He wound his hand in my hair. I twisted away and gasped as my strands nearly tore from their roots. "You know you want this."

His ragged breathing and feverish eyes repulsed me.

Christ, the psycho is enjoying this.

"Not so high and mighty anymore," he hissed as his hand slid over my breast and squeezed.

Oh my God! This is really happening.

With blind panic, my limbs flew out, bucking and kicking. He responded by tightening his hold on my hair and I cried out.

Helpless again. At the mercy of someone's whims. This wasn't supposed to happen. Not now. Not after leaving the weak girl behind.

If you don't stop this, it will be your *fault.*

I closed my eyes and forced myself to focus inward, to reach the sanctuary I'd relied on as a child for my survival. Quiet, unfeeling, and dissociated from pain, the burden of emotion disappeared and my options clarified. I tempered my instincts and raised a surprisingly steady hand to his cheek. "You're right," I said. "I want this contract."

"That's more like it." Eager to claim his prize, he loosened his grip to move down my body. I suppressed a shudder while my fingers grazed up his face. In one swift movement, I ground my thumb into his eye socket and stabbed hard.

He howled—somewhere between a wounded animal and a little girl—and leaped up. I followed him and drew my leg back, prepared to do all womankind a favor and kick the Bryce family jewels so hard, even people who resembled him would become impotent.

"I distinctly heard the lady say 'no'," a familiar deep voice interrupted.

5

I paused mid-kick, lost my balance, and landed hard... on my ass.

Why does this keep happening around him?

Shaking with rage, Bryce whirled to confront the interloper. His irritation turned to surprise then concern. With a few steps back, he straightened his jacket and adopted an aura more suited to exiting a business meeting than a botched molestation attempt. Once clear, he scurried away. I glared at his vanishing figure, disappointed at my lost opportunity to neuter him.

A black-clad arm impaired my view and, in a repeat performance, hauled me to my feet where looming in front of me, sexy as hell, stood Dangerous.

Damn, he cleans up nice.

He exuded masculine elegance in a black suit that flattered his tall, well-built frame to perfection. I drank in his broad shoulders, narrow waist, and long muscular legs. His rumpled hair curled around his collar, and my fingers twitched with the urge to bury themselves in the thick waves.

James Bond has nothing on this man.

He seized my arm and pulled—no, yanked—me alongside him toward the entrance. Between his long legs, my heels, and the cobblestone path, I may as well have been navigating an obstacle course. I stumbled all over the place.

This time if I fall on my ass, it's on him.

He slowed and muttered something under his breath, probably about my klutziness. When we reached the glass door, he jerked it open. As I passed, I deciphered the words 'damsel' and 'distress', punctuated by curses.

My knight in black-tie armor.

We reached an empty corner where I turned to face him. "Thanks for the rescue, but I had it under—" The remaining words died on my lips. Although he displayed no outward sign of emotion, his eyes burned with fury.

Dangerous was pissed.

"Of all the goddamn, reckless, fucking idiotic..." he barked loud enough to attract attention from halfway across the room. "Do you know what could have happened if I hadn't come along? Fuck!" He ran his fingers through his hair and the waves fell in a sexy mess.

"Keep it down," I hissed. So much for maintaining a low profile with a lunatic ranting at me.

He paid no heed to my request. "Do you even have a brain inside that pretty little head of yours, Princess? What the fuck did you think you were doing?"

"Fighting off a psycho's slimy hands," I snapped, "and doing a fine job of it before you showed up."

His eyes flashed. "What was the plan? Lure him outside, tease him, get some business thrown your way? How could you be so goddamn dense?"

I vacillated between laughing in his beautiful face and

planting my fist in it. Given the stares he'd already attracted, violence would have to wait. That left me with good old-fashioned indignation.

"Listen to me, you arrogant jackass. I rely on nothing"—I stabbed my finger in his chest and his surprised expression brought a twinge of satisfaction—"outside my intelligence and exceptional work ethic to achieve my goals. My reputation speaks for itself, and I'll be damned if I'll listen to some halfwit, male-chauvinistic, double-oh-seven wannabee tell me otherwise. Bryce is a lunatic and I'm beginning to think you're not far behind." With a final jab, I spun on my heel and stormed off to locate a well-deserved drink.

With less alcohol than cough syrup, the watered-down rum and Coke did nothing to ameliorate my anger. Dangerous may have been catnip in a suit, but he was a judgmental ass. I downed the remaining contents, slammed the glass on the bar, and slid off the stool. In the interest of decency, I paused to yank down my dress.

"Hi, Jasmine," a voice startled me.

Now what?

Wayne Parker appeared at my side, impeccable in a dark gray designer suit. His conservative, close cropped blond hair and genial smile contributed to the cleaned up, boy-next-door visage. He didn't fill out his clothes like Dangerous—what man could?—but he carried himself with a dignified nature.

The purpose for my being here claimed the stool beside me. "You seem a million miles away."

"Wishing I was."

"I must admit, I concur." His brown eyes filled with mock horror. "Another cat and ferret story, and I'd be at risk of committing myself to an asylum."

I think I'm already in one.

Wayne ordered another round, which I interpreted as my cue to sit back down. I still wanted that damn contract, and if that meant more small talk, so be it. While sipping liquor-flavored water, our conversation turned to Wayne's not-so-humble 'Leave it to Beaver' childhood. His teacher mother and orthopedic surgeon father were still happily devoted to each other.

Gag! I stifled an eye roll.

After private school, Wayne graduated from NYU and accepted a job as a developer at Lyndham, where he dedicated the next ten years to climbing the corporate ladder, culminating in the youngest vice-presidency in company history.

There must be a dark secret lurking. Maybe he's a kleptomaniac or into BDSM or— Crap! Nicki is right. I can't have a conversation with a generic man and not dehumanize him.

Wayne was normal. Unlike Dangerous, who practically came with bright yellow '*proceed with caution*' tape stuck to his forehead.

My attention wandered around the room, passing over a group of gamers huddled in a corner, glued to their smartphones. Kudos to them for venturing out of their parents' basements. I observed the nice-ass young man hitting on a woman too old for him and then my eyes locked with brilliant green ones. My skin prickled, an apt response to a first-class prick. His face was etched in a mask of displeasure.

Waiting for me to rip off my dress and mount Wayne to land my next job?

I delivered the coldest look in my arsenal, but a busty redhead in a miniscule silver dress ruined the effect when she paused to gain his attention. His focus shifted past her, so I attempted a repeat performance which this time lost impact to a blonde. Two exceptionally evil looks thwarted. I abandoned the effort as wave upon wave of women competed for his attention, some subtle, others bold, but all unanimous in their ignorant admiration.

Throughout the perpetual stream, Dangerous remained oblivious. A few were attractive. All obviously easy. Why didn't he respond? I knew firsthand he wasn't gay.

My answer appeared in the form of a tall, statuesque woman, radiating sex appeal like sunlight. She sashayed towards him and laid a hand on his arm. The two made a striking couple. Dangerous, resplendent in black-tie and Miss Dangerous, dazzling with glossy black hair, exotic almond eyes, smooth olive skin, and more curves than a mountain road, all showcased by her snug white floor-length gown. She poured her voluptuous body over Dangerous like maple syrup cascading over a stack of ridiculously hot pancakes and whispered in his ear. He threw his head back and laughed while she preened.

Oblivious to my short attention span, Wayne continued to chat. With no inkling how the conversation had evolved, I opted for the safest route and nodded like an idiot. It proved sufficient because he stood and offered his hand. "Would you care to dance?"

We stepped onto the dance floor where his body defied science by morphing from man to wooden statue. He stumbled twice, both times threatening my toes with bodily peril. I opened my mouth to suggest an alternative pastime but stopped when I noticed him counting.

"Doing math?" I teased.

"Shhhh," he said with an infectious grin. "I'll forget where I am. One, two, three, one, two, three..." he continued while confining us to a tiny patch of floor, much like walking in place. As we box-stepped within our two-foot section, I inadvertently searched the room for nobody in particular.

A tall, dangerous nobody in particular.

Probably making out with Miss Exotic in the elevator.

Wayne said something I didn't catch... again, and I experienced a pang of remorse. He deserved better. He'd been nothing but pleasant, unlike—

"You're distracted," Wayne noted. "Is it the presentation?"

No. "Yes."

"Don't worry. You're extremely talented."

"Thank you." *You have no idea.*

"Tell me more about Jasmine Monroe."

And let the interrogation begin.

"Not much to tell," I said. *I come from a criminally psychotic family and engage in activities of which I'm sure you'd disapprove.*

"Where are you from?"

"Southern California." *Affectionately referred to as hell.*

"What brought you to New York?"

"Work." *To get away from aforementioned psychotic family.*

"What do you do with your free time?"

"I run a company. What's free time?"

He laughed. And planted his foot squarely on mine.

"My apologies," he said. "I can direct an international technology department, but I'm unable to talk, dance, and count at the same time."

Throw chewing gum in the mix and he'd be a basket case.

"May I cut in?" a familiar deep timbre interrupted.

I inwardly groaned. He was like a bad penny, always showing up.

Wayne's already rigid posture stiffened to where a firm breeze could crack him. "What's the matter, Hale? Can't accept a beautiful woman dancing with another man?" He delivered his words in a teasing manner, but an underlying edge poked through.

"More like I can't accept a beautiful woman hobbling on crutches tomorrow," Dangerous countered.

I silently pleaded with Wayne to take a page from drug education and 'Just Say No', but his perfect breeding and etiquette prevailed. "I look forward to another dance."

Unencumbered by similar manners—I had lousy breeding—I attempted to follow Wayne, but Dangerous snaked an arm around my waist. He gathered me in close and the heady scent of earth and spice, layered with something wonderful, enveloped me.

Not again.

I resigned myself to one dance, but remembering what happened at our last meeting, maintained strict eye-to-chest contact.

Eye to broad, solid, handsome chest. Dammit!

We began to move—no, more like glide—with a grace that astonished me. A far cry from Wayne's intrusive feet, Dangerous guided me across the floor, and in his arms, my usually awkward movements elevated to light and poise. As I sailed with him, electric pulses hummed in harmony to the music, and his formerly aggravating energy filled me with exhilaration.

My knees dissolved to jelly and I swooned. Yes, I actually swooned—a word I reserve for women in their sixties with an overactive flair for drama.

And then he ruined it by talking. "I don't believe we've formally met."

"Your wild insinuations were enough of an introduction," I spoke into his shoulder, still not trusting myself.

"That's ancient history."

"Ancient?" I repeated. "Maybe if you have the lifespan of a fruit fly."

"I'm Chase," he said. Not to be outdone, his hand introduced itself by sliding along my back.

I forgot where I was.

"Chase Hale," he added.

I'd heard the name. Owner of Predator Industries, the

company launching Wolfe. Also one of the wealthiest men around. Not that it mattered. He could be the fucking president of the free world and he'd still be a dick.

"Am I supposed to be impressed?"

"No, it's just a name." He waited... and waited... "And I should call you...?"

"A cab would be ideal."

He chuckled. "'Princess' it is." He whisked me to the edge of the floor and back to the center. "You look beautiful tonight."

"All part of my plan to whore myself out to unsuspecting executives."

"Still dwelling on that, huh?" he asked. "I prefer to move forward."

"I'd like to move forward to the end of this dance."

"And I'd like to know why I've never seen you at these functions before. What brings you here tonight?"

"The gardens are renowned for sexual predators," I answered. "It's in all the guidebooks. In fact, now that I crossed it off my bucket list, I should go." I attempted to pull away, but his arms remained wrapped around me like steel bands.

What do these people do for fun? Practice restraining women?

"Not yet, Princess," he said. "I'd rather learn more about Jasmine Monroe, the owner of Monroe Consulting."

"If you know who I am... why would... ugh!" I stomped my foot and stumbled. His arms tightened to keep me upright, and memories of his savior routine in the elevator warmed my cheeks.

His mind must have gone to the same place. "Aftershocks from the killer purple dress?"

That dress wasn't alone in entertaining murderous tendencies. I scowled up at him and— Christ, was it possible for him to be even more beautiful than I remembered? All thought abandoned me. This guy was trouble with a capital 'Get The Hell Outta Here'.

"I asked around," he explained. "And to my surprise, learned my princess in distress is the elusive Jasmine Monroe." He shook his head. "How you've stayed under the radar this long baffles me. A few of my acquaintances have used you."

I had a brief flash of how he could use me then pushed it away. "It's nothing you'd be interested in."

A provocative smile spread across his mouth. "Too late."

My pulse quickened. "You had better be talking software."

We glided by Wayne's two-foot box, and I took a moment to send silent condolences to his latest victim.

"I have a professional question, if you don't mind," Chase said.

"And if I do?" I inclined my head to his arm circling my waist. "Do I have a choice?"

"No. Just being polite."

"Why start now?" I grumbled. "And why do you care about the opinion of a woman who can't land a job without using her body?"

As if invited, his green eyes embarked on a lazy stroll down the length of me, the visual caress as intimate as a physical one. "And what a shame it would be for a body like yours to be left unused."

My libido short-circuited. The dance floor was becoming a minefield.

"As I'm sure you're aware," he continued, seamlessly switching to business. "My company, Predator Industries, is currently developing a security software solution that will be launching soon."

"Yes, I know. Wolfe. From your most recent acquisition."

"I'm curious, Princess. As an independent security programmer, are you worried?"

My eyes widened. "About my business?"

"Yes."

"Why would I be?"

"Because Predator will be rolling out a superior product."

"Don't flatter yourself."

"Why's that?"

I stretched upwards and brought my lips a breath away from his ear. I fought the impulse to sniff him... or do more. "Because I'm very, very good."

He inhaled sharply.

Ha. Two can play at this game.

A lascivious glint entered his eyes. "Still talking software, Princess?"

Mercifully, the band chose that moment to end what seemed like the longest song in history. "Normally I would thank you for the dance, but I'm not going to. Goodnight." I waited for him to free me.

"Eager to leave?"

"Yes, but the men here seem to have trouble letting go," I challenged. "Is it something in the punch?"

He dropped his arms so abruptly, I blinked. And then he grabbed my hand. "I have a proposition I'd like to run by you." Without waiting for an answer, he urged me away from the guests. Confused, I didn't protest when we exited the familiar doors that led to the gardens. He halted and his brows furrowed. "Are you okay being out here?"

"Yes, but—" That's all he needed. He ushered me forward and chose a path illuminated by fairy lights, one that led in the opposite direction of the Neptune fountain.

I pulled my hand free but continued, my curiosity overriding my sense. As intense as Dangerous' presence was, I experienced no fear for my safety. My mind, on the other hand...

We continued along the path, and like before, the unparalleled wonder of my surroundings consumed me. Every detail brought to life a world of fairy tale enchantment and with it, the rare indulgence of breaking from reality. The guidebooks referred to the gardens as Nature's Paradise, a gross understatement when witnessed in person.

A unique sight caught my eye, and I stopped for a closer look. A stargazer lily sat nestled amongst the leaves, its rare purple shade emphasizing the contradictory qualities of fragility and boldness. Its face burst towards the sky in a grandiose gesture.

I brushed a finger along the petal and recalled the day I saw my first stargazer.

My mom had woken me that morning, her face flushed with excitement. At first, I thought something was wrong. She never spent time with me. "Get up, Snuggles." She flung my covers aside. "I'm taking you to my favorite place today. I want to show you something special."

The Los Angeles Arboretum boasted one of the largest floral collections, and I remember my awe as she guided me through the magical land, my small hand entwined with hers. "This is jasmine." She pointed to a cluster of bushes with tiny white flowers. "Don't they smell wonderful?" I delicately sniffed and then gulped in a greedy lungful of the potent sweetness.

Next, she steered me to a group of bright flowers so stunning, they captured my breath. "These are stargazer lilies." She smiled with approval at my reaction. "Lovely in their innocence and purity, they remind me of you." I could still feel the warmth of her hand against my cheek. "See how it faces upwards, stretching toward the sky? They bloom towards the heavens and in return, the heavens bestow a blessing upon them." She winked at me. "And on anyone who has a stargazer lily."

We ended the excursion in the gift shop where, in a surprising show of maternal affection, she purchased the stargazer lily pin and affixed it to my pink overalls.

That was one month before she left.

Gravel crunched and I glanced up to find Chase watching me

with a quizzical expression. Embarrassed, I averted my eyes while ignoring his outstretched hand. "What do you want to talk to me about?" I asked.

"Over here." He pointed to a metal bench. He sat then pulled me down beside him, much closer than appropriate. I wish I'd minded more. He watched me closely as shadows from the torches played upon his face, and his eyes intensified, either in contrast to the dark or with desire, I couldn't tell. Until his next words left little doubt.

"I want you, Princess."

My skin erupted in chills I blamed on the cold metal beneath me. "Are we still talking software?" I said in a small voice.

He quirked a brow.

With a sigh, I surrendered the pretense. "What makes you think I'd agree?"

He leaned forward and my breath hitched. "We both know the answer to that."

Nicki's voice echoed in my head. *No more screw-ups. No more bad boys. Just a lonely girl and her vibrator.*

This man fit right into my former relationship model—self-absorbed, obnoxious, and arrogant. No wonder I was so attracted. I groaned.

"Did I miss something?" Chase asked.

"Your window of opportunity."

He frowned. "I'll rephrase the question. I want to have sex with you."

I didn't hear any question in that sentence but decided to ignore it. "Has it occurred to you that I might not want you?"

"No," he said with a cocky grin and inched closer.

As if fighting off a force overlooked by physics, I resisted the impulse to touch him. "Well, I don't."

He lowered his head and his breath tickled my neck. "Then why so nervous?"

Warning bells pealed in my head like a church on Sunday. "I'm perfectly fine."

"Then it won't bother you if I do this." I jumped when his teeth grazed my earlobe.

Now would be an excellent time to retreat.

I stayed glued in place.

"Or maybe this." His mouth rubbed along the curve of my throat. I white-knuckled the edge of the bench as my world spun.

"But I would much rather do this," he said then crushed his lips to mine.

6

Even his kiss was dangerous—an intoxicating blend of passion and guilty pleasure that made my lips part for more. He cupped a hand behind my head and when his velvet tongue danced across mine, sparks ignited through my nervous system that put the garden colors to shame. Lost to everything but him, my impatient fingers snaked around his neck to delve into his thick hair. I practically purred at the feel of those silky strands.

Hands jostled my hips and the frigid bench beneath me disappeared, replaced by his warm lap. I nuzzled into him and groaned at the answering arousal that swelled in response.

His lips broke from mine to trail heated kisses along my jaw. When his mouth reached the sensitive spot below my ear, I released a sound between a whimper and a moan and shivered against him. He hissed out a breath and ran his tongue along the curve, sucking harder.

Sensations overwhelmed me—the heat between my thighs, his hardness pressed unbearably close, warm fingers stroking my naked back, and his mouth latched on to that sweet spot along my throat.

A dizzy whir filled my head and my hands flailed for something solid. The whir turned to a choppy sputter, my legs stiffening, pressure mounting. "Oh God," I moaned as I reached the edge. A hiss exploded in my head.

And then cold water pelted me.

I shrieked.

What the—?

One by one, the realizations hit.

I'm on a bench.

No! On Dangerous' lap.

Close to an orgasm.

And being drenched by... sprinklers?

"Bloody hell!" Chase yelled and scooped me in his arms before bolting. He hurried to a dry location where he lowered me to my feet. Water dripped from his thick hair, but his chest and pants remained dry, having had the benefit of my body as a shield. His only other casualty, the once prominent bulge behind his zipper, now deflating like a pricked balloon.

I didn't need a mirror to know I was doused.

"Something about this fucking garden," he muttered. He retreated a step and flung his head from side to side. Water sprayed in all directions like Ginger after a bath.

In normal circumstances, I would have laughed at Dangerous' Golden Retriever impression, but tossing aside my inhibitions on a park bench did not qualify as normal. More like lunacy.

He stopped mid-shake, eyes widening.

I followed his stare and cringed. My wet dress! It clung to me like a second skin.

The bulge began to re-inflate.

"Eyes up here." I pointed to my face.

He dragged his gaze up and the lustful expression turned triumphant. "Damn, Princess, if that's how you don't want me, you'll be the death of me when you do."

I concealed my humiliation with what I hoped was a casual shrug. "I won't apologize for liking sex. Old habits but I'm reformed now."

"From what?"

"Dead-end relationships with womanizers. In fact, I think there's a support group for your kind—Jackasses Anonymous."

"I don't recall mentioning a relationship." His voice dropped to a husky tone that set my radar buzzing again. "I'm talking about sex. Wild, sweaty, unbridled, orgasmic, scream-worthy, dehydrating—"

"Enough with the adjectives already."

"I can move on to verbs if you like." His eyes flickered over my indecency.

I crossed my arms over my chest. "No need. I get it. You're a hit-it-and-quit-it type of guy."

He smiled. "Oversimplified, but close enough. I like to keep my personal and professional life… simple."

"And women upset this natural order?"

"Women have a tendency to be dramatic. They become sensitive, attached, and demanding. When that happens, things become messy. I don't have the time nor patience for dealing with those situations, so to avoid misunderstandings, I set clear ground rules."

"Please, enlighten me."

"One, no commitments or expectations. We're two people enjoying ourselves. Outside of that, we do whatever we please. Two, no involvement in personal issues. I enjoy my privacy and don't feel the need to share every aspect of my life. And three, which is most important, never mix personal and professional. No exceptions."

I snorted. "What? No scheduling demands, clothing criteria, or mandatory positions?"

"We can always add an addendum."

"And what if someone doesn't agree to these rules?"

"Then she doesn't belong in my bed."

"You're kind of an asshole, aren't you?"

Hypocrite, my inner voice admonished. *How is this different from the superficial relationships you specialize in?*

Okay, so I used sex as a temporary reprieve to fill the void inside me. Albeit brief, it helped me feel something other than the numbing cold that never thawed. Sex provided the perfect escape, one that distracted, felt good, and allowed me to stay in control. Enough to prevent doing anything stupid like blurting out incriminating secrets. Was it dysfunctional? Absolutely. But I at least acknowledged it. His scenario read more like a business arrangement.

The parties agree, in consideration of the herein contained three mutual rules, to perform sexual acts in consideration for...

What idiot would sign on the dotted line?

An image of long black hair and almond eyes flashed in my head. Was he ousting her from the inner circle or looking to add to his harem?

"And how does it end?" I asked.

"When it stops being fun for either of us, we walk away."

Translation—when I meet my next piece of ass, I kick yours to the curb.

"We both know it would be better than good." He stepped forward to place his hands on my shoulders. "In fact, if not for the lamentable irrigation system here, I believe you'd be a satisfied woman right now."

"You don't know what you're talking about," I grumbled.

His wolfish smile could have devoured me whole. "Frustration makes people grumpy. Let me finish what we started and then we'll talk." His hands slid down my arms as if to rekindle the memory of those fingers.

I hustled back a few steps to break contact. My brain went on a hiatus when he touched me. "Thanks, but I've got it covered."

"Boyfriend?"

Now he asks? "You might want to lead with that next time."

"That's not an answer."

"No."

"Then?"

"Battery operated solution. I'm a liberated woman."

His eyes gleamed. "I'd love to get in on that equation."

I couldn't suppress my shudder of excitement.

He mistook my reaction for the chill in the air and removed his suit jacket. He draped it across my shoulders. "Let's get you inside before you freeze."

We walked in silence while my mind raced. Not accustomed to transparency, his honesty threw me. Instead of showering a girl with false promises, he openly admitted what he thought of women—as unflattering as it was. Ultimately, he'd screw around like all men, but he never feigned monogamy to begin with. This behavior aligned with my low expectations of humanity on which I based most of my decisions. People always lived up to their worst selves but seldom admitted it and much less prepared you for it.

This was refreshing.

Which meant it couldn't happen. According to Nicki, the book titled *Emotionally Healthy Relationships for Dummies* contained one page, which read:

What would Jasmine Monroe do?

Now go do the opposite.

The End.

How could Nicki understand that what she deemed as my destructive impulses were a necessary evil? My past rendered any relationship with a respectable man impossible. Not that I believed one even existed and were merely rumored to have been sighted like Sasquatch or the Loch Ness Monster.

That meant Nicki's friendship—even built on lies—was the closest I'd come to personal interaction. Given that realization, adhering to her request became a minor price to pay.

Dangerous paused at the door and drew his coat tighter around me until it concealed my dress. "Keep it closed. One peep at you from his functioning eye and Bryce will go apoplectic." He pulled his phone from his pocket and pressed a button. "Meet me in front, please." He disconnected, placed a hand on my back, and used it as a rudder to steer me.

"I should say goodbye to Wayne," I protested. "I don't want to be rude." *And I want the contract.*

Chase didn't slow. "Would you like to explain the man's coat over your wet body or should I?"

I quickened my pace.

A well-built, brown-haired man with a ruddy complexion waited beside a glossy black Mercedes. From his stance, I guessed former military.

"Richard, please take Princess home," Chase requested.

Richard smiled at me while opening the door.

Oh, a nice thug.

"This isn't necessary," I protested.

"Not open for discussion. I have some business to take care of here."

Does your business have sleek black hair and exotic eyes?

I shrugged the jacket off, but Chase stopped me. "Keep it on until you get home."

"But it's—"

"Too lethal." He maneuvered me into the car. "You don't need every man leering at you like some prize."

"Besides you?"

"That doesn't count." He leaned in and brushed his lips lightly over mine. "I'm going to see you naked." He closed the door before I could respond.

"An elevator and a park bench?" Nicki shrieked. "Has this guy heard of a bed?"

The thought of rolling around in tangled sheets with Dangerous revved up both my imagination and my pulse.

Nicki's interrogation had begun the moment she spotted my damp dress and limp hairdo. Thankfully, I had left Dangerous' coat in the car. No reason to cross paths again.

"I've got to see him for myself." Nicki departed and quickly returned with her laptop. She stretched across my bed and moments later, an image of a chiseled face, tousled black hair, and startling green eyes filled the screen.

"Fuck me!" Nicki shook her head and her curls sprang up to second that opinion. "I've never thought of going straight before, but this one is welcome to try and flip me."

"What are you? An omelet?" I ducked into the bathroom to peel off my sodden dress. I donned Bugs Bunny pajama bottoms and a tank top before opening the door wide enough to see her.

Though my explanation of the night's events included Chase's outrageous proposal—one that I explained as the Pinocchio request where I trade in my vibrator for a real human—I had omitted my slutty response. I couldn't bare another lecture tonight.

Nicki read aloud. "Chase Alexander Hale, thirty-two years old, born in Colorado, founder and owner of Predator Industries. Older brother named Derek. Lost both his parents in a car wreck when he was fifteen."

Hmmm. The silver spoon has some tarnish on it. Oddly, that offered some consolation. I didn't trust perpetually happy people.

"Seems our boy has a wild streak," Nicki commented. "Got into some criminal trouble in high school."

Go figure. Our common ground lies in derelict behavior.

Except I don't get caught. Amateur.

I turned on the faucet and splashed water on my face while Nicki raised her voice. "He attended NYU and in his sophomore year, created an online game called Hale Spawn. The game went viral, he made a killing, quit school, and started Predator Industries with a classmate named Cory Burns. He eventually bought Cory out and went on to create a billion-dollar company that branched out from developing games to acquisitions of software companies plagued by poor management or a lack of capital to launch their products." She released a low whistle. "Damn, the guy's rich. We're talking like 'has a patent on air' type of rich."

"If anyone could make a fortune playing games, it's Dangerous."

"I'm more interested in the bad part of him." After a few more clicks, Nicki looked up. "I can't find anything about the criminal record. What say you use your computer hocus-pocus?"

"Nah," I mumbled around my toothbrush. "It would be rude to snoop."

"When has that stopped you before?"

When it meant admitting I cared enough to make the effort.

Which is why I also didn't bring up shamelessly pumping Richard for information on the car ride home. As a former Navy Seal, he'd been hired as security for one of Chase's events and subsequently been hired by Chase for his personal security. Expecting to hear horror stories about his arrogant boss, I felt disappointed to learn nothing negative and was downright shocked when he told me how much his ten-year-old son adored Chase.

That man should not be allowed to corrupt America's youth. What could he possibly teach them? Seduction 101? The art of annoying women? Hopefully, Chase refrained from doling out any dating advice or he'd be dooming that poor kid to a life of solitude. A point I brought to Richard's attention. I could still hear his laugh.

"Check out his bevy of beautiful women," Nicki interrupted my thoughts, a huge grin on her face. She was enjoying this way too much. "This hunk of man meat is quite the eligible bachelor."

"Because it's illegal to marry your own reflection."

"Just think." Nicki rotated the computer as if I needed evidence of Chase's decadent lifestyle. "You could be plastered on the cover of some rag like this."

Curiosity won out and I moved closer. Monday night was a buxom redhead with legs up to her throat. Tuesday was a voluptuous blonde who probably came with her own pink Corvette and dreamhouse. Wednesday, a human embodiment of a blow-up doll, and Thursday depicted a familiar brunette with exotic almond eyes.

I returned to the sink to spit out equal parts toothpaste and disgust.

Nicki tilted her head. "Man, he's smoking up my screen. Check out that tattoo on his arm. You think he has more?"

I pictured the swirling design that wrapped around his firm bicep and continued up to parts unknown. The one that made me want to rip off his shirt and trace every last curve with my tongue.

Oops! Wrong answer. "Don't know."

"But it's hot."

"Don't care."

"Excellent." Nicki closed her computer. "You passed the test. The last thing you need is a man who gets laid more than railroad tracks. He's the very definition of why us lesbians are grateful to lead a dick-less life."

I nodded but my agreement stemmed from alternate concerns. Beneath all my objections and bravado, Dangerous scared the living hell out of me. I lost my mind around him and losing control made me vulnerable.

"Stay strong," Nicki said. "And remember, he's an anomaly. There are plenty of men out there capable of teaching you the wonders of human connection."

"What am I? A cyborg?"

"Nah, there's a beating heart in there somewhere. It's just a little hard to find beneath all the chains, thorns, layers of concrete, landmines, poison da—"

"I get it. I'll be good."

7

I woke from a dream filled with stargazer lilies. Something about lying naked on a bed of them while vivid green eyes—

I bolted upright.

I'm losing my fucking mind.

Not less than twenty-four hours ago, I was sprawled across Dangerous' lap like a horny senior on prom night, and now my subconscious mind wanted to finish the deed. And using none other than my favorite flower—a symbol of purity, no less—to do it.

I dragged myself from fantasy to sexually unfulfilled reality and tossed aside my sweat-dampened sheets. As I made my way to a colder than normal shower, I eyed my lily pin on the dresser. Traitor or innocent bystander? I chose forgiveness and hustled to get ready. Inappropriate sex dreams wreaked chaos on timetables.

Abandoning my morning walk for a cab, I made excellent time. Thirty minutes later, I stepped into the office elevator.

My body tingled.

Seriously? I'm developing an elevator fetish? Try explaining that one to a therapist.

Sue sat at her desk, sucking on a sludge-flavored smoothie. "Good morning," she said, resembling an adorable color-blind cheetah in a snug bright orange and black-dotted dress. Fire-engine red striped her hair.

I eyed her drink with morbid curiosity.

"Alfalfa sprouts, beet juice, and cod liver oil." She offered me the glass.

"I prefer food not off the Fear Factor menu. If you want to save time, why not go straight to the source?" I pointed out the window. "There's a patch of grass out back you can graze on. I won't tell the landlord."

"I'll check it out for my mid-morning snack," she replied with a grin and handed me a stack of messages.

Client. Keep.

Salesman. Trash.

Helena. Shred.

My hand froze. Chase Hale? Why couldn't he leave my waking life alone?

By 11:30 A.M., my morning granola bar had long ceased to control my hunger, and I was debating a food run when the outer door chimed. "I'm here to see Ms. Monroe," a familiar voice said.

I eagerly poked my head out. "Wayne, please come in."

He tore his focus away from Sue's slimy cuisine, and warmth flooded his brown eyes.

"Can I get you anything to drink?" I offered. If I waited for Sue, we'd dehydrate to nothing.

He shook his head, and I led him to the round table in the corner of my office. This had to be about the contract.

"I apologize for barging in," he began, "but I finished a meeting nearby and wanted to update you in person."

It's mine. This is it. Stop bouncing in your chair.

"Considering this morning's events, we're postponing the decision."

Huh? Those weren't the right words. "What events?"

He puckered his brow. "Leonard Bryce's employment was terminated. One minute, he's at his desk, and the next, security is escorting him out. I'm unclear why."

Justice, karma, vindication.

"I heard rumors of impropriety," he added, "but saw nothing to support that."

Lyndham must have a terrible vision plan.

He cleared his throat. "Sorry. I shouldn't divulge so much. I would hate for you to run screaming from us."

I thought of Leonard's stubby little meat hooks. "Not a chance."

"Good. I can tell you we've narrowed it down to two consultants—yourself and Teresa Stark."

"Stark." I repeated the name but came up empty. Sometimes staying in my little bubble left me at a disadvantage. "I appreciate you letting me know," I said, faking my enthusiasm. Another milk bottle knocked down.

"You're welcome. Did you enjoy the event the other night?"

"Um, it was..." *Dangerous* "Interesting."

"I was hoping for another dance after our first was so rudely interrupted."

Not without iron shoes.

"An unexpected situation come up," I explained. "Sorry if I left you alone to fend off more cat versus ferret stories."

"I'm afraid I sank to an all-time low and pretended my phone was vibrating with an urgent call."

"Excellent survival instinct."

"If you don't mind my asking, did Hale steal you away to

recruit you for the Wolfe project or because he needed the most beautiful woman in the room paying attention to only him?"

"Um, neither, I think." The only proposal forefront in my mind involved me naked on my back, or on top, maybe on my knees. *Stop it.* I dragged my mind back to the PG rated man in front of me.

Wayne clasped his hands together and his face puckered. "Heed my advice. Do not get involved with him. His indulgent pursuit of women is legendary, and you're far too good to become one of his casualties."

Couldn't argue with that. Except the part about my being too good. "You sound like you know him well."

"We went to the same college."

I raised my brows. Somehow, I couldn't imagine them pledging a fraternity together.

"Forget about him," Wayne blurted. "Have dinner with me instead."

I took a second to let the surprise wear off. Per Nicki's definition, Wayne belonged in the respectable man club. A conservative specimen with no outward vices. Someone I could stand beside without dodging flying sparks. But how would it play out? String him along until he learned the truth about me and then watch him bail? Why would he stay? No one ever did.

Not that it mattered. Because a more pressing concern existed. "I'm flattered but you're a key decision maker for a project I'm bidding on. At best, it's a conflict and, at worst, appears as influence."

Like Dangerous accusing me of flaunting my assets to get ahead.

Wayne's face must have resembled mine a few minutes ago. "I assure you, it wouldn't affect my decision."

"Perhaps not, but perception is reality. It's not wise to mingle personal with professional."

Rule Number Three.

Fuck! Why did everything keep coming back to him?

"I understand," he said, though his pout didn't agree. "Thank you for your time. I'll be in touch when we have a decision."

Not a minute after Wayne's departure, Sue bounded in. "Sounds like somebody's got a crush." She perched on the edge of my desk. "If you rock his world, we can bill our premium rate."

"Why is everyone dead set on whoring me out?" I grumbled. "And we still have to land the contract. Thanks to Leonard the Pervert, it's postponed. Even when something good happens, it screws us."

Sue grinned. "I guess Leonard Bryce finally messed with the wrong woman."

"I didn't do anything." I held my hands up. "Other than the litany of STDs added to his medical records and onslaught of gay porn sent to his office."

Sue burst out laughing. "Firing is too boring for you, boss." She cocked her head. "While you were with Wayne, Chase Hale called again. Care to tell me how we know the CEO of Predator?"

"We're pretending we don't."

"And why is that?"

"Don't you have work to do?"

"Always," she sighed. "My boss is a slave driver."

The following morning began well—and by that, I mean zero sex dreams. With no scheduled appointments, I decided to savor the temperate weather and dawdle my way in to work. Feeling extravagant, I stopped at a coffee cart and treated myself to a frothy drink with too many syllables and even more calories. As I sipped my indulgence, I meandered past a magazine vendor and… choked on a mouthful of foam. I stopped, setting off a chain reaction of stumbling pedestrians. The man closest to me swore, and I mumbled an insincere apology while I snatched an issue off the top rack. The caption read:

Software Mogul and Playboy, Chase Hale, Attends Business Function with Most Recent Love Interest.

Pictured below was Dangerous himself, elegant and gorgeous—his suit jacket noticeably absent—while the almond-eyed beauty clung to him like Saran Wrap. I paid the vendor and stuffed the copy in my bag.

With my magical morning tarnished, I gulped down the rest of my decadence and quickened my pace.

I entered the elevator, pressed the button, and acknowledged the rush of desire from my newfound fetish. Welcome to my new normal.

As I approached the office door, voices drifted. Sue in an uncharacteristically polite manner spoke, followed by... a familiar smooth chocolatey tone.

You have got to be fucking kidding me!

I slowed, every nerve suddenly vibrating. How could his voice alone do this to me? Especially on *my* turf. *My* territory. If someone was going to gain the upper hand, it better be me. Which meant canning the childish swooning and putting on my big-girl panties.

I charged on in.

Upon seeing me, Chase unfolded his long legs and stood. He wore black slacks and a charcoal gray button-down shirt, sleeves rolled to his elbows.

Who the heck has sexy forearms?

I caught myself searching for a glimpse of his tattoo.

So long to my big-girl bloomers.

"Late morning, Princess?"

Sue's eyebrows rose, but I kept a poker face and crossed to my office. As I passed, he whispered low, "Battery boyfriend keeping you up late?" I flushed. More like tawdry sex dreams with him in the Oscar-worthy lead.

"Can I get you some coffee, Chase?" Sue asked.

Seriously?

"Don't bother," I answered. "He won't be staying long."

Chase bent to collect his briefcase, and Sue almost toppled over her desk checking out his ass. 'Wow!' she mouthed as he followed me into my office. With an eye roll, I shut my door on her.

Chase cocked his head to the reception area. "What the hell is she drinking?"

"Probably something she dredged from the bottom of the lake." I placed my bag on the floor. It toppled to its side and the magazine slid out.

Crap! My eyes flew to his face but he hadn't noticed.

With a swift kick, I sent the magazine careening under my desk.

"Nice view," he commented on the large window.

I eyed him up. *Yup. Damn nice view.* "What are you doing here?"

"I thought you may not be receiving my messages." He settled his frame into a chair, and my office collapsed to the size of a shoebox. His presence commanded any space he occupied, including mine. So much for home advantage.

"I got them." With a sigh, I circled my desk and sat down. "And if you're planning on stalking me, please do it cyber-ly so I don't have to see you."

His lips quirked. "Where would the fun be in that?"

"Is that why you're here? For fun?"

"No. We have unfinished business."

"If you're referring to your proposal for no holds barred sex restricted by your control-freak rules then take my silence as your answer." I pointed to the door. I hated being considered a foregone conclusion.

He made no move to leave.

I huffed. "This may be a game to you, but we're in my workplace. Not some locale for one of your cheap romps."

"I don't know about that." He flattened his palms against the desk and those sexy forearms flexed. "This seems durable enough."

And the right height too.

Shit!

"Why me?" I asked with genuine curiosity. "You have more groupies lined up than women at a Black Friday sale. Throw a dart and pick one."

He grinned. "I'm more partial to the lottery method."

"Sorry. Neanderthal Power Ball is not my thing."

"I beg to differ," he said with a knowing smile.

I cursed the answering flush on my cheeks.

"However," he continued, "as much as I enjoy winding you up, I'm here to hire you."

"You're joking," I said.

"Nope."

"Then let me save you some time. Abso-fucking-lutely not."

"Not even a little curious?"

"Nope," I said, impressed with how much apathy I could muster into one word.

"Why the hostility, Princess? I'm asking nicely."

"Oh, did someone spike your oatmeal with anti-rude pills this morning?"

"It appears I'm not the only one in need of a prescription," he countered. "Can you at least attempt to be professional?"

"Me?" I shrieked. "I'm the grown up here. You're the one... You're so..." I flung my hands up. "God, if annoyance could be weaponized, we'd all be done for."

He chuckled and leaned back, lithe and casual.

A waiting game.

"Fine," I snapped. "I'll give you two minutes. On one condition."

"Name it," he said.

"When I decline, you will stop propositioning me, and that includes hinting, inferring, suggesting, coercing, implying, or insinuating."

"Someone's been poring over a thesaurus," he said and reached for his briefcase. "I trust any discussion from this point forward will be in the strictest confidence?"

"I make my living in security. If I blabbed proprietary information, I *would* have to use sex to stay in business."

His eyes twinkled. "It would make negotiating far more pleasurable."

Fuck. Being around Dangerous was... well, dangerous. I named him that for a reason.

I pointed at my bare wrist. "Tick tock."

He extracted a sheaf of papers and aligned each side until not a millimeter protruded.

Serves him right if he gets a paper cut.

He placed the stack on my desk and waited.

I responded with zero effort. It could have housed the secrets to the universe for all I cared. Unfortunately, as long as I resisted, a pair of unsettling green eyes drilled into me. I snatched the papers and feigned interest.

WOLFE PHASE 2. With a modicum of civility, I rifled through the summary, calendar, and milestones. Unimpressed, I skimmed until I reached the quality assurance phase. I frowned at the data.

He scrutinized my reaction. "Anything strike you as unusual?"

"The results have discrepancies." I fought valiantly against it but curiosity bested me. "What happened?"

"I've been asking that same question and have yet to receive a satisfactory answer."

"So ask better questions."

"When I acquired the company that created what will eventually be Wolfe," he launched into the history as if I cared, "I inherited a lead programmer named Sterling. I kept him because he created the original concept and initial beta project. No one has more native knowledge. But something's not right and if there's one thing I know, it's how to read people."

I almost laughed in his face. If that were true, he wouldn't be here.

"There's something I'm missing," he concluded.

"That would be sincerity." I pushed the stack over to him. "Are we done here?"

"Sterling is hiding something, and I'll be damned if I launch a product with my name on it unless I'm one hundred percent confident it aligns with Predator's vision."

Gone was the flirtatious man who propositioned me in the garden. This was Business Dangerous, professional, no nonsense, and the man who, as a college student, created what is now a billion-dollar company. I had to admit I admired this side of him.

But not enough to get involved. "And I'm concerned about this... because?"

"I want you to dig deeper."

"Why me?"

"I need an outsider." He leaned forward and the scent of spice and earth floated across the desk. "And as I recall, you're very, very good. Remember?"

Damn my big mouth.

"How do I know this isn't a thinly veiled scheme to feed your new hobby of harassing me?"

"Are you implying I would stoop so low as to use my company's good name to seduce a woman?"

"Yup."

He paused for a beat and then smiled. "Okay, maybe I would, but that's not what's happening here." He held up his left hand and extended three fingers. "Scout's honor."

"Wrong hand. And the answer is still no."

"Why?"

Because my freaking synapses stop firing around you.

"Because Wolfe is a potential competitor." The words weren't out of my mouth before I acknowledged the absurdity of them. Wolfe and I catered to different markets. My smaller, custom niche ranked nowhere near its magnitude. In fact, Wolfe presented a coveted opportunity. The Holy Grail of software. Any sane programmer would leap at the chance.

Too bad he made me insane.

I opted for an alternate tactic. "I'm too busy to take on anything else."

"The Lyndham bid?"

I nodded.

"Fuck Lyndham. Well, not literally. Erik Lyndham's too old for you and he's already balls deep in women trouble. You should let that one go. Give it to Stark."

"Why would I do that?"

"Because it may never happen. They postponed it with no definitive date."

"I know. Wayne came by to tell me."

"Prep School making house calls now?" He scoffed. "Why bore women over the phone when you can do it in person?"

"He happens to be pleasant company."

"Sure, if you run out of valium," Chase said dryly. "Trust me when I tell you Lyndham's a bad call. Let it go."

"Nope."

"Fine. Then give Wolfe a cursory evaluation while you're waiting on their decision. You either find something or you don't. What's the worst that could happen?"

Option C where I lose it, tear his clothes off, and mount him like a jockey, vying for a spot in the Kentucky Derby.

"You're a programmer," I pointed out. "Take a stab at it yourself."

"I developed games. Feel free to call me when you want cheat codes to power up. You're the self-proclaimed expert. If you live up to your own hype, you'll find something long before Lyndham gets back to you." He eyed my dubious expression. "I'll pay triple your fee."

"All problems cannot be solved with money."

Triple?

"*Most* problems cannot be solved with money," he corrected. "Lucky for me, this isn't one of them."

Damn my bank account. Why had I decided to go legit?

"Five times my fee," I announced. "Consider it hazard pay for dealing with a colossal pain in the ass."

"Done." His face broke out in a dazzling smile that stole my breath.

Wow! Happy Dangerous is sexier than Angry Dangerous.

"I'll give you the weekend," I clarified. "If I find nothing by Monday, I'm finished and I bill for all time spent." I took a breath and addressed the taboo elephant stuffed in my office. "And no funny business."

"Agreed," he said. "Rule number three. No mixing business with personal." He shot me a wicked smile. "Until Monday."

Dear Lord! I just made a deal with a devil in Wolfe's clothing.

8

I entered the apartment in time to see a curly blonde whirlwind whoosh by me. "I picked up an extra shift," Nicki called out. "Dinner is in the fridge and my computer is on the counter. It's on the fritz again."

"Stop downloading porn," I yelled back.

Nicki's muffled reply came through the closing door. Something about living vicariously through Google.

I had barely set my purse down when someone knocked at the door. A minute later, I possessed a manila envelope that contained my access information and a handwritten note. Chase didn't waste any time in business or pleasure.

Looking forward to working together.

-C

. . .

I tossed the note in the trash then changed into Tasmanian Devil pajama pants and a tank top. I heated the lasagna my saint of a roommate left me while I turned on her computer. When competing against the woman who fed me, Dangerous could wait. I cleared the cache, rebooted, and smiled. Same thing every time. If only all my clients were this predictable.

I logged in to Predator Industries next and laughed through a mouthful of pasta when I saw my limited access. Adorable. I tempered the urge to peruse it all. No reason to get further involved.

An hour later, I swapped my empty plate for a bag of Cheetos —I did my best thinking while crunching—and as much as I hated to admit it, Chase was on to something. The information didn't gel. I was officially hooked. I never could walk away from a puzzle.

I woke Saturday, still mulling over the anomalies. After a quick shower, I emerged in a yellow tank top and black leggings—my bumblebee ensemble. I skipped the makeup and fastened my hair in a ponytail before hurrying out to the living room. As I scrolled through more code, I realized something was missing. With a groan, I accepted my next move and picked up the phone.

Chase answered on the third ring. "Princess?" he said, his voice punctuated with quick breaths as if I'd caught him mid-strenuous activity. Good Lord. Was he having sex?

Right. What kind of moron answers the phone during sex?

"Am I disturbing you?" I couldn't help asking.

"Finishing a workout. Got something already?"

"I suspect there are duplications of Sterling's code. Maybe an external storage device if your company allows it, although he probably would have removed it from the office."

"Unlikely. I've had security on him like mirrors on a cheap hotel room ceiling. I'll get back to you."

An hour later, Chase stood at my front door and my mouth turned to sand. The universe had committed a grave injustice arming one man with so much sex appeal, but I'd have to curse it out later. Right now, I was all about admiring its mistake. His tight faded jeans looked like the ones he'd worn in the elevator. Coupled with the white T-shirt stretched across his broad chest, he gave off a 1950s movie star vibe. James Bond by night, James Dean by day.

Footsteps approached behind me. "I'm leaving for the restaurant. Who was at the door?" Nicki's blue eyes grew to Power Puff girl proportions at the sight of our guest. "Google be damned," she breathed.

Chase introduced himself but she ignored the gesture. Instead, she slid her gaze down, lingering on his bicep and the tattoo that flexed from the weight of the box he carried. Her eyes narrowed and I could guess the thoughts bouncing around in her frizzy-haired head. *Work related or a prop for an illicit tryst?* Her answer came in the form of a "Hmmm" that conveyed more doubt than any sound should before she walked around him and out the door.

With an amused expression, Chase entered and placed the box on the coffee table. He withdrew a laptop, external hard drive, and two flash drives.

"All yours." He gestured to the spoils.

"Thanks for bringing these so quickly."

"No problem. I just tossed his office."

"Isn't he going to be mad?"

"It's my fucking company. I can do whatever I damn well please."

I shrugged and inserted the first flash drive. "I'll need some time to sort through these." When he did not take the hint, I looked up. "I'm sure you have better things to do than hang around here. The women in Manhattan aren't going to seduce themselves."

He chuckled and inclined his head. "Anything else I can get you before I leave?"

"A cup of tea would be nice," I joked. Like a megalomaniac would serve me.

He headed for the kitchen.

"I wasn't serious," I called out. "I can get it myself."

"You're too expensive to waste on beverage service. Stay put."

"Top right cupboard. Earl Grey. Cream and two sugars." *A shot of Irish whiskey would be nice.*

He returned a few minutes later, holding a steaming mug. "I apologize in advance if I drooled in your tea. I couldn't help it when I saw what's on the counter."

"That would be Nicki's chocolate raspberry torte." *One of my bribes from our 'no more assholes' agreement.*

"It looks delicious."

That sounded funny coming from a mouth that ranked higher on the appetizing meter.

Chase handed me the mug then sat beside me, brushing against my bare shoulder. I suppressed a shudder by taking a quick sip.

He leaned in. "Two more days."

I swallowed down more nerves than liquid. "Until what?"

His voice lowered to a delectably dark tone. "Until I hear those sweet sounds that you made for me in the garden."

Before I could respond, "Talk Dirty to Me" blared from his pants. I lurched and yelped as hot tea sloshed down my tank top. Chase reached for his phone.

Saved by glam metal music.

"Hale." Chase listened for a bit. "Is he crazy? No, I do not agree to those terms. I'll review it and get back to you." He stabbed the screen and shoved the phone in his pocket.

"Eighties hair bands?" I said as I tugged at my soggy tank. "Really?"

"What can I say? I'm a product of—"

"Bad taste?"

"—my older brother." He stood and headed for the door. "I have a deal in the works that's going south due to the owner's personal drama. I need to go do damage control. If you need anything else, call me."

Finally devoid of distractions and clothed in a clean tank top, I settled in to get some work done. I opened Sterling's first file.

Ewwwwwwww!

I closed it fast enough to sprain my fingers. Thank goodness I skipped breakfast. What the hell was wrong with that man? I subjected myself to three more files before I gave up on that thumb drive—and possibly food for the rest of my life. A lobotomy couldn't delete those images from memory.

The next one yielded fewer disturbing results and more of what I hoped. As I sifted through chunks of discarded code, I became convinced Sterling had altered the program. Now, I needed to trace his files and locate the hidden code.

I lost count of how many obsession-filled hours lapsed before a knock disrupted my analysis. I grumbled and dragged myself to the door. "What?" I barked as I opened it.

Chase held up a huge bag of Chinese food. "Something tells me you have one of those compulsive, workaholic personalities."

My stomach rumbled before I could close the door. "Any chance I can send you away with a tip?"

"Here's a tip." He strolled in and placed the food on the table. "Studies show productivity declines in proportion to growing hunger."

"Same goes for annoyance." I went into the kitchen and returned with plates and utensils. "I know why you're really here. You want that torte."

"So cynical for one so young." He began opening cartons and spooning out food. "Can't I just be a nice guy for feeding you? I'm guessing you're not the domestic type."

As soon as I spied the shrimp wontons, my stomach convinced me to cut him some slack. "Fine. You got me there. My culinary talents end at oatmeal or grilled cheese and tomato soup."

"Both tempting if I were eighty-five years old." He scooped kung pao chicken on my plate before adding some to his own. "So how long have you been in New York?" he asked as he opened a container of orange chicken. The pungent sweet and spicy scent filled the air.

"Ten years."

"From?"

"California." I opted for a fork over chopsticks. I wanted the food to reach my mouth.

He took the chopsticks. *Of course he did.*

"Why did you leave?"

"New York is on the other side of—" What the hell? This wasn't confession time. I shoveled an enormous bite of Mongolian beef in my mouth.

If he noticed the awkward lull, he didn't comment. "Why do you avoid software functions? They're a great networking tool for a sole proprietor." He dunked a pot sticker in a puddle of soy sauce and popped it in his mouth.

"Because people annoy me, especially when they ask lots of questions or require inane small talk."

"Like droning incessantly about pet ferrets?" He held up his thumb and forefinger. "I came this close to punching him in the face."

"What do you expect when you throw a bunch of nerds together in a social setting?" I pointed out. "Witty banter?"

"Present company excluded."

"I wouldn't be so quick to rule me out. I've been to my share of Comic-Cons."

"As have I."

"Please tell me you didn't dress up."

"Absolutely not," he said with a deadpan expression. "I reserve that for Star Trek conventions."

I laughed and choked on a stray noodle.

"Careful, Princess," he advised. "I have another day of labor to collect."

"In that case, shut up. I'm not coordinated enough to eat and talk."

He took the hint, and we continued in silence. As we neared the end of our meal, he fished in the bag and with a flick of his wrist, tossed a fortune cookie to me. I tore the wrapper, cracked it open, and released an unladylike snort.

Chase reached over and plucked the tiny paper from my hands. "*Your true love may be right in front of you*," he read. "I don't know whether to be relieved or offended by your reaction."

"Offended?" I repeated. "Have you met you? Or do you need a reminder?" I held up an index finger while doing my best to imitate his posture. "Rule number one. No emotional relationships. They're messy and confusing, and since I'm easily confused, relationships are forbidden. When women get emotional, mass hysteria ensues, and during their looniness, they inexplicably Velcro themselves to me."

I held up two fingers. "Rule two. No conversations containing personal information. Only nonsensical babbling please. I'll accept incoherent sounds if there's no embedded code. Or better yet, while in the throes of passion, feel free to shout out my name. In fact, I'm so magnificent, I might yell my own name out."

He threw his head back and his laughter echoed throughout the room. "Nice impersonation," he said, still grinning. "But I can think of better uses for that smart mouth."

Whoa!

"My turn," he said, "Though, I doubt I'll be able to top that precocious performance." He snapped his cookie and read. "*Someone near you may not be who they appear*. That's accurate."

I stilled.

"Fucking Sterling," he muttered.

My heart took a few seconds to start up again. Damn my paranoia. Would it ever get easier?

I stood to gather the dishes. "Thanks for dinner, but I have a lot of work left." I noted his eager expression and rolled my eyes. "Seriously?"

He nodded.

"Fine," I sighed. "One slice and then you leave."

He grinned while collecting the cartons then followed me into the kitchen. He eyed the dessert with the same longing women directed at him.

I plated two slices then opened the fridge to remove a tall can. I vigorously shook the container, upended it, and the sound of compressed air filled the room as a mountain of whipped cream blanketed my dessert.

"Are you sure that's enough?" he asked as he eyed the mini ski slope on my plate.

"Not yet." I tilted my head back, positioned the spout above my open mouth and—*shwwwwwwft.* I waved the can at him. "Your turn. Like a baby bird."

He shrugged and angled his head back. I stood on the tips of my toes and hovered the can above his mouth.

And sprayed... and sprayed... and sprayed.

With a strangled noise, he shoved my arm away and a blizzard of white foam exploded. He sucked down the mouthful and followed it with a gulp of air. A blob detached from his white beard and plopped on the floor.

I hooted with laughter.

"You're crazy!" The sexy, freakishly tall garden gnome grabbed the can from my fingers. "This stuff makes you even more unstable." He turned on the faucet and splashed water over his face.

Still chuckling, I dampened a washcloth and rid the kitchen of all signs of debauchery before Nicki returned and strangled me.

He straightened and I handed him a towel. "You missed a spot," I said. Without thinking, I reached up and rubbed the remaining foam off his jaw.

I froze, my hand on his face.

Before I could withdraw, he caught my wrist.

Mischief glinted in his green depths as he brought my thumb to his mouth. He flicked his tongue over the tip and a wall of lust nearly knocked me over. I fought back a groan as my finger begged to slide inside that erotic mouth.

He released me before I could act on it.

"Monday," he said and headed out of the kitchen. "And I'm bringing the whipped cream."

Oh God!

I sagged against the counter. Now that my sex-crazed harlot had come out to play, kenneling her would be a bitch. I hummed a Christmas carol, recited the alphabet, and named the last ten presidents before I deemed myself presentable enough to join him at the table.

I deemed wrong.

I was toast the instant he took his first bite. "Bloody hell," he sighed. "Your roommate is a saint." His face ignited with pleasure as he drew out the experience to exact as much gratification from the bite as possible.

Is that how he treats a woman in bed?

"I can't believe someone hasn't snatched her up for her culinary skills." He scooped another forkful, his face a mask of sinful bliss.

Please don't saddle me with a dessert fetish next.

"What's her deal anyway?" he persisted. "Single?"

He practically caressed the fork with his tongue. I swear I heard the tines moan.

Lucky utensil.

I averted my gaze before my heart gave out. "Why? Interested?"

"Not my type."

"Female, beautiful, and breathing? Sounds like a winner to me."

"Something tells me I'm not on the right team."

I looked at him, surprised by his astuteness. Then again, he would know. He consumed women like they were on clearance.

A gleam entered his eye. "Have the two of you ever…"

"No. Scrub that kinky brain of yours."

He wiggled his brows. "A guy can fantasize, can't he?"

"Give me a break. One snap of your fingers and you could summon an orgy faster than ordering a pizza."

He didn't disagree.

9

"Good morning," Nicki thrust her face inches from mine. "Excellent. No sex."

"How can you tell?" I maneuvered around her to slice the last bagel and pop it in the toaster.

"No sated glow, no remorse, and still uptight."

"Nice work, Sherlock," I said. "Now do you believe it's just business?"

"I know little about offices, but I'm certain water cooler buddies don't drool at each other like Fred Flintstone over a slab of brontosaurus ribs."

Now I was craving ribs. Maybe I could talk her into making some. "I'm helping him solve a problem while earning good money. That's all. It's a win-win."

"I guess there's something to be said for him wanting your brains *and* your body. That's more than most of the men you go for."

"They want more than *my* body," I protested. "They want the bodies of every other female they see."

"The fact that you make that sound normal concerns me."

I shrugged. "It's the way of the world."

"And your view of the world scares me even more."

If she ever got a true glimpse of it, she'd never leave the house again.

The toaster dinged and I shifted to slather a hefty amount of cream cheese on my bagel.

"I'm off to the restaurant for vegetable delivery day." Nicki grabbed her keys and cell phone. "I thought about setting you up with my produce guy, but the bastard saddled me with squishy tomatoes last week, so instead of a date with a hot girl, he's getting my foot up his ass." She took the bagel off my plate and blew me a kiss. "Behave yourself."

I bade my absconded breakfast farewell then settled for a bowl of cereal. With a courier scheduled to collect Chase's work product later, I wasted no time attacking Sterling's computer. Based on yesterday's experience, I covered my eyes and peeked through my fingers. This time, instead of the threat of blindness, I found file transfers to an external network. No surprise when the network yielded encryption up the wazoo. Impressive, but nowhere near my league.

Without breaking a sweat, I hacked through the firewall and gawked at the windfall of data. Talk about an information hoarder. I wanted to bust the bastard on principle alone for jerking me around. *Five times my normal bill rate*. I repeated the mantra several times before attacking the mess.

A few hours later, I had my answer.

Checkmate, you son of a bitch.

And that's when I realized my mistake.

A hefty chunk of my survival relied upon avoiding attention, which meant maintaining a delicate balance between skill and mediocrity. I applied enough of my genius to run a successful company but reined it in before attracting unwanted notoriety. Sometimes maintaining the equilibrium took more energy than the work itself.

So how could I explain what I'd just accomplished? This was some next-level shit.

But damned if I let some two-bit hacker outsmart me.

And damned if I admitted this was my ego talking.

A knock interrupted my mental quandary. I answered the door. "Sorry but I need a little more—" Chase rested against the jamb, casual in jeans and a black T-shirt. I averted my eyes before his tractor beam of lust sucked me in. Too late. My body already had liftoff. "What happened to sending a courier?"

"What happened to relinquishing my property?"

"Do you want this done or not?"

He stepped inside. "If you don't have anything, it's okay."

His calm acceptance of failure confused me. Unless he doubted my abilities. "You don't believe I can solve this?"

He shrugged. "It was worth a shot, but I can find someone else to crack it."

"Are you insinuating I'm incompetent?"

A smile tugged at his lips. "At least you have your looks to fall back on."

"Unbelievable." My molars ground together. "Have you always been shallower than a beach at low tide?"

"You could see it as a compliment."

"Would you be flattered if people assumed you're useless based on how you look?"

His smile widened into a full-on grin. "You think I'm good-looking."

"That's not what—" I noticed the gleam in his eyes and stopped. Why did I let him goad me?

However offensive, his low expectations offered a solution to my dilemma. Table my pride, play dumb, and accept the title of bimbo. Being underestimated did come with advantages.

But damned if I let an insufferable rich boy call me incompetent.

And there goes my ego again.

But something more sinister loomed, serious enough to usurp my pettiness. If Sterling succeeded, people could suffer, and though my expertise excluded moral gray areas, wouldn't that make me complicit? I hated involving myself in matters unrelated to me. Not my business. Not my problem. Words that kept me safe.

But I already struggled with the weight of *my* sins. Were my shoulders strong enough to add someone else's?

Shit! I was about to do something stupid.

"Chase, I need to—"

He was on the couch, feet propped, phone in hand.

"Please, make yourself at home," I mumbled, irritated with how he commandeered my sanctuary. I was running out of sacred locations.

With less enthusiasm than the achievement warranted, I grabbed Sterling's laptop and settled beside Chase. "As you know, Wolfe captures account info and credentials using sophisticated encryption." I directed him to the screen. "Here's the issue. This code creates a backdoor that sends the data to Sterling's private server. The encryption is on par, so the firewall won't detect it. It masks as an information packet when in reality—"

"—it gives him open season on any business using Wolfe," Chase finished.

"It's nothing tricky," I lied, downplaying the brilliant execution and, hopefully, the brilliance of the woman who discovered it. Never mind that Sterling had broken the code into so many circuitous and complex pieces, it took a warped mind, the patience of a monk, and the tenacity of one pissed off woman to piece it together. "When he executes this section here—"

"—he can drain my end users blind!" Chase sprang up with enough force to rattle the couch. "That two-bit, dickless, son of a worthless whore. I will fuck that man's career in so many directions, he'll be begging for a job in a fucking video arcade."

I'd witnessed Angry Dangerous before—usually with me as the catalyst—but as an innocent bystander this time, I settled back to watch the show.

First, he paced, his long legs making easy work of my living room. Next came a vein throbbing in his neck. His fists clenched as if searching for an outlet then relaxed to allow his fingers to stab through his thick mane. It flopped in all directions, still maintaining its boyish charm, which contradicted the litany of expletives pouring from his mouth, most colorful enough to make a sailor blush. I raised my brows and committed a few to memory. I'd have to look them up later.

While Chase continued to rant about a rain of hellfire descending upon Sterling's picked over carcass, I tilted my head forward and grimaced at the tightness. Two straight days hunched over a computer, coupled with the tension he managed to inflict on me, and my taut muscles were ready to snap. I weakly massaged the stiffness.

Warm hands pushed mine aside, causing tingles along my skin. "Chase, don't..." I protested, but his strong fingers began targeting my muscles. My head lolled forward as my aching knots melted, and I practically purred. Maybe I was enjoying his hands on me too much, but I didn't care. After my weekend marathon session, I deserved pampering.

The home landline shrilled.

"Stay," he commanded as if my wet-noodle-like limbs would allow anything else. His magic fingers skimmed along the column of my throat and a wall of heat slammed through me. I think the phone rang again, but I couldn't hear over the blood roaring in my ears.

Click.

"Hey, Jas," Nicki's voice filled the room. "You're not answering your cell. You better not be violating our deal over Sir Screws-A-Lot—"

My eyes popped open. *The answering machine!* Why did she insist on plugging that archaic piece of crap in?

"—because you agreed to follow Operation No More Assholes—"

I scrambled to rise, but Chase's powerful grip held me in place.

"—and if you're tempted, remember how dangerous hotness can be. Like that Greek story where that dumbass built wings from paper—"

"Move!" I shoved Chase away.

"—and flew into the sun. Poof! Splat! Greek roadkill. The moral of the story… if you break your promise, you are toast."

I almost face-planted lurching for the handset. But it didn't matter. She and her big mouth had already hung up.

Like an idiot, I stood with the receiver in my hand. Maybe if I came clean about Nicki's scheme regarding sex-crazed hooligans, he'd understand and abandon his pursuit.

Not likely when he was their leader.

Alternate plan. Be a confident idiot. I grabbed an empty file box and walked towards him. "Here." I shoved it in his midsection. "Don't forget anything."

He packed up the materials while making no effort to hide his amusement. When finished, he stepped into the hallway and turned towards me. "It's wax."

"What?"

"Icarus' wings were made from wax. He flew too close to the

sun and they melted, causing him to plummet into the sea and drown, thus negating *his* hotness. You might want to update your roommate."

"Shut up." I slammed the door in his self-satisfied face.

There was no mistaking the sound of laughter from the other side.

10

Sue smiled at me the next morning, her eyes sparkling brighter than her hot pink beret. I waited for an explanation but when none came, proceeded to my office. The answer hit me in a wave of floral perfume, emanating from the enormous bouquet of fuchsia and purple stargazer lilies on my table.

I flushed as I recalled my dream.

Great. Let's add lilies to my growing list of sexual fetishes after elevators and desserts.

I eased into my chair and lowered my forehead onto the cool wood, adding a few thumps for good measure. Only Chase possessed the ability to transform a symbol of purity into depravity.

"What are you doing?" Sue entered my office.

"Kick starting my brain."

"Well hurry it up so you can divulge. Are they from Wayne Parker?" When I didn't answer, she snatched up the card. "Amazing work, Princess. Looking forward to future endeavors. Yours Truly, Chase."

I glanced up. "Before you get any ideas in that blue-streaked head of yours, it's a thank you for some last-minute weekend consulting."

"Weekend consulting, eh?" The dimples in her cheeks flashed. "Is that what people are calling it these days?"

"Last time I checked, smartass was not in your job description."

"Sure it is." She mock saluted as she backed away. "Under 'other duties as assigned'."

The phone rang and I braced myself, waiting to hear Chase's name, but Sue announced a client instead. The next was a vendor. Then another client. And so the day progressed, anticipating every call with dread, none of which lived up to my expectations.

As closing time approached, I exhaled my first full breath of the day. Strange how much energy I expended preparing for something that never happened. Even odder was how closely relief resembled disappointment.

I arrived home to find Nicki on the couch, painting her nails a traffic-stopping red. She examined my face. "Excellent. No sex."

Wow! While clueless about my plethora of secrets, she could read my coitus status like a cookbook. Unbelievable.

"I'm proud of you," she continued. "Especially with the way Dangerous drools over you like a monkey over a banana split." She wiggled her glossy tipped fingers. "What do you think? It's called 'I'm Not Really a Whore'." She waved her arms, and I ducked to avoid a smack to the face. "I'm not sure if I like it."

"Maybe it's the false advertising."

She made a face at me.

"No judgement," I said. "A whore is just a woman with a man's morals."

A sharp knock interrupted us. "Expecting anyone?" I asked.

She didn't hear me, too engrossed with scrutinizing her fingers. "I don't think it's wanton enough for me."

"I assure you," I said as I swung open the door. "You exude sluttiness in spades."

"Why, thank you," Chase responded. "Though I was going more for the hard-to-get vibe."

"Considering you're here, I don't think you've grasped that concept."

As usual, my eyes contradicted my surly tone by drinking in every inch of him. *If he looks this gorgeous at the end of the day, how the fuck does he start out?* Today, Business Dangerous stood before me dressed in a dark blue suit and white shirt, the first few buttons undone. I liked that he'd ditched the tie. Why a man began each morning by putting a noose around his neck baffled me. Maybe because most deserved a good old-fashioned hanging.

"What do you want?" I asked.

"Answers." He folded his arms over his broad chest. "There's something off about you."

"Just because a woman rejects you, doesn't mean she's not right in the head."

"That's debatable but not the issue," he said. "I'm here about your findings."

I sighed and stepped aside. I suppose five times my rate included follow-up questions.

He entered and turned to zero in on me. "When you explained Sterling's code, I failed to recognize the magnitude of it but upon closer analysis, what you did in a short amount of time is mind-blowing. Few people can blow my mind."

"Maybe because they're too busy blowing other parts of you," I said. Nicki snickered behind me.

Chase's features hardened. "That caliber of investigation resides in a class of its own. So who was it?"

"Who was what?"

"The person who helped you."

"Uh oh," Nicki mumbled from her perch on the couch while applying another coat. One more and flames would shoot from her fingertips.

"That's your take-away?" I hissed. "Why? Because in your fucked-up, misogynistic, pig-headed world, no woman can think for herself?"

"No," he said calmly, "because if you're capable of pulling this off, you wouldn't be an underrated programmer barely a tick above breaking even."

Okay, he had a point.

"When I confronted Sterling," Chase continued, "he said few people possessed the talent to uncover his hack, because he embedded it with genius complexity. Not to mention the encryption you had to crack. He was practically salivating to find out who broke it."

"You didn't tell him, did you?"

"Of course not. At first, I chalked it up to hubris. All hackers believe themselves exceptional, but then I showed it to Kunnen, and you know what he said?"

I assumed the question was rhetorical. And who the hell was Kunnen anyway?

"He said that even if someone beat the tricky security, nobody in their right mind could piece together that level of deception so quickly."

"Maybe I'm not in my right mind," I retorted. Not a flattering comeback but my fight was fizzling, probably doused by the sweat running down my back.

"I'm aware of that." His unwavering green eyes pinned me. "But there's more."

Fuck! Fuck! Fuck! No good deed goes unpunished.

"Hold up a minute." Nicki placed her polish down then raised her hands. Whether to take up arms on my behalf or dry her nails, I didn't care. She made an excellent distraction. "Jas saved your ass from a catastrophe that could have been one of the worse embarrassments since… since…" She turned to me. "A little help please."

"Windows Vista?" I offered.

"Okay. That." She directed her annoyance back to Chase. "And you have the audacity to storm in here and accuse her of…" She paused again. "What exactly are you accusing her of?"

"This isn't about gratitude," Chase said. "It's about confidentiality. She allowed a third-party access to my proprietary software, which violates our agreement."

Seriously? I could crack that security while half asleep and hungover. "If I assure you it was me, can we drop this?" I asked.

"No, because that raises more questions. Such as why a computer phenom is pursuing second rate projects that don't showcase an iota of her capabilities?"

"I'm going after Lyndham."

"I rest my case."

"Maybe we're not all glory mongers who crave attention, status, and money."

"Is that what you think of me?"

"If it gets you to leave, then yes."

"Not a chance. Either someone helped you or not. Which is it?"

I shifted from one foot to the other. "It's not that simple."

"Then explain it in small words, and I'll try to keep up."

"Why can't you take my word and leave it alone?"

"Because if my company has taught me anything, it's to deal in truth over trust. If you're not providing answers, I'll find them on my own and I promise, when I learn whatever it is you're hiding, you will not like how this ends."

I wasn't liking it right now.

Normally, I'd exhibit minor concern for a random individual poking around my past. I'd covered my tracks so thoroughly, you'd never know if a freight train used them, but his tone felt more personal than business, and not only did he wield the resources to dig until he never saw daylight, but he also had that extra push of motivational juice to unearth every pebble. Which meant uncovering answers to much more than this one question.

Fuck! Fuck! Fuck! How could I have been so stupid?

With nothing left but damage control, I gestured to the couch where Nicki sat, still flapping her arms like a bird on meth. With a suspicious look, he obliged, maneuvering away from her flailing limbs.

I sat in the recliner and mentally calculated the amount of information necessary to appease him.

"Well?" Chase said.

Nicki's hand connected with the side of his head. "Oops."

A shame she didn't hit him harder.

"I wasn't lying about being very good," I started. *I just lie about everything else.* "I downplay my skills when it suits me. In this case, it didn't."

He shook his head. "I don't buy it. I researched your company. If you're so talented, why aren't you more successful?"

Of course the nosy bastard did. "*My* business choices are none of *your* business."

"They are when you breach our agreement."

"I kept my word," I snarled, offended over the slight on my integrity. So what if I lost it years ago? He didn't know that.

"I'm done here." He moved as if to get up.

"I figured it out because it takes one to catch one."

"What the hell does that mean?"

"It means I'm a hacker," I shouted. "Like Sterling. Only better.

Kind of a big deal. Well, more than kind of. At least I used to be. That is, I don't do it to the degree I used to, but is it something you do or what you are? I still dabble... eh, more than dabble but not illegal, okay, not *as* illegal. Assuming there are shades..." I realized I was rambling about the fine points of breaking the law. My next words came out in a rush. "So help me, Chase, if you screw me over on this, I will..."

What would I do? Hack him to death? This wasn't his fault. I screwed up.

Surprise flickered across his features before he dropped his face in his hands. His shoulders shook with fury. I'd witnessed a multitude of emotions from Dangerous: anger, disapproval, lust, but never condemnation. How would contempt look on him? I dreaded finding out.

He'll never trust me again.

Probably thinks I sabotaged his project.

Doesn't want to sleep with me anymore.

Wait! What!?

The silence extended, stretching my nerves along with it. *Bring on the damnation already.*

But he remained quiet, shoulders still vibrating.

I approached my snapping point. "Dammit, Chase. Say something."

He threw his head back and released a howl that ricocheted around the room.

Stunned, I pointed at the crazy man laughing in front of me. "You're seeing this too, right?" I asked Nicki.

"Yup."

"What's the protocol for a mental break?" Cheetos and ice cream worked for me. Who knew with Chase? Whiskey and a slutty blonde?

The hoots eventually subsided, and he sagged against the couch, sucking air through the dopey grin on his face.

Positive he'd misheard, I tried again. "I am a high-level hacker. Someone who, by definition, engages in illegal activity, punishable by prosecution under penalty of the law." When he didn't respond, I leaned forward and enunciated. "A cri-mi-nal."

His smile broadened.

"What are you? Daft?" I thumped my chest. "I've done things. Horrible things. Because that's what I am. A horrible person." One who did not deserve forgiveness, mercy, or recognition. Only a validation of the self-loathing I harbored within.

That got his attention, and he instantly sobered. "What are you talking about? You're fucking incredible. Just when I think I have you pegged, you completely throw me."

"Then you understand what I am?"

"A criminal? Yeah, I got it the first twenty-six times." His eager eyes honed in on me. "What do you hack? People? Companies? Assholes who cut you off in traffic? What type of encryption? Come on. Spill."

"You want me to confess my crimes to you?"

"I'm not planning on exposing your rap sheet. Chalk it up to professional interest."

Relieved by his reaction—and a bit disturbed—I considered his request. I'd already waded in this far, why not? "I started with school attendance records."

"Ditched a lot, huh?" he teased. "I figured you for a rebel."

More like too bruised to show up. "Typical teenage crap. Concert tickets, grades, petty theft." *Food, shelter, survival.*

He winged an eyebrow.

"I may have skimmed money from companies known for fraud and illegal activities."

He steepled his fingers. "Companies with more to lose by opening their books to the authorities. Nice."

It felt strange discussing this part of my life. And a bit fun. Nicki and Sue both knew about my hacking but adopted glassy-eyed looks at any detail beyond the Cliffs Notes version. Still, I omitted scenarios that ended with me locked up in a federal penitentiary. "The rest is dull by comparison. College transcripts, employment records, Nicki's culinary school grades."

"What?" Nicki jerked to attention.

"After that rocket fuel you passed off as a lavender martini, no way you got an 'A' in mixology."

She scoffed. "I'm better at consuming drinks than making them."

"What about for fun?" Chase asked. "Ever fucked with people you don't like?"

"I considered adding Leonard Bryce to the National Sex Offender Database."

"Don't waste your energy. He'll make it there on his own. What else?"

I recalled my fantasy of adding my dear sister Helena to a deportation list, but as always, the thought of declaring all-out war pierced my gut with fear.

Never pick a fight you can't win.

"An overcrowded animal shelter received a generous donation from a crooked political action committee. An insurance company reversed their regrettable decision to decline a kid's cancer treatment. All allegedly"—I curved my fingers into obnoxious air quotes—"of course."

"God, Princess. Even when you're breaking the law, you're adorable."

The compliment had me lowering my eyes before he saw the shame in them. No one could ever know about the acts that kept me up at night or all the pain I'd caused. Those were mine alone to bear and not even a lifetime of charitable deeds could erase them.

"Since we're discussing this topic." His expression grew thoughtful. "I got a speeding ticket last week. Think you can help a fellow out by—" I targeted a throw pillow at his head and he fell back, laughing again. The man was a sector short of a hard drive. Though, when you reached his obscene level of wealth, people politely referred to it as 'eccentric'.

Nicki pointed to the guffawing lump on the couch. "I told you anyone with half a brain would see how awesome you are."

"A shame he doesn't own the other half," I mumbled. When he finally lifted the pillow, his ebony hair was tousled, breath shallow, and a glow tinged his cheeks.

Whoa! Is this what he looks like during sex?

My body clenched with the urge to find out.

Misunderstanding my discomfort, Chase spoke. "Don't go getting all shy on me. I'm not finished with you."

Wrong choice of words. "Er... what now?"

"Why haven't I heard of you? In my circles, I'd know about someone with your skill level preying upon the public."

Because I took pride in my anonymity—a necessity with my family. Plus, I went by my moniker, which I shared with nobody. "The supremely talented are known only if they choose to be."

"That sounds like some Yoda bullshit. Are you really as good as you say?"

I threw him an indignant look. "I had no problem with Sterling."

"True, but the rest of that resume is as outdated as my Uncle Virgil's argyle sock collection. Anything recent?"

My face must have given it away because he jumped to his feet. "I knew it! You are still in the game!"

"This conversation is over."

"Okay, no more talking."

"Finally."

"Because I want you to show me."

"What?"

"A demonstration."

"What part of 'this is over' do you not get?"

"All of it," he answered. "I'm not suggesting you rob the U.S. Mint. We'll find something challenging with minimal risk."

"You're asking me to hack into an institution? Have you lost your damn mind?"

"Depends on who you ask. The goal is to witness your skills, not send you up the river." His forehead creased in thought. "Something more daunting than poaching a movie from your cable company yet secure enough to—" He snapped his fingers. "I got it. Hack into Predator."

"That's ridiculous."

"Why? It's not a crime if you have my permission."

"And what if you turn on me or use it as leverage?"

"You don't trust me?" He looked taken aback as if the thought had never occurred to him.

"Says the man who deals in 'truth not trust'."

"Touché."

"Don't take it personally," Nicki interrupted. "She doesn't trust anyone."

The mischief vanished from his eyes, replaced by a soft dewy green that reminded me of spring after a rain. "I may be a lot of things, Princess, but petty is not one of them. I would never ask you to do anything against your will nor use this to hurt you."

The unexpected sincerity tugged at the knots in my belly, threatening to unravel the frayed edges, but a wave of unease fought it back. "At least tell me what you'd gain from this."

"A perverse curiosity, or even better, call it a quality assurance test. I have a state-of-the-art security program that stands up to the best. In fact, I doubt you can break in. Not in twenty minutes."

My eyes widened. "You're going to time me?"

"Can't have you floundering all night. I need my beauty sleep." He removed his jacket, laid it on the back of the couch then sat down. "Don't tell me you're afraid?"

"You do realize I don't fall for juvenile provoking."

"Then I won't triple dog dare you." His eyes took on a thoughtful gleam. "Perhaps a legitimate wager?"

"I don't want your money."

"Who said anything about money?"

My stomach did a loop-de-loop. Naturally, he'd go straight to sex. I parked my outrage on standby, ready to unleash it at his terms.

"I want to hire you," he said instead.

"Huh?" That was unexpected. And insulting.

"A mind like yours is a rarity that should not be wasted."

"And my body isn't?" I blurted, before my brain caught up.

"On the contrary." His lips quirked as his eyes raked over me. "I'd love to show my appreciation for all your qualities." His gaze lingered long enough to raise my temperature another thousand degrees. Maybe that nail polish had rubbed off on me.

Nicki snapped her fingers in front of Chase's face. "Focus."

He laughed and pushed her arm down, careful to avoid her wet nails. "I'll extend it to thirty minutes."

My embarrassment gave way to pride. "Don't insult me. I can do it in fifteen."

"Cocky. I like that in an opponent. If I win, you relinquish Lyndham to Stark and take me on as your client."

"I told you, I—"

"No hinting, inferring, suggesting, coercing, implying, or insinuating." He counted each on his fingers. "You said nothing about betting."

"I must have missed that one. And if I win?"

"What do you want?"

"To be left alone."

"Amen to that," Nicki muttered.

For the first time, uncertainty penetrated his confidence. "Then that's what I'll give you," he finally said.

With newfound exuberance, I sprang up to shake his hand.

"Sucker," Nicki mumbled.

I set up my computer on the dining table while Nicki downloaded a stopwatch app on her phone. Chase stretched on the couch and closed his eyes. Apparently, he wasn't kidding about his beauty sleep. Not that he needed it.

Nicki raised her arm. "GO!"

I lovingly ran my fingers over the keyboard, savoring this part —when the inner conqueror faces the challenge of discovering what secrets beckon from the other side. Nothing but me and the rush of anticipation.

"You gonna buy it dinner first?" Nicki interrupted.

I began to type. Satisfied, Nicki entered the kitchen to start what I assumed was a victory meal. Hopefully, ribs.

I followed my routine and applied the infiltration software I'd written. Some tweaking to adjust for his security and *BAM!* Chase's company data appeared on the screen.

Now, that's what I'm talkin' about.

No more insufferable seduction attempts, unwanted attention, incessant questions, inappropriate propositions, or unwelcome surprises. Nothing but peace and freedom. And most of all, no more temptation. Maybe I'd even stop having those damn sex dreams.

You'll also never find out how the real deal compares.

Not that I intended to anyway, right?

All I needed to do was get up, announce the win, and move on. But I couldn't budge. As if holding me hostage, my body sat immobile and silent, while my mind raced. Why did winning suddenly feel like losing? What was I losing anyway? Didn't that imply having something to lose in the first place?

Stop thinking, get your ass up, and claim your prize!

I opened my mouth, but before any words came out, a series of annoying beeps interrupted.

"I'm in," I said weakly.

Chase bounced off the couch. "Too late, Princess. You lose."

"*What*?" Nicki appeared at my side. "You *what*?"

"Not now." I shot her a half apologetic, half shut-up look. With a scowl that told me I'd pay for this later, she retreated to the kitchen. Probably to eat my ribs.

Chase circled the table to stand behind me. "Show me." He placed a hand on my shoulder and leaned in.

I tried to ignore the warmth coursing down my arm while I scrolled through the information.

"Employee records?" he requested.

Tap, tap, tap. "You should offer your Human Resources Director, Mildred, a better retirement package. She's been with you longer than time itself."

"Noted," he said. "Financials?"

Tap, tap, tap. "Damn, I should have charged you more."

"Ongoing projects?"

Tap, tap, tap. "I didn't know you were doing due diligence on—"

"We're done." He closed my laptop. "I'm feeling an odd mixture of admiration and terror right now."

All I felt was his thumb making delicious circles at the base of my neck.

"It's safe to say we need to enhance our security. Thankfully, I just won the best consultant money can buy. You're mine now, Princess."

Oh, God! What had I done? Whatever it was, I blamed him. Prior to Dangerous, I never allowed stupidity to rear up and bludgeon me on the head like this. I was the girl who analyzed the pros and cons of a hairdo, the one who never made a decision on a whim or even worse... a bet. But around him, all rational thought short-circuited. I pleaded temporary insanity. Except now that I'd accepted a role as his minion, it was looking more permanent.

Fuck! Fuck! Fuck!

Against my body's wishes, I tilted forward to break contact. No more distractions. Time to salvage something from this fiasco. "I will not be cheap."

"You mean you also want to get paid?"

I ignored the joke. "Chase, this was merely an audition. You have no idea what I'm capable of. I can help make Wolfe legendary, but I want something in addition to my rate."

"Judging from your behavior, I doubt it's publicity."

"No. Something down the road."

"Delayed gratification? Now, I'm listening."

"Compensation proportional to sales. Half a point for a year. A quarter for the next two."

"Royalties?" Chase exclaimed. "Are you serious?"

"Do you want me or not?"

"I do," he said simply, "but I need to focus on business right now."

"And that's all you'll focus on. Rule number three. Remember?"

Chase lowered himself into the chair beside me, his expression none too happy about abandoning that endeavor.

Was he pouting?

"Can you handle it, big guy?" I taunted.

"My employees trust me with their livelihoods and rely on me to make solid business decisions. They reciprocate with loyalty and sacrifice. They're killing themselves to make Wolfe successful, and if I have a resource as impactful as I know you will be, I can't deprive them because of my personal wants."

This was Business Dangerous. The responsible CEO who had built his empire through sweat and hard work. The side of him I reluctantly admired.

And then he heaved a dramatic sigh. "Unfortunately, you don't get to the level I'm at without making sacrifices."

I rolled my eyes. "Only you see relinquishing a tumble in the sheets as martyrdom. You truly are a giver."

"If I were any other man, I might be concerned by how much you're enjoying this." He curled his fingers around my wrist and smirked when my pulse jumped. "Good thing I know better."

I yanked my hand away. "Do we have a deal?"

"Not yet." He leaned forward and kissed me, stealing every ounce of breath until the room spun. When he pulled back, his smile held equal parts satisfaction and regret. "Now we have a deal."

11

I woke early on Monday, quickly showered, and took much greater care than necessary in choosing a fitted pinstripe skirt and button-down white blouse. I accessorized with light makeup, pulled my hair in a twist, and added my lily pin. Satisfied with my conservative yet professional appearance, I departed for Chase's office to begin work on my new project.

Too bad. You'd rather work on him.

No. He is nothing more than a colleague.

That sucks.

No. It's a good thing.

Sucking can be a very good thing.

Shut up.

I entered Predator's lobby for the first time. With tall windows, chrome fixtures, and splashes of bold color, it reflected the company's reputation—cutting-edge, unconventional, and alluring—much like its CEO, who stood waiting for me, impatience etched on his face.

I paused to admire the view. I wish I was referring to the building.

Whether dressed in casual attire or the navy-blue Brioni suit he wore, every piece of fabric he owned accentuated his perfect build. Even a garbage bag would worship that body.

"You're late." Chase approached. He placed a tall cup in my hand.

"No. You're early. Stop being a tyrant." I took a sip. Earl Grey, cream, and two sugars. He remembered.

Chase responded by ushering me towards the security office where he surprised the man behind the desk by requesting unrestricted access.

"Are you sure, sir?" He eyed me with trepidation. "She's a consultant."

"Trust me. It won't make any difference." Chase's response puzzled the man further but he obeyed. Fifteen minutes later, equipped with my ID card, I followed Chase on an abbreviated tour of the vast facility. From the state-of-the-art kitchen, arcade games, open design, and seemingly happy employees, the place encouraged collaboration and creativity.

We ended on the second floor in a corner office, twice the size of the others. With three desks, four computers, and a long table scattered with papers, I expected multiple occupants but a sole man in the room approached.

"Meet Brandon Kunnen," Chase introduced. Brandon's lean frame stood around six feet, lithe and toned with a swimmer's build. Appropriate since his shoulder-length blond hair, board shorts, and flip-flops exuded more California beach bum than computer guru. I pictured him propped on a surfboard, hair whipping in the breeze, his blue eyes mirroring the ocean depths.

Cowabunga!

"Brandon, this is Princess," Chase said.

"Jasmine," I corrected.

"Princess Jasmine?" Brandon flashed a million-watt smile. "As cartoon babes go, she's the cutest."

Chase rolled his eyes.

"So you're the brainiac who thwarted Sterling's evil plan." Brandon pumped my hand. "Dude, you are way too gorgeous to be an egghead. What gives?"

I laughed at his infectious grin. "Right back at you."

"If you two are finished with your mutual admiration," Chase interrupted, "Brandon will be your point of contact. He reports directly to me." He moved to the door. "Take care of her, Brandon."

"With pleasure," Brandon said, his voice filled with gusto.

Chase groaned. "Lucky you're useful because you are a pain in my ass."

"Your fault for hiring your college buddy," Brandon yelled back as the door closed.

"Is that how you know each other?" I asked.

Brandon gestured to a desk. "We were roommates freshman and sophomore years."

I made my way over and deposited my belongings. "You knew him when he started all this?"

"I'll never forget it."

"Tell me." I settled in the chair. Ooh. Ergonomic. Only the best around here.

Brandon began sorting through papers in what looked like an effort to organize them. "A few of us were on a gnarly video game bender. Like mondo hard core." He attacked another stack, leaving more of a mess behind. "Eight hours in and Chase is whiffing on the game faster than when he wiped out on his first wave. Suddenly, he hurls the controller and yells, 'This game fucking sucks. I can write something better than this piece of shit'. We were all wasted at the time, so we laughed and forgot about it. Not him. Dude goes on to crank out the most bitchin' online game ever. Next thing, he's a freaking zillionaire. Quits school, starts his own company, and here we are."

"I read that he launched Predator with a classmate. Cory Burns?"

"Yeah. Cory was a business major. Chase isn't the type to become quick amigos with newbies, but when we met Cory, we vibed. Eventually we all rented a place off campus. When Chase's game went viral, Cory took over finances and brought in some investors through family connections."

"What happened to him?"

The wattage in Brandon's smile dimmed. "Chase bought Cory and the investors out and became sole owner. He was the one with the vision and talent. It was always his company." He swung his arms around. "This is all Chase."

He relocated another pile of papers, and I refrained from telling him to stop. The place was looking like the aftermath of a hurricane. "How did he sucker you into working for him?"

"That wily son of a bitch insisted on paying my way through school, knowing he'd own my soul. Now I'm nothing more than an indentured servant." He released a persecuted sigh which lost its effect when coupled with his smile. "At least he let me choose my title."

"Which is?"

"Vice-President of Awesomeness. Though, it's been six years and I'm still waiting on the business cards."

Within a few hours, he had me sold on that title. While Marie Kondo would have run screaming from Brandon's organizational madness, his insane talent, diligence, and creativity made my head spin with glee. It didn't hurt that he was sharp and funny as hell. His vocabulary alone had me in stitches, communicating advanced concepts through intellectual geek-speak one second and laid-back slang the next.

Brandon was explaining Wolfe's scanning features when the hairs on the back of my neck prickled.

Chase appeared at the door. "Hey, Princess, ready for lunch?"

I must have done a poor job curtailing my surprise because he frowned. "Consider it an introduction to Predator."

"You never fed me my first day." Brandon pouted.

"That's because I've seen you eat." Chase looked around. "How's everything going?"

"Couldn't be better." Brandon looped an arm around my shoulders. "Thank you for bringing her to me. It's like we were meant to be."

"Oh, for fuck's sake," Chase snapped. "Stop hitting on my consultant. You would not believe what I went through to get her here."

Brandon unsuccessfully smothered a laugh which followed us into the hallway. "Idiot," Chase grumbled but the corners of his mouth lifted.

We stepped onto the busy sidewalk, and a gust of wind smacked me, freeing strands from my elegant twist. I glanced at Chase. Not a hair out of place. Figures nature wouldn't deign to mess with him. We merged with the lunch throng and Chase placed his hand on my back to guide me. I attributed the warmth to the increasing temperature outside.

We chose a small Greek restaurant where Chase pulled out my chair. As I sat, his hand floated up my back, delivering shivers beneath my blouse.

Deliberate or accidental?

We placed our orders, and he leaned forward. "Any first impressions on Wolfe?" His knee brushed against mine.

Deliberate or accidental?

Christ, he was making me crazy. And why was I analyzing every tiny gesture? From my experience, he adhered to his own rules. Borderline fanatical even. But he wasn't above seizing any opportunity to remind me of his presence. Always a game. Always an angle. Always Dangerous. I shifted my leg away.

"Maybe a few." I launched into a summary of my thoughts.

"Not bad," he commented. "What do you think of Brandon?"

"He's fantastic," I gushed. "Intelligent, witty, creative, funny."

"Easy there, Princess. He's developing software, not donating a kidney."

"I can't believe how much fun I'm having." Especially for someone who prided herself on solitude. "Being his college roommate must have been a blast."

"He's good for a few stories."

We paused as our server delivered our food. Layers of gyro meat piled high atop fluffy pita bread. It smelled amazing.

"Such as?" I opted for divide and conquer and ripped the sandwich apart. I took a large bite. Delicious.

Chase couldn't help but smile. "Night before fall semester started, Brandon, Cory, and I were at a bar when this girl walked in. Brandon insisted she was his soulmate. Problem was she only dated foreign men, went nuts for their accents. Poor little American Brandon had no chance but instead of cutting his losses like a normal person, he manufactured the worst English accent I've ever heard—something between a Bond villain and a Muppet—then fabricated some bullshit backstory about transferring here from England. He was pretty pleased with himself the next morning."

"Impressive commitment to a cause," I noted.

"It was until she showed up in his Economics class the following day and turned out to be the professor's daughter," he laughed. “He had to speak in that atrocious English accent for an entire semester.”

“And the soulmate?”

“She dumped him for an Irishman who sounded like he had marbles in his mouth.”

I envied the joyful expression on Chase’s face. As someone who missed graduations, proms, parties, and every other milestone people took for granted, I had no friends or nostalgic memories to define me. Nothing to dilute the wickedness my family cursed me with.

I shook off the darkness. “What about Cory? Do you guys still get together?”

“No,” he responded with finality. “How about you? Does that over-analytical brain of yours permit you to have fun?”

“Nah, I’m boring. Ask Nicki.”

“I don’t believe that for a second.” An un-boss-like gleam entered his eye. “And I’d rather find out for myself.”

My purse buzzed, saving me from a response. I reached for my cell phone.

Chase leaned over to read the display. “Why is Prep School calling? Didn’t you withdraw from Lyndham?”

“Not over voicemail.” I sighed at his disapproving expression. “I want to explain. I feel bad.”

“They’ll be fine with Stark. I did you a favor. And now, I’ll do you another one.” He reached over to press the green button on my screen.

“What the—”

“No time like the present.”

“Jasmine, are you there?” Wayne’s voice sounded faint.

I cursed Chase with my eyes while I raised the phone to my ear. “Hi, Wayne.”

"My assistant said you called. Is everything okay?" I pictured his puppy dog eyes filled with concern.

"It's regarding the project." I lowered my voice and Chase bent forward. I braced a hand on his shoulder and shoved him back.

"We'll be announcing our decision shortly," Wayne said.

"About that… I'm withdrawing." I narrowed my eyes at Chase's gloating smile.

Silence on the phone.

"Um, thank you for the opportunity," I continued.

More silence.

"Perhaps we can work together someday?" I added.

Chase rolled his eyes. I scooped up a cucumber slice and tossed it at him then stifled a giggle when it bounced off his nose.

"Did you accept something else?" Wayne finally spoke.

"Yes."

"Predator." Wayne made the word sound dirty. "I knew that bastard would try something. Is he poaching you or attempting to seduce you?"

Does mind-fucking count? "It's just a contract."

"What's he saying?" Chase asked.

I made a shushing motion and threatened him with another cucumber slice. He plucked it from my fingers and popped it in his mouth.

"Does this mean you'll have dinner with me now?" Wayne said.

I'm not sure why his request surprised me since he'd alluded to it in the past. Maybe because of the busybody green eyes scrutinizing me. "Um, sure, I'd love to."

"Wonderful," Wayne exclaimed. "I'm leaving the country on business tomorrow. Is tonight too short notice?"

I visualized the dessert I'd leverage for this. "No, that works. I'll see you tonight."

"Unbelievable," Chase exclaimed when I hung up. "Only you can decline a job offer and walk away with a date."

I ignored him and finished my lunch, grateful to return to Brandon's office with no further incidents. Chase accompanied me to the door. "Good luck on your date with Prep School tonight." He walked away but paused long enough to call out over his shoulder. "Don't forget to take a book."

I entered to find Brandon flipping through notes. Was it possible the place looked even worse? He popped a french fry in his mouth. "What's this I hear about a date? I figured a bodacious betty like you had to be taken. Who's the lucky guy?"

"You may know him from college. Wayne Parker."

He thought about it while chewing. "You could do worse. How's Chase taking it?"

"It's personal, which by his own admission, makes it none of his business." One of the few times we agreed.

"Ah… yes," Brandon said knowingly. "Company and assets shalt not fraternize without incurring the wrath of the gods. The sacred rules."

Geez. Was there a laminated copy hanging in the break room?

"What's the deal with those anyway?" I asked. "Does he ever loosen up on them?"

"Never." He offered me a fry which I declined.

"Why so tyrannical?"

Brandon shook his head. "Sorry, babe. That's his tale to tell."

Something told me not to expect a story anytime soon. "Can you at least share what's going on between him and Wayne?"

"That's easy. As computer science majors, we all embodied the geek stereotype—ostracized by the cool crowd, zero chance of nailing a hot girl."

"But not Chase."

"Effing freak of nature," Brandon chuckled and shoved more

fries in his mouth. "He could have any girl on campus flat on her back in less than ten minutes. Drove Parker gonzo. Especially since a few of them were his girlfriends."

"Chase seduced Parker's girlfriends?"

"From what I saw, they moved in on Chase but depends who you ask."

"Is the word 'no' not in his vocabulary?"

"Not when it comes to Parker." He finished off the last of the fries and tossed the container in the trash as if shooting a basket. "With those two, it's always a competition or more like a slaughter, but you know Chase. If he can get a rise out of you, he'll prod for the sheer hell of it."

I knew too well. "So I probably shouldn't mention Chase tonight."

"Not unless you want Parker to go all aggro."

"Noted," I said and resumed analyzing a piece of code until a poke in my arm startled me. "What the hell?"

"Time to come up for air, babe." Brandon poked me again. "Don't you have a date?"

I thought for a second. "I do. Crap. I have to go." I jumped up and grabbed my purse. "Thanks, Brandon."

"Remember," he called out after me, "no glove, no love."

As I exited the building, I noticed Chase's driver, Richard waiting at the curb. I smiled and raised my hand, but it dropped when I noticed Chase. Or rather, Chase's date. I pivoted away as the almond-eyed beauty wrapped her arms around him.

Stealth. The restaurant's odd name made sense as soon as I entered into darkness. The posh establishment catered to the elite, as only a well-advertised gimmick could, yet despite its crammed capacity, it remained eerily hushed.

The place gave new meaning to the term 'blind date'.

"Jasmine, over here," Wayne called out. I followed his voice until I bumped into him. I grabbed his arm for balance. Solid. Muscular. Not bad. He wore a gray suit—I think it was gray—with his short hair tidy as usual. He presented a bouquet of white daisies—I think they were white—and helped me into my chair.

"You look lovely," he said.

How would he know?

He handed me a menu, and I withdrew my phone to turn on the flashlight app.

They must save a fortune on their electric bill.

"Good evening." A creepy waiter appeared by my side. I jumped and angled my phone towards his face. A scowl looked back at me.

"Turn that off," Wayne whispered.

I obliged before the waiter threatened to haunt me.

Instead, he presented a bottle of wine and my eyes acclimatized enough to see Wayne delicately sniff, swirl, and taste the liquid. He nodded his approval, and the server filled our glasses before taking our orders. He blended back into the shadows.

Who trains the staff? Ninjas?

"What do you think?" Wayne gestured to the bottle.

"I'm afraid my knowledge of wine is limited to red and white, and I can't tell the difference with my eyes closed." *Or in here.*

"I'd be happy to lend some insight," Wayne offered. "My family enjoys vacationing in Napa every year."

"Thank you but I'm content with my ignorance." I took a sip and wrinkled my nose. Yup, fermented grapes.

Wayne raised his glass. "To the first of what I hope will be many dates with a beautiful and amazing woman."

My smile faltered. I hated acting like I was a better person.

Do it for Nicki.

With that thought, I threw myself into the evening as if I stood a chance at a normal dating life. Child's play for someone who elevated fiction to an art form. Surprisingly, as the night progressed, I found myself acting less and enjoying more. Wayne regaled me with amusing stories of past trips to foreign lands and the cultural blunders visitors committed. The India anecdotes were the best, especially the ones involving a spitting camel.

"How did Hale convince you to work for him?" Wayne asked, throwing me with the abrupt change of subject.

"Um." Something told me he wouldn't appreciate the bet angle. "He pitched me on the potential and I couldn't resist."

"A reaction shared by most women," he said.

"It's just business."

I seem to be saying that a lot lately.

Ironically, all attempts at seduction had ceased as soon as my employment began. Problem not completely solved though. Frequent sightings placed a strain on *my* libido. Treating him more like unattainable eye-candy and less as the object of my sexual frustrations helped. Although, the more-than-occasional 'accidental' contact left me with discomfort in certain body parts.

Crap. Wayne was saying something.

He shouldn't talk while I'm fantasizing. I paused to listen. He'd moved on to family. Ugh. I preferred fantasy.

"What do your parents do for a living?" he asked.

"I'm afraid they passed away," I lied. After years of practice, facts from Jasmine Monroe's contrived backstory rolled off my tongue with a pathological ease that would frighten any mental health expert.

"I'm sorry. Any family?"

"A cousin I don't like much." I effortlessly wrote Helena's new role into my fictional past.

"That's a shame. My parents' support has always been—"

The sound of an old-fashioned telephone ring interrupted. "Ni hao," Wayne answered his cell phone then fluently launched into a Chinese dialect. He stepped away from the table.

Impressive.

After seven emails, two games of Minesweeper, and a dozen dirty looks from the waiter—at least I think they were dirty—I was less impressed.

When Wayne returned to the table, he stumbled while pulling out his chair. I suppressed a smile. Not that he would have seen it. He wisely waited for his sight to adjust before picking up his wine glass, "I'm sorry about that. I'm working on a critical overseas deal and since it's mid-morning in China, I occasionally get disturbed. If the deadline were not so close, I wouldn't have let it interrupt our wonderful evening."

As a businesswoman, I understood. "It's okay."

He reached for my hand and held it until our meals arrived. One taste of the miniscule entrée, and I decided the chef was also cooking in the dark.

As the evening wound down, Wayne cheated by checking the time on his cell phone. "Don't tell," he said. "I'd love to continue this, but I leave for Beijing tomorrow morning."

We exited and he hailed me a cab. "May I see you when I return?"

"I'd like that."

He bent his head towards mine and I raised my mouth. The kiss was pleasant. Not panty-combusting like Chase's, but warm, safe, secure, and above all else... normal. I wound my arms around his neck.

His phone shrilled and he pulled away. “Sorry,” he apologized while ushering me into the cab. “Ni hao.”

The following week flew by with unprecedented speed, and I ended up back in my office, playing catch up. I was dedicating a disproportional amount of time to Wolfe but enjoying myself too much to care. Even Chase’s impromptu visits left me smiling and for some inexplicable reason, amused the hell out of Brandon.

I added an item to my expanding to-do list and frowned when I heard a commotion in the outer office. Sue poked her head in. “Someone is here for you.”

“Who?”

“Teresa Stark,” she whispered as if afraid to say the name aloud.

I frowned. “I don’t know her. She got the Lyndham gig after I withdrew. What does she want?”

“Beats me, but I’m sending her in before she puts a hex on me.”

I stood to welcome my unexpected guest. “Hello, I’m Jas—” My greeting died as familiar exotic almond eyes zeroed in on me.

12

Her bronze skin glowed against a snug white pantsuit, an ensemble destined for disaster on a mere mortal. I'd have spaghetti stains all over it within minutes and that's without going near Italian food. But on her, the wardrobe choice snubbed the laws of nature by remaining crisp and pristine. Her glossy black hair was pinned in a sophisticated chignon and her makeup applied with meticulous precision. An ocean of professionalism.

An ocean Dangerous was dipping into.

"Jasmine, nice to finally meet you." She extended a manicured hand, the tips painted white of course. "Chase has told me so much, I feel like I already know you."

With a cat-like grace I envied, she settled into a chair and crossed her legs. From her well-endowed curves to perfect posture, she radiated poise. The kind that, by sheer proximity, reduces others to a frump.

I realized I was staring and sat my butt down. "Congratulations on the Lyndham contract," I offered while straightening my spine with a sudden urge to appear taller.

"About that..." A delicate frown creased her perfectly shaped eyebrows. "I'm afraid I've done you a disservice."

This is strange. "You have?"

Remorse ran counter to her self-assured composure, but she attempted it with valiance. "I'm sure you've learned that Chase and I are very close."

And getting stranger. "That's none of my concern."

"True, but you need to understand he doesn't engage in conventional relationships. Ours is the closest to a commitment he'll ever experience. He dotes on me as a husband would. Treats me like a queen."

Queen trumps Princess.

"Why are you telling me this?"

"Direct. I admire that." A genuine smile lit up her face, transforming it from lovely to downright beautiful. In that moment, I saw why Chase wanted her. "Occasionally, he crosses the line to make me happy. It's flattering, except a man of his means doesn't account for collateral damage. I'm afraid this is one of those instances."

For someone who appreciated getting to the point, she remained far from making one.

She propped her hands in her lap. "When I heard about Lyndham, I knew it was perfect for me, so in typical Chase fashion, he intervened to remove my sole competitor."

"You're referring to me?"

"You held out longer than most." Her exotic eyes glimmered with admiration. "But what woman wouldn't give up everything to be near him? Especially when his motives are camouflaged with so much charm."

"I don't understand."

"I think you do." The admiration took a downward slide into condescension. "Chase said you were intelligent, so I'm surprised you didn't catch on. Right when Lyndham is on the brink of a decision, Chase appears with a tempting alternative. Oddly convenient, wouldn't you agree?"

"No, I saw a promising opportunity in Wolfe and seized it. *I* decided."

"You initially posed a challenge which caused him to deviate from his plan of compliance through seduction"—her eyes raked over me as if questioning his original method—"to securing you a position, but seldom does that man not achieve his goal."

None of this made sense. If true, wouldn't it bother her to accept a job she never earned instead of cherishing it as a loving gesture from Chase? No wonder he thought I exchanged favors for work. To these two, sex equaled currency. "If Chase manipulated me into backing out, he must have believed you were incapable of winning it on your own."

Her eyes sharpened, adding to the feline image. "His actions have nothing to do with my skill. He was showing affection towards me. I'm confident I would have prevailed anyway."

"I'm not sure about that." She may have appeared flawless on the outside, but I'd seen it before. Flash over substance.

"You clearly don't understand relationships," she chastised, a fact that rang true. "Chase wanted me on Wolfe, but because of his rule separating business and pleasure, we made a choice. As good as we are in the boardroom, we're far better in the bedroom. Which is why he secured me the only other viable contract worthy of my talent."

I pushed away an image of them together. But not before acknowledging how perfect the picture looked. "Why come here and tell me?"

"To preempt any issues." Her mouth turned upwards in a

placating smile any politician would approve of. "You're running in the same circles as us now, and I'd hate to be the cause of bad blood. Especially with how important Wolfe is to him. In the end, we all got what we wanted. I have Lyndham and you landed a role you would never have attained otherwise. In fact, you may be the true victor in all of this."

I considered her explanation. This couldn't have been about clearing the way for her. I hacked into his company. I solved his Sterling problem. He was impressed by my skill.

Because he never expected you to have any.

He didn't know a damn thing about me when he waltzed into my office, brandishing an offer too good to refuse. In fact, he lacked faith in my ability to crack Sterling's code. He only showed up with a job after his seduction attempts failed.

Fuck! Fuck! Fuck!

My mind replayed the countless times he tried to convince me to relinquish Lyndham.

Let Stark have it.

Give it to Stark.

It's in good hands with Stark.

And when I refused, what did he do?

Shifted tactics from seduction to employment.

My insides began a slow descent.

"That son of a bitch," I whispered.

"Don't feel bad about being a means to an end," she said. "Chase and I share a special bond. I know things about him others would never understand. You could say he owes me." She stood, not a crease in her pantsuit. "It was nice meeting you, Jasmine. I'm happy we're on the same page now." Without waiting for a response, she and her shapely ass exited my office.

I slumped in my chair. How could I have fallen for his sham?

Stupid and pathetic.

Her only incorrect statement was assuming it was not personal. After years of hiding in the shadows, being appreciated felt incredible. Which is why I'd gobbled up his validation like a starving child desperate for a crumb of attention.

The worst part? I still wanted it.

Which meant in all these years, I had not learned a fucking thing.

This is why I stayed away from people. They lied, cheated, and used you to further their own ends. Nothing had changed since childhood.

Especially me.

For all my reinvention, I was still the same dumb girl falling for the same dumb tricks. I may have faced worse men and survived, but a man who worked your emotions wielded a more dangerous weapon than one who used his fists. A lesson worth remembering.

"FUCK ME!" I banged my fist on the desk and cursed again when my stress ball rolled off the edge. I bent to retrieve it, and a flash of color caught my eye. Curious, I picked up the magazine I had purchased from the street vendor what seemed like ages ago.

Ignoring the sage voice telling me to burn it, I flicked through the pages until I spotted Dangerous with his voluptuous almond-eyed whore. How could someone—Chase, not the whore—be so beautiful yet so demented? Is that what had swayed me? I should know better. Helena had taught me that lesson years ago.

Like a masochistic stalker, I devoured the text, pumping the stress ball harder with each word.

'In uncharacteristically smitten behavior, billionaire playboy Chase Hale has been frequently seen in the company of independent software consultant, Teresa Stark. Could she be the vixen worthy of taming our most eligible bachelor?'

I hurled the magazine at the wall where it bounced off with an unsatisfying flutter.

I can hack into the Pentagon, but I have no clue who that green-eyed snake is screwing?

Talk about a monumental fuck-up. I'd even told him about my hacking skills. Had he told Teresa? No, she seemed like the type to gloat over information. Not that he'd have any proof to back it up. Foolish admissions aside, tying me to any crimes, pre and post Jasmine Monroe, would be near impossible without knowing my actual identity.

Still, I liked to cover my ass. And the best way to do that? Keep my name associated with Wolfe. Business Dangerous would never risk his product's reputation by outing one of his top programmers as a criminal hacker. Assured mutual destruction. A respectable strategy.

Which meant completing that dickhead's project. So much for my urge to tell him where he could ram his hard drive.

You got this, Jasmine.

Nothing in the contract stipulated being nice.

You got this.

I'll funnel my work through Brandon.

You got this.

"Chase on line one!" Sue yelled.

Fuck! I don't got this!

By lunchtime, I'd avoided three calls from Chase. Sue poked her head in my office. "I'm going to run an errand. Are you okay?"

I briefly glanced up from coloring devil horns on Teresa's picture. "Fine."

Sue frowned. "This goes against every well-nourished cell in my body, but I'm willing to bring you back a Twinkie if it'll make you smile."

I must have looked awful for her to offer what she referred to as 'creamy death in a spongy exterior'.

"It's just a headache. I'm going home soon."

By the time I entered my apartment, my fake headache had grown into the real deal. Even the roots of my hair hurt. I donned Bugs Bunny pajamas, grabbed a container of Haagen-Dazs, and flopped on the couch to lose myself in mindless TV.

A knocking sound woke me. I opened my eyes to an ambulance-chaser commercial and a carton of melted ice cream. The knock came again. Nicki must have forgotten her keys.

I opened the door.

"You're a difficult woman to reach." Chase brushed past me to enter.

"Please come in," I mumbled at his back.

He turned to evaluate me. "Sue said you weren't feeling well. Is Brandon overworking you?"

"No." I took offense on Brandon's behalf. "He's the best thing about this ordeal."

"Ordeal? What does that mean?"

"It means that nowhere in our contract are home visits included."

"I'm checking up on my investment."

"Making sure your efforts weren't wasted?"

His forehead creased. "You're acting odd. Do I need to drug test you?"

"No. You need to leave."

"Why so eager to get rid of me?" He glanced down the hallway towards the bedrooms. "Is someone waiting for you?"

"Why is everything about sex for you?"

"Answer the question."

"You're my boss, not my mother, and you still haven't given me a reason why you're here."

"To see if you need anything."

"Yes. For you to go away."

"I was thinking more like chicken soup, but now I'm leaning toward prescription meds."

"Your *investment* is fine and will continue to do her part. You'll get everything you want, as usual."

He flashed a smile laced with his diabolical charm. "If that were true"—he gestured toward the bedrooms again—"we'd be twenty feet down that hallway right now."

I hated my body for warming at the thought. But I hated him more for barging in here looking like sex-on-a-stick. "Is there nothing you believe you're not entitled to?" I asked, my voice heavy with disgust. "You're unbelievable."

"I'm not about to apologize for wanting to fuck a woman."

"Wise move. You wouldn't have time for anything else." Using sex appeal as a manipulation tool. How had I fallen for it? Especially since I'd been warned. "I should have listened to Wayne. He was right about you."

"Prep School?" His eyes narrowed to green slits. "Why are you listening to that cocksucker? I thought you were smarter than that."

No, you didn't. Or you wouldn't have come at me with your machinations.

He glanced down the hallway again. "Is he waiting for you right now?"

"Don't blame Wayne. This is on you." And on me.

He eyed me for a few seconds before speaking. "If you're unhappy with our agreement, I'll give you an out. Wolfe is too critical to be at the mercy of your tantrums."

I wanted to accept, but I wanted my insurance policy more. "I'm not leaving Brandon. Why should he suffer for his terrible taste in friends?"

"Heaven forbid you don't do right by *Brandon,*" Chase mocked as he opened the door and stepped into the hallway. "Remember, Princess, you work for me, and I expect to get what I'm paying for."

"I have it on good authority you already did." I closed the door in his face.

13

I sighed and wondered for the hundredth time how Brandon had talked me into this. With Wolfe's release in the books, we'd been riding high, giddy as proud new parents—by far my best work of the legal variety. But how I let him take advantage of my post-project buzz and convince me to attend Chase's launch party baffled me. Especially since the venue was Chase's penthouse. At least Wayne had agreed to join me as a potential buffer and like-minded Chase-despiser. Or as I had presented it to him... a date.

With my date running late, I ventured solo into the mouth of the lion—er, Chase's home. The living area alone could swallow up my apartment while still leaving it hungry for seconds. A mammoth fireplace ran along one side of the room, giving the enormous space a cozy feel, while the remaining walls were painted a warm caramel color, accented with ivory crown molding and colorful prints.

I peered out the floor-to-ceiling windows and gasped at the view that made my coveted office window feel like a porthole.

I made a face at the unexpected elegance.

What did you imagine? Posters of pin-up girls and muscle cars?

With smooth jazz filtering through surround sound and penguin-attired servers offering appetizers artfully arranged on silver trays, it had the makings of a lovely party.

If not for the host.

I honed in on his tuxedo-clad form and my chest constricted. Standing a full head taller than his guests, he projected undeniable authority, likeable approachability, and a hypnotic sensuality. If someone figured out a way to bottle his aura—Eau de Dangerous—they'd be set for life.

Curious which Jessica Rabbit wannabe won the lottery, I stood on tiptoe to catch a glimpse. The air whooshed out of my lungs when I saw Teresa plastered against his side, challenging a speck of dust to intervene. Myriad women attempted to approach Chase, some making a play, most paying homage to their boss, but they presented no challenge for Teresa. Dramatic in a snowy white strapless gown that pushed up her cleavage to unnatural proportions, the white devil had come to play. With her Elvira black hair and frostbite smile, she utilized her deadly aura to deflect each advance and stake her claim.

Just plant your flag in his ass and get it over with.

Where the hell was Wayne?

Probably making out with his phone somewhere.

Not that I'd seen much of him. Between my Wolfe deadline and Wayne's crazy travel schedule, we'd managed a handful of dates, each one ending in a three-way between Wayne, me, and his Chinese buddies. Then followed by an apologetic bouquet of daisies.

If we wanted to progress past heavy petting, we'd have to switch to morning trysts.

And why did he think I liked daisies?

I was drooling over a limited-edition Star Wars lithograph when Brandon approached, looking dapper in grown-up clothes. "I should have known you'd be admiring nerd art." His words ended in a whistle. "Damn, girl. Egghead by day. Diva by night." He snapped his fingers like a fashionista.

Relenting to Nicki's insistence, I had allowed her to dress me in a clingy purple gown which left one shoulder bare and hung in a straight line to the floor. The slit starting high on my left thigh lent an air of indecency but made walking possible. She had pinned my hair into a loose updo and, for effect, fastened it with a jeweled clip.

"Not too shabby yourself." I studied Brandon's dark suit. "New duds?"

"You don't think I own nice clothes?" He scowled. "I take offense."

"You forgot to cut the tag off."

"What? Where?" He jerked his head and spun like Ginger chasing her tail. I smothered a grin, and he dropped his arm. "Very funny."

I gave him an impromptu peck on his cheek. "I'm going to miss you."

"Not if you agree to stay and work on Warrior with me."

My mood soured at the reference to Predator's next software project. Warrior tracked and analyzed company transactions to flag anomalies. The genius lay in its ability to identify security risks by adapting and learning patterns. It was cutting edge, challenging, and revolutionary. And it was *my* creation. I'd conceived it while coding on Wolfe but not in time for the current release. Now it sat in limbo, waiting for development as an autonomous project that I itched to complete. Unfortunately, per my contract, it belonged to Chase and while it pained me to walk away from both

Brandon and Warrior, I refused to spend another second in Chase's domain.

Brandon gestured to Chase. "I'm not sure what went down with you two, but now is the perfect time to make him grovel. Do it for me. He's been a ginormous tool lately."

"Nah, he looks like he has his hands full." More like multiple handfuls from the size of Teresa's jugs.

He chuckled. "Teresa, huh?"

I nodded. "They make a perfect couple." *In a soul-sucking sort of way.* "What's the deal with them anyway?"

"They go way back. She was one of his first employees."

"Why did she quit?" *Don't say Rule Number 3. Don't say Rule Number 3.*

"It's complicated."

Ah. The universal copout when hiding something. "I thought Chase liked things simple."

"He does now," Brandon clarified. "But that's after going through one hell of a rough ride. She helped him through it."

"So not one of his renowned sexual conquests?"

He shot me a why-do-you-want-to-know look.

I raised my hands. "Just wondering why she's shooting death rays at me." I wasn't exaggerating. Ever since I entered the penthouse, she'd been directing visual daggers my way.

"Ignore it. That's her normal state."

"Resting I'm-going-to-murder-you face?"

Brandon laughed. "Something like that. After everything that went down, she's a little protective of him."

I'd seen panda bears less defensive of their young.

"There you are." Wayne approached. He planted a kiss on my cheek before greeting Brandon. Apparently, his animosity for Chase did not extend to all former classmates.

"Dude." Brandon shook Wayne's outstretched hand. "How's

the hush-hush project going? Word on the street is you've run into some issues."

"What have you heard?" Wayne asked.

"Something about being under plan and over budget."

Ha. Figures. That bucket of curves in white wasn't close to the programmer she fancied herself. No wonder she had to sleep her way into jobs.

I strained my neck to locate her, wondering if she'd allowed Chase off-leash. He'd taken a position at the front of the room while she stood by the kitchen, chastising a waiter. Not that he appeared to mind when the tongue-lashing gave him an eyeful of her ample cleavage. Damn, her rack could put Kansas City ribs to shame.

Wayne was saying something. I missed it. As usual.

At least this time I wasn't obsessing over Chase.

No, I was fixated on his date's tits... much better.

Brandon chuckled. "Maybe if you hadn't dropped the ball on the best coder to ever touch a keyboard..." He gave me a wink.

Wayne frowned and I shot Brandon a stop-stirring-shit-up look, which only broadened his grin.

"Ladies and gentlemen, if you'll indulge me for a moment." I tensed at the masculine voice commanding the room. "Wolfe dropped yesterday morning and it is already making waves in the software community. This is an unprecedented achievement." Hoots and cheers erupted before Chase hushed them then launched into a speech about the inception of the project, punctuated with humorous anecdotes. He spoke easily, his smooth cadence enthralling his audience. "This could not have been possible without you." His eyes briefly found me and took an audacious trip down my dress, pausing infinitesimally at my thigh-high slit.

I flushed and looked around, but no one seemed to notice.

Chase continued. "As a sincere thank you for the long hours and sacrifices, you will see my gratitude reflected in your next paycheck." Thunderous applause filled the room.

"Always the center of attention," Wayne sneered. "If only he knew about the deal I'm working on..."

"I'm interested in hearing about it," Brandon said.

Wayne ignored him and glanced at me. "It must be tedious working for Hale." He paused as if waiting for confirmation. When none came, he continued. "Constantly fending off the lecherous advances of your boss."

"It was madness," Brandon interjected. "J barely got any work done. Dang, the girl can run."

"Don't listen to him," I said. "If the job required cardio, I never would have stayed." Why was I defending Chase? Maybe because the clichéd accusation conjured ludicrous images from the fifties of horny bosses chasing their secretaries around their desks.

In truth, for being a lousy person, Chase was an impressive leader. While his intelligence came as no surprise, his management style did. Instead of throwing his title around, he earned the respect of his employees by listening and working in the trenches with them. His people loved him.

The female ones perhaps a little too much.

Wayne's expression darkened. "Just once, I want him to feel the sting of watching someone else attain what he desires."

My movements stilled. Is that why we were together? As part of some boyish pissing contest? Color bloomed on my cheeks. Not again. Always a pawn. Always an ulterior motive.

Either Wayne caught up to the conversation, or he noticed my expression because his eyes filled with apology. "That's not what I meant." He clasped my hand. "It's Hale's fault. He brings out the worst in people. You're a wonderful, smart, beautiful woman. Any man would be fortunate to have you."

If he knew how far off that was, he'd understand why my theory fit better.

A ding interrupted the awkwardness, and Wayne withdrew his phone to read the text. He looked up, eyes shining with excitement. "It's Erik Lyndham. I've been trying to schedule time with him, but he's been preoccupied with personal matters. He can meet tonight for a drink. I need to go." His lips brushed mine and he was off, happier than a bear with a honeypot—crap, now I was using Nicki-like analogies.

Brandon watched Wayne exit. "Is that normal?"

"To be cock-blocked by his phone? Every single time."

"There really is an app for everything," he quipped and extended his arm. "Forget about that idiot. I've got something that'll make you happy."

"A time machine?"

"Better."

I accompanied him to the rear of the penthouse where he stopped at a set of double doors. He threw them open and flipped on the light. I squealed at the enormous game room, complete with ping-pong, air hockey, foosball, and vintage video games. An old-fashioned popcorn machine stood in the corner.

After two ping-pong games, an atrocious showing at foosball, and multiple rounds of Pac-Man, Brandon pointed across the room. "Up for getting your ass kicked by the air hockey master?"

"Sure, let me know when he gets here."

"Funny." He grinned. "Care to back up that cocky attitude with a wager?"

"What do you have in mind?"

He activated the table and a rush of air whooshed in. "If I win, you do Warrior with me." He flashed his sparkling 'I should be in toothpaste commercials' grin. "You can't deny we make an epic duo. Like software superheroes." He propped his fists on his hips and puffed out his chest. "Wolfe-man."

I groaned, in part at the terrible pun but mostly from the mention of another bet. "I can see why you and Chase are friends. Let's go with loser buys lunch."

"Agreed." He launched the puck which I smoothly deflected. "Genius got game," he teased. He was good but not as good as someone who spent their childhood afternoons in an arcade, avoiding her home life.

After several games, Brandon threw his arms in the air. "I surrender and bow down to the air hockey queen… or should I say 'Princess'," he snickered. "Go again? This time my pride is on the line so feel free to let me win."

"Pity victories are so empty." I twirled the paddle. "You'd never respect yourself in the morning."

"Try me. I have excessively high self-esteem."

After another trouncing of his excessively high self-esteem, Brandon broached the taboo topic. "What's going on between you and Chase?"

The puck sailed into my goal.

"That's what I thought," Brandon set his paddle down. "Why am I losing the most bitchin' partner I've ever had over some dick move he made?"

I understood the sentiment. After months of late nights and weekends, Brandon and I had forged a unique bond, solidified by takeout and sleep deprivation. As a self-proclaimed solo act, I lucked out with Brandon as my first collaborator. Not to say I wanted another one. People still sucked.

"Chase wouldn't agree to my staying on anyway," I said. Not with the attitude I'd been throwing around. Over the course of the project, Chase and I had come to a tacit agreement. He appeared only when necessary, and I refrained from hurling office supplies at his head. It took more fortitude to ignore the random Teresa sightings.

"I can think of one reason he wouldn't, and it falls between rule number two and four."

"He has a fourth rule?"

"Nah, I just added it for dramatic effect." Brandon's humor vanished, the change out of place from his perpetually jovial self. "I don't know what happened, but can you please work it out with him?"

"I've been wondering the same thing," Chase spoke.

I whirled to see him standing in the doorway.

"That's my cue," Brandon said and walked towards the doors. "Good luck, man." He slapped Chase on the back and left the room.

"Where's Teresa?" I blurted the first question that popped in my head.

"Gone, like everyone else."

I picked up my cell phone and gasped at the time. "I should leave."

"Not so fast, Cinderella. We need to talk."

The thought of more lies spewing from his seductive mouth made me ill. I eyed the escape route he blocked.

"Try it and I'll throw you over my shoulder and haul your ass back here."

"How very kidnapper-meets-caveman of you," I said but my traitorous body perked up at the thought of his hands on me. Having my mind and body at odds was a bitch. "Now get out of my way. I don't have time for this."

"For the love of my goddamn sanity," he barked. "What the fuck did I do?"

"You used me," I snapped.

"For what?"

"For your white-clad little slut." And with that admission, I exploded like a volcano, erupting all over his lying ass. "You and your damn knight-in-armor delusions gave her everything she wanted. Swooping in and fucking with my head until I walked away from Lyndham. Congratulations. Your girlfriend got a job she didn't earn, and you two can continue to fornicate like little minxes."

As if speaking the words purged their toxicity, I inhaled a cathartic breath, my first since Teresa's visit.

Chase, on the other hand, grew more disturbed. "This is about Teresa? I told you I don't do relationships. What part of that did you not get?"

"The part where you're a lying sack of shit," I said. "This isn't about who you're screwing. It's about screwing *with me*. Do you deny trying to keep me from Lyndham?"

"No."

"For Teresa?"

"For you. You're too intelligent to work for those idiots."

"You didn't know about my intelligence when you first showed up in my office."

"No."

"So you admit you were there under false pretenses."

"Yes."

"Because you wanted to manipulate me."

"Because I wanted to fuck you."

A rush of heat shot through my core. *Not now. Focus.* "Then why hire me?"

"Because once I discovered you're a genius, it would have been irresponsible not to." When I stayed silent, he rolled his eyes. "Contrary to how the media portrays me, I don't make all my decisions with my dick."

Don't think about his dick! Don't think about his dick!

"Have you fucked Teresa?" I blurted.

Because his dick in someone else is so much better.

His lip twitched. "I thought it didn't matter who I was screwing."

"That means 'yes'."

He sighed. "It started with sex, then she helped me with a problem and it progressed into a friendship, and then a combination. Not a relationship."

"Well *someone* didn't get the memo."

"Look, Princess, I have never, nor will I ever be stupid enough to put myself between two women." The corners of his mouth lifted. "Unless they want me to."

I released an undignified snort which had him crossing the floor to stand in front of me. He gripped my shoulders and exasperated green eyes locked onto skeptical blue ones. "I'm the first to admit I'm far from innocent, but I coerced you from Lyndham because I'm a prudent businessman. I don't give a flying fuck who they hired as long as it wasn't you."

I stared into his eyes. His steady, unflinching, guileless eyes. Either he'd been trained to withstand interrogations, had sociopathic tendencies, or he was telling the truth.

Fuck! Fuck! Fuck!

Teresa had me so scrambled, you could serve me up with a side of bacon.

"Besides," he smiled, "considering the deal you struck, who screwed who?"

"Just because I profited, doesn't excuse your intentions."

His thumb drifted along my collarbone, and I struggled to keep from leaning into his touch. "Which one? To hire one of the smartest women I've ever met or to fuck one of the sexiest women I've ever seen?"

"Um, neither? Both?" I forgot the question.

"We checked off the first so how about moving on to the second?" I gasped as his hips pinned me against the air hockey table, giving me a dizzying preview of what I could have. An undeniable rush of wetness answered between my thighs.

"I should... um, go." But that's the last thing I wanted.

"You can leave any time, Princess." His voice was pure silk over sex. "But if you stay, you're mine."

I hesitated, still thinking I had a choice.

But that was an illusion

Because I damn well already knew what I was about to do.

I raised my head, the answer clear in my eyes, and his mouth crashed down on mine.

14

Whiskey and sin never tasted sweeter. With every slide of his tongue, he swept me deeper, making daylight a distant memory. His lips moved from mine to the bare skin of my neck and—Oh Christ! My head fell back as he sucked, making my nerves sing. Fire followed his path as he nibbled his way lower, and when his teeth grazed my nipple through the thin fabric, lust arrowed straight through my core.

I grabbed for him, eager for his mouth on mine again, but he dropped to his knees and draped my leg over his shoulder.

Thank the stars for the slit in my dress.

My fingers gripped the table behind me for balance as his fingers tugged my thong to one side. I gasped when he buried his face in my aching pussy. His tongue began a slow swirl.

"God, Princess. You're as sweet as I imagined." The vibration from his words alone had the power to set me off, but they were nothing compared to his talented mouth. He licked and teased and probed until I lost control of my limbs. My fingers clutched harder. My head rolled back.

God help me!

With a swift lashing of his tongue, everything inside me stilled before erupting into a white-hot blaze. I cried out, shaking from the rush, while he continued lapping through my tremors. He pinned me against the table, latched his lips around my clit, and with a rhythmic suction, catapulted me to another explosive climax that collided with the first and would have brought me to my knees had he not been propping me up.

I was losing my mind.

He rose to his feet, the ghost of his tongue still working me through the aftershocks, and I fell trembling into his arms.

When his eyes found mine, they were brimming with lust and a twinge of male pride. How did they shimmer so hot and dark at the same time? It was mesmerizing.

He was mesmerizing.

"Thank you." I whispered before my brain caught up.

Did I just thank him for making me come? What the fuck? This is what happens when you let your body rule your head. Stupid shit comes out of your infatuated mouth.

His lips curled in that sexy way that made me want to feast on him. "Save that sentiment for when I'm inside you, Princess."

I groaned at the fresh wave of lust.

"Let's go," he said and gathered me in his arms. His long legs forged a path to the bedroom where he hit the light switch.

Dangerous' lair.

We landed hard on the bed, a tangle of tongues and limbs. I greedily wrestled off his shirt, sighing at the hard planes of his chest. Warm, smooth, and firm... even better than I dreamed—and my dreams of him were pretty damn good.

When he lowered my zipper, I couldn't shimmy out of my dress fast enough. My thong and strapless bra followed, and I hissed as he took my nipple in his mouth. He sucked hard.

And then he went still.

What the—

It took me a second but when I glimpsed his face, I understood.

He was focused on the circular scars scattered across my midsection. This had never happened to me before. The men I chose were too self-centered to notice graphic details about my cruel childhood. They only cared about getting off.

But Chase wasn't any man.

Mortified, I attempted to roll away, but he pinned my body beneath his. This time, when his breath fanned my skin, it wasn't from arousal but in a calculated appraisal. The scars had long healed to a mottled pink, but no amount of time could fully erase the past.

When he raised his head, I recoiled at the sight. As a kid, I'd conducted an experiment where I threw copper into fire, turning the flames a ferocious green. That fury was nothing compared to what stared back at me now.

"Are those what I think they are?" he said through a clenched jaw.

Memories curdled my stomach. Strong hands, searing pain, and the acrid odor of cigarette smoke mixed with burning flesh. Smells I'd never forget.

"Princess?" Chase snapped me back to my current hell. "I asked you a question."

Panic stirred enough to make me feel sick.

His eyes weren't looking at me. They were looking *through* me, the intense green embers determined to penetrate every tawdry layer until nothing remained but the ugliness I struggled to cover.

He'll strip my soul bare.

I twisted away but he collected my wrists in one hand while gripping my chin with the other. "Who did this?"

Restrained, vulnerable, and at the mercy of another, my panic accelerated. "GET OFF ME!" I screamed.

He released me.

I nearly ripped the sheets bolting out of bed. Spinning in circles, I searched for my clothes, but only found my bra draped over a lamp. With a frustrated curse, I tugged it free.

"What are you doing?" Chase asked.

"Leaving."

"Like hell you are!" He sprang from the bed and snatched the lace from my hands.

"Chase, I don't think—"

"You think too much." He wrapped an arm around me and pulled me into a deep kiss, his tongue relentlessly attacking until the doused spark rekindled. The lust caught fast and combined with my anger, shame, and adrenaline, ignited into a powder keg on the verge of going nuclear. I needed an outlet. Fucking or fighting. It didn't matter.

As if understanding, he held me tight, slid a hand between my legs and worked me, rough and hard until I came, the release a heady mix of healing and pleasure.

With a gentle nudge, he toppled us onto the bed, kissing, nibbling, and licking until my world caught fire again. I pulled his remaining clothes off and hungrily reached for his erection. Damn, his cock was magnificent. When he pulled away, I made a sound of protest, but he rolled on a condom then returned to ease inside me, his eyes melting into liquid pools of black that seemed to devour me whole. I moaned as my pussy stretched with an exquisite fullness, and unable to formulate words, clamped down, pulling him deeper.

He released a sharp hiss. "Princess, you keep gripping me like that and this is going to be a quick ride." He reared back to thrust into me, and I held on as he drove us into a fierce rhythm. The harder he plunged, the more I bucked. The more he gave, the crazier I became. I closed my eyes as he flooded my senses, pushing me to the edge all over again.

"Look at me, Princess," he ordered.

One glance at the raw need reflected in his eyes and the world around me shattered into blissful fragments. He pulled out abruptly, slid down, and buried his head between my thighs.

Holy hell!

I thrashed and bucked as he consumed my excitement with greedy licks, flicking my hypersensitive bundle of raw nerves into a mix of inevitable ecstasy.

And alarm.

A twinge of fear crept in, and I began to resist. I saw myself teetering on the brink of an unknown abyss. Never pushed this far. Never out of control. I couldn't afford to let go.

But I was losing the battle.

He slipped two fingers inside me and with a twist of his wrist, hit a spot I thought only existed in fiction. I clutched his hair and pounded on his shoulder. Anything to center me.

"Chase... too much... I can't."

"Stop fighting, Princess. Let go."

"I... can't."

But I was already gone.

It unraveled from somewhere deep and seized me in a series of spasms so forceful, I could have pulled a muscle and not noticed. He waited until I began my descent then reared up on his elbows and slammed into me. I came unhinged and the room filled with loud, erotic whimpers I vaguely recognized as mine. The world tumbled away and along with it, any illusion of control. I was left vulnerable and unprotected and for the first time in my life, I didn't give one single damn about it.

He collapsed beside me and we lay motionless, our labored

breathing the only sound in the room. My body was delectably sore, my limbs heavy, and my mind numb.

I had never felt more alive.

"Finally," Chase said, his voice thick with contentment. "With our track record, I expected the fire alarm to go off."

Sirens went off all right.

He planted a kiss on my lips, swung his feet to the floor, and walked into the adjoining bathroom.

Languid, cozy, and ensconced in a high-thread-count cocoon, my limbs rebelled against rising, but I never stayed overnight at a man's place. I stretched and wiggled, waiting for blood to return to my extremities. Just a few more minutes...

My eyes blinked open to a vaulted ceiling that did not belong in my apartment. Neither did the muscled arm wrapped around my torso. From the beginnings of streaking sunlight, I guessed it to be early. Early like when vampires go to bed and overachieving nutjobs wake up. Damn these luxury sheets. With a sigh, I extricated myself from Chase, or tried to. His arm tightened and I found myself pulled closer.

I relented and stayed still while my mind did the opposite. As someone who placed a high value on detachment, my life was relegated to a string of pointless encounters. Never at the mercy of another's behaviors or questions. Comprehending that was easy. Deciphering last night... not so much. After more than my share of good sex with bad boys, I had learned they all exhibited a common trait. They cared more about satisfying their own egos than the woman beneath them.

But not Chase.

Sex with him was... words eluded me. Probably because he fucked me stupid. He'd shattered expectations, taken me to incredible heights and through it all, treated my body with a reverence that astounded me.

No surprise he scratched the yearning that had plagued me since the night in the garden. Hell, since the elevator. But only in this moment did I truly understand what I sacrificed by living on the periphery with my managed expectations and measured reactions. How I protected against vulnerability at the expense of my sensuality.

And I wish I'd never realized it. Vulnerability was a luxury in which I could not indulge.

I glanced at the catalyst for these unsettling admissions. Sleep softened his features, lending him an innocent quality.

Ha. Even Genghis Khan probably looked sweet in repose.

I studied his sculpted cheekbones, full lips, dark lashes—why would a man need lashes that long?—and thick hair, tousled from sleep. What woman wouldn't be tempted?

He shifted and the bold lines of his tattoo caught my eye. The design blurred and I shook my head, blaming sex-addled hallucinations when I started seeing letters. "Catherine?" I whispered. Why would the most noncommittal man on the planet have a woman's name inked on his arm?

"She was my mother."

I shifted my gaze to find sleepy green eyes observing me. "She and my father died when I was fifteen. Car accident." An inflection in his voice betrayed emotion but just as quickly, it disappeared.

I skimmed a finger over the pattern, beautiful in the way it curved and molded with his sinewy lines. "What does the rest mean?"

"It's a compilation of my life... what I've lost... things I've done... what saved me." He grinned. "You may find this hard to believe, but I haven't always been the pillar of virtue you see before you."

I snorted but kept investigating. Seldom do you find a road

map into someone's inner self. Chase was turning out to be more complex than I imagined. More letters formed. *MM*.

Minnie Mouse? Hard shelled chocolate? Slim Shady?

In a casual move, he tucked his arm away, depriving my eyes from further probing. "Do you have any tats?"

After the attention he paid to my body last night, I doubt he'd have missed a mosquito bite. "No, but I have thought about getting one."

"Let me guess… a lily?" He surmised correctly. "Maybe right here?" His lips brushed over my shoulder and I shuddered. "Or how about somewhere in this vicinity?" His tongue traced a lazy pattern down my side until he reached my hipbone. He parted my legs and nuzzled my inner thigh. "But I'm partial to…"

All investigative thoughts vanished.

I woke to the same luxurious thread count but no occupant beside me this time. Instead, his annoyed voice filtered through the cracked door. "Another bidder?" he shouted. "How the hell did that happen?"

I wrapped a sheet around me and headed to the bathroom.

"He's not supposed to be soliciting other offers." Chase's irked voice grew louder. "This better not be a ploy to drive up the price. Especially after all the extensions I've granted him to work his personal shit out. If he can't get it sorted, I'll knock down the bitch's door myself and make her sign…"

I closed the bathroom door and sighed at the over-sexed harlot staring back at me in the mirror. Tangled hair, glowing skin, and satisfaction oozing from every pore, she looked quite pleased with herself.

When I reentered the bedroom, Chase was pacing, clutching his phone tight enough to crush it. He slowed when he saw me. "Sorry if I woke you. This fucking acquisition is squeezing the life out of me."

"It's okay." I scooped my thong up from the floor.

"Opportunistic money-hungry tools," he grumbled.

"Uh huh." *Where is that bra again?* I checked the lamp. Not this time.

"Why can't anyone honor an agreement anymore?"

"Can't say." Not under the bed.

He noticed my actions. "Going somewhere?"

"Home." I continued my kinky scavenger hunt. Shoes... check. Still no bra.

"Why?"

"Because that's where I live." I shook out the covers. "And I have stuff to do."

"Like what?"

Like screw my head on straight.

"Um... I need to... re-grout my bathroom."

His lips curved. "I was wondering how long it would take."

"For what?"

"For you to freak out."

"I'm not—"

"We're consenting adults who no longer work together. Stop analyzing and enjoy it." He grinned. "If the scratches on my back are any indication, you already did."

I held up my dress and grimaced. I'd seen road maps with fewer creases.

"You can wear something from here."

"From the Chase Hale Jilted Lover's Collection?" *Let me guess... white clothing.*

"I meant something of mine," he said. "I'll take you home after we shower. I've been imagining you naked and lathered up for months."

Slightly creepy but hot.

"What's it going to take?" he asked. "A game of air hockey?"

I couldn't help but laugh, which turned into a squeal when he lunged forward to tug at my makeshift toga. It crumpled to the floor. He reciprocated by pulling his T-shirt over his head. His pajama bottoms followed.

My mouth dried to parchment at my first glimpse of Chase in full naked daylight splendor. His body reminded me of a sculpted Italian statue, painstakingly carved from smooth marble, lean and defined with hard muscle and eight-pack abs, all tapering to that sexy V that drove women crazy in Calvin Klein underwear commercials.

His hands cupped my backside and molded that work of art to me. He was already hard. With a kiss, he turned and walked toward the bathroom, granting me an extraordinary view of his amazing ass.

His body was a temple.

And I was about to go Lara Croft all over it.

Chase's midnight-blue Ferrari roared down the street. *Holy shit!* I held on for dear life while my cheeks flapped against my ears.

Speakers blared "Living on a Prayer"—an appropriate song choice—while Chase deftly maneuvered the car, displaying glimpses of an alter madman ego.

Where did he get his license? Mr. Toad's Wild Ride?

He turned onto my street and parked in front of my building.

"Thanks for the—" He disappeared and seconds later my door opened.

"I'll walk you upstairs," he said.

"No." I pried my knuckles from the handle before allowing him to pull me from the soft leather. "I'd rather Nicki not see you."

"Are you ashamed of me?"

"Like you would ever believe that." He wouldn't know the word humble unless a stripper adopted it as her name.

"I'm getting the feeling she doesn't like me," Chase observed.

"Gee, I wonder why. Playboy, philanderer, womanizer..."

"Nah, she just doesn't know me. Once she does, she'll love me."

"If history is any indication, you won't be around that long."

He pulled me into a kiss that melted my insides. "Then it's a good thing I'm irresistible. See you soon, Princess."

I waited until his penis-on-wheels rounded the corner before heading upstairs. Not two feet into the apartment, Nicki came barreling out of her room, all nosy curls and sweetness. "Good morning, Miss Walk of Shame." She assessed my wet hair and oversized clothing. Her face and curls deflated. "Why would Wayne have a sweatshirt with Predator's company logo on it?"

Damn, I should have taken Chase's NYU sweatshirt.

"What did you do?" Nicki's stern voice reminded me of Mrs. Tyler, my seventh-grade teacher who would punish me whenever I screwed with the class computer. Seventeen years later and I was still in trouble for screwing things I shouldn't.

"Really?" Nicki glowered at me, all Medusa hair and fury. "Another man-whore?"

"Not technically. I didn't leave any cash on his dresser."

She didn't crack a smile. This was bad. "You will never have a normal relationship if you keep engaging in this behavior."

"News flash. I will never have one anyway."

"You don't have to settle for Dangerous. You can have more."

Back to the proverbial milk bottles she called expectations—or as I called them... pre-meditated disappointments. I rubbed my temples, combatting the brewing headache from her disapproval —or from sleep deprivation. "Please get it in that frizzy little head of yours that this is who I am and what I want." Wanted, deserved, cursed... Whatever.

"Jesus Christ! Even your dysfunctions have dysfunctions. There's so much wrong with that, I don't know where to begin."

"How about with leaving me the hell alone?" I snapped.

Nicki's face fell and I instantly regretted my words. Here I was alienating the one person who gave a damn and for what? An ephemeral man. For the millionth time, I wished I could explain but with so much at stake, the more superficial the relationship, the better. And Chase checked off that box. "I'm sorry I can't be the house-in-the-suburbs type of girl you want."

She thought about it for a second then sighed dramatically. "You're not dumping Wayne, are you?"

Thinking of Wayne while the smell of Dangerous' body wash lingered on me seemed wrong. "I haven't thought about it."

"Bang Dangerous, date Wayne, swipe right, play the field, and find someone better."

I needed a flowchart to follow that statement. "I spent one night with Dangerous. Don't get ahead of yourself. You have your crazy hair for that."

She swatted my arm. A good sign. She was softening. "He won't give up. I've seen how he eyes you. Like a Great Dane drooling over a Scooby Snack."

"Do you have any analogies that aren't food related?" I asked, genuinely curious.

"Like you don't compare every person to a computer."

"True. And Dangerous is an open-ended program which means I can do whatever I want. Rule number one, remember?" I trusted Chase to promote monogamy as much as I trusted Hollywood to release another quality Star Wars movie. But that's what made it perfect. No strings, no accountability, no questions, which meant no lies. Ironically, he could be my most honest relationship.

"So..." A curious glint entered her eyes. "Does Mr. Little Black Book fuck as good as he looks?"

“I’m pretty sure he’s illegal in a few states.”

She quirked a brow. “That good?”

“I’ve never seen stars before... and little cartoon bluebirds.”

“Did he fuck you or hit you over the head with an anvil?”

“Brain damage either way.”

15

I studied the post-coitus bouquet perched on my desk. Deep red roses against a backdrop of white lilies. Passion and purity. Even Dangerous' flowers conflicted. Though there was nothing pure about our night together. Two days later and I could still feel his touch tingling across my skin.

I swiveled to gaze out my window but rotated a full three-sixty and ended up staring at the flowers again.

Ugh! He was like a drug.

And damned if I didn't want another hit.

What a rush!

What an idiot! Getting involved with the one man in Manhattan whose dating life played like a reality television show.

Do not jeopardize everything you've built for a fantastic fuck.

But damn, can that man fuck.

I pushed him from my thoughts and attempted to tackle the proposal sprawled across my desk. So much for my laser-like focus. An entire morning devoted to a bid for a family-owned pet supply chain and all I had to show for it was a slew of terrible ideas.

None of which related to the proposal.

"Wayne Parker on line one," Sue announced.

Wayne? Was he privy to my night o' sin already?

"Jasmine." Wayne's voice was warm, and I imagined him as always... neat, tidy, and safe. "I wanted to let you know my meeting with Lyndham went well."

"That's great." *Not that I asked.*

"Which is why I'm flying to China tonight. I'm sorry to cancel our date tomorrow. I hope you're not upset."

"Not at all." Because I had no recollection of making it. "Thanks for the update. Travel safe."

"I also wanted to apologize for abandoning you at Hale's party. Of all the places to leave you... I'm sorry. Did he at least behave?"

Like a gentleman? No.

Like a hot-blooded fuck-god? Absolutely!

"Yes."

"Good to hear it." He sounded relieved. "From the way Teresa speaks, you'd think he has mind control abilities over his conquests. It's abhorrent how he takes advantage of that sweet woman."

You mean the woman who would happily icepick me if she knew I'd screwed Chase?

I rolled my eyes. Between Bryce, Teresa, and myself, Wayne couldn't accurately judge a person's character if they came with a lie detector test. The only one he pegged correctly was Chase. I guess it's true what they say... 'even a broken clock is right twice a day'.

"Hale." He made that word sound obscene. "He is arrogant and manipulative."

And can make a woman come more times than you answer your phone.

"And have I told you," Wayne continued, "how he added insult to his already unconscionable acts?"

What now? Pyramid scheme?

"He went and offered me a job," he said.

I waited for more but nothing came. "That's it?" I asked mockingly. "Oh, the horror."

"Why would I subject myself to that injustice?"

"They have foosball in the lunchroom?"

The line went silent.

"Uh, Wayne?" I said. "You still there?"

"You're sleeping with him," he said flatly.

I sighed. Yup. He had Chase pegged.

"How could you?" Wayne's voice was filled with hurt. "I thought you were too intelligent to become another notch on his headboard."

Best not to mention Chase's headboard was wrought iron.

I tried to muster up some compassion. To Wayne, this represented nothing more than another tick in his expanding defeated column. Nobody liked to lose. I knew that better than most. "I have work to do." *Okay, so I suck at compassion.*

"Before you go, please remember something."

"I'm listening."

"When Hale discards you for a newer model, know that a better man appreciates and cares about you." He hung up.

Newer model? Did he just call me old?

But I couldn't argue with the rest of it. Chase wasn't the better man. He was better *for me*. Which meant the best thing for Wayne was to move on. He didn't belong around people like us.

Not five minutes later, the phone rang again. "Sender of beautiful flowers on line one," Sue announced.

Ugh! This is going to be one of those days.

"Hey, Princess." Warmth rushed through me at the sound of Chase's voice. "You free for dinner?"

"I'm—"

"I'll pick you up at your office." He disconnected.

Effective tactic. Hang up before the target declines.

As if pulled by a magnet, I raised my head, not surprised to find Dangerous standing at the door. He smiled at the flowers before turning that sexy grin on me. "You ready?"

Only he could make two innocent words sound like foreplay.

End it. NOW!

He approached my desk and leaned over to capture my mouth in a dizzying kiss.

Maybe in a few minutes.

A low growl from my stomach interrupted.

Chase pulled back with a frown. "Have you eaten today? And before you answer, Cheetos are not a food group."

I was lucky I remembered underwear.

My stomach rumbled again, as if sensing my intention to cheat it out of a meal.

"Enough. I'm feeding you." He rolled my chair to the side. "I'll even throw in chocolate if you don't complain."

Already threatening to deny my body the best sex of its life, adding chocolate deprivation just bordered on evil.

I reluctantly agreed then locked up and followed Chase to the waiting Mercedes. "Ms. Monroe." Richard smiled. "Nice to see you again."

Why do I feel like a slut being led to slaughter?

We exited near a brick building, framed by a jaunty red

awning. My stomach growled again at the smell of fresh-baked bread that reached us before we walked through the large red door. A short Italian man, his face half hidden behind a thick mustache, greeted Chase warmly. I imagined him in coveralls, hopping over barrels to save Princess Peach from a giant gorilla.

"Meet Franco," Chase introduced. "His family makes the best Italian food in the city."

Don't let Nicki hear that. She already wants to poison you.

Franco seated us in a corner booth where I propped my elbows on the checkered tablecloth and regarded the collection of black and white photos grouped on the wall. Franco's relatives, judging from the resemblance. The sentiment eluded me. I never wanted to lay eyes on my family again much less display them. Unless plastered on a wanted poster.

I decided to get straight to the point. "What are we doing and why are we here?"

Chase leaned back and regarded me. "Because you're a dangerous one to leave alone too long."

Me? Dangerous? Ha. "Afraid I'll come to my senses?"

"Not at all." A slow smile spread across his lips. "I rather enjoy knocking them out of you."

I nearly groaned from the adrenaline surge.

"And *this*— " he spread his arms wide—"is dinner. Unlike Prep School, I prefer a woman who doesn't consider a lettuce leaf a meal."

"Shocking, judging from your Barbie dates." I regretted the words the second they came out.

"Keeping tabs?"

"Merely an observation. Speaking of which, don't you usually move on about now? You know, the whole women are disposable principle?"

"Razors are disposable," Chase responded. "And just so you

know, I have engaged in sex with the same woman multiple times."

"How very green of you," I said. "What if *I'm* ready to move on?"

"Then you'd be lying." He leaned forward, his eyes darkening with intent. "Because I've learned what it means when you're looking at me like that."

Franco chose that fortuitous moment to return, carrying a basket of garlic bread and two orange-colored drinks. I sipped the Bellini that I never ordered and smiled my approval. Not one for fancy toast, I retracted my position the second I bit into the homemade goodness.

"Wait until you try the ravioli!" Franco said with a bow before shuffling off.

"I guess I know what I'm ordering," I commented.

"You never had a choice."

"Seems to be a common theme."

Chase reached over to cover my hand, sending heat up my arm. "You always have a choice, Princess."

Tell that to the fire you just stoked.

Which meant I needed to get Dangerous out of my system or risk insanity—not to say he didn't instill a different kind of crazy. Besides, with the world so messed up, was it wrong to accept a moment of pleasure when offered? After years of deprivation, hadn't I earned a brief detour in my otherwise well-calculated life?

The master of rationalization at work.

"Okay," I agreed. "But I have a rule of my own."

"You're supposed to disclose all terms up front. Not *after* the man gets a taste and will do anything to be inside you again."

I struggled to stay on point. "Call it effective negotiating."

"I call it extortion."

"This stays in the bedroom. I'm not interested in a public association with the world's most notorious playboy."

"Add shower and game-room to the list and you have a deal."

I thanked Richard and started towards my apartment but paused when Chase opened the trunk and removed an overnight bag.

Am I sleeping with a man so pretentious, he carries an 'I'm going to get lucky' valise with him?

The apartment was thankfully empty as we made our way to my room. I removed the lily pin and placed the cheap costume jewelry in its overkill velvet box while watching Chase hang a suit in my closet. I found the scene unsettling, too comfortable in its surreal depiction of a normal couple at bedtime. Even now, he invaded my space with an ease that disturbed me.

"Nice." Chase admired my Darth Vader lithograph with *'Who's your Daddy?'* printed on the bottom. "Any chance you have a Princess Leia gold bikini stashed around here?"

"Are you making fun of me?"

"You're speaking to someone who has an R2-D2 trash can in his office."

"Maybe there's hope for you yet." I headed for the bathroom to take a shower, knowing full well I was inviting the inevitable.

I was reveling in the hot needles pummeling my skin when *inevitable* opened the door behind me. My wet hair was swept to one side and strong hands gripped at my hips. My body came to life, my nipples tightened, and the cascading stream transformed into an erotic caress. I tried to turn, but his arms locked around me.

"Lift your leg," he growled in my ear.

He held me in place as I braced a foot on the shelf, and all I could do was close my eyes as his hand dipped between my thighs.

"Tell me that's not from the shower." His voice rumbled with appreciation. He pushed two fingers inside me and groaned at how easily they slid in.

My hips moved instinctively, imploring his fingers to fuck me while a sense of shame washed over me at how much I wanted this. His fingers slid free, parted my pussy lips, and it was my turn to groan as he found my clit. I gasped when he squeezed then rubbed his fingers together, pinning my clit in the most intense massage. Everything spun as wave upon wave of insane pleasure radiated. I swayed against him and my moans turned to errant whimpers.

"God, your noises make me want to fuck you," he growled and pressed his erection against my back.

I cried out when his teeth found my neck and my clit was pressed so damn hard, I almost came, but he resumed rolling in sweet circles, the friction making me ache with need. My muscles tightened, my nerves pulsed, and sweat slicked over me faster than the water could whisk it away.

With a trembling hand, I clawed at his thigh, frustrated when my fingers slid off his wet skin.

"You're already shaking," he whispered and bit down on my neck again in what was sure to leave a bruise. "But we're not there yet, Princess."

I reached behind to bury my hands in his hair while his fingers persisted around and around, his other hand stretching a nipple. "Chase... I need..." My words trailed off into a moan. I gripped his roots. Dammit, he knew exactly what I needed.

"What's that, Princess?" he practically purred. He was loving every second of this. "Answer me one question and I'll let you come."

He pulled his hand away to turn the water off.

"No," I whimpered. "Please don't stop." The words came out without my consent. I'd never begged for anything in my life.

He chuckled but resumed his torturously patient rhythm and I moaned all over again as he brought me back to the brink within seconds.

"You will answer one question," he ordered.

"Yes," I relented.

"How long, Princess?"

"Huh?"

How long did it actually take you to hack into my company?"

"You knew?" I panted. With his fingers playing me, I could barely remember.

"How long?" he repeated and pulled back.

"Five minutes!" I yelled.

"Not so immune to the Hale charm after all." He rewarded me with a severe pinch of his fingers, and I gasped from the unexpected sting then screamed as I came in a blinding shockwave. My knees buckled but his embrace kept me up.

When he spun me to face him, I almost thanked him again.

Once my breath returned, I scowled. "So you're one of those men who gets off on making a woman beg?"

"No. I enjoy making women scream." His smile turned devious. "I enjoy making *you* beg."

Not for the first time, I questioned my ability to survive Dangerous. The self-assurance and rationalization I fancied as protection became a joke when naked and trembling in front of him. I needed something to level the playing field. Something to reclaim control. Anything so I'd hate myself less for my weakness.

My hands trailed his thighs as I sank to my knees. "Is that so?" I murmured and licked my way down his flat stomach, flicking beaded water droplets off his smooth ridges and paying special attention to the solid V at his hips.

Every inch of him was tongue-worthy.

Incredibly hard and heavy in my hands, I admired his erection before wrapping my fingers around it. I squeezed and was rewarded with a sharp hiss. With gentle flicks, my tongue caressed his tip, tasting the salty droplets from his arousal. His anguished groan was all I needed, and I relaxed my throat to take him deep inside my mouth.

He slapped a hand against the wall. "Fuck, Princess that feels incredible."

I warmed from the compliment as I drove him in and out, enthralled with how his abs contracted in time with his breathing. I splayed my palm over the cut muscles, emboldened by the rapid movement.

Replacing my mouth with a firm hand, my lips coasted lower to cup his smooth balls. I swirled the silky skin between my lips and felt pride at the string of expletives he released. A heady rush came over me as the air grew thick with his intoxicating scent. Knowing I could make him moan with pleasure was beyond empowering.

I pulled him into my mouth again and tightened my grip, grazing him with my teeth, voraciously sucking while increasing the pressure, ready to watch him skyrocket over the edge. He responded with a growl and gripped the back of my head, fucking my mouth with eager thrusts. His breathing turned to grunts and with a jerk, a rush of warmth shot down my throat. I sucked every drop until he was dry.

When he hauled me to my feet, the sexual haze in his eyes left no doubt I'd accomplished my mission.

Did he feel like thanking me or was that my thing?

16

I'm too young to die.

Chase handled the Ferrari with his usual grace and confidence, sprinkled with a hefty dose of crazy. He opened the throttle, plastering me against the soft leather then took a hairpin turn. I waited until we stopped at a red light before peeling my fingers off the dash, unsure if they would straighten again.

His phone rang. “Hale.” He spoke into his earpiece. “I'll be right there.” With a squeal of the tires—or it might have been me—he flipped a sharp U-turn. “I need to make a stop to sign some papers for the acquisition. Then we can get on with the rest of our night.”

That sounded funny since we'd just finished dinner and the rest of our night comprised of getting naked and burning off calories. Although Chase had agreed to my dates-equal-sex–and-not-food agreement, in the past month of sexing it up together, he'd routinely coerced me into meals, especially when my obsession with the pet supply chain bid caused me to forget them.

We continued in comfortable—albeit death defying—silence

until Chase turned down a tree-lined street scattered with affluent homes. "My brother's place," he answered my unspoken question as we pulled up to a modern two-story house. "Derek's my attorney."

The front door opened and a man with familiar ink-black hair stepped out. "You must be Jasmine." He directed a smile towards me.

The brothers resembled each other, but while Derek held his own in the looks department, he lacked his younger brother's gut-punching beauty. Shorter than Chase, he carried a few marriage pounds, wore his hair tidy, and where Chase's piercing green gaze frequently held mischief, Derek's brown ones shone with maturity.

My heels clicked on glossy marble while I followed the men through the house to the backyard. A woman was standing at a grill, flipping burgers like a pro. Her short dark hair jutted out in a contemporary style and a cooking apron enveloped her small frame. She hugged Chase then turned to me. "I'm Lynne. Are you two staying for dinner?"

"We're only here for a few minutes. Be right back." Chase followed Derek into the house, leaving me alone with this strange lady.

She turned off the grill and invited me to sit at the patio table.

"Chase said he used your services on his latest project," she said. "Games, right?"

"That's his thing. I do security software."

"Whatever you did, you made quite an impression." She grinned. "I believe his words were 'It's freaking scary how her mind works'."

I flushed at the unexpected compliment. At least, I took it as one. "That might be his way of saying I'm a little off."

"We all are. It's a prerequisite for putting up with him."

"How long have you known Chase?"

"He was in high school when I met Derek."

"Let me guess. A good-looking, sullen teenager who got the head cheerleader and homecoming queen?" Probably in the same night.

"Girls were never the issue," she agreed, but her next words added an unexpected element. "It was his need to beat the crap out of every guy. After their parents' death, Chase went off the rails, caused a lot of problems. But no matter what type of trouble he got himself into, Derek never gave up on him. That's one of the reasons I fell for Derek."

"I had no idea." And I preferred it that way. We all carried trauma from our pasts, but hearing vivid details made them real. Made *him* real. And I favored the objectified version to a humanized one.

"Any plans to collaborate again?" she asked.

"According to him, not a chance."

"Ah, yes," Lynne said with a knowing look. "Rule number three."

What the fuck? Does everyone get a wallet-sized copy?

"Sorry." Lynne stifled a laugh. "I didn't mean to embarrass you. As a psychiatrist, I find them very insightful."

Chase left me alone with a head doctor? If she pulls out inkblots, I'm bailing.

"How about your family?" Lynne questioned. "Parents? Siblings? Where did you grow up?"

"In California." Hopefully, one out of three answers would suffice because that's all she was getting. "May I use your restroom?" I scrambled away as fast as my psychoanalysis-adverse legs could carry me. People who earned a living prying into people's heads creeped me out.

When I exited the bathroom, I dilly-dallied down the long

hallway. Anything to avoid my hostess. Ironically, I probably needed therapy more than most. But not from my fuckbuddy's sister-in-law.

I stopped at a portrait hanging on the wall. A blonde woman with gentle green eyes radiated sweetness while the man beside her wore a silly smile, in contrast to his ebony black hair and large stature. Two boys crouched at their feet. Even back then, Chase's impudent smirk and sparkling eyes stood out.

To lose good parents at a young age hardly seemed fair. Especially while the undeserving ones lived.

I heard my name.

"So what's the deal with Jasmine?" Derek was saying. "It's rare you bring a girl around. Who was the last one... Terry, Tara?"

I sidled close to the wall, remaining out of sight.

"Teresa," Chase corrected.

My insides clenched. Always fucking Teresa.

"Yeah, that's it," Derek said. "Lynne thought she was disingenuous."

Maybe Lynne's a decent shrink after all.

"If it wasn't for Teresa, I would be—"

"I know," Derek interrupted. "I'm well aware how she saved your ass."

I heard pages shuffling and then Chase's annoyed voice. "These terms are unacceptable."

"I figured as much. Sign here."

More papers rustling.

"Jasmine seems pleasantly different," Derek said.

"Very," Chase chuckled. "Most women can't wait to be associated with my name. Not Princess. She's so insistent on avoiding the limelight, it's an argument to take her out to dinner." I could hear the grin in his tone. "Says my unscrupulous reputation will make her look bad."

"Smart woman," Derek muttered. "At least you know she's not after your money."

"She appears to be after nothing."

"And that's a problem?"

"Everyone wants something."

His body. His hands. His tongue. His very generous dick. And to get the hell out of here. Not necessarily in that order.

"Sounds ideal for you," Derek remarked. "Zero entanglements."

"Something like that."

"You know Lynne's hoping Jasmine will make you renounce your wretched lifestyle."

I retract my previous thought. She's an idiot.

"She hopes that of every woman. It's annoying."

"This may be a radical notion but maybe you might keep one around for a while."

"And maybe you might mind your own fucking business." Chase's voice floated across the room as if he were walking. "Or are you forgetting that I tried that once?"

Dangerous settling down? Hah!

"Is she still calling?" Derek asked.

"Straight to voicemail."

I frowned. Who? Not Teresa. I wished Chase would send her to voicemail.

"She wants something," Derek said. "And you know how manipulative she can be. She'll blindside you and anyone near you if she gets the chance."

"I'm well aware of how she fucking operates," Chase responded with a coldness that gave me a chill. I'd never heard him like this before. "And I'm also aware of what you think I should do since you've told me. Repeatedly."

"So how about you listen to your big brother for once?"

"And how about you blow me?"

"Nah," Derek said. "You have enough willing participants."

Chase laughed and just like that, the tension diffused.

Before I could wrap my brain around any of it, Derek spoke again. "How's the sex with Jasmine?"

Yikes! I almost bolted. Did I want to hear the answer? Not really, but I stayed anyway, feminine pride on the line. Finally, Chase spoke. "Do you remember in college when I hooked up with that drama chick?"

"Parker's girlfriend?" Derek laughed. "How can I forget? You said you saw God that night."

"Sex with Princess makes me look like an atheist back then."

Awwww.

"I think we're done here," Derek said.

I scurried away to join Lynne. Moments later, Chase joined us and we said our goodbyes.

"I hope Lynne didn't talk you into a stupor," Chase said as we drove away.

"Just tidbits about your hellion days."

He shrugged. "I was working out some anger issues. I've since learned to channel my energy into more constructive outlets."

I warmed at the thought of all those delicious outlets. "And I more than approve of your current stress relief methods."

He choked out a laugh. "I was referring to martial arts, though I'm happy to redirect my testosterone into other endeavors for you."

Oddly, I found a twisted camaraderie in his dysfunction. The more fucked-up, the more I could relate.

"Attracted to bad boys?" he teased.

He had no idea how much. "What was your worst fight?"

"In college, I mouthed off to a group of Paul Bunyan

wannabees in a redneck bar then made out with one of their girls. I ended up getting jumped by a pack of lumberjack giants."

"What happened?"

"Have you ever seen a Jackie Chan movie where he fights off multiple attackers by using everything in the room as props?"

"Yes," I said, growing impressed.

"It was nothing like that," he snorted. "I got my ass kicked. I still can't see flannel without breaking out in hives."

I laughed. No flannel threats in my closet since Nicki had purged all my comfortable clothing.

"I deserved it," he admitted. "I could have walked away, but I chose to stay and entertain my death wish instead. Have you ever done something you knew was tremendously stupid yet couldn't stop yourself?"

Yup. I was sitting right next to it.

I reached out and pouted when instead of hard muscle, my hand brushed against paper. My eyes opened to see an envelope on his pillow. Confused, I opened it and gasped at my Wolfe royalty check. *Holy shit!* With a squeal, I leaped up and bounced like a six-year-old on a sugar bender. I knew Wolfe would be lucrative, but I never imagined... not in the first check. The first of many. I collapsed on the bed, gasping—I needed to start exercising. Why would he agree to an arrangement that paid me so much? Granted this was couch cushion change to him but still... I rolled on my back and held it up as if evaluating its authenticity. That's when I noticed the note attached.

. . .

Had to leave early. More acquisition delays with more blood-sucking leeches. Use some of this money for bail in the event I strangle someone today.

-C

P.S. Still think I got taken but do what you did for me last night again and we'll call it even.

A faint blush crept up my cheeks. Yup, last night had been interesting.

"I believe it's time I get acquainted with my competition." Chase had gestured to my nightstand.

Huh? Wayne couldn't fit in there.

When he opened my drawer, he surprised me by forgoing my vibrator for the deceptively small egg-shaped bullet. "It suits you," he murmured, and I wondered what you could glean about a woman from her sex gadgets. I'm sure I could find a quiz about it somewhere on the internet. I'd once taken a test that determined my personality type based on how I ate an Oreo. It told me to stay away from furry animals and seek professional help immediately.

"You gonna show me some moves?" I joked.

He laid it beside me. "I'm not stupid enough to train a woman out of my bed."

"Surely the virile Chase Hale is not intimidated by inanimate devices."

"Baby, I'm irreplaceable," he said with a cocky grin. He moved between my legs and kissed my inner thigh. Then he sat back and waited.

"Um, you gonna use it?"

He glanced up at me. "No. You are."

"What? No."

His eyes glinted with desire. "You have no idea what it's like watching you come. What it does to me."

"I don't think—"

"The noises you make, how your body moves. I want you to do that for me. Please."

The more he spoke, the more his words became an aphrodisiac, urging me to obey. I reached for the plaything, shocked at my acceptance. Why couldn't I say no to him? A question to be asked the next time I chastised my selfish body.

I flipped the switch to the lowest setting and a buzz filled the room.

"Spread wide for me, baby," he coaxed.

With the fingers of one hand, I separated my lips and, with the other, rubbed the tiny cylinder on my exposed flesh, too self-conscious to enjoy it.

No way I'd orgasm.

"Damn, Princess." His eyes darkened to a deep midnight green as they followed my movements. "I wish you could see how fucking gorgeous your pussy is." His cock stood proud, his breathing jagged, and I could feel excitement radiating from every inch of him. But it was how he looked at me with those mesmerizing eyes—like no one ever had—visually ravishing my body with a dark hunger as if I were the sexiest woman alive.

An exhilarating sensation came over me and with a depraved exhibitionist side I never knew existed, I parted my legs wide, giving him the explicit view he requested. His own private show compelled by the insanity he instilled in me. Wetness pooled between my thighs and the bullet glided effortlessly, injecting sweet vibrations throughout my nerves. It didn't take long before my body tensed and I cried out.

"My turn." He lunged forward, wrapped his arms around me and rolled us over until I sat astride him. With his hypnotic gaze locked on mine, he gripped my waist and pushed me down hard, filling me deep in one heavenly move.

Oh my fucking God!

I moved my hips back and forth, moaning when his cock rubbed the perfect spot inside me. Arching my back, I rocked faster until I was mindlessly grinding my pussy against him and the delicious friction had me struggling to draw breath. Something hard slipped between my legs, but I didn't care. Until the high-powered vibrator clamped down on my clit. Setting: Insanity. A scream ripped from my throat and I exploded, bucking like a possessed woman while mercilessly riding him into oblivion.

I left Pettery Barn's corporate office with a signed contract and retainer check in hand. The family-owned pet chain account baffled me. Unless they intended to house state secrets, their demand for excessively encrypted software translated to overkill, but they had agreed to my exorbitant quote without balking. Not that I needed to worry about money anymore.

"Good morning," Sue said when I sailed past her. She followed me into my office and watched as I powered up my computer. "You're looking content," she commented. "Scorching CEO getting the job done?"

I ignored her and typed. The printer hummed and spit out a sheet of paper.

"What's it like to mattress dance with such a hunk?" Sue asked for the millionth time.

I snatched up the check and walked over to dangle it in front of her. This ought to shut her up.

"Why is that made out to me?" she asked.

"Because it's your bonus." I placed it in her hand. "None of this could have happened without you." If Chase was rewarding his folks for Wolfe, Sue deserved the same.

I jumped when she flung her arms around me. "I knew you would do amazing things when let loose." She pulled away and her eyes misted. "Thanks for taking a chance on a weird kid not even out of college."

"You were cheap and I never could refuse a bargain." I extricated myself from the hug. Jasmine Monroe did not do emotion. Even for someone as adorable as Sue. "Now go earn that bonus by getting back to work."

With an enormous grin, she complied, bouncing like she'd attached springs to her purple boots. As much as I wanted to share in her joy, I couldn't. Not while plagued by a burning curiosity about the woman Chase had mentioned last night, the one he always sent straight to voicemail. Should I brace myself for an ambush from another one of his manipulative she-beasts? Did occupying Chase's bed paint a target on my back?

With my patience depleted, I gave Sue the afternoon off. I wanted answers and to get them, I needed privacy.

I'd conducted background checks on men before. Once, I'd confirmed a hunch that my date's family had been fleeced by mine. I considered it proactive and sometimes essential. And if the situation didn't qualify as either, I'd make up another justification.

Besides, he'd never know.

Affluent people hit both extremes of the hacking coin. As public figures, scandals and gossip littered the internet, which in Chase's case, translated to his legions of beautiful women. I grimaced at the sight of almond eyes and long dark hair. That bitch had been around a while.

On the flip side, wealth afforded discretion, which meant the rich could hide the condemning stuff better than the average yokel.

It didn't take long to hit pay dirt in the form of a buried court reference that someone had taken great effort to hide. Though not well enough. From there, I followed the breadcrumbs until I uncovered the original legal document.

My fingers froze.

A marriage certificate? Chase was married?

Nine years ago to Missy-Mae Callahan.

MM.

17

"Who's my what?" I asked.

"Your date," Helena screeched into my ear. "For my wedding. So you don't look like a loser sitting beside an empty chair."

Like I would subject another human to her toxicity or have them bear witness to the eggplant. Nobody deserved such trauma.

With no worries of bothering Sue, who had left hours ago, I punched the speaker button and swiveled my chair to face the window. So much for staying late to make headway on the pet supply project.

"You're there to make me look good, not broadcast what a failure you are." Helena's blaring voice blanketed my office with obnoxiousness. "I swear, what type of idiot can't get a date for a weekend?"

The type that's too exhausted to deal with this right now.

After the initial shock from discovering Chase's clandestine marriage, I'd spent last night digging around until I worked myself into such a state, even the annulment voiding the marriage did nothing to ameliorate my anxiousness. Sizeable sums of money had changed hands with the intent of concealing the event, which only piqued my curiosity. Especially when I found the unmarried Miss M&M Callahan residing in a fancy Texas home, driving a Mercedes, and maintaining a bank account that until recently, held a sizeable sum. All with no obvious source of earnings. It didn't take hacking into Chase's financials to solve that mystery.

If he felt guilty enough to support her, what had he done to her?

And how was this any of my business? That being the pertinent question.

So why did I continue searching until I found myself staring at a picture of a petite blonde woman with guileless blue eyes and an adorable heart-shaped face? Even in two-dimensional print, she exuded a sweetness I'd never see in the mirror. If Dangerous had once been attracted to that type, something had derailed him to the dark side, because as much as I loathed to acknowledge any similarity between Teresa and myself, neither one of us possessed an innocent bone in our bodies.

And why does any of this matter?

Because I'm a fucking hypocrite.

"...so I'm going to help you." Helena's condescending tone snapped me back to my current predicament.

"Help me with what?"

"I found you a date." Her smugness poured through the speaker, making my hairs stand on end. This couldn't be good.

I reached for my stress ball. "Instead of playing OCD matchmaker, why not change the seating chart?"

"Are you crazy?" Helena shouted as if I'd recommended we dance naked around a campfire. "I spent months grueling over it with Phil's mother, and I refuse to kiss that tyrannical purse-strangling bitch's ass any more than I have to. And definitely not for you."

"Then I'll bring Nicki."

"That harpy is *not* welcome."

Moot point. Nicki would sooner bake with Bisquick than attend Helena's wedding.

"Like… I… said…" Helena dragged out the words like my bra size trumped my IQ. "I already found someone. His name is George Junior. He's Phil's cousin and a dentist from Hollywood."

And has two heads and breathes fire. "I'd rather not."

"Unbelievable," she yelled and suddenly, my office became too small to contain her wrath. "I'm doing you a favor and this is the gratitude I get? You already ruined my life when you made Mom leave. I will not let you ruin my wedding too. Honestly, I don't know how you can live with yourself."

I pushed down the old wounds her words conjured. Now was not the time for self-pity. "Then why do you want me there?" That question still ate at me.

But she wasn't listening. When Helena dove into insulting mode, she went deep. "You have no clue how impossible it is to make you sound tolerable. Like Dad used to say… the only chance you have of keeping a man is by getting knocked up. You're going to die old and alone."

"Since you know so much, can you tell me if it'll be quick?"

"Joke all you want," she spat. "But since you're the nitwit who can't get a date, you're going with George Junior. Who knows? If he feels sorry enough for you, maybe you'll get laid."

"Why the hell would she want to do that?"

I kicked my chair around to see Chase standing in the doorway, a thunderous scowl marring his face.

Fuck me! That man could moonlight as a ninja at Stealth.

"How long have you been there?" I mouthed.

"Long enough," he answered at full volume.

"Who's that?" Helena demanded.

I shushed him. "I'll be off in a minute."

"Who's with you?" Helena repeated.

Chase eyed the phone receiver.

"Don't you dare," I warned as we simultaneously lunged for the handset. He beat me to it with his damn ninja reflexes. I fumbled to disconnect the call, but he easily held me off.

"This is her date for whatever you're discussing," he barked.

Helena said something indecipherable that, judging from Chase's expression, must have been one of her caustic classics.

"I don't give a damn," Chase bit out. "I'm coming with her—"

"Chase, don't," I implored.

"—so back the fuck off."

I slumped down. Fantastic. Prod the beast who held my livelihood in her claws.

Helena started in again but Chase interrupted. "That's *your* problem. We'll see you there." He slammed the phone down. "Who the hell was that cunt and what did I just commit to?"

"My cousin," I groaned. "Her wedding."

"Someone is marrying her? She sounds as appealing as herpes."

"It's shocking how people you least expect to get married make it to the altar." The words slipped out without thinking.

Thankfully, he didn't notice. "Where's the wedding?"

"San Diego."

"At least it's a decent spot. We'll take Predator's jet."

"No." I was supposed to be deterring him, not securing transportation. "Don't you have obligations?"

"What's the point of running my own business if I can't take time to enjoy life?"

"You're confusing enjoyment with torture. There's a reason I never discuss what's left of my family. They're a bunch of dicks... no, that's an insult to dicks."

"All the more reason to not go solo."

"We agreed to a strictly physical relationship, which I'm sure precludes crashing obligatory family events." *You stay out of my past and I'll stay out of yours.*

"This is different," he justified. "It sounds... interesting."

"You do not get to change the rules based on your whims."

"After hearing the end of that phone conversation, there is absolutely no scenario where you're going alone."

"I can handle it."

"I'm not saying you can't. I'm saying I don't want you to."

"And I'm saying it's not your decision."

"For fuck's sake, Princess, will you please, just this once, shut up and let me do something nice for you?"

"And will you please stop assuming you know what I want?"

He reached the door in two strides. "I'm not spending tonight fighting. Maybe after you think it through, you'll come to your senses."

And just like that, my chivalrous hero disappeared to leave me alone with the aftermath.

Stupid white knight syndrome.

I squeezed the stress ball harder. If this kept up, I'd have fore-arms like Popeye.

What to do?

Take him with me, play my role, and force feed him lies?

Isn't that what you do every time you open your mouth?

Maybe he's doing the same.

With that sickening thought, I gave up and gathered my purse. If I planned an evening of self-flagellation, I may as well relocate to a setting conducive to ice cream. As I exited the building, I considered hailing a cab but decided to walk. Maybe the brisk evening air would inspire a way out of my dilemma.

The nightlife street crowd differed little from the morning throng. Flashier dressed obstacles trekking to more entertaining destinations yet still exhibiting the same single-minded aggressiveness. I hardly noticed. Fixated on Chase's obstinance, I barreled through the crowd in a similar trance.

A sturdy shoulder crashed into mine. Thrown off balance, I stumbled back while large hands seized my arms to steady me, or so I thought. Until they dragged me into an alley instead.

Confusion delayed my reaction and then reality crashed into me. I struggled and kicked, trying to hit anything sensitive. My knee must have connected with something important because I heard him grunt, but any hope was short-lived when he slammed me against the wall. A fist came out of nowhere and lightning exploded across my cheek. My head snapped to the side as I crumpled and would have hit the ground if not for his meaty hand circling my neck.

"Dumb bitch." His sour breath curdled my insides. Through watery eyes, I made out a broad figure wrapped in a black hoody. His body twitched in jagged and erratic movements.

Drugs?

I tried to speak, to tell him to take my purse, whatever he needed to go away and get his next fix, but the vice around my neck was tightening, stealing my words along with my breath. Spots obscured my vision and darkness loomed. If I passed out, I'd be at his mercy to kill… or worse. That visual sent me into a frenzy and with a surge of desperation, I clawed and scratched at anything within reach.

And then blinding pain filled my head.

Burned, bruised, broken, but never mugged before.

It's crazy what goes through your mind when you're falling.

18

I woke to a body wracked with pain. Another beating. I tried to remember what I'd done to make him angry.

A scuffling noise. *He's coming back. Hide!*

"I think she's stirring," a female voice said.

Helena? Of course she's here. She never missed a beat-down.

"Princess, can you hear me?" A man this time.

Princess? Why would he call me that?

My eyes slowly opened to see a blurry figure. A few blinks and it transformed into a breathtakingly beautiful face, shrouded by a halo of light.

An angel. I'm free.

"She looks terrible."

And my afterlife is insulting me.

"Get the doctor."

My angel disappeared and the soft glow transformed into a harsh fluorescent glare. I was lying in a hospital bed with Nicki spinning above me.

"You were mugged," she explained.

Fragments of a dark alley, giant hands, and rancid breath skipped through my mind. A wave of nausea hit, and I turned to dry-heave into a bucket that magically appeared. Sweaty and exhausted, I collapsed. "What did—" I gasped as flames shot up my throat.

"And strangled," Nicki added. "And you hit your head pretty hard."

That explained the marching band playing in my skull.

Chase entered with a jovial looking man wearing a white coat. A stocky nurse in green scrubs followed, her expression as severe as her tight bun.

The doctor gave Nurse Bunhead a look and with no-nonsense efficiency, she ushered Nicki and Chase out of the room. The next fifteen minutes involved a gamut of tests, a quiz on current events I couldn't have passed when healthy, and questions regarding childhood injuries that left medical professionals concerned. Although not uttered in years, the crafted fiction of sports injuries and childhood dares spilled out with not so much as a fluctuation in my heart rate. Not bad for someone in my current state.

The doctor was delivering his verdict when Nicki and Chase returned. The list included a head gash, concussion, strangulation...

I stopped paying attention.

Until he spoke again. "You were unconscious for two days, so you'll be staying with us for a little while. You need to get your strength back."

My eyes widened. "No," I mouthed. "Meeting. Pettery Barn."

"It's under control," Chase assured me, but the loud spike from my heart rate monitor said otherwise. "Brandon," Chase elaborated. "He's taking time off from Predator to become the newest temp at Monroe Consulting."

Bloody hell! I mimicked typing on a computer.

"No work!" the doctor ordered before he and Nurse Bunhead left the room. Nicki took off after them with a list of questions.

Chase balanced a hip on my bed. Careful not to disturb the IV, he intertwined his fingers with mine. "You were found in an alley," he answered my questioning look. "No purse or phone and your dress was torn here." He pointed above my right breast. "He took your lily pin."

My heart sank at the loss of my only childhood memento. Brutally taken at the hands of violence. How could I argue with such a poetic ending?

The following days flew by in a haze of sleep, pain, and drugs. I frequently woke to find Nicki reading or an occasional Chase sighting. Nicki mentioned other visitors, but I missed them while floating in and out of oblivion.

Which was best given a fun fact about strangulation—the red eyes and nose bleeds. Something about anatomy and tiny blood vessels. Throw in the bruises and swollen jaw, and I was a sight to create sore eyes. They would fade with time, but even the police officers who came by did a double take. They chalked it up to a routine mugging, invited me to look at mugshots then hastily retreated as if I would hex them.

On day something or other, I woke to find Chase watching me.

"I know I'm a mess," I confirmed but perked up when the words came out without daggers scraping my throat.

"What are you complaining about," he joked, "we're the ones who have to look at you."

"So why are you here?" I asked, genuinely curious.

"What type of man would I be if I deserted you now?"

"The normal kind." Which I preferred. Altruistic actions made me uncomfortable. They didn't align with people's true natures and always came with a catch.

"I'm going to assume that's the head injury talking," he said then grinned. "Besides, I still find you sexy, so what does that say about me?"

"That you watched too many horror movies as a kid?"

"Perhaps." He placed a replacement cell phone beside me. "For emergencies only or the doc will sic psycho-nurse on me."

I nodded though I had no intention of obeying. Not after being forcibly separated from my company. "I'm not sure I'm okay with the work situation you arranged."

"Are you questioning Brandon's skills?"

"I'm questioning your motives."

"In all his years with me, Brandon has asked for little, so if he requests a sabbatical to help a friend, I'm not standing in his way."

I'd take it up with Brandon later. What little energy I possessed was fading and any protesting only chewed it up faster. I settled back against the pillows.

I woke to find myself alone and reached for the cell phone. A text message from Chase popped up.

I know what you're doing. Make it quick.

Sue answered on the second ring. "Hi, boss. Feeling better?"

"Much. How's my company faring with Brandon at the helm?"

"He's incredible." Her tone turned wistful. "Tall, sweet, funny, gorgeous—"

"And likes long walks on the beach," I finished. "Please make sure you're spending more time working and less time canoodling."

"No worries there," she grumbled. "He treats me like a kid sister."

"Did you postpone the pet store deadline?"

"No. Jerry said if you can't meet the schedule, he'll hire someone else."

I groaned.

"Brandon took the meeting."

I groaned louder.

"Have a little faith. He's good."

"Details."

"No can do. I'm under orders to not indulge your workaholic tendencies."

"Orders from whom?" I asked though I already suspected. "You know you work for *me*, right? Or am I looking at a coup?"

"Your company is safe," she assured me. "Both Brandon and Chase signed confidentiality, non-disclosure, and proprietary agreements. Considering how heavy those documents are, I assume we're covered."

"Yup," I said with pride. "They're five pages longer than the CIA's."

"Should I ask how you know that?"

"Not unless you want to be an accessory," I answered. "Can I speak to Brandon?"

"Nope. Everything's covered. Gotta go." She hung up.

Useless. On to Plan B. Brandon immediately answered my IM.

Brandon: *Hi, J. Checking up on me?*

I typed back. *I have trust issues.*

Brandon: *With good reason, I was waiting until your recovery to tell you we lost some clients.*

Me: *WTF?!?!*

Brandon: *Just kidding. Sorry. I'll shut up before your concussed self comes down here and kicks my ass.*

Me: *Bring me up to speed and I'll forgive you.*

As Brandon elaborated, my blood pressure normalized. Though I itched to get involved in my projects, in my current state, a monkey could run my company better. Luckily, Brandon's skills exceeded a primate's. Good thing I received that royalty check. No way he came cheap.

Me: *How much did I agree to pay you while I was unconscious? Sue will write you a check.*

Brandon: *Wipe out the hundred lunches I owe you. The rest is taken care of.*

Me: *How?*

Brandon: *Chase is still covering my salary.*

Me: *I can't have him do that.*

Brandon: *Why not? This was his idea.*

"Woo-hoo! Freed from captivity." I danced into my closet to search for a specific outfit.

"You're returning to work, not being released into the wild," Nicki responded. "Are you sure you're ready?"

"I was ready two weeks ago." I escaped into the bathroom before she convinced me otherwise. Another day of internment—with her as my jailkeeper—and I risked going native on her ass. Not that Chase was any better. When he wasn't yelling at me to be careful, cursing about his never-ending acquisition, or off doing whatever I had no right to ask about, he'd been at my apartment *not* having sex with me. Anything physical and he shut me down faster than an overheating processor.

"Don't overdo it," Nicki nagged through the door. "You leave for San Diego soon. You need to be rested and alert."

"I prefer alone and medicated." After numerous attempts to discourage Chase from going—including subliminal messages while he slept—I had decided on drastic measures which meant leaving him behind and dealing with the consequences upon my return.

"Maybe it's not a terrible idea to take him."

I exited the bathroom and shot her the incredulous look she deserved. "Since when?"

"Since a junkie almost killed my best friend."

"Why is everyone overreacting?" I dabbed some makeup over the mild discoloration that remained on my jaw. A few more days and it, along with the fading bruises around my neck, would be gone. Nothing a scarf couldn't conceal in the meantime. As I loosely tied it around my neck, I cringed at the familiarity of my actions. I may have upgraded my armor from childish long-sleeved turtlenecks to expensive silk accessories, but the message remained the same. Still a victim. Still hiding.

"I can take care of myself," I announced and brushed past her towards what I hoped would be a return to normalcy.

I realized that was not going to happen when Richard intercepted me on the sidewalk. "Good morning."

"What are you doing here?"

"Escorting you to work." He opened the car door.

"Thank you, but after my incarceration, I need air. Even the polluted kind."

"I have my orders and I couldn't agree with them more."

"Fine," I griped, reluctant to blemish my first day with a pointless argument.

Sue and Brandon proved no better with their excessive doting. Only when Brandon finished his debrief did I forgive him. Not only had he saved my ass, but no one could have done it better... except me.

"You've done great work," I said.

"Don't sound shocked," he replied, feigning affront. "We may not all be geniuses, but some of us can still hold our own."

"Are you sure you want to go back to working for a tyrant?" I asked as he gathered his belongings. "I could use a man of your talents and I'm much nicer."

"Amen to that but the big man needs me. Who else will tell him when he's acting like an idiot?"

"You must be very busy."

"It's like having a second job," he laughed and gingerly wrapped me in a hug as if I were made of expensive crystal.

I reached up to kiss him on the cheek. "I owe you." And I intended on squaring up as soon as possible. Everything came with a price, and I liked to keep my side of the ledger clean.

"Consider us even. Chase is less annoying with you around." He waved to Sue. "See you around, kid."

Sue's gaze lingered on the door long after Brandon had disappeared. Poor girl had it bad. So bad, she didn't hear the phone ring. I went into my office and answered.

"You okay?" Chase asked.

"I will be once everyone stops asking."

"I'm coming over tonight to check on you."

"If it's for a check-up, we'd better be playing doctor."

His denial earned him a dial tone, which did not deter him from calling throughout the day. After the third time, I instructed Sue to inform him I remained amongst the living then hang up. Reestablishing my software throne demanded concentration.

When I exited the building that evening, exhilaration pumped through my veins. Ready to resume life with a vengeance, I embraced the night air and... walked straight into Richard. "Chase is meeting me at the apartment."

"And I'm escorting you there." He opened the car door and waited.

"I'm fine." I held my hands up. "See? Not even a paper cut."

"Excellent. Now get in the car."

With an overdramatic sigh, I complied. Maybe an amenable attitude would raise my odds at seducing Chase.

I was chatting with Richard when my phone buzzed. I snatched it up without looking. "I'm still in one piece," I snapped. So much for amenable.

"Um, Jasmine?" Wayne hesitated. "How are you feeling?"

"Fantastic." *And ready to tear the head off the unlucky bastard who asks next.*

"Did you get my flowers?" he asked.

"I did and thank you," I said, recalling the bouquet of white daisies. A sweet gesture that screamed missionary position next to Chase's enormous bouquet of lilies.

"If you're up for it, I have something I'd like to discuss with you. It's regarding a time sensitive business opportunity."

I agreed to dinner the following day then hung up when my building came into view.

As promised, Chase arrived soon after with the bonus of take-out. Although the food smelled delicious, I planned on it getting cold.

"How are you?" He clinically assessed my person for signs of damage.

"No nausea, headaches, pestilence, floods, or famine."

"I'm relieved to hear we averted the apocalypse."

I hesitated to remove my scarf, annoyed at my embedded instinct to hide my wounds. Chase had witnessed worse—like my recent resemblance to something out of a Stephen King novel — yet the bruises still represented my vulnerability, a fear I had cultivated for too long to just toss away.

Luckily, I could still move forward with my plan.

I approached him for a kiss. As expected, he reciprocated with a peck. Nope. That would not do. Which is why I had chosen a specific button-down dress for this occasion. I unfastened the top two buttons.

"What are you doing?" he asked warily.

"It's warm in here." Another button followed.

"Princess," he cautioned.

Another one and my dress fluttered open, teasing him with a glimpse of what lay beneath.

He crossed his arms, jaw set. "In case you failed to notice, abstaining has not been easy for me either."

"Then I'm about to make it harder."

And from the looks of it, that's not the only thing getting harder.

His eyes followed my determined fingers. "You're not going to stop, are you?"

The dress slipped off my shoulders, revealing his favorite sheer bra and panty set. I stifled a smile as his eyes darkened to liquid emerald pools. Bolstered by his reaction, I unknotted the scarf and let it fall. He didn't notice.

"Your move," I challenged.

He closed the space between us. "I do all the work, understood?"

Poor guy never stood a chance.

19

Unsurprised to find Richard outside my apartment the next morning, I flashed him a grin before cooperating. My actions garnered a suspicious look, but he wisely accepted his good fortune without comment.

How could I not be ecstatic? Not only had Chase been amazing last night, but the sex had landed us back into superficial relationship territory. Smack in the middle of my comfort zone. Right where we belonged.

I had just reached my desk when Jerry from Pettery Barn called. By the time I hung up, he'd saddled me with a crazed list of demands and a splitting headache —one that I would never mention lest everyone freak out imagining post-concussion symptoms. Already fortified on par with Fort Knox, Jerry's demand for additional security irked me, but as long as he continued to pay my invoices, I would lock my opinions up tighter than his system. I swallowed two ibuprofen capsules before tackling his exhaustive requests.

At the end of the day, I departed the office for my next destination, a dinner date I now regretted making. I stepped onto the street and stopped.

Crap! I forgot about Richard. Using Chase's driver to meet another man? Could that be any tackier? Especially if that man was Wayne.

"I'm not going with you tonight," I said.

He groaned. "I knew this morning was too good to be true. Why not?"

"I have dinner plans."

"Then I'll take you."

"I'm meeting someone," I explained.

"Good. Dining alone is bad for digestion."

I looked him square in the eye. "I'm having dinner with somebody... *else.*"

His face clouded with disapproval. Give me a break. Surely, he'd been working for Chase long enough to understand his boss' proclivity for open relationships. "That changes nothing," he said stiffly.

"I think Emily Post would disagree. Goodnight." I walked down the street and hailed a cab.

The restaurant was called N.Y.O.L—pronounced 'Nile'—which stood for *Name Your Own Lobster.* The sign hung above an enormous tank crowded with them. I cringed. If I named a living creature, I'd adopt it, take it home, and allow it to live its remaining days in comfort. Not smother it in butter sauce and plate it.

Where did he come up with these places?

Wayne rose from the table and attempted an awkward embrace as if he seemed unsure what to do with me. Unlike Chase who had zero trouble deciphering my body's needs. And there I was... thinking of Chase when I should have been paying attention to the man in front of me. Long live old habits.

I took pity and sat down. Relieved, Wayne did the same.

"I'm sorry for your ordeal." His brown eyes brimmed with sympathy. "I hope you were well cared for, though I can't fathom someone as selfish as Hale pulling off the Florence Nightingale role."

My befuddled expression answered for me.

"I saw him at the hospital," Wayne explained. "He told me to go away."

I shook my head. Idiot boys.

"I came by to deliver this." Wayne pulled a box from his pocket and opened it to reveal a bracelet of deep green stones.

The same color as Chase's eyes when he was aroused.

Could I be any more improper?

"I meant to give this to you while you were working for Hale, but let's call it a get well present now." He removed the bracelet and fastened it around my wrist. "The Chinese man I purchased it from said anything created from jade is imbued with powers to ward against evil."

Perfect for throwing at Helena when she walked down the aisle.

"You shouldn't have," I said and meant it. All this niceness was starting to weird me out.

"You deserve it. And you deserve someone better than Hale. Wear it as a reminder of that."

Fearing a spiral into Chase-bashing territory, I spoke quickly. "You mentioned a proposal?"

"Yes. Teresa is working on an encryption system to secure our financial data."

"I know." *I bid on the project. Duh.*

"A recent development has given rise to the need for additional resources."

Like discovering she's an idiot?

"Is she not making enough progress?" I asked sweetly.

"Not at all." He leaped to her defense too quickly for my liking. "She's wonderful. I can't imagine any of this is her fault."

Then my imagination is better than yours.

"I've altered our marketing strategy," he continued. "I want to hype security as a cornerstone of our software."

"Sounds promising."

"It is," he concurred with his own idea. "I have investors lined up contingent on the demo of a beta version. Erik Lyndham is announcing his retirement soon and with the influx of cash, I'll be the logical choice to take over."

"And I'm here because...?"

"Brandon mentioned your work on Wolfe." He must have noticed my expression because he hastily added, "He also mentioned your aversion to attention. Something I will respect should you accept my offer. With your skills, we'll deliver a superior product, lock the investors in, and I'll take over Lyndham. Then, with you by my side..."

We'll rule the galaxy... <Insert maniacal cackle here>

"...we'll mold the company however we see fit. I'm offering an executive position with full creative control. Hale made an enormous mistake when he let you slip away."

Finally. Someone who didn't have a copy of those infamous rules.

"What about Teresa?" I asked.

"You'll enjoy working with her. She's delightful."

The absurdity of that statement made me want to laugh in his face.

So I did.

His brow puckered. "Something amusing?"

"Your idea," I said flatly. "I'll work with that woman the day parkas become standard issue in hell."

"But think about—"

“What the hell are you doing?” Chase’s voice startled me. I spun my head in a move I’m lucky didn’t land me back in the hospital with whiplash.

Chase marched to our table, anger rolling off him in waves. “What is so goddamn difficult about getting into a goddamn car and being driven to a goddamn destination?”

Wayne nervously glanced around. “Listen here, Hale—”

“Shut your fucking mouth, Parker,” Chase snarled. To my surprise, Wayne complied, opting to shoot visual daggers instead.

“Pussy,” Chase muttered.

Wayne stiffened but remained silent.

Not me. I stood and gestured to the door. “Outside. Now.” Chase may not care about making a scene but for the hell I planned to unleash, I needed fewer witnesses and room enough to shove my foot up his ass… assuming his head would move over.

We exited to a busy street, bustling with pedestrians and traffic. Audience or not, I whirled on him. “What the hell is wrong with you?”

His lip curled in disgust. “Of all the men in this city. Un-fucking-believable.”

“Is this about Wayne?”

“It’s about you. Do you know how careless you’re being?”

“No, but if you hum a few bars, maybe I’ll catch on.”

“This isn’t funny,” he said.

“Do you see me laughing?” I shifted to allow a young couple to pass. They cast us curious glances then sped up. “Because unless you lo-jacked me, which would be equally disturbing, Richard followed me.”

“Of course,” he replied as if stalking was perfectly acceptable behavior. “You’d think an ex-Navy Seal could manage one civilian female.”

"Enough with the overprotective alpha-male bullshit," I ordered.

"I'm looking out for you," he said through gritted teeth. "It's called being nice."

I snorted. "I don't know which pack of wolves raised you but in common society, storming into restaurants and abducting women is not nice. It's psychopathic."

A group of teenagers ambled by and one broke away to undress me with glossy eyes. I wrinkled my nose. Any closer and I'd have a contact high.

Chase shoved the kid towards his fellow hooligans. "Keep walking," he growled, confirming my wolf theory.

"See? That's what I mean." I pointed to the departing figure. "I don't need a bodyguard."

"And I'm not offering," he replied. "Not if you let Richard do his job."

"Job?" I repeated. "What am I? A babysitting to-do item on your list? Somewhere between 'seduce my latest bimbo' and 'make another cool million'?"

"For fuck's sake, Princess. Why can't you do what you're told?"

"Because last time I checked, I didn't have your brand seared on my ass," I snapped. That attracted some odd looks from nearby pedestrians. "And I've been saving said unbranded ass my entire life."

His eyes filled with challenge. "If you're so capable, why haven't you gone to the police station to review mugshots?"

Because I don't do law enforcement. Call it a family trait.

"And if you're so responsible," he continued in a lecturing tone that made me want to slug him, "why was the hospital unable to find a next of kin? With no directive, they had no instructions for your care. Max was searching for your bitch of a cousin when you woke up."

My head jerked. "What?"

"My investigator," he explained. "Helena's your only relative that Nicki knew of. Max didn't have much to go on. Just her first name and city."

Coldness gripped my insides. "And what did he find?"

"Helena Brooks, lives in San Diego. Then you woke. I spoke to Derek and he'll draft..."

His words faded to white noise as my meticulously fabricated life flashed before my eyes.

Fuck! Fuck! Fuck!

Time to bolt! Now!

But I stopped myself.

No! That's the old you talking. You are now Jasmine-fucking-Monroe and you did not create her so some egomaniac with an overdeveloped savior complex could fuck with her.

"ENOUGH!" I shouted. The street appeared to freeze then chaos reigned as people scrambled to get away from the screaming crazy woman.

Not Chase. He stepped in closer. "Most women would be flattered I'm making the effort."

Most women don't have life-threatening secrets they're protecting.

"Because the women you consort with are simpering sycophants who indulge your bullshit knight-in-shining-armor fantasy. I can't imagine how fragile your billion-dollar ego must be if this is how you feed it." A sneer formed on my lips. "And before you hurl another rock, you might want to move out of your glass penthouse, because I don't see you inviting others to rummage through *your* life."

Like your fucking marriage.

"And people say *I'm* self-destructive," he muttered. "What part of you feels compelled to reject anything good for you?"

I let out a caustic laugh. "That you consider yourself good for any woman is delusional. Go back to your bimbos and stay the fuck away from me." I opened the restaurant door and stepped inside, relieved when he made no move to follow. I slumped into a chair beside the enormous tank and blankly watched its inhabitants skittering by.

A lobster drifted over that appeared particularly interested in my predicament. "I don't understand," I addressed it. "For a man who enacts privacy rules, why is he so quick to invade mine?"

My companion remained silent, but his glare turned disapproving.

"Don't look at me like that," I defended. "*He's* the one who violated the foundation of our agreement."

Not even a flinch.

"Oh, shut up."

Stupid condescending crustacean.

20

"I don't like you going alone." Nicki was sprawled on my bed, cringing while she watched me jam clothes into a suitcase. "Can't you call Chase? Play nice for one weekend?"

The week had passed with no contact from Chase, zero Richard sightings, and no attacks on my person. For some, finding a twenty-dollar bill meant good luck. For me, not ending up as a back alley punching bag was just as good. We all have our standards.

"Nope. Our program ran its course."

"Life is not software. No matter how much your processor brain wishes it so."

"Close enough." With my code, I controlled the ending with precision. No sloppy infinite loops that ran on in perpetuity, nor did any of my variables become obnoxious and start disrespecting other lines of code by trampling over their boundaries.

"Maybe something good can come of it," Nicki mused. "Weddings are an excellent place to meet men. That's a silver lining."

I threw a tank top at her head. "Only if you're color blind."

Nicki folded the tank into a perfect square and layered it in the case.

"I'm done with men." I wadded up a pair of jeans and mashed them into the fray. "Fucking rules. What about the fine print stating everything is subject to change whenever he damn well feels like it? What type of man does that?"

Nicki reached over to rescue the jeans. "The overprotective type with control issues, extensive resources... and a private jet." She pleated the fabric into flawless creases before repacking it.

"I'd rather backstroke to San Diego than travel with that megalomaniac." I balled up a T-shirt in my fists. "Anyway, it doesn't matter. I'm over it."

"Clearly," she said and elbowed me aside, assuming control of the disarray. "I think you should let him come... with his private jet."

"Since when did you become a card-carrying member of the Chase fan club?"

"Since they threw in a set of steak knives." She held up a bikini and to my amazement, nimbly transmuted it into an equilateral triangle worthy of an origami expert. "He's growing on me. Besides, any man that comes with a—"

"If you say 'private jet' one more time, I will post your recipes online." I scanned the room. "Where's the eggplant?"

"In a garment bag by the door."

"Is it still intact? You didn't maybe, accidentally on purpose, fling it in an incinerator?"

"Not even fire can vanquish that depth of ugly." She zipped up my efficiently organized case and placed it on the floor. A shame I would return with it in shambles. Let's hope my life didn't mimic that fate.

"Do you have everything?" she questioned as we walked down the hallway. "Garlic necklace? Silver cross? Holy water?"

I thought about the jade bracelet on my dresser. While I didn't subscribe to superstition, I couldn't think of a better time to test its evil-warding properties. "I'll be back." I dashed to my room to fasten it around my wrist before joining Nicki at the front door.

I stopped short.

"You ready, Princess?" Chase asked.

Nicki grinned and straightened her arms, tilting from side to side in a flying motion.

Without waiting for a reply, Chase seized my luggage. "I'll meet you downstairs."

"What the... how can... why is?" I sputtered at his retreating figure.

"Calm down and use your words," Nicki prodded.

"Did he just kidnap my bags?"

"Yup and I advise you go after him if you want to see that dress again."

I never wanted to see that monstrosity again but with no choice, I shuffled over the threshold in time to see my suitcase rounding the corner.

"Drink heavily and don't kill anyone," Nicki called after me. "That includes on the flight."

Richard was stowing my bags when I arrived. I sidled over to him. "Sorry about ditching you," I whispered.

He grinned. "That's okay. You're spry for a civilian."

"Now that we're buddies again, can I have my luggage back?"

He answered by closing the trunk.

Dammit!

After a car ride full of withering looks—all my doing—we pulled up alongside a plane with the Predator logo emblazoned on its side. The instant I boarded, I offered Nicki a silent apology. Something about a luxurious cabin eased my irrational fear of heights, adopted when Helena lured me onto the roof of our house and attempted to push me to my death. Or at least to a couple of broken bones.

As we took off, I conjured soothing memories of my soon-to-be-seen beloved Pacific Ocean. Anything to trick my brain into forgetting Chase's attendance at the imminent torture-fest waiting for me. At least, I had no worries of Helena outing me. Not at the wedding. With her overdeveloped ego, she would never share the spotlight. A minor consolation.

Chase spoke first. "I don't understand what made you blow a gasket the other day, but I have a proposition for you regarding Richard."

I turned to face him. "I am not betting you for it."

He smiled. "Richard drives you in confidence. You retain autonomy yet I'm assured of your safety. See? I can compromise."

"And why this crazy obsession with my safety?"

His voice grew quiet. "I left you alone that night because I got pissed off. If I had stayed, it wouldn't have happened."

I released an exasperated breath. "I am not your responsibility, nor do I need you to pity me because you feel guilty about something that is not your fault. I am a grown woman and I make my own decisions."

The plane bounced and I gripped the armrest.

"Relax," Chase said. "It's only air."

"Where I come from, air is not bumpy."

He pried my fingers free and placed my hand in his. "Do we have a deal?"

"Richard is going to follow me anyway, isn't he?"

"Yes," he said, absentmindedly playing with my jade bracelet.

I sighed. "Fine, but I need you and Max to butt out of my life. I'm a grown woman—"

"—who makes her own decisions," he finished. "Got it." He

looked down at my wrist. "You don't wear bracelets. Where did this come from?"

"A gift."

"From?"

"Wayne brought it back from China," I said, daring him to make an issue of it.

He gave a disgusted snort. "What type of moron tries to seduce a woman with jade?"

"A thoughtful one," I countered and his lips quirked. "*Person*," I corrected. "Not moron."

I waited for a sarcastic follow-up but instead, he planted a kiss on the inside of my wrist. "It looks pretty on you."

Maybe he would behave after all.

We exited the jet to unblemished skies and sunshine that somehow blazed brighter on this side of the country. I raised my face and inhaled deeply. The pungent salty air made my skin itch to take a dip in the ocean, especially when the hotel turned out to be across the street.

Corinthian style pillars lined the entrance, an ornate preview of the extravagance to be found within. A few steps into the lobby and my mouth dropped at the twin spiraling staircases reminiscent of something from Gone with the Wind. My eyes followed them upwards to a dome lined with imitation Roman frescoes. Or from the crazy affluence around here, maybe they were real.

Damn, Phil's family must be loaded.

I mentally thanked Helena for negotiating reasonable rates on the exorbitant room prices, although she probably finagled mine so I'd end up in a closet under the stairs like Harry Potter. In a place like this, it still might be nicer than my apartment.

"Come on," Chase's voice shook me out of my trance. From the keys he held, he must have checked us in while I was gawking like a tourist.

When we entered our room, my jaw dropped again. Our suite consisted of a lavish living area, a nook with a rolling desk, and the best part, French doors that opened to a wide patio overlooking the beach.

I wandered into the bedroom and my mouth fell open again, making me question why I bothered to keep closing it. Unable to control myself, I flopped onto the king-size canopy bed and sighed when my body sank into the feathered comforter. Even the fabric softener smelled wonderful.

"That's not the best part." Chase pushed open the bathroom door with a flourish. "Ta-Da!"

I craned my neck to see if he had miraculously conjured a bunny, but he was referring to the jacuzzi, modestly masquerading as a bathtub.

"Temperature controlled, pressure sensitive jets." He waggled his eyebrows. "With room for two."

"More like room for an orgy," I said. "This is your doing. Isn't it?"

"Given your propensity to spontaneously combust every time I mentioned this wedding, I wanted you as comfortable as possible."

"You did enough with the plane. You didn't have to—"

"At the risk of sounding repetitive, shut up and let me do something nice for you." He walked over to the bed and scowled at me.

"Thank you," I mumbled.

He stretched out beside me. "A decent effort but I'm not much for words. I prefer more physical demonstrations of gratitude."

"Such as?"

"You can start by undressing until you're wearing nothing but a smile."

In truth, I had acquiesced to Chase's compromise only because an encounter with Helena was akin to fighting a war, and no decent strategist would willingly battle on two fronts. But one glance at the seductive curve of his lips and melting green eyes and I eagerly stripped until nothing remained but the bracelet. When I reached for the clasp, he stopped me.

"Keep that on."

"Why? You know it came from Wayne."

"Yes," he said. "And after today, you're not going to look at it again without remembering what I'm about to do to you."

"There is something seriously wrong with you."

"And you love it. Now get on top of me."

I straddled his waist, but he shook his head and prodded me forward until my thighs were balanced on either side of his wicked smile. "Now grab that headboard, baby, and ride me until you can't see straight."

Holy hell!

Confused by the lack of signage, I circled the courtyard seeking assistance, or anyone wearing epaulets. Unsure about my first meeting with Helena, I'd insisted Chase remain in the room and work. No need for his presence at the rehearsal. He'd have plenty exposure at the fancy dinner and cocktail party tonight.

A cute blonde, wearing a creased maid's uniform, stumbled out of a nearby closet. I almost approached her but reconsidered when I noticed her jumpy demeanor. She tugged at her dress, smoothed her hair, and walked in the opposite direction. Moments later, a tall man with lazy brown eyes and a self-satisfied, lipstick-covered smirk emerged from the same door. His shaggy brown hair jutted outwards as if recently gripped by frantic fingers. He ducked into a nearby bathroom.

This really is a full-service hotel.

I wandered the grounds until finally coming upon a sign with the names *Helena Genevieve Brooks and Phillip Douglas Toliver* written in tiny letters.

Brooks.

My former last name. A name I never wanted to be associated with for the remainder of my life. Just seeing it in print made me queasy.

I followed the directions and emerged in a display of such ostentatious taste, my body viscerally recoiled as if smacked with a baseball bat.

Did the Lucky Charms leprechaun throw up in here?

After he dropped acid?

The horror started with rows of purple chairs, an enormous orange flower wrapped around each. They parted to allow for a shimmery gold strip of fabric down the center, flanked on either side by fuchsia, tangerine, and lime-colored flowers. It all led to a heart-shaped arch beneath suspended angel wings, accessorized with pink, orange, and green bows. I spun around and cringed. The blast radius of bad taste even extended to the surrounding foliage, degrading it with paper lanterns and strands of pink lights.

If Sue were here, I'd lose her.

Sadly, the spectacle overshadowed a breathtaking ocean backdrop, but it could have been worse. At least the tree trunks weren't pink. I glanced around, confirming no unopened buckets of paint.

A rotund woman with rosy cheeks and a business-like persona bustled over. Her bright yellow and pink floral muumuu draped over a sizeable frame and her chubby fingers gripped a jeweled clipboard. Fluorescent pineapple earrings bobbed around her friendly face. "You must be Helena's cousin, Jasmine," she said with a smile almost as bright as the rest of her. "I'm Rita, Phil's mom."

And the décor suddenly made sense.

She beckoned for me to follow while scribbling something. Multiple rings glinted in the sunlight with every word she wrote. Enormous and sparkling, much like Rita herself. "Jasmine, this is Phil, your soon to be cousin-in-law."

I froze.

"Hello, Jasmine." Phil's lazy brown eyes raked over me. His brown hair lay flat now, damp from the water he'd recently combed through it, and his clothing was reassembled, but the self-satisfied smirk—minus the lipstick—remained. It widened into a lecherous grin. "You're almost as beautiful as your cousin."

Gag!

"I see you've met my fiancé." My heart jumped at Helena's voice. She approached with a petite, curvy brunette in tow. Gabriella. Helena's childhood partner-in-sleaze. "Good to see you, cousin." Helena planted a perfunctory kiss on my cheek.

Bogus displays of affection? Wow! She must really need to sell this relationship.

"I'm thrilled you're here," Rita gushed at me. "Family is the measure by which one is judged. And when Helena said she had no close relatives, I wasn't sure what to do." Her voice took on a sympathetic tinge. "Especially after everything she went through with the tragic circumstances surrounding her father."

The only tragedy is being related to him.

"Which is why I insisted on meeting you. Tell me everything." Rita's pen hovered above her clipboard as if conducting an interview. "Has Helena always been so giving and generous?"

What the fuck?

"Um, sure," I stammered, wishing I had an advanced copy of the playbook we were following. "She's always been one to share." *Do sexually transmitted diseases count?*

"Excellent." Rita scribbled something down. "The only way to know a person's true self is to meet those who've grown up with them."

I was beginning to understand why Helena needed me. Wacky Rita considered family as some sort of vital background check.

"What about me?" the brunette piped up. "I know Helena better than *she* does." She pointed a finger at me which Helena lowered.

While Helena had traded her slut apparel for a modest sundress she probably hated, Gabriella's skin-hugging jeans and tight blouse stayed true to her teenage tastes. Even Gabby's brown hair remained frozen in time, teased high in a do worthy of a Texan who owned stock in a hairspray company.

"Family is best," Rita said, dismissing Gabby. "I'd rather hear it from Jasmine."

"Jasmine?" Gabby scowled, cracking her heavily spackled face. "Who the hell is Jas—" Her words turned into an *ooof* as Helena's elbow connected with her ribs.

Gabby quickly recovered, no doubt accustomed to Helena's method of communication. She sized me up with narrow eyes and finally decided to address me. "Well, well. Looks like the ugly duckling grew up. Too bad she didn't turn into a flamingo."

It's a swan, you dumb-fuck.

"She's joking." Rita spoke to me, misunderstanding the dynamic. "You're stunning. Helena didn't tell me how beautiful you are. With your height and those eyes, you could be a model." Her face lit up. "Are you a model? That would be so exciting. Please tell me you are."

This sweet lady is the tyrannical purse-strangling bitch?

"Sorry," I said. "Software programmer."

Rita's smile grew even wider. "Beautiful *and* smart. Sweetie, you're the total package."

Helena's face darkened. I couldn't help but grin.

The rehearsal began and, much to Helena's annoyance, Rita took an instant liking to me. Too bad that didn't deter the matriarch from getting in my face every time I botched a step. From sweet mother figure to five-foot tall drill sergeant—complete with whistle—the transformation was frightening. The only thing missing was camouflage. I'm guessing it didn't come in a muumuu.

Halfway through the fourth iteration, my brain rolled over and took a nap. My job entailed wearing an ugly dress and walking in a straight line. The most challenging part? Not suffering a seizure from the decorations.

Finally, Rita released us—though I suspected it had more to do with adhering to the schedule than our performances—and I went upstairs.

I found Chase already dressed in a dark suit, on the phone, pacing. I waved and crossed to the bedroom, pausing to admire his tall, broad-shouldered frame. Damn, he was easily the most gorgeous human I'd ever laid eyes on. I sighed. This crazy lust-filled infatuation had to cease at some point. Relationships were not meant for longevity. Even superficial ones.

When I emerged from the bedroom, I found him still on the phone. "That part is non-negotiable. I've already made enough concessions regarding his personal—" He went motionless when he saw me. "We'll finish this later." He disconnected, his eyes never leaving me.

With my bruises healed, I confidently stood in sparkly silver sandals that matched my snug, strapless mini dress. All courtesy of Nicki. Thanks to her instructions, my blue eyes emitted a smoky vixen vibe, complemented by my long hair which flowed free in loose waves.

I shrugged. "If I'm doomed to be a giant, purple dinosaur tomorrow, Nicki thought I should make up for it tonight."

"Mission more than accomplished," he breathed. "Tell me we can be late."

I shook my head. "I am not getting on Rita's bad side."

"Then we're leaving dinner early." He extended his arm, and we rode down the elevator while I did my best to feign calmness. If all Helena required was an endorsement of her fictitious pious image, this should go off without a hitch.

So why did my dread increase with each passing floor?

Because nothing was ever that easy.

21

No surprise that the rehearsal dinner was being held in the most upscale of the hotel restaurants. We stopped at the sign that read *Reserved for Toliver/Brooks Wedding Event* so Chase could unhook a pretentious velvet rope. I took that moment to brace myself. Seeing Helena was always unbearable but twice in one day could only be described as a special type of hell.

As soon as we entered the bar area, a bright orange pumpkin descended on me. Rita, psychedelic in a tangerine floor-length dress, wrapped me in a plump hug.

It was official. I liked Rita.

"You look spectacular, honey," she raved. "Every single man here would give an eyetooth to meet you, but I'll only take you to the worthwhile ones. You're much too precious for just anyone."

"I agree." Chase moved forward and wrapped an arm around me. There was no mistaking the irritation on his face.

"Oh, dear." Rita's booming laugh rang in my ears. "This makes much more sense. Helena mentioned Jasmine was unattached, which is crazy given how wonderful she is. Silly me, offering to find her a man when she clearly already has one." She patted Chase's arm then squeezed his bicep. "And what a man you are." She shot me a thumbs-up.

Nothing subtle about Rita.

Chase's expression softened. No one could stay annoyed with Rita.

We followed her as she introduced us to the other guests. Unfortunately, her love of family was not exaggerated and for the next grueling hour, we met cousins, aunts, uncles, and countless others I purged from memory. I plastered a cordial smile on my face while enduring the wanton looks Chase received from the females in the room. I wasn't sure what bothered me more. That so many women wanted to screw him or that I cared.

We approached a man wearing a hideously loud yellow and green patterned shirt, the top four buttons undone to display gold chains layered over a thick mat of chest hair. From my vantage point of a few inches, a small animal had chosen his head as its hibernation spot.

If the Pillsbury Doughboy and Joe Pesci produced a love child, I was looking at him.

Rita introduced us. "Meet my nephew, George Junior. He's a dentist in Hollywood."

Helena's date for me? Ugh! What the hell was she thinking?

Oh yeah, she hates me.

I mentally thanked Chase for bulldozing his way here.

"Dentist to the stars," George Junior corrected, in an accent adopted from watching too many mafia movies. "You're Jasmine? Nice." Junior's spray-tanned face scrunched in concentration while he evaluated me as if purchasing a thoroughbred. Except no breeder would stare at a horse's chest like that. "When Helena said

I gotta be your date, she didn't say nothing about how fine you are." His toupee shifted with his nod of approval.

Chase moved but Rita interceded with shocking speed for a woman of her girth. In one motion, she steered us away. "I'll catch you later," George Junior called out.

"He's lucky he's a dentist," Chase growled. "If he eye-fucks you again, I'm going to knock out every one of his fucking teeth."

Rita led us over to the bride and groom. "Kids, you already know Jasmine. This is her date, Chase. I'll leave you all to catch up."

Helena and Gabriella's eyes went so wide, I imagined them bugging out to a honking sound. Not that I blamed them. Chase could have been en route to a GQ photoshoot instead of some lame rehearsal dinner. Phil went through the motion of shaking Chase's hand, but his lazy eyes roved up and down my body as if searing every inch to memory.

"So you're the one who took pity on my pathetic cousin and tagged along," Helena addressed Chase, the chill in her voice as icy as the reflective blue dress she wore. In contrast, Gabby's indecent black number flaunted her sexuality like a siren. The wetsuit material barely stretched over the important bits. Her hair was balanced precariously high on her head, the updo equivalent of a Jenga tower.

"No," Chase answered smoothly. "I'm the one with the privilege of escorting the most beautiful woman here."

Helena stiffened while the insult flew over Gabby's head, mountain of hair and all. Gabby was too busy sizing him up anyway. The hamster jogging on the wheel in her head must have been pumping overtime because her eyes glimmered with rare shrewdness.

"Chase Hale," she exclaimed. "Predator Industries. One of the top ten wealthiest men according to Forbes magazine."

She can't put M&M's in alphabetical order, yet she's got the who's who of rich men memorized?

A seductive smile formed on her collagen induced lips. "And even hotter in person." She angled closer and brushed her ample boobs against him.

"I need a drink," Chase muttered but before he could move, his phone buzzed.

"Fucking acquisition?" I guessed, which elicited a smile from him. When he made no move to answer, I nudged him. "Go take care of it."

"Okay, but don't get molested while I'm gone. That's my job."

As he walked away with Gabby's eyes glued to his retreating ass, Helena waved someone over.

"Hey, foxy." George Junior sidled up, beaming like a dullard. "You know lots of other chicks wanted to be George Junior's date, but I ain't with them 'cause Helena said to wait for you, so that's what I'm doing. I'm all yours, cupcake."

"Not interested."

"Helena said you got no idea of a good thing." He puffed out his chest, severely testing the resilience of his shirt. "But you'll learn when you hear people talk. George Junior's a big deal."

Either he wasn't listening or unable to hear anything over that shirt. "For the sake of your dental work, please go away. You don't want to be here when Chase returns."

"That hoity-toity guy you're with? Everyone knows he don't wanna be here." He turned to Helena. "Ain't that right? Poor schmuck owed her a favor." He took Helena's sly smile as confirmation and leaned in, his scent a putrid mix of Aqua Velva and garlic. "George Junior will do him a solid and take you off his hands."

Helena may have been willing to keep my secret for now, but that didn't preclude her from a little torture, and from the satisfied expression on her face, this was it. “Oh, look,” I pointed to a random spot in the room. “I see Rita beckoning.” I quickly walked away and headed for the bathroom. Hopefully, George Junior had enough wits about him not to follow.

I was starting on my second round of lotion samples when a heavy floral scent rolled in… followed by Gabby.

She noticed me at the counter. “I thought you were gone for good.” She never was one for tact.

“It wasn’t my idea to come here.”

“No. Gone like in dead. It was super creepy when I saw you in New York. All spooky and shit. Like a ghost.”

“*You* saw me?” I questioned.

She dug into her gigantic purse to unearth a tube of lipstick. “Didn’t Helena tell you?” She coated her full lips with an unneeded layer of red and puckered them like a blowfish, which, if you factored in all the men she serviced, wasn’t far-fetched. “Typical. Always taking credit for my stuff. Like this one time when I said we should fuck these twins and—”

“Save me the exposition,” I interrupted, “and answer the damn question.”

She blinked. “Why would you expose yourself?”

She and George Junior would be perfect together. Mr. and Mrs. Pet Rock. “Where did you see me?” I asked.

“On a shopping trip in New York. That’s when I got this dress in a tiny boutique off Fifth.”

Skanks Emporium?

She replaced the lipstick and withdrew a can of hairspray from her handbag. “I didn’t recognize you at first. Like you look totally different but still the same. I thought you were one of those dopey gang members. You know, people who look like you.”

“Doppelgangers?”

“Whatever. But then I saw that dumb flower pin of yours.

What's with you and stupid flowers anyway? Smart women want diamonds." Using her fingers, she teased her hair an inch higher before unleashing a torrent of toxic fumes. Maybe that contributed to her depleting brain cells.

"Then what?" I coughed out.

"Then men give me diamonds."

I groaned. "*After* you saw me. Then what happened?"

"Helena said to follow you. I don't know why. The day you went missing was the best day of her life. We celebrated by swiping a bottle of champagne and getting wasted."

I didn't know what to make of her explanation. Neither my plan nor my abilities had failed me. It was sheer dumb bad luck—and in Gabby's case, extremely dumb. That and the lily pin. In hindsight, that memento had given me nothing but problems.

"Perfect timing too." Gabby uncapped an eyeliner pencil. "I thought Helena was nuts for inviting you but now that you brought that fine hunk of man-meat, I forgive her. He's got everything I want in a man."

"A pulse?"

Her eyes widened. "Have you ever screwed one who didn't have a pulse?"

This conversation was becoming too stupid for an audience.

She traced over the already thick lines surrounding her eyes. "My last guy turned out to be a lying weasel with not a penny to his name. Invented paper clips, my ass. But Chase... he's hotter than hell and oozing cash. I don't know how you suckered him into coming but he's mine now. No one can stand being around you anyway."

I had no delusions of Chase sticking around, but my stomach churned at the thought of those two cozying up together.

"Finally, a rich man I want to fuck," Gabby said excitedly. She dipped a hand in her neckline and propped the milky white tops of her enhanced breasts to front and center. Next, she shimmied her dress up until it barely covered her ass.

I was looking at more breasts and thighs than my last bucket at KFC.

"You think he'll like this?" She jutted her hip and raised a shoulder. "Or how about this?" She jiggled her cleavage.

Without a word, I made a beeline for the exit. And walked straight into Chase.

"There you are," he said. "I was worried Junior abducted you."

My response was drowned out by Rita's drill-sergeant voice. "Everybody to the dining room now. Get your meat in your seat." The crowd obeyed as a unified whole, and I swore when I saw George Junior's name on the card to my left. Chase plucked my card off the table and exchanged it with his, which vaguely read *Guest*. An arriving George Junior began to protest, but Chase's murderous glare silenced any further whining.

Unfortunately, that didn't stop Junior from talking. From our spinach and goat cheese salads through the prime rib and whipped potatoes, he flapped his jowls, yapping about his Hollywood dentist clients and name dropping at every opportunity.

Like he really knows Brad Pitt's flossing routine?

A birdlike woman who I remembered as Phil's something-removed cousin blessedly interrupted. "Did you plan the wedding?" she asked Rita. "This location is lovely."

Rita beamed with pride. "Yes. I almost went with the cathedral on Sixth—"

But realized Helena would burst into flames if she stepped into a church?

"—since Phil and Helena met at that church."

I emitted a strangled choke that earned a glower from Helena.

"A shame the exorcism didn't work," Chase muttered.

Servers cleared our plates and replaced them with champagne

filled flutes, signifying speech time. Gabby spoke first, lying through her plumped-up lips as she portrayed Helena to be a sweet, loving, saint of a woman whose motivation to help others originated from her own tragedies. I tensed when she fabricated the despair Helena felt at the disappearance of her little sister but no one noticed.

Chase leaned over. "How are any of these idiots buying this?"

And they were. The entire clan sat listening with rapt attention, admiration shining in their eyes. I didn't care. The sooner the charade played out, the sooner I'd be flying home.

Until Rita called on me. "Jasmine, as Helena's cousin, will you say a few words please?"

Shit!

Helena's piercing gaze lasered into me. The message was clear. *Make it good or you're dead.*

I pushed to my feet and cleared my throat longer than necessary. "I can't express what it means to be invited to my cousin's wedding. Helena is one of the most interesting, creative, and resilient people I have ever known. Through sheer determination and will, she can make anything happen. Phil is a lucky man to have someone like her." I raised my glass.

Huh! For a master at lying, every word was true. Maybe not that last part. Phil was cursed to live with a banshee.

Next, a wiry man with a mop of white hair stood up. "As Phil's uncle, I also have the honor of being his godfather." He paused to check out a server's ass as she bent over to pick up a napkin.

Next was Phil's best man and cousin and an even bigger douche. He was working on his sixth bimbo wife and, from his slurred speech, twentieth drink.

The list went on... a cousin with an amphetamine habit, another on parole, a grandma with a gambling problem, and my personal favorite—the uncle mandated to court appointed sex addiction meetings.

I watched with amusement as the cavalcade of vices poured out faster than the champagne. Girls, liquor, drugs. The table was a treasure trove for a twelve-step program.

No wonder they welcomed Helena. They were just as cursed as we were. Except for Rita who seemed blinded by loyalty.

This holier-than-thou act was for a one-woman audience.

Confirmation came when Rita assumed center stage. "My dear family," she began, "after years of enduring your spirited antics, each of you holds a dear place in my heart. I love you all."

"Not enough to release our trusts," a young man quipped, eliciting chuckles from the table.

"True," Rita responded. "The conditions still stand. Before receiving your share, you must demonstrate the ability to lead a responsible and upstanding life. Like my dear son, Phil."

A round of applause followed.

"And part of being responsible is settling down." Rita spared a glance for the six-time married douche. "Now that Helena Brooks, someone equally as lovely as Phil, has captured his heart—"

"I'd be more worried about his balls," Chase mumbled.

"—she and Phil will ensure the Toliver legacy continues."

And receive Phil's trust. Bingo! I finally understood the end game.

Chase slipped his hand under the long tablecloth and placed it on my knee while Phil's uncle assumed the spotlight to sing Phil's praises—or confess his sins. Same difference. Phil bailed him out after an arrest for flashing. Classy.

"Your legs look so damn sexy in that outfit," Chase whispered while his hand traveled up my thigh. He toyed with the edge of my dress, his gaze locked on the speaker. "I haven't been able to keep my eyes off you all night." His fingers sneaked beneath the hem then continued to inch higher.

I jerked. "That's not your eyes."

He grazed over my thong while a chuckle vibrated low in his chest.

"Chase," I breathed, "Stop."

"No," he said simply. "I'm finally having fun."

The speaker's voice faded as Chase began to caress the flimsy silk between my thighs. My eyes widened when he slipped a finger underneath the elastic and ran it along my lips. A soft moan escaped me.

"Shhh," he whispered. "You'll give sweet Rita a heart attack." He grazed over my clit and a hot flicker shot through me.

"We can't... ohmygod." My legs separated of their own volition.

This was so wrong.

And I was loving every second of it.

His finger began torturing me with easy, practiced circles, and I fought the noises bubbling in the back of my throat. There was nothing I could do about my hips though. They took on a life of their own as they undulated against his hand, urging him to speed up and take me somewhere I should not go.

"That's it, baby," he whispered. "Use my hand to get off."

His words made it worse—or better—I couldn't tell.

"Jasmine, are you okay?"

Fuck!

Rita's voice hit me like a slap and Chase's hand stilled. "You look flushed." Her round face was creased with concern.

"I... um," I stammered.

Chase started stroking me again.

Bastard.

"I'm... I'm just warm." I sounded like an overworked porn star.

"It is stuffy in here," she agreed. "Drink more ice water, dear. It'll make you feel better."

A fucking fire extinguisher wouldn't help.

I nodded and everyone returned their attention to cousin-who-cares.

Chase strummed my clit faster and I white-knuckled the edge of my chair. The conversations around me garbled beneath the pounding in my ears, and I bit my lip to stifle my sounds. I was going to come. Right here. Right now.

And then his hand abruptly disappeared. "No," I yelped but it was drowned out by scraping chairs.

"Go. Now." Chase pulled me to my feet.

Denied, disoriented, and driven by an unbearable desire in my pussy, I blindly followed him through hallways until he chose an empty conference room. I caught a glimpse of the dark lust in his eyes before the door closed behind us and we were shrouded in shadows. Hands whipped me around and folded me over the nearest table.

I almost sobbed with relief when his fingers slid beneath the string of my thong and then gasped when he tugged, grinding it into my over-sensitive lips. I would have come from the contact alone, but he yanked the fabric down to my ankles.

"Jesus, Princess." He pushed two fingers inside me. "You're fucking drenched." I let out a muffled sound and greedily rocked back against his hand, needing more friction, needing more... him. He took control and pumped me hard, enslaving me to his rhythm. He added a third finger and I spasmed, tumbling into the abyss.

When I heard the sound of his zipper, I swear I'd never heard anything so sweet.

"Hurry," I practically begged. "Take me. Now."

In one stroke, he buried his entire length into me, and I braced myself against the table. But it still wasn't enough. "More," I moaned. I wanted... no, needed... to feel more. To feel everything. Anything to fill the void. I reached back to grab his thigh and sunk my nails in. "More," I repeated. With a grunt, he reared back and drove into me with such force, my eyes watered. "Yes. Yes." My muscles frantically pulsated around his cock. "Fuck me. Please."

He fisted a hand in my hair and jerked... hard. My head snapped back and scorching heat shot straight to my clit. Pain intensified pleasure and I arched my back, inviting him to give me something I didn't understand. But he knew exactly what I wanted. Powerful hands pushed my strapless dress down and grabbed my breasts, twisting and pinching my nipples, rough enough to bruise. I found myself growling as my muscles flared and I gave in to the dark delight.

"Fuck, Princess." His fingers moved down to brutally dig into my hips, anchoring me in place. And then he fucked me harder. Merciless thrusts that battered my pussy. Ruthless and rough. Flesh slapping flesh. Beautiful and vicious. He sent me right to the edge, every thrust a blissful punishment that promised the sweet release of freedom. The air grew thick, sweat burned my eyes, and my ravaged flesh burned raw but none of it mattered. I was too far gone. Too consumed with my mindless need to be taken.

With a curse, his hard body folded over mine and the air rushed from my lungs. Heat engulfed me and my raw instincts leapt into a frenzy. His fingers wrapped around my neck like a cage. I was pinned beneath him, at his mercy, helpless, and trapped.

And I fucking loved every second of it.

I came in an explosion, bucking and jerking, and gritting my teeth as waves of euphoria slammed through me. I yelled out his name along with a string of incoherent words until he twisted my face to kiss me, greedily swallowing the screams of a woman thoroughly unhinged. A shudder wracked his body and he let loose a deep grunt and slumped on top of me.

Nothing existed anymore.

Only him.

And it felt like the road to Heaven.

Chase was waiting when I exited the bathroom, his suit and demeanor impeccable. No one would guess he had just fucked the lifelong convictions out of his date in a room down the hall.

Until they saw me.

"Uh oh," he said. "I recognize that look. You're about to freak out on me."

"I'm fine," I said but we both knew that was a lie. Especially with how I bolted out of the room as soon as he released me.

"You're more than fine." His green eyes filled with awe. "You're incredible. I knew once you finally let go, you'd be amazing. But I had no idea… fuck, I have no words for that."

I did: Stupid? Careless? Irresponsible?

Everything about the sex had been wrong. And by wrong, I mean so damn good, it was terrifying. He'd threatened my inhibitions before but, Christ, I'd sped into insanity so fast, I didn't even see the onramp. I'd been defenseless, reckless, and vulnerable.

And for that moment, gloriously liberated from the empty ache that lived inside me.

Which meant as soon as we arrived in New York, we needed to part ways for good.

"I'm tired." I started down the corridor though I had no idea where I was going. I'm sure Chase could have navigated us back to the elevators, but he seemed content to let me lead. Maybe hoping we'd stumble across more empty rooms and have another go at it.

I hated that my body perked up at the thought. When I saw a sign for the lobby, I quickened my pace, rushed around the corner, and walked smack into an approaching woman.

"Excuse me, young lady," she said.

"Sorry, I wasn't paying—" I stopped and my body froze.

I was standing face to face with... the woman who had abandoned me as a child.

22

Her petite physique, pale blonde hair, and remarkably unlined face brought back vivid memories of a person who had once played a prominent role in my life. Yet if time was dependent on change, then the last twenty-five years were nothing more than a blink.

I hesitated, afraid she'd vanish in a puff of smoke if I acknowledged her.

But her eyes remained blank.

She has no idea who I am.

I retreated a step and bolted.

With no destination in mind, I ran as if I could leave the past standing in the foyer of the hotel. When I stopped, I found myself facing the entrance to the bar.

"Princess, wait." Chase caught up with me. "Jesus, you're white as a ghost."

Because I just saw one.

"Come on." He took my hand and led me into the room. Although Helena and Phil were nowhere to be seen, many wedding party stragglers remained, most bombed out of their minds. Chase sat me down in a booth towards the back and I barely registered when he disappeared. He returned with a shot glass which he placed in my trembling hand.

"Drink."

The liquid fire seared my throat but did nothing to cure the disbelief.

Chase settled beside me. "Who was that?"

"Nobody." I couldn't do this. Not now. Not ever. In all my calculations, this scenario never registered as plausible. But that's what made my family so insidious. Every time you presumed to understand the playing field, they changed the rules. Usually by cheating.

Before he could probe further, a woman's voice cut in.

"I don't believe it."

I raised my face until I was staring into dark blue eyes identical to mine. They widened with astonishment. "After all these years, how can this be possible?"

I struggled for words but came up blank.

"The odds are so slim," she continued in a cultured tone I didn't remember her having.

"Of… seeing me again?"

"No, of *you*. Look at you," she exclaimed, growing animated with every word. "Last I recall, you were too gawky for any sort of attractiveness. There was a remote possibility you could grow into something presentable, but given your plain looks and gangly frame, I wrote it off as impossible. Yet somehow you blossomed into an absolute beauty." Her eyes filled with wonder. "Utterly amazing. You're exquisite. So tall and stunning."

Chase scowled at her. "She's more than just a pretty face." Even misunderstanding the dynamics, my knight in shining armor was quick to defend.

"Can we please speak?" My mother gave Chase a pointed look. "In private."

I hesitated. Was I ready to listen to the explanation I'd dreaded most of my life? To risk devastation if she confirmed my suspicions? Did she leave because of me? Sometimes the pain of uncertainty was preferable to the misery found in truth.

But if I didn't pursue this opportunity, I'd only be adding regret to my long list of burdens.

I shot Chase an imploring look and he acquiesced, heading to the bar, but from his expression, our conversation was nowhere close to finished.

My mother sat on the bench facing me. "A distasteful young man," she commented, but her eyes remained on me. She continued her scrutiny as if preparing to publish my anomaly in a scientific journal. Though if anyone at this table warranted a study on defying nature, it wasn't me. Her skin glowed smoother than a woman's half her age, without so much as a wrinkle to mar the perfection. Either she'd been stored in a jar of formaldehyde or had exceptional work done.

But the most surprising transformation lay beneath the superficial—a regal highborn elegance commonly bred from birth but in her case, acquired post disappearance. It certainly didn't come from our family's genetic cesspool. What had happened to her?

"Try pulling your hair back," she suggested. "It will accentuate your cheekbones. But keep it long. Men love long hair on women. Also, less eye makeup. The way it's smeared on your face means you applied too much. You should attempt a more natural look."

I didn't understand. Why was she discussing beauty tips?

"Your skin is a little dry," she continued. "Ingesting coconut oil—"

"What are you talking about?" I blurted.

She stopped and raised an eyebrow, not even a wrinkle creasing her forehead.

Oh, fuck it. I yanked off the proverbial Band-Aid. "Why did you leave?"

She reared back and shot me a disappointed look, as if a direct question represented the height of poor manners. "Subtlety is an art form a lady uses to achieve her goals. You should try it."

"Was it because of me?" I steeled myself for the answer that carried the power to decimate.

"What?" Her smooth face creased slightly with what would have been a frown on anyone else. "Don't be absurd."

That response should have unfurled the dread in my gut yet it remained, coiled as tight as a wound-up snake, ready to bite. I may not have been bad enough to make her leave, but I sure as hell wasn't good enough to make her stay.

Something inside told me to heed the snake and tread lightly but I pushed it aside. I couldn't stop now. "Then why?"

She displayed a similar hesitancy to continue the conversation, prolonging her response with some sort of swami breath—a deep inhale through her nose followed by three quick exhalations via her mouth.

"It's quite simple," she finally answered. "I was meant for more than what your father offered."

Her idea of 'simple' clearly differed from mine. "But you married him."

"Yes. When he was teetering on the brink of financial greatness. Back when he led me to believe he had the potential to provide the life I deserved. But cruelty is born of weakness, and I underestimated his propensity for both. We could have—no, should have—had everything, but instead, he settled for a mediocre whiskey-soaked life. Once I realized he'd never fulfill his obligations, his other propensities became inexcusable and embarrassing. I was not placed on this earth to live as an impoverished woman. Especially when he was so close to parlaying his skills into millions. He was the best con artist there ever was, until he let the bottle best him. I am assuming that's what eventually led to his arrest."

She assumed incorrectly but that was a story I had no intention of sharing. Besides, I still had too many questions. "But he started drinking because of you. After you left."

"You are mistaken, child, but what do you know? You were too young to remember. I concealed his vices and kept him going. He may have been the talent but I was the mastermind. He was nothing without me. Had I stayed, he would never have been caught."

Again, she was wrong. "You knew what he was doing?"

"Don't be naïve," she said brusquely. "I pride myself on knowing all my options. Thank goodness I left before his arrest and the ensuing scandal. And well done to you for disappearing before it happened. A shame Helena did not have your sense of timing. You were extremely fortunate."

No. I knew exactly what was about to happen since I had caused it.

"Anyway," she added as if this concluded the story, "it all worked out for the best."

Except it didn't.

I had expected a story fraught with tears, remorse, and concern. Any indication of human emotion would have placated me but instead, she remained collected and unruffled. My inner voice reiterated the stupidity of continuing but being a masochist at heart, I ignored it. "What was it? The drinking? The lying? The brutality? Or something I missed?"

"Yes," she said. "With his financial future degenerating, all those vices magnified. When he stopped listening to me, I concluded it was time to act. I implemented my plan and after a few attempts, was finally rewarded with the success to which I was entitled." Her dark blue eyes shone with victory. "You have no idea what I endured, living with his ill-treatment, knowing I was destined for better."

I refrained from pointing out my firsthand knowledge of that VIP experience, except no one had ever suggested I was worth more. "You left your children behind," I pointed out that important, yet absent, fact from her story.

"Why is that an issue? You turned out perfect. Absolutely exquisite."

The *issue* was all the nights spent buried under the covers, wracking my immature brain, trying to figure out what I could have done to make her stay. Wasted hours wondering if I'd been smarter, nicer, sweeter, whatever-er. When the truth is, she never gave a damn. I had made her my world when I was never even an afterthought."

That pissed me off.

"So let me get this straight. Dad was too abusive for you to stay, but cuddly enough to leave your children with? Sounds like splendid parenting."

"Don't be melodramatic," she admonished. "It all worked out. You're—"

"Pretty," I interjected. "I know. And in your estimation, that makes everything okay."

Her features sharpened. "You survived just fine."

"Surviving and living are two different concepts," I shot back. "Why didn't you take me with you?"

"It was impossible to take children."

"Where did you go? The Island of Misfit Adults?"

"Do not mock me." Her expression hardened and I wondered

if my eyes crystallized like that when I was angry. “I’m surprised how disrespectful you’ve become.”

I almost laughed. “Chalk it up to poor parenting. Where did you go?”

“If you must know, I met somebody and—”

“You left for a man?” Any last shred of hope withered at the utterance of those words. Perhaps I’d still been naively holding out for something semi-redeemable like an escape to a convent or some sort of refuge. Nope. She had waltzed out on her own terms which meant leaving me had been easy. Which begged the question… What about me made it so easy?

“Not just any man,” she said. “An obscenely wealthy, handsome European tycoon with a weakness for American women and one unwavering stipulation—no children, past or future. He had already fathered three with his deceased wife and would have refused to take me had he learned of my own.” She smiled wistfully. “He whisked me to Italy where we lived in an enormous villa. It was glorious.”

I swallowed the lump in my throat. “Such a shame the price of admission was your children.”

“I’m truly astonished by your attitude,” she scolded. “The daughter I knew would never put herself above those around her. She cared about the happiness and wellbeing of others. What happened to that kind and compassionate girl? Have you become so selfish that you prefer I squandered my one chance at happiness because you weren’t included? Would you rather we all maintain a miserable existence rather than one of us live our dream? Any good daughter would not wish that upon her mother. Are you telling me you do?”

“Of course not.”

“Then why are you saying such hurtful things?”

How had this become my fault? I never begrudged other

people their happiness. And never would I desire the abuse I received be thrust on others. Especially my own mother. What type of monster would that make me?

But given the choice, would I have given her my blessing to pursue her happiness? We would never know since she robbed me of the opportunity to sacrifice my life for hers. What mother would put that responsibility on a child anyway? It was too much to understand. Which is why she decided for all of us. She chose herself.

"You should be proud to have a mother who accomplished such an insurmountable task," she continued, "especially after the damage having a second child inflicted. It was not easy to return to my competitive form after I had you." She patted her flat stomach through her silk Armani suit. It cloaked a body that showed zero evidence of any hardship. In fact, her perfect figure represented the best money could buy. Nature did not bounce high and firm like that. "A little nip and tuck and I reinvented myself as a brand-new woman." She gave me a significant look. "Something we seem to have in common from what I hear, *Miss Jasmine Monroe*."

Her meaning was clear. While I never succumbed to physical enhancements, I'd taken equally drastic measures to transform myself into an unrecognizable person. Both of us driven to extreme actions by the same abhorrent man.

Except I didn't willingly sacrifice others. Yes, the long list of sins in my ledger proved I was no angel, but ever since that fateful night, any collateral damage I left in my wake was intentional.

Maybe hers was too.

"How do you know anything about me?" I asked.

"Oh, please. I asked before I came in here and while I approve the effort, the name you chose is a little pedestrian, don't you think? 'Jasmine' rings more like a stripper than a refined woman."

That statement hurt more than any of her other revelations.

Not the disapproval over a stupid name, but that she had no recollection of the day we spent at the gardens where she had purposefully shared her love of stargazer lilies and introduced me to the most wonderful smell a little girl had encountered—the jasmine flower. The day she bought me the lily pin.

The pin I wished I still owned so I could throw it in her face.

"Too late to change it now," she said. "No matter. Once it is followed by the last name 'Hale', no one will care."

"Huh?"

"Although I find him distastefully rude, his net worth more than compensates for the attitude. I thought Helena had done well in her marriage, but should you entice Chase Hale to the altar, you'll surpass even her calculated efforts."

I never thought I'd be competing with Helena for Gold Digger of the Year.

Speaking of gold digging... "Where is your Italian tycoon?"

"Demetri passed away a month ago." Even with her lack of facial expressions, she exhibited no signs of a grieving widow.

"I see," I said, unsure where to go from here. "Look, um..." I mentally applied the title of 'mom' but found it distasteful.

"Brenda," she stated. "I've exerted too much effort cultivating my youthful persona. The admission of kids adds at best nothing and at worst, ruins it altogether. I am too young to have two full grown children. Consider me a friend of the family. No relation to you or your sister."

Looks like we're all rewriting our pasts. Except she was smart to adopt the persona of a non-relative. Any relation and Rita would pounce.

"Not sister," I informed her. "My cousin, Helena. Jasmine Monroe has no siblings." *And I will never go back to being a Brooks again.*

She waved a hand. "Fine. Cousin. It doesn't matter. I am not here to get involved in whatever drama you and Helena cooked up."

"So why are you here, *Brenda*?" I emphasized her first name. "To support your daughter on her wedding day?" It stung that she would want to be there for Helena when she clearly had no feelings for me.

"Weddings are the perfect venue to meet eligible bachelors."

Especially when the family was crawling with men waiting for their trusts to be released. "Let me guess. Demetri left you nothing."

"Every penny to his spoiled brats," she spat. "And after I gave him the best years of my life."

Years that should have been mine.

A calculating gleam entered her eyes. "Although, when you marry Chase, my efforts might be better served tapping into that pipeline. He can certainly afford it."

I stiffened. "That's never going to happen. Use Helena as your golden goose."

"Nonsense. I'm sure even with your caustic personality, you can accomplish it. With proper persuasion, men are malleable creatures."

"We're talking about people, not Play-Doh. And Chase and I are not together."

"Not if you allow that to continue." She pointed at the bar.

I turned to see Chase seated on a stool while Gabby crawled all over him like a lapdog in heat. "It's fine." Though the sudden urge to punch her said differently.

"It is unacceptable," she snapped. "Be sensible. Your looks will only accomplish so much. The rest is strategy. Claim him but make it appear like the union is his idea. Then hold that acerbic tongue of yours until you have a ring on your finger." She said the last bit with skepticism, as if doubting my ability to pull it off. She rose to her feet. "If you remember anything from tonight, remember that piece of wisdom. You now have the knowledge to make him yours. If you fail, you have only yourself to blame."

And with that warped maternal advice, she floated away, leaving behind a lingering trail of Chanel.

That's more than she left the last time.

I leaned my head back and closed my eyes. Although I never remembered her as the maternal type, had she always been this cold and manipulative? And was it the same innate force that drove me to be so calculating?

Gabby's tacky scent attacked my mother's fragrance with the subtlety of a hammer. I groaned. "Leave me alone," I mumbled.

"No can do," Chase replied.

My eyes opened to see him alone. "I am not in the mood and Gabby's slutty body spray is not helping."

He wisely chose the seat across from me. "Who the hell is that awful woman?"

Apparently, I wasn't the only one saddled with the blunt gene. "Brenda is a family friend. A close friend of my mother's." I wasn't sure why I added that last part, but it seemed right to connect the two.

"I'm sorry. You both must have been devastated when she died."

My gut twisted at Jasmine Monroe's backstory. It was one thing to talk about it in the abstract, but it felt indecent to have others partake in the charade. Especially when the truth just left the bar.

"You never talk about your parents," he said. "What were they like?"

Selfish bastards who ruined my life. One by leaving. The other by not leaving.

I sighed. "I never really knew my mother. She abandoned me when I was five." Bitterness kept my words honest.

"What caused her to leave?"

"She wanted a better life with a different family."

Chase's astute eyes studied me. "Do you believe she left because of you?"

I hesitated. Although my head now knew the truth about my dad, the five-year-old in me still clutched to the guilt like a security blanket. After carrying it around for twenty-five years, it was ingrained in me.

He grabbed both my hands and squeezed. "You're wrong."

"How would you know?"

"Because she had a responsibility to you. Not the other way around. I don't care what you were like as a child, her job was to protect you. A job she failed at miserably by leaving you behind."

"The man was rich and didn't want her kids."

His lip curled in disgust. "There is no way that had anything to do with you."

And that was the problem.

"Don't you get it?" I said. "If she left because of me then at least I would have mattered, but I didn't. I never even factored into the decision." After years of condemning myself as the cause, I'd never considered the alternative. That I was so inconsequential, leaving me was neither easy nor hard. It was nothing.

I didn't know which was worse.

"Listen to me, Princess." He waited until he had my full attention. "I have firsthand experience dealing with this personality type. The kind that will do anything to ensure an easy life regardless of how much fallout they leave. They consider their needs tantamount and relegate others as pawns. We're not people to them but tools to achieve their goals. When they discard you, it's human nature to question your own worth instead of evaluating theirs, but something is wrong with them. If she placed material wealth over her own daughter, nothing about you could have derailed that outcome. Not because you don't matter, but because of her narcissistic fucked-up priorities. Place the responsibility where it belongs. If this happened to some other innocent child, would you condemn them?"

His intense gaze never wavered and through the compassion in his eyes, I felt a strange sensation of comfort. Like a light, it flowed through me, shining on the depths of my soul, illuminating even my darkest shadows. My heart swelled with emotion.

And terror.

I pulled away.

He continued to watch me intently. "You know, Princess, you're finally beginning to make sense."

"What does that mean?"

"It means if you couldn't trust your own mother, why expect it from anyone else?"

"Please don't psychoanalyze me."

"You want to know what the real tragedy is," he said softly. "You, more than anyone I know, deserve to be happy."

The fact that he actually believed that nearly broke my heart.

23

I woke to a thick marine layer hovering over the horizon that mimicked my feeling of suffocation. Yet, unlike my oppression, the dense canopy would burn off by mid-morning to yield a pleasant day.

I ran through my mental checklist for the day: keep Chase away from Helena, avoid Brenda, stay as far away from George Junior as possible, survive the wedding, then return home to end things with Chase.

In a minefield of horrific options, why did that last one bother me most?

I pushed myself out of bed and reached for Chase's shirt. *Ugh!* Gabby's toxic perfume cleaved through my brain. Where'd she get the stuff? A rocket fuel store? I wadded it up and lobbed it into the trash. He could afford another one.

Shrugging on a fluffy hotel robe and slippers, I padded into the sitting room to find Chase working on his computer. He wore jeans and a T-shirt and from his damp hair and fresh scent, he'd already showered. Relief washed over me. Now that I had made the decision to end things, I could not afford any complications, which included his naked and chiseled body soaped up beside me.

"Are you feeling better this morning?" he asked, the compassion returning to his eyes.

Not really. While today had all the makings of a grandiose cluster-fuck, at least I trusted Brenda was here for reasons unrelated to me—I guess that was the upside to being inconsequential—but Helena had known about her and had chosen to withhold it. More mind games to worry about.

On the other hand, as much as I hated to admit it, Chase's insightful characterization of my mother's personality type had made me feel better.

A characterization that was too insightful. Who in his life was he referring to?

"Chase, last night, you mentioned having firsthand experience with somebody like my mother. Who were you talking about?"

"No one. Just generalities I've learned from having a psychiatrist as a sister-in-law." He sidestepped the question like a pro. I would know.

"But you said—"

His phone buzzed and he answered quickly. "Derek," I noted the relief in his voice. "Has the jackass finally settled his divorce so we can move forward with the sale?"

My first guess would have been Teresa. A bitch with narcissistic tendencies? Absolutely. But the way he dodged the question made me think it was something else. *Someone* else. Maybe related to his mysterious marriage that was none of my business?

With a loud sigh, I headed for the bathroom. It sucked being on the receiving end of a lie.

Since I'd rejected Helena's offer—prompted by Rita—to have my hair and makeup professionally done, I was on my own. I wouldn't put it past Helena to slip the makeup artist a fifty and have me turned into Bozo the Clown. Not that it mattered. The eggplant would upstage it anyway. What did it say about my life that being humiliated by that dress didn't even rank as one of my top concerns today?

With no more reasons to procrastinate, I approached the garment bag, yanked the zipper down, and found myself staring at the wrong dress.

What the hell?

Did Nicki make a mistake? Maybe she packed two dresses in case I changed my mind. Frantically, I ransacked the garment bag but found nothing else. How could she have forgotten it? And how did she find another dress in the exact deep shade of purple? Confused, I held it up and my eyes widened. It couldn't be. How could this gorgeous dress have once been the eggplant when it bared no resemblance to the original atrocity?

I gingerly slipped it on and... holy shit! It was amazing. Gone were the puffy sleeves and constricting bodice, replaced by delicate straps and a slightly rounded, but tasteful, dip between my breasts. Instead of the floor-length deathtrap, it now safely ended above the knee, the spiky lace tiers still intact but somehow quirky and stylish instead of demented and psychotic.

Nicki had even sewn a tiny hidden pocket for lipstick or some other utilitarian function. In that moment, I could not have loved her more.

Chase entered as I was applying a final coat of lip gloss. "Whoa." He halted and his eyes mimicked mine from a moment ago. "What happened to poufy, scary...?" His arms traced a wide hula hoop motion around himself.

"Eggplant 2.0, courtesy of Nicolette Simms." I spun. "What do you think?"

"Heart stopping." He smiled. "But there's something missing."

I looked down at the dress and matching shoes. "I can't think of anything."

He withdrew a velvet box from his pocket and flipped open the lid. A delicate flower-shaped diamond pendant lay nestled inside.

"Chase, no."

"Look closer."

"You're not going to pull a Pretty Woman on me and snap the lid, are you?"

He quirked an eyebrow.

"Never mind." I bent to study the pendant. "It's jasmine."

"I know nothing can replace the lily pin you lost, but I thought this might help."

Ha! Comparing my shoddy glass bauble to this refined piece of jewelry was like equating a Yugo to a Lamborghini.

But it was too much. When he removed it from the case, I shook my head. "I can't accept this."

"Why?"

"Because we're not... I'm not..." *Because we're done in two days.* "This isn't what we are. Please stop being so nice."

"Is this going to be like those damn dinners all over again?" He firmly gripped my shoulders and turned me to face the mirror. "It's a gift. It doesn't have to mean anything. So unless you want to start an argument and risk Rita's ire by being late, I suggest you cooperate."

With a guilty sigh, I lifted my hair and allowed him to clasp the delicate silver chain around my neck. The diamonds shimmered against my bare skin.

"It's beautiful," I said, vowing to return it as soon as we returned to New York.

"It's just an object." The green depths of his eyes shone as lustrous as the diamonds. "You're beautiful."

I had no words. Not when I knew they wouldn't matter after tomorrow.

When I reached the Toliver/Brooks wedding party, I located Rita immediately, impossible to ignore in her mother of the groom ensemble—a fuchsia skirt puffed out by layers of netting coupled with a fuchsia and orange striped bolero jacket. A wide brimmed hat sat atop her head, almost normal if you ignored the orange sparkly bow wrapped around the base.

From the opposite direction, Helena approached to the obligatory 'ooohs' and 'aaahs' required of even the most hideous bride. Not that Helena qualified as one. She looked beautiful in a tasteful designer gown. Based on her personality, I expected something tight and squeezy, but though the bodice fit snug, long lace sleeves covered her arms and the skirt billowed out, covered in dainty, delicately stitched pearls. Slightly smaller than the ones wound into her pale blonde updo.

The wicked sister had donned her fairy princess costume today.

Helena stopped short when she noticed me—or more likely, the dress— and stumbled, causing Gabby to comically tumble into her back. Unfortunately, both stayed upright. I waited for her tantrum, her livid expression indicating her desire to have one, but before she reached DEFCON 1, she cast a sidelong glance at Rita.

Man, I could have used a 'Rita' while growing up.

Gabby, who on a good day possessed the IQ of a shrub, did not follow Helena's example. "What the hell are you wearing? That isn't the dress we—ooof!" Helena's elbow connected with her ribs.

"Jasmine, your dress is gorgeous," Rita weighed in, never one to be shy with her opinion. "Alluring and flattering"—she glanced at Gabby's outfit with distaste—"while perfectly respectable. You look sensational."

Gabby's scrap of fabric deserved that remark. With a hemline six inches shorter than mine and a cleavage dip alarmingly low, she looked like she'd be more comfortable turning tricks in the hotel bar.

But neither Helena nor Gabby's attention remained on my dress for long. "What's this?" Helena gestured to my neck. Both she and Gabby stared at it, dollar signs practically registering in their eyes.

Rita beamed. "A gift from that handsome beau of yours?"

I offered a slight nod.

"Oh, it's exquisite." Rita clapped her hands. "Just like the two of you. I can't wait to see what your babies will look like. They are going to be stunning."

Helena and Gabby both released a strangled sound while I searched for any method of escape. Thankfully, a photographer gestured to us.

By the time we finished with pictures and were summoned to begin the wedding, the sun had begun its descent. It emblazoned the sky in a radiant display of orange and magenta that strangely adhered to the wedding's color scheme.

Even Mother Nature wouldn't piss off Rita.

A string quartet, glowing radioactive in lime green vests, began playing and, on cue, I dutifully hustled down the gold path. I tensed when I saw Chase, seated between two blonde women, each clawing for his attention. I offered him a half smile to which he responded with one so dazzling, it put the decorations to shame.

I refocused on my steps and headed towards the lascivious jackhole at the altar. The one undressing me with his eyes. Decked out in a black tuxedo with purple cummerbund and tie, Phil resembled a magician. A shame he couldn't transform himself into a decent human being.

Gabby followed next, strutting her wares like a runway model on a makeshift catwalk. With no desire to earn an ass-kicking from Rita, I suppressed the urge to yell, 'Work it, baby'. She ended her jaunt by striking a flirty pose beside me.

The guests stood in unison as the death march—er, wedding march—started, and a hush fell over the crowd.

"We are gathered here... blah, blah, blah," the minister began, and I took that as my cue to zone out.

"—be true to her, forsaking all others—"

Unless they have a vagina.

"—for richer or poorer—"

You got half that right.

"Better or worse—"

What if they're both the worst?

"—You may now kiss your bride." We exited to applause, and I headed for the reception area where I found Chase waiting at the entrance. One of the blondes still hovered, eagerly chirping in his ear. He left her in mid-sentence.

We entered to wildly festive streamers, balloons, and an explosion of party favors. Definitely the right place. Maybe we'd have a piñata later, though putting a baseball bat in my hands might not be smart with Gabby in the same room. We located our places at a round table thankfully not shared with Helena, but I groaned when Gabby plopped her ass in the seat beside Chase. She scooted closer.

Before I could digest that, Brenda appeared and took a seat across from me. The antithesis of Rita, she was spring personified in a flattering lavender zippered jacket and matching skirt. She zeroed in on my necklace and shot me an approving look.

"Chase, you look so handsome." Gabby's voice dripped with targeted seduction.

Brenda's approval turned to irritation.

Awww. How supportive. My mommy wants me to land the billion-dollar man.

"What did you think of the ceremony?" Gabby cooed and leaned forward until her tits almost fell out of her dress. "I'm so jealous of Helena, meeting the perfect man. Do you ever think about getting married?"

Mentioning marriage to a self-committed playboy? Rookie mistake. Did she not read chapter one of *Gold Digging for Dummies?*

This was going to be a long night.

As if on cue, George Junior swooshed over to claim the empty chair near me. I say '*swooshed*' because that's the sound his powder blue—more than likely flammable—crushed velvet suit made every time he moved.

Who dressed him? Queer Eye for the Pimp Guy?

And so the evening progressed with Gabby pawing at Chase, Brenda growing irate at another woman stealing my cash cow, Chase watching Brenda too intently for comfort, and Junior trying to convince me to leave the table for a romp on the beach. The chicken was the best thing around... and it tasted like old tires.

"Come on," Junior was coaxing. "It'll be fun. So what if you get a little sand up your—"

"Dear Lord, please stop talking," I interrupted.

Brenda fixed Junior with one of her haughty expressions. "You are a glorified tooth polisher. Make something of yourself before expecting her to give you the time of day."

Trust Brenda to ignore the skeevy factor and make this about his bank account.

George's sloppy smile turned bitter. "If you don't start being nice to me, I'm gonna tell Helena. She'll be mad. You ain't gonna like Helena when she's mad."

When was she anything else?

Gabby rolled her heavily lined eyes. "Chase, you haven't said anything about my dress. What do you think?"

That a dead hooker wouldn't be caught wearing it.

The band began the clichéd chicken dance, and I cringed as throngs of people rushed to the dance floor, flapping their elbows and clapping their hands, nearly knocking over the servers as they attempted to distribute slices of wedding cake.

Gabby angled closer to Chase and raised her voice to be heard over the music. "It comes off really easy."

"You're not listening," George Junior whined, pulling my attention back to him. "I'll throw in a free teeth cleaning."

Brenda declined the server's offer, her figure too vital to squander on indulgences. I, on the other hand, accepted the largest piece of lemon cake on the tray, which caused my mother's mouth to tighten. "What?" I said around a mouthful. "It's fruit." Her judgmental attitude was starting to piss me off.

Along with the attention whore vying for Chase's attention.

And the repetition of the damn chicken dance.

As if reading my thoughts, the band kicked it up a notch.

Gabby followed the band's lead and upped the ante on her little game. She scooped up a forkful of frosting and squealed, "Oops, clumsy me." The piece landed on her protruding bosom, perfectly lodged in her cleavage. She dipped a finger in the frosting and seductively licked it off.

"Hell yeah," Junior whooped. "Frosting tits." Before I could stop him, he scooped up a handful of cake and smeared it across my chest.

"What the fuck?" I cried out.

With blurred speed, Chase reached across me to clutch a fistful of blue velvet.

"It's not my fault," Junior whined. "She's not playing nice. Helena said she'd spread her legs for anyone."

I grabbed Chase's arm. "Don't do this here. Please." As tempting as it was to see Junior's obnoxious face pulverized, I couldn't risk the attention. "Please," I begged. "For Rita."

Chase's biceps coiled beneath my fingers and I thought Junior was toast, but then just as quickly, Chase's arm went slack. "Get the fuck out of my sight." He shoved Junior away.

Junior scurried off like the rodent he was.

That's one down.

"Let him have her," Gabby said. "They deserve each other."

Chase shifted his murderous glower onto her. "Go clean yourself up. You're embarrassing yourself."

"Do you want to come with me?" She fluttered her eyelashes.

"Let me be clear," he enunciated. "I'd rather stick my dick in a blender than fuck you with it."

Her face went from shock to rage and for a moment, I thought she was going to slap him, but instead, she shoved her chair back and stormed off.

And that makes two.

"We need to go before I kill someone," Chase said. "There's a place I know not too far from here. You up for it?"

I nodded and pointed to the sticky frosting coating my skin. "Let me clean this up first. I'll be right back."

I made it to the bathroom with no distractions, and after a few paper towels soaked in water, I was frosting free and eager to leave. I exited and headed back to Chase. For the first time in what felt like days, my lungs expelled a long breath. In a few minutes, we would be gone and I would never have to lay eyes on another member from my cursed family. I had played my part, Helena got what she wanted, and now I was—

"Where do you think you're going?" Helena said before sharp talons painfully dug into my arm and pulled me through a doorway.

24

I tripped over an honest-to-God pineapple piñata before regaining my footing. We were in a musty backroom littered with boxes of decorations, racks of packing materials, and camera equipment. A dim bulb cast a glow over the small space.

"You." Helena's contorted face ruined any illusion of the beautiful bride. She jabbed a French manicured finger in my chest, and I stumbled again in my effort to move away. "How dare you swap dresses?"

With unsteady hands, I smoothed down the target of her wrath.

Never show weakness.

"I didn't," I said. "Look closer. Nicki's a whiz with a needle and thread."

"Your obnoxious roommate did that?" Helena's eyes widened and for a moment, admiration replaced rage. Then, just as quickly, the cobra returned. "You had no right. I chose it for a reason."

"She can't help herself. I didn't know until today. I swear." Why did I even bother? In her eyes, I'd committed the ultimate sin—

deprived her of an opportunity to humiliate me. "Today is your big day," I reminded her, in hopes the auspicious occasion would garner some favor. "Can't you enjoy yourself and let it go?"

Even the Godfather granted requests on his daughter's wedding day.

But not Helena. She was practically vibrating with anger. "You think because it's my wedding day, you get a free pass to do whatever you want? That you're special? A worthless bastard child like you? What a joke."

Her barbs usually landed straight on, but this one eluded me. "What does that mean?"

"It means you're literally a—"

"Helena, stop," Brenda ordered. I turned to see my mother in the doorway, one of Phil's uncles in tow. Given the disappointment on his face, the two had not expected to find the little room occupied.

Helena shifted to face her. "Give me one good reason why I shouldn't tell her."

Brenda whispered something in the uncle's ear and with hunched shoulders, he skulked away. Satisfied he was gone, she zigzagged through a maze of dusty boxes until she stood between us. "Because it is not your place," she said, and like a ref in a boxing match, guided Helena to the opposite end of the room.

"Awww, poor little princess," Helena mocked. "Heaven forbid we hurt her feelings."

I flushed at the nickname I'd grown accustomed to hearing as an endearment. Coming from Helena's mouth, it sounded tainted. Even inadvertently, she sullied everything in my life.

"Not a word," Brenda ordered.

Helena protested. "But—"

"No," Brenda snapped.

My eyes bounced from Helena's bitter expression to my mother's stern one. When it became apparent no one was going to divulge anything, I blurted. "Will someone tell me what's going on?"

"You're a bastard," Helena spoke quickly, drowning out my mother's objections. "Like literally a bastard. Illegitimate. You're not my dad's kid. Not my family. You're nothing to me."

Brenda glared at Helena. "She's still a half-sister," she corrected, this time to Helena's displeasure.

I shook my head. "I'm not following."

"I'll make it simple so your simple brain can understand." Helena's gloating smile widened. "My father is *not* your father. You are *not* my family."

"Still your half-sister," Brenda repeated, earning her another nasty look.

"Where do you think your freakish height comes from?" Helena persisted. "Not from my family of perfect proportions."

While five-foot ten was hardly Amazonian, compared to the rest of my family, I may as well have been jolly and green. But still... that wasn't exactly scientific proof. And Helena wasn't the most reliable source.

"Is this true?" I directed the question at Brenda.

My mother said nothing, but my answer came by way of her large blue eyes. Eyes identical to mine from the wariness they reflected to the lies they held. I saw that look in the mirror every morning.

"Tell me," I demanded.

My mother answered by brushing debris off a metal chair before perching on the edge. Not so much as a speck sullied her immaculate suit. With an erect spine, she crossed her legs at the ankles and folded her hands, the regal posture incongruous with our environment but somehow fitting for her. She performed one of her swami breaths. "Before you were born, I met a man—"

Does she have any story that doesn't begin with that phrase?

"—who was in town to present a paper at a science conference. He was brilliant, wealthy, handsome, and capable of lavishing me with the attention and lifestyle your father could not. We engaged in a relationship which was perfect until..." Her tone shifted from nostalgic wistfulness to disappointment. "Until I became pregnant with you. Then he was livid."

Already deprived of a sense of belonging, I thought it impossible to feel more adrift. I was wrong. My past may have been miserable, but at least it was mine. The identity I had willingly burned to ashes had been *mine*. Ashes that I used to craft my new life. But as it turned out, that foundation was fake too. Was anything about me real?

"Why did he become angry?" I asked in a thin voice.

"Because he already had two children and if there were to be more, he preferred his wife bear them."

I reeled back. "He was married?"

Helena snickered.

My mother continued as if simply sharing a tale and not bulldozing the very bedrock of her youngest daughter's life. "Instead of leaving his wife, which would have been the proper thing to do, he presented me with an ultimatum. When I refused to terminate the pregnancy, he ended our relationship." Her eyes lifted and I recoiled from the accusation in them. "I know if we had stayed together, he would have divorced her and chosen me. Instead, I had no choice but to give up the one man I wanted and remain with your father. All to give *you* life."

Stunned, I could only stare. Helena was right. I did ruin her life. And she did blame me. I'd always sensed that searching for her would yield nothing but regrets, but I never thought *I'd* be the regret.

My fate had been sealed before I was born.

"God, I wish I had a camera," Helena laughed. "Your face is priceless."

"Did Dad know?" I asked.

"*My* dad," Helena countered. "Not yours."

Brenda shifted her hips, either discomforted by the folding chair or more likely, our topic. Either way, she maintained her impressively rigid posture. "He eventually suspected enough to order a paternity test. Once confirmed, I knew I would suffer at his hands for my mistake—"

Which one? Having an affair or having me?

"—so I focused my efforts on leaving. That is when I met Demetri who offered me the life I truly deserved."

Slowly, her words sunk in… and with them, the awful truth. "You left me with an abusive alcoholic who knew I wasn't his kid?"

"Were it not for my pregnancy, I would have departed sooner. I endured far too much for that blunder."

I barely registered being called a 'blunder' because that was nothing compared to what she had already done. She had sacrificed me to a monster knowing full well I'd be the currency he used to pay for her sins. "Did you stop to think… did you even care…" I struggled to get the words out through gritted teeth. "What would happen after you saddled Dad with—"

"His name is Anthony," Helena interrupted. "*Not* your father."

"—with another man's kid? That he would redirect your punishment towards me?"

"That was beyond my control," she sniffed.

"It happened *because* you left," I said.

"At least I didn't abort you like your biological father demanded."

"Maybe you should have."

She lifted her chin. "Abortion is a sin."

"So is adultery," I yelled back.

"Told you," Helena taunted in a sing-song voice. "I told you it was all your fault."

"Will you shut the fuck up?" I barked, without a thought for who I was talking to.

"How dare you?" Helena lunged forward but jerked when her dress caught on a tripod. After a few unsuccessful yanks, she wrenched the delicate fabric, tearing the beautiful lace to shreds. Thankfully, she stayed on her side of the room.

"Who's my father?" I asked Brenda. An image of my '*Who's your Daddy*?' Darth Vader poster came to mind. How could real life be more fucked-up than science fiction?

Brenda hesitated.

"No more games," I snapped. "Who is he?"

"He's a well-respected, world-renowned physicist. A veritable genius, famous for his contributions to the scientific community."

"I didn't ask for his fucking resume. I want a name."

"I'm afraid I'm not at liberty to say. He remains married and has since ascended to a revered status in his field. The mere suggestion of infidelity, let alone an illegitimate child, would jeopardize his impeccable reputation."

I curled my fists as the pressure in my head threatened to explode. "He dumped you for getting knocked-up and you're protecting him? I'm not buying it." No way this selfish, opportunistic bitch would grant a favor without something in it for her. "What aren't you telling me?"

She performed another one of her annoying swami breaths while I resisted the urge to leap across the room and throttle her. "Let's just say that when he ended our relationship, we came to an understanding that made it worth my while to exercise discretion."

Just when I thought I couldn't be more repulsed, she always

found a way. "What's the going rate for keeping a daughter from her father?"

"He can afford it."

"That's not the point," I said.

"He deserves to pay after forsaking me."

But I don't.

"Best. Wedding. Present. Ever," Helena hooted and bounced up and down, her tattered skirts billowing around her like a jelly fish. "How does it feel to be so hated? To know that both your parents despise you?"

Like the bottom had plummeted from my world and dropped me straight into hell. But she already knew that. Because she had planned this revelation. This twisted showcase that went beyond cruelty. It was downright demented.

"What is your problem?" I asked Helena. "What did I ever do to you?"

Her pale eyes flashed with so much hatred, my skin heated. "If it weren't for you, Mom would have stayed and Dad would have been happy."

"You can't be serious."

"*You* made him hate her. *You* made him drive her away. *You* ruined everything. Everything bad that happened is because of YOU!"

"Because I'm the one who forced her to spread her legs for some brainiac boyfriend?" I shot back.

Brenda gasped while Helena's face twisted. "She should have done everyone a favor and aborted you like your father wanted."

I flinched. The words hurt, maybe because the same thought had occurred to me. Why bring a child so hated into the world? "Perhaps you're right, but you're delusional if you think she would have given up her lavish meal ticket to stay with a failure of a husband." I glanced at Brenda for confirmation, but she remained silent.

"You're the failure here," Helena hissed. "Running and hiding like the coward you've always been. Thinking you were better than us. Well now you know the truth. You're not good enough to be one of us. You were never part of the Brooks family."

Helena's words hung in the air.

You were never one of us.

I am not one of them.

A slow smile spread across my lips. I'd been looking at this all wrong.

"What the hell is so funny?" Helena barked.

Between the extortion, adultery, and Anthony's evil soul, Helena never stood a chance at inheriting one redeemable chromosome. But I would gamble that even with the mystery shrouding my real father, compared to Anthony, his DNA won the genome lottery any day of the week.

"Because I'm not like you," I said simply.

"And that's a good thing?" Helena shrieked. "You're gutter trash who never should have been born. Nobody wanted you then. Nobody wants you now. You would be doing everyone a favor if you went off and killed your —"

"That's enough!" Chase's voice boomed.

25

He was looming in the doorway, his jaw set in a rigid line I knew well. He was furious.

"Are you fucking insane?" He strode over to my side, his glower still fixed on Helena. "Who the hell do you think you are, speaking to your cousin like that?"

All three of us paused to remember who that was.

"And you." He turned to Brenda. "How can you sit and do nothing while that bitch abuses your best friend's daughter?"

Now everyone was confused.

I masked my alarm by plastering an artificial smile on my face. "It doesn't matter. I was just leaving." I tried to nudge him to the door, but he stood rooted like a mountain.

Damn knight in shining armor.

Brenda rose to her feet as if sharing my idea of a quick getaway, but Chase pinned her with his hard gaze. She made a show of brushing a speck of non-existent fluff off her immaculate suit instead.

"Please, Chase." This time I grabbed his arm. "It's nothing. Just old family drama. Come on."

Go now! Before—

"Don't you mean *her* daughter?" Helena said.

Oh, fuck!

She was rewarded by Chase's blank stare.

"It seems my dear *sister* likes to keep secrets while making up stories," Helena continued, suddenly more than willing to claim the familial relationship. "Especially about our mother over there."

Fuck! Fuck! Fuck!

I was now tugging on his arm. "Let's go. I promise I'll explain everything."

Just not here. Not like this.

But he wasn't listening. Instead, he spared a long look for each of us. First my mother, who registered apathy. What did she care? Her ass wasn't in the crosshairs. Next was Helena, who stared back with cold eyes. Vicious, shark-like, and hell-bent on demolishing her prey.

And me? Well, I could only imagine how I looked—like I'd been sucker-punched by a wrecking ball.

Suspicion replaced the confusion on Chase's face. "I thought your mother was dead."

"Um, no, but she did leave. That part is true. I didn't..." *know how to finish the sentence.*

Unfortunately, Helena suffered from no such limitations. "Haven't you figured it out by now or are you a bigger idiot than she is? There is no Jasmine Monroe. Never was. She's been manipulating everyone around her and playing you for a fool. Laughing at you behind your back this entire time."

"That's not true," I said quickly. "Not all of it. I never—"

"I'll tell you exactly who she is." Helena spoke over me, her voice a combination of glee and loathing. “She’s a selfish, spoiled brat who abused the family she never should have been a part of. She’s a schemer who took advantage of our generosity when we opened our doors to her. We gave her everything and she threw it back in our faces.”

“Chase, I didn’t—wait, what?” Helena’s words grabbed my attention. “Were you even in the same house?”

“See?” Helena pointed at me. “She appreciates nothing. Just takes and takes and expects everyone to cater to her.”

“That’s bullshit,” I said. “No one has ever given me a damn thing in this world. Especially you.”

“Really?” Helena countered with a sneer. “You were lucky we didn’t throw you out like the mangy rat you are. Lucky we took pity and let you stay, even though you did nothing but make our lives hell.”

“You don’t know the meaning of hell.” The blood in my veins boiled and a sea of red clouded my vision. “Hell was waking up every morning, terrified of the bruises and broken bones he was going to give me. Wondering if every day would be the one where he landed me in the hospital or finally put me out of my misery. He was a sadistic monster who beat on me for sport and laughed while I bled. If you think I’d be grateful for a father like that, you are out of your tiny fucking mind.”

Chase’s eyes drifted to my abdomen. “Are you saying…?” His eyes swam with horror. “Your own father?”

“He’s not her father,” Helena growled. “He’s mine. And quit your whining. You brought it on yourself.”

“Jesus, Princess,” Chase murmured.

“Don’t.” I recoiled from the pity in his eyes. I was already spiraling down a one-way trip to a fragile place I kept locked away for a reason. I did not need to speed up my descent.

“No.” My mother gripped the back of the folding chair and shook her head with enough force to dishevel her perfectly coiffed hairdo. "You turned out fine," she muttered, more to herself than anyone else. "Absolutely fine." She executed an obviously painful swami breath then visibly regained her composure as if absolved of any wrongdoing, a skill perfected over time, no doubt. "It all worked out fine."

"I take it he's also alive?" Chase asked but he already knew the answer. "Where is he?"

No sense hiding the truth now. Not with Helena, the mouthpiece, in the room. "In prison," I answered. "He defrauded his clients by enacting what history considers a Ponzi scheme on steroids. I'm sure you've heard of the infamous Anthony Brooks."

Chase's eyes widened. "The embezzler?"

Just hearing it aloud brought a fresh wave of shame crashing over me.

Chase's brow wrinkled as he recalled details. "He had two daughters. The older didn't amount to much."

"At least I didn't run away like a selfish little bitch," Helena retorted.

"But all kinds of speculation followed the younger one," Chase continued as if she hadn't spoken. "She disappeared right before he got busted. Though she was a teenager, rumors had her involved somehow. They could never piece it together. What was her name?" His eyes dropped to my chest, more specifically, the former resting place of the lily pin. He exhaled sharply. "Her name was Lily. You're Lily Brooks."

Hearing my real name struck hard. And with it came the memories. Each one broken, scarred, and buried for a reason.

"Lily," Helena spat. "Such a dumb name. Mom picked it because of a stupid stargazer lily flower. The ugliest flower ever."

A spark registered in Chase's eyes and I knew he was remembering our first night in the garden. Then the emotions followed—

shock, pity, anger, fury, and an underlying hurt that pierced me deeper than I thought possible. When he spoke, his voice was devoid of any of the reactions I'd just witnessed. "You should have told me."

A pang of guilt flickered, but I shoved it into my vault of disallowed feelings. I couldn't afford the luxury. Not after the sacrifices I'd made to protect myself. Not when every piece of my carefully constructed life had been tightly woven out of desperation and justification. One thread of doubt could unravel it all. Erase the fabric of my being. Erase *me*.

I could not let that happen.

"You do not get to persecute me," I said. "Not after you stipulated the rules."

He shook his head. "You would have done the same thing no matter what guidelines I proposed."

"You mean not divulging to a random sexual partner that I'm the daughter of one of the most hated men in America? Damn right I would have."

"You are not his daughter!" Helena shouted.

"Right," he barked out a harsh laugh. "Fuck buddies. Nothing more. I should have—wait." He turned to Helena. "What did you just say?"

"He's *my* father," she repeated as if she was stuck on a loop. "Not hers."

"You're not Anthony's kid?" Chase asked me.

"No."

"But you are the youngest daughter who everyone was looking for?"

"Yes."

"Christ." Chase rubbed his temples. "This is worse than a Jerry Springer show."

"It gets better." Helena sneered. "Her own dad is too embarrassed to claim her."

"Who's your father?" Chase voiced the million-dollar question.

I shrugged and we all turned to Brenda who stood firm, her vow of silence intact. I answered for her. "Some scientist with genius level smarts and an even higher level of paranoia."

"That's the first thing that's made sense today." Chase gestured towards Brenda and Helena. "There's no possible way your brains came from this lot."

Helena snarled. "Who do you think you are?"

"Someone smart enough to hire the best resource my company has ever had." Chase's eyes landed on me and the betrayal in them felt like a slap. "But not smart enough to know I was being played the entire time."

This is why I held on to my secret. No one could comprehend living beneath a cloud of fear. Knowing your life could be stripped away at the whim of another person. The lengths you would go to be safe.

And who the hell was he to throw guilt around when they were *his* rules?

"Stop playing the victim," I said. "We agreed to casual, which makes my life none of your business. I did nothing wrong."

His eyes flared. "How about lying to my face every fucking day?"

"I did what I had to do."

"You did what you wanted to do."

No. I did what I needed to. Which meant never acknowledging Lily again. Not after the things she had done. The weakness she represented. I could never go back to being her.

"What would you have done if I'd told you?" I challenged him. Condemned me? Run away? Destroyed me? I wanted him to say it. To say I deserved all the above.

"I guess we'll never know." He headed for the door.

"Chase, wait," I called out.

He stopped and turned back.

"Are you going to tell anyone?" I asked.

His face twisted in disgust.

"Forget him," Helena cackled. "I can't wait to blow up your perfect little life."

Why couldn't she shut up? It was over. She'd won. Why wasn't that enough for her?

Because her pleasure did not come from winning. It came from tormenting me. There was no goal, only the act itself. Which meant there would never be an end. She'd continue to annihilate anything I showed the slightest affection for.

I would never be free.

The realization gripped me like an icy fist.

Show no weakness.

That wasn't enough.

Show no weakness.

I had to do more.

Show no weakness.

"NO!" someone shouted and from the three pairs of eyes staring, I realized it was me.

My heart hammered and I imitated my mother's swami breath. Useless. But I couldn't back down now. Not with so much at stake. "Helena." I hated how shaky my voice sounded. "I always wondered how you got by when Anthony's assets were seized and the house confiscated. How someone with no education or skills could make it."

"What are you blabbing about?" Helena said.

"Then I got to thinking. You always had one fallback."

"You don't know anything."

"The Butterfly Club," I announced and experienced a glimmer

of satisfaction when she stiffened. It bolstered me to continue and my voice grew stronger. "You think Rita will release the trust when she learns how her son met you?"

"Whatever you think you know, Rita won't believe you. Especially when she finds out what a liar you are."

"What liars *we* are," I corrected.

"She'll listen to her son, not some attention-seeking whore she just met."

"You sure about that?" I fished in the tiny pocket Nicki had fortuitously sewn for me. She meant it for lipstick, but she would have approved of this far more. "You know why I love technology?"

"Cause you're a nerd with no friends?" Helena said.

"Because there's no hiding who you are. It's all right there for the taking. If you're good enough to find it. Even the oldest profession—say, a glorified whorehouse—uses electronic records." I held up a thumb drive. "Phil was a great tipper."

"What the... how could..." Helena was practically frothing at the mouth. "You hired someone to investigate me? That's pathetic. I'm not afraid of you."

"If you were smart, you would be." I tossed the drive to her and she nearly tumbled over her shredded skirt to catch it. "You've done some very bad things. Things I found in less time than it takes to order room service. Imagine what I could do with an entire afternoon."

"You're lying."

Whether it was from the rush of newfound power or the need to prove myself, I dove in and went for broke. "How do you think Anthony got caught? The little FBI fairy?"

"Oh no, Princess," Chase muttered. "What did you do?"

My mother gasped. "You? But why? How could you?"

"How could I not?" I shot back at her. "After all the suffering he caused? Everything he did to me?" I could still feel the fear paralyzing me that night. How I'd almost backed down until desperation had driven me over the edge. But I would never admit that to them. "He deserved much worse."

"I would have killed the motherfucker," Chase growled.

Helena held up a hand. "Don't listen to her, Mom. It's impossible. She's too stupid to pull that off."

"Stupid?" Chase snorted. "She's a fucking genius. Do you not know one goddamn thing about your own sister?"

Sadly, they knew nothing about me other than the roles they cast me in—villain, scapegoat, victim. Labels assigned before I was even born, designed to give them a false sense of control.

And like a puppet cutting her strings, I renounced those titles. "Helena, you blame me for Anthony and Mother leaving." I pointed at Brenda. "She would have left whether I was born or not because she's a selfish bitch." I expected Brenda to protest but she still seemed to be in shock over my part in Anthony's arrest. "But your father? Hell yeah. I am one hundred percent responsible for getting that sociopath off the streets. And I would do it again in a heartbeat."

Helena snarled. "You cost me everything." She lunged at me.

Chase grabbed her and with little effort, lifted her off her feet. He set her aside. "Stay," he ordered as if talking to a dog.

I pointed to the drive in Helena's hand. "He got what he deserved and now it's your turn. Except I'm not going to blow up your perfect little life. I am going to rain holy hell down on you."

Helena looked at me as if seeing me for the first time.

I stared back and, as if a filter had been removed, the woman before me stood in perfect focus. I no longer saw Helena my torturer. I saw a pathetic excuse for a human who relied on others for her wellbeing. I saw weakness. I saw prey.

I was the shark now.

"You've got more to lose," Helena threatened but the quiver in her voice betrayed her. "I'll tell everyone who you are and what you've done."

My lips tilted in a mocking smile. "Mutually assured destruction? Are you that dense? Who do you think will claw her way back up? I've done it before. What have you accomplished when not on your back?"

"You're bluffing. No way you'd risk your cushy life for me."

My insides burned with the need to make her suffer. I wanted to watch her go down in flames then dance on her fucking ashes. But she was right. Given the money I'd scammed for Anthony and my subsequent life of hacking, I would be collateral damage.

And as much as I relished this newly discovered power, I wasn't them. The blackness I feared should I ever go down this path did not inherently live inside me. If I went dark side now, I'd be choosing to infect myself with the same hatred and spite I sought to escape from.

"I'll leave you alone," I offered quickly before I reconsidered, "but if I get an inkling of you so much as saying either of my names, as God—or whatever demon you worship—is my witness, I won't just ruin you, I will erase your very existence. You will have nothing. Not even your name."

Helena looked to our mother but Brenda, as usual, opted for self-preservation. "I told you her father's brilliant. Leave me out of this."

"That's not going to happen," I said. "By this time tomorrow, I'll know the name of your baby daddy."

Brenda's translucent skin paled to ghostly white. "I would never forgive you."

"Why should I care?"

"If you do, he'll stop paying."

"Then I'll make you the same deal. Forget about me and I'll stay out of your life."

"Are you blackmailing me?" Brenda asked.

I shrugged. "It's the only language this family understands."

"Agreed," she replied without hesitation. "My children have caused me nothing but grief. I am more than happy to eradicate their faces from my memory."

"You're talking about Lily, right?" Helena pointed at me. "This is all her fault. She's the one who—"

"Enough." Brenda held up a hand. "Your obsession with your sister has always clouded your judgement, but now, your paltry vendetta has brought the madness to *my* doorstep and I will not allow *you* to jeopardize my livelihood."

"Half-sister," Helena corrected.

"Stop it!" Brenda shouted. "You have not changed at all. You are still the same petty, jealous, obnoxious child I remember. At least Lily was tolerable."

"You always favored her," Helena whined. "Everything was always about Lily."

"That's preposterous." Brenda scoffed. "I never paid any attention to her."

The fact that she used neglecting her child as a defense for good parenting was truly a warped testament.

"Then why won't you admit we'd be better off if Lily never existed?" Helena pressed.

Brenda fisted her hands on her hips. "Stop talking before you cost me everything. We are accepting Lily's deal. Move on and forget about her. She's not worth it."

"Fine," Helena mumbled.

In that moment, they actually sounded like mother and daughter. It would have been amusing were I not smack in the epicenter of my own personal train-wreck. With that in mind, I turned to deal with Chase.

But he was gone.

26

My Looney Tunes ringtone interrupted what was supposed to be a distracting Star Wars marathon but I ignored it. I didn't need to look at the display to know it wasn't Chase. I also didn't need my heart to lurch every time the stupid thing rang.

A week since the incident I'd dubbed *The Broom Closet Massacre*, and Chase had been avoiding me as if I were a live grenade.

Not that it should have mattered. I was planning on ending it anyway.

Just not like this.

After his disappearing act that night, I'd tossed in bed alone, watching the clock numbers bleed together until finally relocating to the balcony where the ocean kept me company until sunrise.

I remembered as a kid, spending hours mesmerized by the waves, fantasizing about them sweeping me away to a magical land far away from my life.

Pathetic how, twenty years later, I was still wishing for the same thing.

When Chase returned the following morning, he had impatiently gathered our bags with no words and even less eye contact. After a tense elevator ride, he took two steps into the lobby, dropped our luggage, and banked left. Confused, I followed his movements and groaned when I realized his destination. George Junior had just emerged from the hotel restaurant, whistling to himself.

Without preamble, Chase blocked his path, drew his arm back, and landed a punch squarely on George Junior's flabby jaw. George Junior's round head snapped back and then he crumpled to the floor in a doughy heap, his toupee askew. Onlookers pointed and snapped cell phone pictures while Chase returned to collect our bags and exit the hotel.

A tedious plane ride ensued in which not even the luxury of Chase's private jet could offer any comfort. He immediately disappeared into a back room and I never saw him after that. Richard had met me at the runway and taken me home.

In Chase's eyes, I was no longer Jasmine Monroe, accomplished hacker/cyber-nerd who had launched his software product into the stratosphere. All he saw now was Lily, the street urchin who came from nothing but darkness and, according to his disdain, deserved exactly that. And he wondered why I did not tell him.

I also wondered what he would do with the information.

I wanted to believe he'd do nothing and leave it alone, but I had never seen this side of him before. Scorned Dangerous. Who knew what he was capable of? I couldn't take the risk. Which is why I needed to talk to him. To determine if he required persuading. I knew his buried secrets. And I would do anything to ensure his silence.

I hated that my mind went there.

The phone rang again, and I cursed when my heart did the involuntarily flippy thing. Dammit. I was going to end it with him anyway.

This time, I checked the display then answered.

"Hi, Wayne."

"Jasmine, how are you?"

"I'm fine," I lied. "How's the business venture?"

"Excellent. In fact, that's why I'm calling. I'm hoping you'll reconsider and join Project Stryker as lead programmer. That's the name we assigned. Catchy, huh?"

With the pet supply chain job winding down, I needed another project—more like a distraction—to keep me busy. I thought about Warrior, the software idea I'd created while working on Wolfe. The brilliant algorithm that analyzed company transactions and adapted to their patterns in order to flag anomalies and security breaches.

The one that belonged to Chase.

He had yet to develop it, so maybe now that I'd never see him naked again—I pushed the image of his sculpted body away like I was performing a mental exorcism— he'd let me collaborate with Brandon to bring my vision to fruition.

I knew even entertaining the idea was absurd. First, though it would benefit his company, his approval was as likely as barn animals flying around on jetpacks. Next, it would also mean seeing him in the office, tolerating the disdain in his eyes, and constantly being reminded about never seeing him naked again.

Christ! I was going to end it anyway.

"Jasmine, are you still there?"

"Yes." Same old patterns. Wayne talking. Chase dominating. "Stryker. Right. Catchy. I thought Teresa was..." *fucking it up? Wasting everyone's time?* "Running it," I finished.

"I'm afraid she's not producing like we hoped. This position requires focus, but she's too distracted with her private life. I thought she understood that but in light of her recent personal choices, I have my doubts."

"Why do you care what your workers do on their own time?"

"I care when it concerns Hale. I thought she had more sense than to allow him to get his hooks in her again, but he has manipulated her into doing just that. Now that they're back together, I find myself unable to trust her judgement. Or my company's proprietary secrets, especially since we added a new layer of complexity to the product."

I nearly dropped the phone. "Since when?"

"Since we've upgraded to a new platform. It is truly astounding. Nothing on this caliber has been done before. It will revolutionize financial based security."

"Not that," I snapped. "About Chase and Teresa. Together."

"Ah, yes," he answered. "Hale has a tendency of moving on quickly, or rather backwards in this case. Congratulations on dodging that proverbial bullet by the way."

What the hell was happening? And why was it happening so soon? Did Chase instruct his PR department to send out a press release the second we were over?

"You didn't know?" Wayne asked.

Not a huge leap, considering my response.

I sensed him trying to withhold his *I told you so* but apparently, not hard enough. "I'm sorry to be the one to say, 'I told you so'."

"Then don't."

He sighed. "If you still have doubts about his extracurriculars, check your phone. I'll be in touch soon."

Within seconds of disconnecting, a text popped up. I stabbed at the screen, missing the icon twice before it opened to display, in high pixelated glory, an image of Chase and Teresa.

My breath rushed out as if the pic had gone 3D and punched me in the gut.

They sat huddled together, heads bent in private communion, discussing something I assumed contributed to the satisfied glow on her face. The date stamp confirmed it as last night.

Always fucking Teresa.

I hurled my phone at the wall.

I did my best to subdue my violent urges before marching over to retrieve it. Good news… I threw like a girl so it was unharmed. Bad news… the stupid picture was still on the screen.

Fucking bastard!

Technically, I was the illegitimate one but if anyone dared mention that now, I'd punch them in the throat.

I hurried to my room, changed into jeans and a T-shirt, jammed my feet into a pair of sneakers, and bolted out the door. I hailed a cab and gave the driver Chase's address. I needed to make sure he kept his mouth shut anyway. Now seemed as good a time as any.

I tossed the driver a few bills before racing into the immaculate lobby. The doorman must not have received the press release because he escorted me to Chase's private elevator.

Chase met me wearing nothing but pajama bottoms and a severe scowl. The glass of amber liquid in his hand explained the smell of whiskey in the air.

When he made no move to invite me in, I took a page from his protocol manual and marched past him, straight into the great room.

He followed me, the scowl never leaving his face.

"Is your little slut here?" The last thing I needed was for Teresa to show up while I was negotiating his silence. That is why I came here, after all.

"What are you talking about?"

"Teresa."

The grooves in his forehead deepened. "What the fuck business is it of yours?"

"Were you with her last night?" Okay... maybe I had two reasons for being here.

"Still none of your fucking business but yes."

A stab of jealousy pierced through my wall of indifference. Though I'd seen the picture, hearing his admission twisted the knife deeper. "Worried your bed will cool down if you don't stuff a body in it right away?" Dumbass choice since that woman emitted as much warmth as a subzero freezer. Yet, he couldn't stay away from her. Why? What made her so damn special that he kept jumping back into her waiting claws? Hell, maybe he'd never left them. That *is* what she told me. Maybe she was telling the truth. "Have you secretly been with her this entire time?"

"Be very careful where you're going with this," he warned in a tight voice. "You're one to talk about secrets."

"Is that what this is about? Retaliation? I withheld personal information, so you leap into bed with the one woman I despise?" I shook my head. "You really do live up to your reputation as a philandering, callous, insensitive..." I ran out of adjectives. Dammit. Why couldn't I be as colorful as him when it came to ranting?

"I suggest you rethink your strategy of playing the victim here," he said, his eyes as frosty as the ice rattling in his glass. "It mistakenly assumes you possess a shred of moral high ground."

"You want an apology?" I snapped. "Fine. I'm sorry it happened."

"In other words, you're not sorry for lying. You're sorry I found out."

I remained silent. Denial would be another lie and we both knew it.

He let out a cynical snort. "That's probably the first honest thing you've said to me."

"As I recall, *you* pursued *me*. I did not force anything between us, nor am I the one who orchestrated those ridiculous rules keeping us out of each other's drama."

"No. You just conveniently hid behind them."

"It's not my fault they made you more attractive to someone in my predicament."

"Making me the perfect sucker," he said bitterly.

"This isn't about you, Chase. This is my life and I do whatever's necessary to protect it."

"From whom exactly?"

"From everyone." I swept my arm around. "The press, my sister, the man I grew up thinking was my father, every perennial bottom feeder out there. Take your pick."

His jaw tightened. "Good to know you hold me in such high company."

"Am I wrong? As soon as you found out, you hightailed it out of my life so fast, I'm surprised you slowed down long enough to dial Teresa's number."

"I have her on speed dial," he responded.

"You are such an asshole."

"It's truly astonishing how you can paint me as the bad guy." He raked his fingers through his hair, causing his muscles to ripple beneath his smooth skin.

I lost concentration for a half second. But it was enough.

He smirked.

"Dammit, go put a shirt on," I ordered.

"You're the uninvited guest here." His impudent smile widened. "If you want to fight on equal ground, feel free to strip."

My lip curled. "You're so predictable, it's boring. Do you ever think about anything besides sex?"

"Why would I?" His sharp tone ricocheted off the walls. "As I vividly recall, I'm nothing more than a fuck toy, minus the batteries. And now you have the audacity to storm in here and persecute me for following your lead?" With a wry smile, he raised his glass in a mock toast. "Congratulations, darling. You take hypocrisy to an unparalleled level." He knocked back the contents and was already halfway to the bar before he swallowed.

I averted my gaze from his taut back as he pulled the stopper from a decanter. "You could bang any red-blooded woman in this city, what is it about her you can't stay away from?"

He poured a generous refill before turning back to face me. "Maybe because she never lied to me."

"I lied to *everyone*."

"That's possibly the worst defense I've ever heard."

"I don't owe you an explanation."

"Ditto."

I glared at him.

He glared back.

With a loud huff, I broke eye contact. "You could have warned me before I saw you with her."

"Like you did before I walked in on your family reunion from hell?"

"You should have picked another woman," I yelled.

"And you should have told me who the fuck you really are," he shouted back.

"She's a manipulative whore."

"Your entire life is a manipulation."

"Everybody lies."

"Not like you they don't."

"Then why didn't you tell me about your wife?"

He froze.

Oh, shit.

I had no idea how much time passed but when he finally spoke, his voice was controlled fury. "Did you hack into my life?"

I knew I'd crossed the line, but there was no turning back. And why should I? My world had been torn open for him. Time for him to open a vein. "Obviously. And speaking of hypocrites, I'm not the only one keeping secrets."

"That's not a secret. That is none of your goddamn business."

"Cut the innocent attitude. You intentionally hid your past from me just like I did from you."

"Then tell me, Princess." There it was. That emotionless tone I'd heard him use in his office. The one that chilled me straight to my bones. "What entitles you, as my random fuck buddy, to hack into details of my life while you use my rules as a get out of jail free card?"

"In my situation, I can't risk unknowns. There's too much at stake. I had to make sure you weren't hiding something that could put me in jeopardy."

"And were you satisfied with what you found? Perhaps something to hold over me should I divulge your truth? Blackmail seems to be the way of your family."

I looked away, ashamed that I had considered it. But I would only use it if he drove me there. If I had no choice. "Will you divulge my truth?" I finally voiced the question I had come to ask.

"Don't worry." His voice was laced with disgust. "There'll be no need to use your insurance policy."

"Hey. I'm not responsible for the stupid shit you did. I didn't make you a liar. You were plenty good at it when I met you."

"I suppose I should take that as a compliment, coming from the master."

"Good enough that God knows what else you've been lying to me about." My eyes widened as I realized the implications. "Have you been playing me this entire time? Was Teresa telling the truth? Did you seduce me away from Lyndham so she could get that contract?"

"For fuck's sake. Are we back to that?"

"Have you been screwing with me from the start?"

He scrubbed his hand down his face. "I swear, every time you open your mouth, something crazier comes out."

"That's not an answer."

"Because you don't deserve one."

"This is why I don't get close to men," I seethed. "They're not satisfied until they fuck you in *and* out of the bedroom."

"Like women are any better," he retorted. "You're all untrustworthy, dishonest, and fully deranged." He gazed up at the ceiling as if pleading for divine intervention to drop a sane one in his lap. "I don't think there's a rational one on this planet."

"You should know," I said as I headed towards the door. "You're working your way through them fast enough."

"Damn right," he yelled back. "That's what fuck toys do."

I stomped into the elevator and waited for the doors to close. Seconds later, I heard the sound of glass shattering.

27

"Brandon's on hold," Sue called out. "Are we speaking to him or is he on our shit list by association?"

Only one way to find out. I picked up the receiver. "Hey, Brandon."

"Hey, gorgeous. What's going on between you and Chase?"

After a week-long moratorium on *he who shall not be named*, the mention of him had me reaching for my stress ball. I'd taken to buying them in bulk. "I'm fine, thank you for asking, and nothing's going on. Why?"

"Because we are getting started on Warrior and when your name came up, he blew a gasket."

I winced at the reference to my beloved brainchild. Although I'd been handsomely compensated for my brilliance, money could never replace the opportunity to develop my masterpiece. And no one could do it better.

"If he barks at me one more time," Brandon continued, "you're getting a new partner and I demand Vice President of Awesomeness business cards."

"Don't tease me. You're never leaving him."

"True," he admitted. "He'd be a mess without my stabilizing influence, but even I can't get him off the warpath. I don't know what's messing him up more. You or the Chinese investors. My money's on you."

"I doubt I have that much influence and did you say Chinese?"

"Yeah. They're trying to undercut his acquisition deal."

My instincts buzzed at the news, though my head told me it was probably nothing. Still, I felt compelled to ask. "Brandon, what company is Chase trying to buy?"

"It's confidential until the owner works out his personal legal issues and can sell free and clear."

"I can keep a secret." If he only knew how well.

Brandon sighed. "It's Lyndham. Erik Lyndham is retiring and selling off his company."

Ni hao.

Oh, shit.

I slapped my palm against my forehead. I should have seen the signs. "Why so hush-hush?"

"Lyndham's wife found out he's been dipping his wick in anything with lipstick and she's out for his balls in the divorce. He's dragging the sale until after she signs the settlement papers so she can't touch the profits. The douchebag would rather cancel the deal than give her a cent. Real class act."

First... ewww.

And second... that explains Chase's phone calls.

"Where do they stand now?" I asked.

"Chase and Erik made a verbal agreement. They were working out the final details when another offer appeared. Someone must have leaked that Erik was looking to sell. It's strange though. The offer is weirdly precise and way too generous."

Because their information was being fed to them by an inside man. An inside man who stood to gain a fortune should his play for the company succeed. Chase had no idea Wayne was spearheading the opposition.

Not my business. Not my problem.

"Is Chase going to lose?"

"Nah. I've learned never to bet against him. If he wants something badly enough, he gets it."

Like he once did with me.

"Brandon, what do you know about these Chinese investors?"

Hello? What part of 'Not your business?' is confusing?

Apparently, all of it because I was diving in.

"Alright, egghead, what aren't you telling me?"

The last thing I wanted was for Chase to blame me for causing a panic. Nor did I want him thinking that I cared enough to do so. "After listening to Chase bitch about this deal non-stop, I'm curious. That's all. I won't tell a soul. I promise." I was the most trustworthy liar there ever was.

"Lyndham came to Chase, said he was retiring, and offered Chase first dibs on buying the company. Chase agreed and after some gnarly negotiating, they came to a verbal agreement that would be finalized after Erik fixed his wife drama. Chase accepted his word. Then a consortium of Chinese investors decided to throw their hats in the ring." He paused. "Do Chinese wear hats?"

"It's called a douli. Keep going."

"At first, Lyndham honored his agreement with Chase and told them to go pound sand, but they sweetened the offer, and being the duplicitous jackhole that he is, Erik's now drooling at the windfall. It doesn't make sense, though. Their offer is more than the company is worth. It's like they know something we don't."

Like something Wayne presented to the Chinese investors that made them salivate enough to finance his purchase of Lyndham?

It had to be the project for which Wayne kept trying to recruit me. I tried to recall our conversation. Damn, why did he have to be so boring that I zoned out when he talked?

Something truly astounding... never been done before... blah blah blah... will revolutionize financial based security.

A shiver of apprehension ran through me. What were the odds of two innovative and revolutionary financial-based software ideas simultaneously in play? Nah, it couldn't be. Only Brandon and Chase had seen my code.

Still, the facts spoke for themselves: First, we had two men in competition. Second, they both were after the same company. And third, they were spearheading similar proprietary software projects. As the quote goes, 'Once is happenstance. Twice is coincidence. But three times... that's enemy action'.

And if Wayne had stolen Warrior, then he had taken *my* idea.

I pumped my stress ball faster.

Of all the shady, underhanded, rotten...

And this was coming from a liar and cyber-thief. Go figure.

"You still haven't answered my question," Brandon interrupted my internal rampage. "What happened between you two?"

"It's complicated."

He gave a knowing laugh. "That's grown-up code for 'I don't want to deal, so I'm taking my toys and going home'."

"Hanging up now." I disconnected then dialed another number.

Wayne answered on the second ring.

"Tell me more about Stryker."

Clack, clack, clack.

I attacked the keyboard like it owed me rent money. And for

what? To dig into a far-fetched hunch I didn't want substantiated for a man I never wanted to see again.

When had my life stopped making sense?

I reminded myself it never had.

I also reminded myself that this wasn't for Chase. It was for Warrior. *My* professional legacy.

I typed faster.

"What did that computer do to you?" Nicki asked as she barged into my room. "I can hear you pounding on that thing from the kitchen. Are you picturing Chase's face on it, or is it frustration from not pounding *him* anymore?"

"I told you. In this house, there shall be no mention of that blasphemous name."

"This is unfamiliar territory for you, so I'll overlook the theatrics. But here's a thought. Have you tried talking to him? And by talking, I mean not yelling."

"Nothing to say."

"Spoken by a woman who's doomed to live her elder years in the company of twenty cats. Should I start clipping Purina coupons for you now?"

"Have you forgotten you used to hate him?"

"I used to hate avocados too, but now find myself craving the occasional guacamole. People change."

"No. They don't." Humans always embodied their worst selves. Or, in this case, our true selves. No matter how much distance I put between myself and Lily, I'd never outrun her sins. And no matter how much attention Chase lavished on a female, he would always be a womanizing playboy. "He is and forever will be a man-whore who goes around fucking who he pleases."

"And pleasing who he fucks," she quipped.

I glared at her.

"Sorry. Too soon?" She perched on the edge of my bed. "Look,

I don't know what he did since you won't go into details, but it's not like me to back a losing horse."

"Don't you mean horse's ass?"

She shook her head. "This is the anger stage. Hang on to it. It beats what comes next."

"I don't understand."

"No, you probably don't." And with that cryptic remark, she stood and walked to the door. "How about a Better Than Sex Chocolate Cake to cheer you up?"

I nodded, unwilling to admit that after Chase, it would forever be known as plain old chocolate cake.

I returned to my keyboard abuse. The sooner I finished, the sooner I could forget about the bastard who'd just ruined my favorite dessert. Without breaking a sweat, I bypassed Lyndham's firewall, located Wayne's files, and zeroed in on Project Stryker. Or as I soon determined... Warrior. Yup, on my screen, plain as the Princess Leia Pez dispenser propped beside my laptop, was my code. My poor baby—inspired by a late-night Cheetos and Coke Zero bender—hijacked from its creator and forced to live as a hostage amongst the inept.

Why was I not surprised by my lack of surprise?

Because people suck.

And since Wayne didn't know I created it, the idiot had unwittingly offered me a job to work on my own concept. I would have laughed if I wasn't so pissed off. And curious. How had he stolen my project in the first place? Okay, technically, it was Chase's project but like a helicopter parent long after their child leaves the nest, I would never let it go.

The answer required another hack which, under normal circumstances, classified as a no-brainer but not this time. Not when I had just declared the recipient dead to me.

Screw it. He'll never know.

My typing softened as if I were physically sneaking onto Predator's premises. I frowned at my pounding heart. What was this? Amateur hour?

Get a grip.

Though I expected it, finding the malicious software on Predator's server still made my blood sizzle. The infiltrator allowed the perp access to Wolfe, Warrior, and damn near anything else they wanted. The hidden code was more than respectable. It would have to be to get past Chase's formidable security. But it also seemed familiar. Every hacker had a style, almost like a signature, and I'd seen this one before. Now, if I could just remember where...

My jaw dropped.

Sterling.

Wayne had hired Sterling to steal Warrior!

28

A shrill beep sliced through my brain and my arm shot out, knocking over everything on my nightstand except the infernal alarm clock. That necessitated opening my eyes, not easy after multiple bouts of insomnia.

And it was all Chase's fault.

A month apart and memories of our time together still randomly popped up throughout the day. And as for the nights, they were just plain evil. I missed falling asleep against his hard body and waking to find his strong arms around me. I missed the feel of him beside me and inside me. Lord, that man possessed the ability to make me come like no other. All it took was that devilish gleam in his eyes or a few filthy suggestions and I was reduced to goo.

He was too talented for his own good.

He was too talented for *my* good.

And those were the good nights. On the worst occasions, my visions featured a leading lady—usually Teresa—wrapped around him like a venomous snake. Those dreams had me waking up wanting to scrub my brains out with bleach.

None of this made sense. How could a lifetime of nothingness be so easily obliterated by a man with wealth, beauty, and the accompanying promiscuous lifestyle? A man who rolled out his conditions before touching a woman then watched with amusement as she clamored to sign her name—or more likely draw an illiterate X—on the dotted line.

Say what you will about emptiness, but at least it came with its own numbing agent. Now, I was relegated to feeling things in places that were impervious to logic and reason. Places I never knew existed. Places that scared the hell out of me.

It was too much.

Never one to underestimate the power of denial, I searched for the apathy I knew still lived inside me. It required digging much deeper than before, but when I finally reached it, it enveloped me like a favorite blanket. This I knew. This would get me through another day.

Sue was at her desk when I entered the office, a strange expression on her face. "Uh oh. Don't tell me one of the Pettery Barn employees locked themselves out again." Due to their overkill security, Jerry's workers spent more time barred from their system than working in it.

"Not that." Sue's lime green beret shifted as she pointed. "This."

I followed her finger to the headline displayed on her screen. *Predator Industries Acquires Lyndham Incorporated.*

My ribcage constricted at the picture of Chase, handsome as the devil I knew him to be, shaking hands with a dapperly dressed Erik Lyndham. Although years apart, both men exuded a seductive lady-killing vibe. The kind that promised a good time before leaving you with regret as your breakfast companion. Case in point, this entire debacle started with Erik's inability to keep it in his pants.

"It's weird," Sue speculated. "Do you remember the rumor a few weeks back about the cyberattack on Lyndham?"

"Alleged cyberattack and yes."

"They declared it a hoax, right?"

"Yes." They had no choice but to deny it. Wayne could not report the destruction of a product he stole without incriminating himself. Similar to my inability to implicate Sterling without doing the same. Touché. Free passes for everyone.

"And now Chase buys them out?"

I shrugged.

Sue's gaze on me sharpened. "You wouldn't know anything about this, would you?"

"Me?" My voice dripped with sainthood. "Are you insinuating I launched the cyberattack?"

She raised her brows.

"Why would I—oh, hell." I sucked at being coy, and she wasn't buying it anyway. "Yes. I used *Jasmine's Super Virus* to annihilate a stolen program on Lyndham's servers."

Okay, my program needed a cooler name, but the Trojan's ingenuity surpassed the lousy title. Once unleashed, it tore through Wayne's data like a paper shredder on steroids until no trace of Warrior/Stryker remained.

To make matters worse, I had also discovered that Wayne was responsible for Sterling's original attack on Wolfe. Back when Chase had first hired me and learned about my skills. Back when he had looked at me with respect and not the contempt he wielded now.

I consoled myself by imagining Wayne peeing his pants when he opened the anonymous message waiting for him the next morning. It detailed his transgressions to the accompaniment of menacing music, chosen carefully by yours truly. Nothing says you're a lowdown prick like the proper ambience.

Sometimes it scared me how much I enjoyed being bad.

"Should we expect blowback?" Sue asked, as if I broke the law all the time. Probably because I did.

"Nah. We're the good guys here."

"Uh huh." She didn't sound convinced. "Does Chase know?"

"No. And we're keeping it that way. Especially since it was stolen from him in the first place. Understand?"

"Not really but my lips are sealed."

My loyal soldier to the end.

The office phone rang, and I continued to the kitchen to make a cup of tea. I'd just sat at my desk when Sue's voice interrupted. "Teresa Stark's on hold."

Chalk it up to morbid curiosity but I picked up the receiver. What could that bitch want? Thanks to me, she should be out of a job. A small consolation.

"Jasmine, dear." She spoke too warmly for my comfort. "I heard through the grapevine you're no longer involved with Predator."

A gorgeous, emerald-eyed grapevine? "That's correct."

"In light of the recent acquisition, Chase has decided to take me." I scowled at her choice of words but remained silent. "You are now speaking to the top coder at Predator."

Unless she weaponized the venom in her personality and used it to murder every programmer there, I highly doubted it. I almost asked her who she slept with to attain the fictitious status but sobered when I remembered. "You wasted no time ingratiating yourself to the new boss."

"Chase couldn't wait to get started with me." Again, her choice of words grated, but I refused to take the bait. "As I believe you know, we have a long history together. In fact, he tasked me with implementing the next up and coming breakthrough. I believe you call it Project Warrior though the final name will be my decision of course." Her gloating seeped through the connection as odorous as noxious fumes.

"That's Brandon's project," I said in a tight voice. She had to be mistaken. For all of Chase's many faults, he'd proven himself to be a savvy businessman which meant not condemning a vital project to slaughter. But then again, who knew which head was making his decisions these days?

"Not anymore," she laughed.

Fantastic. In reclaiming Warrior from Wayne's purloined grip, all I'd done was dump it into the hands of another undeserving moron. Once again, no good deed went unpunished.

"And not to kiss and tell," she continued as if confiding in a best friend, "but Chase finally acknowledged our special bond and agreed that with our history, placing rules on our relationship would be silly. We have evolved to a point where work and play are both possible. A true partnership on all levels now."

So much for a sliver of a silver lining. "How wonderful for you. Goodbye."

"Wait. Chase said everything we have so far originated with you." The grudging tone indicated she'd rather break a nail than acknowledge my brilliance.

"It's yours now. Goodbye."

"Stop. Please."

The desperation in that last word made me pause.

She spoke quickly. "I'd like you to deconstruct it for me."

What the fuck?

"I know this is awkward," she hedged.

"No. Showing up at a party with the same white dress is awkward. This is offensive. If you need help, go sleep with someone smarter than you and for the record, you're not my type."

"Need I remind you." Her desperate tone turned to one of chilled superiority. "Your contract with Predator mandates your assistance with any work product you developed. You have no choice."

"Sure I do. Tell Chase to sue me." I slammed the phone down with enough force to rattle the pens in my mug.

"What was that?" Sue appeared at my door, a yellow legal pad in her hand.

"Stupid men making stupid decisions with their stupid dicks."

"I figured as much." She scrawled something on the pad. "If it helps, we can burn a hunky, green-eyed doll in effigy?"

I opened my mouth to ask where in tarnation she'd acquire such an item but thought better of it. Hopefully, she wasn't writing down the ingredients. Then again, if we added a black-haired female, dressed in all white...

What was it about obnoxious women that turned men into drooling dumbasses? Sure, she was sexy and sophisticated and had that slinky Marilyn Monroe vibe, but from the way they clamored to do her bidding, there had to be more. Maybe a hellion in the sack? Visions of her working those talents on Chase made my blood pressure spike.

Can this day get any worse?

"Brandon called. He needs a favor."

Why do I ask stupid questions?

Sue began to read from the notepad. "Predator is holding a retreat next week at a local hotel to assimilate Lyndham's new developers. Brandon's scheduled to give a presentation on Wolfe but can't make it."

"Conflicting surfing competition?"

"No clue but he'd rather not cancel on the grounds that Chase has been a major dickhole lately." She looked up from her notes. "Brandon's words. Not mine."

I held up a hand. "Stop right there. I'm not helping Chase ever again."

"Chase will be tied up in meetings at Predator and doesn't care who does the sessions," she reassured me. "And this is not for Chase. It's for Brandon, the man who selflessly saved our asses after your... accident."

"Not the guilt trip," I groaned.

"It's one session with you and a bunch of fellow nerds worshipping your every word. Nobody knows it better, including Brandon himself. They'll be lucky to have you." She pointed at the pad. "His words again."

Anyone but Brandon and this conversation would have been over faster than *Jasmine's Super Virus* mowed down Wayne's files.

"You owe him," Sue cajoled.

Fuck.

"*We* owe him."

Fuck, fuck.

"Which means I'm not leaving until you agree."

Fuck, fuck, fuck.

She smiled. "I'll put it on your calendar."

I reread the email I'd been typing for the last hour then deleted it again. Much like every other task I attempted, it was gibberish.

By afternoon, I'd snapped at Jerry twice, programmed multiple lines of spaghetti code, and forgot where I'd placed every item I touched. I finally surrendered to my uselessness and opened an online logic puzzle. Better to be unproductive than damaging.

I'd just submitted my answer matrix when Sue entered, a stack of mail in hand. Finally, something I couldn't screw up. She dropped it on my desk then retreated to answer a call.

Since Sue handled client related correspondence, it left miscellaneous items for me. I sorted through workshop registrations and programming magazines before stopping at a nondescript envelope. It felt heavier than the others with my name printed in neat letters. I tore it open and read the note.

Dear Lily,

Yes, I know who you are. If you want to know who I am, meet me at Flo's Diner in Lower Manhattan. Wednesday at 8:00 A.M.

Sincerely,

Your Former Admirer

P.S. I hope you enjoy my gift.

I tilted the envelope and the lily pin fell out.

29

I shifted in the booth while my eyes remained on the entrance. I'd arrived at the diner early to secure a seat with a clear line of sight to the door and easy access to an exit. Not difficult since this metal deathtrap was shaped like one long bullet.

I spared a glance for the waitress as she dropped off a glass of water that I had no intention of touching. Ever since I received the letter, nothing settled in my stomach.

This is a bad idea, I reminded myself for the hundredth time. But what else could I do? Allow some anonymous psycho to lord my past over me?

And then he entered.

Every kid has a monster from childhood. One that lives under the bed or in the far recesses of a closet, waiting for the cover of darkness before emerging to wreak havoc.

Not mine.

Mine walked amongst us in broad daylight, a flesh and blood being who terrorized my waking hours. One who indoctrinated my life with so much fear, it became as routine as breathing. And now he was here, sauntering down the aisle, horror incarnate.

"Hello, Lily." It was the voice of the devil, deep and terrible, and it conjured up a sickening mixture of revulsion and dread. He settled in the bench across from me. "I wish I could say it's nice to see you but we both know that would be a lie."

I could only stare at the man I grew up thinking was my father. Anthony Brooks.

The waitress returned and I watched in disbelief as he ordered a cup of coffee like a normal human being. He offered her a wink and she grinned at the charisma responsible for conning many a sensible person out of their life savings. No one would suspect that the slicker-than-oil smile masked a conniving sociopath.

He looked back at me. "Are you planning on speaking, girl?"

"Prison," I squeaked out. "How?" Had he escaped? If so, he wouldn't be patronizing a restaurant in Manhattan.

"I am a reformed man," he announced with a flourish.

Though I doubted he'd found Jesus in prison, I did notice other changes. He was fit, lean, and in better shape than pre-incarceration. A few extra creases lined his handsome face and gray tinged his blond temples, but other than those characteristics of aging, he appeared just the same.

Which meant just as deadly.

He extended his leg alongside the table to display a flashing security bracelet attached to his ankle. "Courtesy of the US Department of Justice."

That didn't help. Put a vicious dog on a leash and it only made the animal more aggressive.

His pale blue eyes considered me, sharp, calculating, and free from the alcoholic haze I remembered. "You turned into a looker, I'll give you that. Just like your mother."

"The only thing I share with her is the desire to be away from you." An underlying tremor threaded my brave words. I hoped he didn't notice.

A pleased smile crossed his face. Of course he noticed. Bullies drew strength from the fear of others, absorbing it as energy to power their evil. "Kitten found her claws," he drawled. "Another trait you picked up from her."

"Or my real father," I said and waited to see his reaction.

His brows pitted together. "I was hoping to spring that little fact on you. Who enlightened you?"

"Helena," I answered, all too willing to shift his displeasure to her.

"Helena," he scoffed. "She was more than happy to spill her guts about your identity before her wedding, but now that she's sitting pretty, she won't even utter your name. That's what she gets for marrying a pussy. Made her soft."

Helena's silence bolstered me. It represented my first victory against these accursed people. Something I never dreamed of as a child. Maybe there was hope.

Anthony reached for a napkin, and I jerked back from the sudden movement as if zapped by a live wire.

And transported myself right back to my private hell.

He smiled, that same satisfied smirk he wore when beating the shit out of me. "Stop being a baby. If I wanted to hurt you, you'd be back in the hospital. Speaking of… did you enjoy my present?"

"The pin," I whispered. "How?"

The waitress returned with his coffee and flashed him an inviting smile before moving on. I watched with amazement as those weapons—also known as his hands—performed the innocuous task of stirring in cream and sugar. I wasn't fooled. I knew the damage they could do.

When he shifted back to me, his scowl returned. "I assumed even a drug addict could take on a scrawny girl. My fault for hiring cheap labor but in my defense"—he gestured to his ankle hardware—"I didn't have many options."

An ocean of panic reared up. He was coming for me and there was nothing I could do. I'd never make it.

"Answer me this, Lily. How many men would allow their wife's bastard to live under their roof? I'd say that more than a little gratitude is warranted for such an act of goodwill."

Although the last person who said that to me did not fare well, this was an entirely different animal. A much more lethal one who packed a stronger punch. But I'd take that punch any day before I said thank you.

His face darkened, emphasizing the ice in his eyes. "Especially when your pissy little attitude drove my wife away."

"She left you for a Greek tycoon," I blurted.

He reared back as if I'd slugged him. "Who told you that?"

"She did."

"Your mother? You saw her? Where?" He whipped his head around as if expecting her to emerge from the kitchen hoisting a tray full of hotcakes.

Holy cow. He still loves her.

After everything she put him through, the man still wanted her. How fucked up was that? Love truly was some messed up shit.

"Where is she?" he repeated.

"I don't know. She disappeared. She's good at that." Somehow, he'd find a way to pin that on me too.

"Where did you see her?"

"Helena's wedding."

He let out a snort. "Why would Helena invite you? She despises you."

"She wanted family there to impress her new in-laws." *And to let me know how much my own mother hates me.*

"No, she wanted *me* there," he corrected. "Not a charity case reject. But the bastard Feds wouldn't allow it. Because of them, my poor little baby girl had to get married without her daddy."

It took all my strength not to roll my eyes.

"But there are benefits to prison," he said as he raised his cup for another grueling pause. "It gives a man ample time to reflect on life, people, and the circumstances that led to his arrest." He kept his voice low but each word held intent. "You disappeared without any warning right before the job I planned. The one I spent months prepping for. That score was going to set us up for life."

"You mean set *you* up for life." Once he didn't need me anymore, he would have either turned me in or killed me. Either way, I would have been history.

"Soon after that, the Feds showed up with a warrant full of anonymously gained facts like my bank accounts, client list, investors, statements, hell even my calendar entries. Care to explain that?"

I didn't need to. We both knew it was me. He may have been a legend at breaking the law, but I was so much better. A fact his ego would never forgive me for.

His face contorted with rage, and I flinched at the savagery in his eyes. "You left your sister without a family. You deserve to die for that."

Then just as quickly, his mask fell into place, once again the consummate gentleman out for a spot of coffee. I couldn't take much more of this. And neither could my heart. It was already on the verge of exploding from overexertion.

His voice was calm when he spoke again. "Which is why at first, I was livid when the druggie failed. But then I started to think."

A perilous act for a lunatic.

"Maybe prison has made me magnanimous, but I've decided

to give you another chance to finish what we started. You're going to do one last job for me."

"I don't work for you anymore."

"You do when I say you do," he said coldly. "Thanks to your actions, the Feds confiscated my assets, which gives you the perfect opportunity to make amends for your betrayal."

I didn't like where this was headed. "What are you talking about?"

"I'm out while I assist the Feebs with an embezzlement case in their New York office. When we finish, I go back, except you're going to make sure that doesn't happen. I know of a substantial sum sitting in an offshore bank account. You are going to secure those funds and place them in an account under a new identity that you will create for me. Once you do that, I'll consider your debt paid."

A trickle of dread slid down my spine to join the other hundred. "But... I... I can't."

"But... but..." he mocked. "You deserve a fate far worse for what you did. You're getting off easy."

To unleash this monster on the world would be unforgivable. I'd already caused enough harm. I couldn't bear the responsibility of additional damage. "And if I refuse? It's too late to report me to your FBI pals."

"True, but public persecution can be harsher than the law. Especially when people learn that a prominent criminal's daughter, who was complicit in his crimes, has been living with a fabricated identity, preying upon them. I know details of everything you did for me, Lily, and you have plenty to answer for. Don't ever forget that."

I wish I could but I remembered it all. The money I'd stolen, the data I'd manipulated, the innocent people I'd hurt. How he made me target the weak, knowing they'd never fight back. And how he would punish me when I refused. He enjoyed hurting people. Even more than that, he enjoyed making me hurt them because he knew the toll it took on me. Especially that last job. The one that changed everything. I could still feel the darkness branded on my soul.

And now he wanted me to do it again.

"This account isn't yours, is it?" I asked.

He laughed, his amusement like a rusty knife twisting in my back. "What do you think?" He fished in his pocket and withdrew a card. "You have two weeks to make it happen. I'll be in touch." He dropped it on the table and rose. "Thanks for the coffee."

I glanced down at the row of neatly written numbers. When I looked up, he was gone. I shot to my feet, raced down the hallway, and barely made it to the bathroom before I vomited.

30

My Looney Tunes ringtone jolted me from my nightmare. Cursing, I fumbled until I found my cellphone tangled in the sheets.

"Hello," I mumbled.

"Do you know what time it is?" Sue yelled.

"Too early the fuck'o'clock," I groaned. "What do you want?"

"You're supposed to give Brandon's lecture in two hours, and I haven't heard from you since yesterday."

After leaving the diner in a fugue state, I'd gone straight home where I hacked Anthony's records to find the bastard wasn't lying. The government had come to see him as an asset in solving financial cases. I'd also hacked the account he wanted me to steal from and, after tracing it through a zillion shell companies—the laundering version of nesting dolls—I discovered it belonged to the Russian mafia. A group that specialized in creative ways of killing people.

After that, my options went from bad to worse. Not do what Anthony demanded and have him ruin me. Do what he wanted and have him ruin me—I wasn't stupid enough to believe he'd leave me alone—or the scariest option of all... he'd keep me around to do his bidding.

I vowed that would never happen again.

But he couldn't break me if he couldn't find me. Which brought me to *my* final option. My 'In case of emergency, break out new identity' last resort. Paranoid by nature, I'd set up everything I needed to start over for exactly a situation like this. My contingency plans always had contingency plans.

My heart hurt at leaving everyone and everything I'd grown to care about, but that was my fault for allowing sentimental attachments. People like me seldom got a happy ending. It helped if I viewed this as a trial run. Lessons learned. The next go-around would be different.

"Are you there?" Sue snapped.

"What?"

"Get going!" she shouted.

"Okay, okay." I disconnected and ran to the bathroom. A quick shower, minimal makeup, and a comb through my hair took care of the basics. I reached for the first black dress in my closet. Perfect for someone dying on the inside.

I entered the hotel lobby and paused to read Sue's meticulous email which included the conference room, presentation time, a map, and a guilt-inducing list of Saint Brandon's acts of kindness in case I tried to back out. If I wasn't so annoyed, I would have applauded her manipulation tactics.

The room was empty when I arrived, so I used the extra time to do what any productive person would. Curse the jackass who put me here. Of all the asinine, hare-brained, moronic, idiotic—

and every other synonym for stupid—ideas Brandon had ever concocted, this was the worst.

I stopped at the front of the room where Brandon had hooked up his laptop to a projector. A note lay on the table beside it.

Hey J,

I'm sure you can recite this stuff from memory but in case your brain shorts out, the material is loaded on my laptop. Please leave it in my room when you're done. Room #620. Keycard is in the bag.

You're a lifesaver.

Love, Brandon

"Well, this is a nice surprise." A tall man sporting a thick mustache entered. "We thought we'd have to stare at Brandon's ugly mug for the next two hours." The people behind him laughed as they filed in and took their seats.

"Jasmine?" Wayne spoke from the doorway. "What are you doing here?"

I groaned. Seriously? Wayne was working for Chase? The man he stole from? He was either delusional, brave, or stupid. My money was on the latter. It seemed to be a common affliction these days.

Either way, I wanted to welcome him with a knee to the nuts.

A flash of white behind him caught my eye and Teresa stepped forward, a sneer on her beautiful face. "Looks like someone was set straight regarding her contractual obligations."

Oh, how I wanted to smash my fist in her nose and watch blood gush all over her white suit. Instead, I inhaled a swami breath that didn't work—why did I keep trying them?—then opted for another one of Brenda's tricks. I imitated her erect posture followed by her obnoxiously haughty tone. "We're beginning the presentation so either take a seat or leave."

Teresa whipped around and with some lame comment about my lack of qualifications, she disappeared.

That worked better than planned. Unfortunately, Wayne did not follow. Instead, he chose a seat in front, folded his hands, and waited like a model student.

Kiss ass.

I began with an overview of Wolfe then broke down the key components and structure. As usual, my love of the subject matter superseded my annoyance with Brandon, Wayne, and even Chase. I flowed through the material and especially enjoyed it when the Lyndham programmers expressed their appreciation for the ingenuity behind its creation. Everyone but Wayne. The session ended with a few questions, three offers for collaboration, and a request for a date.

"Excellent presentation." Wayne approached when the room cleared out. "But please tell me you're not here in an attempt to sway Hale back from Teresa." The revulsion in his tone, on his face, in his posture, and pretty much oozing from everywhere else, indicated his contempt for that plan.

"Here." I unplugged the laptop cord and handed it to him. "If you're going to stand there and judge, at least make yourself useful."

He sighed and began winding it around his hand. "I'm sorry about Stryker. If we had succeeded, our futures would be brighter than this. It was an incredible idea..."

My incredible idea.

"...in theory. But it proved to be flawed. Too many kinks to work through. We had to scrap it."

I cursed under my breath. Though I never expected him to

admit he was a thieving lowlife, blaming the software was just plain tacky. "Are you sure it wasn't your team that butchered it?"

He blinked. "Of course not. Teresa is top-notch."

And now, thanks to Chase, that bitch was getting another shot at Warrior. Would she recognize the code? Doubtful. Her software skills were as basic as her color palette.

I jammed Brandon's computer into the case then held it open. Wayne placed the cord inside and I zipped it closed. With a final sweep, I swung the bag over my shoulder, grabbed my purse, and exited the room.

Wayne followed. "Please listen, Jasmine. Doing favors for Hale will not get you anywhere. He's already moved on." He fell in step beside me. "I'm only telling you this because I don't want him to make a fool of you again."

We reached the elevators and I stopped to push the button. "I wasn't aware there was a first time."

"Where are we going?"

"To Chase's room where I'm going to fall on my knees and beg for forgiveness. And if it means doing other things while I'm on my knees... well, whatever it takes. You're welcome to come along and watch."

His eyes bugged out. "WHAT?"

"For Christ's sake, Wayne. Why can't you mind your own business?"

"Because we had something special before Hale ruined it, and we owe it to ourselves to explore what could have been. We are perfect for each other. I'll prove it to you."

He planted his mouth on mine.

Taking advantage of my shock, he slid his tongue past my frozen lips. The intrusion snapped me back to reality and I shoved him away. "What the hell are you doing?"

"Didn't you feel something?"

"No, but I'm sure you'll feel this." A satisfying crack echoed as I slapped him across the face. He rubbed his cheek and stared at me, slack jawed.

In the land of perfect timing, the elevator would have appeared or he would have disappeared. But when neither happened, we ended up staring at each other in awkward silence.

"Screw this," I mumbled and went in search of the stairs. Great, now I'd have to haul my sorry ass up six flights because of that idiot.

I still couldn't help but smile. Although inappropriate, his behavior had legitimized a much-needed excuse to smack his stupid face. Not as much fun as punching Teresa, but we take what we're given.

When I entered Brandon's room, I paused to look around. The suite was as big as an apartment and included a comfortable sitting area, an alcove with a large desk, and a door which I assumed led to a separate bedroom and bath. Brandon must be doing something right.

I walked to the desk and placed the computer bag down. Uh oh. Why was a computer already here? And why did I recognize the screensaver?

Oh, shit.

I turned to run but it was too late. The bedroom door opened and Chase walked out. He stopped, shock plastered on his face.

My heartbeat quickened as my eyes drank him in. He was wearing slacks and a button-down shirt with the sleeves rolled up. He looked perfect. Better than perfect. Except for the glower directed at me.

I stupidly held up the key card.

"That went missing yesterday." He walked over and plucked it from my fingers. "Why do you have it?"

"Brandon," I said quickly. "I thought this was Brandon's room."

He put the card in his pocket. "You certainly get around, don't you?"

"No, I'm returning his—" Wait. Why was I defending myself? "Says the man who acts like a horny teenager while making project decisions."

"Is that what this is about? Warrior?" He barked out a laugh. "Get over it, sweetheart. It's my fucking project and I can—"

"Do whatever you damn well please with it," I finished. "Blah, blah, I get it. It's like talking to a wall. There's no getting through to you."

"And your genius solution is to crash my event with your new boyfriend? Very mature."

New boyfriend? Where was that coming from? It didn't matter. If it irritated him, I was all in. I planted my fists on my hips. "Why do you care?"

He stepped closer, his powerful frame invading my personal space, and I could practically feel the anger vibrating off him. "I care when I'm being made to look like a fool."

His move was meant to intimidate but instead, it flooded my senses with his heady scent of pine, mint, and him. Desire clouded my thoughts and I shuffled back. "You don't need my help with that."

"Then why flaunt it in front of my company?" He pressed forward again, his advances fluid compared to my klutzy maneuvering. "What are you trying to accomplish? Retaliation for giving Teresa your precious Warrior?"

"You're out of your self-absorbed mind." I stepped back again and cursed when I bumped into the desk.

He pressed his advantage and in one stride, pinned me against it. "How about we try something foreign for you? Admit the truth. Tell me you're here because of your childish vendetta and we'll call this even."

"You're not getting anything out of me," I said with more confidence than I felt. In truth, after a month of withdrawal, my willpower was as stable as a house of cards in a hurricane. With barely a fight, it collapsed and I breathed him in deep, sighing as he filled my starving lungs.

He instantly detected the change and a predatory gleam entered his eyes. "Maybe I will get something out of this after all."

Dangerous.

There was a reason I'd named him that when I first laid eyes on him. And the thrill that shot through me said little had changed.

I had to get out of here.

As if predicting my move, he curved an arm around my waist. "What's the matter, baby?" His lips quirked in a mocking smile before he brought them to my ear. "Prep School not getting the job done?" He nipped at my earlobe.

Sweet Jesus!

I reminded myself he didn't want me. This was just a convoluted ploy to show he had the upper hand. I planted a hand on his chest, determined to push him away.

But my body was selfish. Even knowing the truth, it was willing to sacrifice self-preservation for a moment of pleasure.

And damn if my body wasn't buzzing with pleasure.

My fingers curled into his shirt and I pulled him in.

"Ah, there she is," he groaned and kissed me.

His wicked tongue pillaged, his hot mouth devoured, and as if a switch flipped, I went from conflicted to insatiable.

Hands hoisted me on the desk, and I couldn't say who spread my legs but when my skirt rode up, he pulled me against him. Tormented by memories of him inside me, I moaned at the feel of his erection while shamelessly grinding my hips against his. Hell, I was going to come from dry humping him with our clothes on.

He broke the kiss to look at me, eyes blazing with triumph and fury. "You may be with that gutless coward..." He shoved a hand beneath my skirt and when he felt my soaked panties, his laugh felt like sandpaper. "But your body never could lie to me." As if to prove his point, he pushed the fabric aside and plunged two fingers inside me.

I gurgled at the mind-numbing ecstasy.

"Fuck, you're so hungry for it," he rasped and added a third finger. The pad of his thumb pressed down on my clit, and I held on for dear life as the room spun.

"Tell me what you want, Princess."

"You. This." I cried out frantically. "Please, Chase." I hated that I was begging, hated that I sounded so pathetic.

His fingers moved with purpose. Thrusting, stroking, teasing. "Is that why're you're here?" he growled. "Cause your limp-dick boyfriend can't get you off?"

Yes. No. Whatever. I didn't care. I was losing my mind as he brought me close to the sweet agony of release. My body trembled, my muscles tensed, and I threw my head back.

And that's why I missed the warning in his tone.

"Because if Prep School is who you want..."

I tumbled over the edge as the orgasm started.

And abruptly stopped when he pulled his hand away. "...then only a slut would be up here letting another man finger-fuck her."

It took a second to absorb the words but when they hit, they hit like a slap to the face.

He turned his back on me and after a few breaths, checked his watch. "Dammit. I'm late for a meeting. Clean yourself up and don't be here when I get back." Without so much as a glance, he left the room.

Humiliation burned the back of my throat so thick, I choked on it. I despised him for the power he held over me, for the weakness he brought out in me, and for the emptiness he left me with. I loathed him so much that the only person I hated more was myself.

I moved slowly towards the door, burdened by the weight of my actions, but the thought of facing anyone in my shameful state made me feel sick. I headed through the bedroom to the bathroom instead. He was right. From the smudged makeup and disheveled clothing to hair that looked like it had been styled by Medusa, I was a walking disaster. Inside and out.

After a half-ass effort to compose myself, I ended up sitting on the closed toilet lid. A tear rolled down my cheek and I angrily swiped at it. What was happening to me? Jasmine was always so composed and self-assured, but ever since Lily's resurrection, she was falling apart. If I had any hope of pulling myself back together, I needed to lock Lily away where she couldn't do any more harm. My future identity depended on it. Unwittingly, Chase had just confirmed my decision to leave Jasmine behind and start fresh. After that reprehensible performance, I was more than ready to walk away.

A knock on the hotel room door made me jump. I shot to my feet. How long had I been sitting here feeling sorry for myself? It came again, more insistent. "Chase? Are you there?" a female voice called out. "Come on, sugar. You promised we'd talk so quit fooling and open the door. Just because we're not married anymore does not mean you can ignore me."

Holy shit!

31

I heard Chase's muffled voice from the hallway seconds before the suite door opened. "What are you doing here?" he was saying. "I told you we'd meet downstairs and then you send me a text telling me you're at my room? What the hell?"

"Privacy is better," she said and then laughed. "You think because you wouldn't give me your room number, I couldn't get it? You know how persuasive I can be. That man at the front desk never stood a chance."

"There seems to be a lot of that going around," he muttered.

I released a small breath when they ignored the bedroom in favor of the sitting area. That wasn't to say they would not end up here. Especially if she was here to reconcile. If so, would he accept? Was she the one that got away? Everyone had one of those. The person they'd give anything to score a second chance with. Well, normal people at least. I barely spared a thought for the men I'd been with.

Except for Chase.

And that is why I needed to see her for myself. What type of woman was capable of ensnaring his heart all the way to the altar? Who had managed what every straight female in America only fantasized about?

From behind the bedroom door, I carefully peered through the crack. The former Mrs. Chase Hale was freaking adorable. She stood no more than five feet tall with petite proportions flatteringly displayed in the fitted bodice and flared skirt of her bright yellow sundress. With the white lace trim and bouncy blonde curls, she epitomized sunshine. If someone handed her a parasol, she'd be a shoo-in for the cover of Southern Belle Monthly.

"Lord, but I have missed you." The cute little pixie spoke with an equally cute southern accent. She stood on the tips of her toes to deliver a kiss that barely reached his jaw.

He sighed. "Missy, what is so urgent that you felt the need to interrupt my business retreat?"

"I wouldn't be here if you would take my calls. I don't like dealing with Derek. He's mean to me." She pouted, which only made her face sweeter.

"Still haven't answered my question," Chase said.

"That's easy, sugar. I'm here 'cause I want you to reconsider."

"What specifically?"

"Everything." She laid a hand on his arm. "I meant what I said. I miss what we had. I miss us."

Something queasy swirled in my stomach. With Teresa already taking up rent space in my head, I could not afford another roommate. Especially one he had loved enough to make his wife.

He shrugged her arm off. "I can't do this right now."

"Of course you can. Don't you recall how good we were together? How everything fit between us? It was like a fairy tale. Girl from a small town in the South comes to the big city. She's lost and confused and doesn't know anyone until she finds work as an assistant for an ambitious young hotshot CEO. They spend their days and nights working together and eventually fall in love. It's so romantic."

That meant there was a time when Chase had not subscribed to his no fraternization rule. Perhaps his crazy rules were not the rigid obsessions of a control freak but from lessons learned. Maybe an adorable little sunny blonde lesson.

"There's nothing romantic about being manipulated," he said.

"That was all a silly misunderstanding. I admit I made some mistakes as I was just fixing to start my career and had no idea what I was doing. Why, if I didn't have you to guide me, I don't know how I would have survived."

"I'm sure you would have managed."

"Come on, sugar. I helped you too. With all that anger you had bottled up, you were wound tighter than my grandma's girdle. You were ready to explode, and it wasn't gonna be pretty. You needed me."

"Do you really want to go there?" Chase warned in a low tone.

"I need to know what happened. One minute we're planning our future and the next, you're gone. Then Derek calls me in, feathers all ruffled, and with no explanation, he shoves a stack of papers in my face and tells me I'm never gonna see you again. I didn't have a chance to ask why. I need to know."

"You know why," he answered. "You just never thought I'd figure it out."

"I don't," she pleaded. "Tell me. Please."

It sounded like a lot of unfinished business was about to be dredged up and none of it positive. Although I couldn't deny the perverse pleasure I'd get from hearing horrible things about him, I wanted nothing more to do with his life. Past, present, or future.

Unfortunately, it was looking like I had no choice.

Chase raked his fingers though his hair and then he seemed to come to a decision. “Fine. Let’s start with those late nights in the office you mentioned.”

And we’re off.

“You’re right,” he continued. “After spending that much time together, I started to see you as more than an employee. You became a friend.”

“And you were mine. It meant so much to me that you felt comfortable enough to open up about your parents’ death.”

Chase’s body tensed and his voice came out tight. “Did you know I never talked about it with anyone? Not Derek, Lynne, the psychologists, my court appointed shrink, no one. Until you. Because you had been through it. You could relate. Which is how you coaxed me. I finally found someone safe with whom I could share the worst thing that had ever happened, because you had experienced it too. Because you understood.”

She smiled up at him. “All I wanted was to help you. To be there for you like you were there for me when you took a chance on a girl with no experience. I wanted to give you something back.”

“Is that what you set out to do?” His voice sounded calm but there was an underlying edge that indicated anything but. Could she hear it too? Probably not or she wouldn’t be smiling up at him as if this was a sure thing.

“Of course,” she answered.

“I have to admit, you were good. You didn’t look at me with pity like everyone else or offer bullshit platitudes about God’s will and time healing wounds. You went at it from the rage angle. And once I started talking, it felt good to unburden myself of all the crap I’d been carrying. I suppose in that regard, you actually did help.”

His tone had shifted to one I recognized. The one I used when disassociating feelings from words. When I needed to shut down the pain from my memories before they threatened to overwhelm me.

Chase was spinning and she had no idea.

Which is probably why she doubled down. "All I ever wanted to do was help you. You were never going to let anyone in with all that anger. Once you let your guard down, I felt so attracted to you. I reckon that's why I kissed you."

This little slip of a girl had made the first move?

Chase scoffed. "Do you realize how conflicted I was about sleeping with you? You were this sweet, sheltered, innocent girl and I was the big bad city predator taking advantage of his naïve employee."

Shards of jealousy slashed my heart. Maybe at one time, I'd been as innocent and sweet, but that was lost so long ago, I couldn't conjure a memory of what it felt like. After the choices I'd made, the word 'innocent' had been stricken from my vocabulary, never to be reclaimed.

"Sweetie," she said, "you could never take advantage because I wanted you just as much as you wanted me. That's why we got married."

"So becoming pregnant had nothing to do with it?"

My hand flew to my mouth.

His voice sharpened. "And due to your strict Baptist upbringing, you would have been shunned for having a child out of wedlock. Isn't that what you told me? You knew I wasn't ready to be a father, but you also knew that since I'd grown up without one, I would never doom my child to that same life."

Had Chase not followed through and bailed on his wife and child? Maybe he cheated on his pregnant wife? Was the money he gave her out of guilt? And did that mean there was a Chase Jr. running around with blonde curls and striking green eyes?

Fuck. *I* was spinning now.

Missy's response sounded soft in comparison. "You are an honorable man who did the right thing. I could tell once you got used to the idea, how excited you were about the baby. And how crushed you were when we lost it."

My heart skipped.

Oh no.

"It?" he repeated. "She would have been a girl." His guarded facade fell, and his eyes deepened with pain. His raw vulnerability stole my breath. And broke my heart. I didn't want to know this. Not now. Not ever. But the wetness in my eyes said I'd already taken in too many stolen moments.

"I am sorry," she said.

As if it never happened, the emotion vanished and a hard mask descended. "Don't be sorry," he said coolly. "I know the baby was Cory's."

My jaw hit the floor. Cory, the college buddy, ex-partner no one talks about?

Missy's lips formed an O shape.

Chase glared at her. "Do you have any idea what it feels like to mourn the loss of something that was never yours?"

Tears welled up in her cornflower blue eyes. "I had no choice. He forced me. He threatened my job. He said he'd tell you that I came on to him and you'd get rid of me. I was so scared. If you'd just asked me, I could have told you what he did to me. But you didn't." Her soft tone turned accusatory. "Instead, you left me."

Oh my God. Had she become prey to the big bad city as Chase had feared? And had he cast her out?

Chase's expression grew even harder. "And did you also not have a choice when you two conspired to steal my company?"

Wait, what?

She faltered. "That wasn't me. It was him. He was jealous of your success. I was only—"

"Leaving your options open until you saw which one of us came out on top. Once I figured it out and kicked him out of the company, you hedged your bets on me. Using his baby to get me to the altar was a brilliant touch. Excellent acting skills."

Oh crap. No wonder he thought I was just another manipulative liar.

Her beseeching tone disappeared. "You know all about that, huh?"

"I know everything," he snapped. "Like how your dead mother is retired and living in Florida with husband number four."

Missy gasped. "How did you find out?"

"I may have been too trusting back then, but I had good people looking out for me. Once I confronted Cory, he denied it at first then admitted everything and jumped on the buyout I offered him. You, on the other hand, were so dazzled by the settlement agreement Derek dangled in front of you, you didn't even ask why I wanted out. In the end, all it took was a creative lawyer and a shit-load of money to erase both of you from my life along with any bad publicity a young and upcoming CEO could not afford at the time."

"Maybe that was true back then, but I've had a lot of time to think and I've changed my mind. Living without you has made me realize how much I miss you."

"No. You miss my money since the payments ended three months ago. Which is why you're here."

Her blue eyes hardened and when she spoke, her words were ice. "Since we're all about truth now, I was relieved when you filed for divorce because I never loved you."

"I know," he said softly.

What the fuck? I wanted to slap that bitch in her evil little imp face. After what she put him through, how dare she take a cheap shot like that?

"Let me guess," she drawled. "Teresa was the snitch that sold me out?"

Fucking Teresa.

And that's why he owed her, a fact she loved to remind me of at every opportunity. I suppose he did owe her. Without her intel, he may have lost everything, though her altruism was as hard to swallow as my cooking. With Missy out of the way, it opened a clear path for her to compete for the title of future Mrs. Hale.

Missy echoed my sentiments with a humorless laugh. "Figures she'd go digging for dirt. That bitch wanted you so bad, she'd make a deal with the devil himself. Let me guess, she gave you a shoulder to cry on which turned into sex, and next thing, you two are an item. Are you still with her?"

Yup. Teresa would always prevail because she and her fancy white suits had him bound by something more powerful than lust. Gratitude.

"You know," Missy continued thoughtfully, "I'm open to a new agreement. How about we start the payments again and I don't go to the press and tell them how you dumped your wife after she miscarried?"

The disgust in Chase's eyes should have sent her packing but her greed far outweighed her sense. "Do you think I give a rat's ass what people think?" he growled. "I'm Chase fucking Hale. Women are always trying to get something out of me. Lying is second nature to them."

Ouch.

She smiled at him. "Except what I'm saying is true."

He gave a dark laugh. "Go ahead. Things are different now. And Derek's been itching for a fight with you and your mother for years. I never cared enough to pay attention to what he's been doing but we can find out together." Chase pointed to the door.

"Now get the fuck out and never contact me again, or I'll let Derek do what he's wanted to from day one and bury you."

"Fine. I don't need you or your money. Y'all can go to hell." She marched out in a huff of yellow that didn't seem as bright as before.

I mentally urged Chase to follow and either go join his retreat or head down to the bar—God knows he deserved a drink—but instead, he went to a sideboard at the far end of the room. Of course, a suite like this would have its own bar. Dammit. I was never getting out of here. Maybe I could sneak out while he was pouring.

"You can come out now, Princess."

Oh, shit.

32

I shuffled out of the room and planned on bolting but instead, found myself walking to the couch. I sat down. He knew I was listening which meant not only had he allowed me to witness his most humiliating moments, but he had bestowed upon me a glimpse of his true pain. Something I'd never had the guts to show anyone. To disrespect that almost seemed sacrilegious.

He approached with two glasses, handed me one, then sat beside me. I didn't care what was in the glass. Any liquid courage would do. I downed the contents in a large gulp and coughed when whiskey burned down my throat. I placed the empty glass on the table while I regained my breath.

"I never meant to hear all that," I started. "Okay, at first I was curious and then I was stuck with no good exit strategy and then your conversation took a turn and then it became awkward." I stopped. I was rambling. "For what it's worth, I'm sorry you went through that."

"Don't be. I had just dropped out of college to start my

company. I was young, immature, and cocky as hell. I needed to be knocked down a peg or two."

"No one deserves that."

"I'm glad you said that." He watched me, an inscrutable expression on his face. "Because imagine my surprise when I finally start caring for someone else only to discover she's another pathological liar stringing me along. Are all women psychos or do I have a type?"

"I didn't know what you'd been through."

"And if you had, would it have changed anything?"

We both knew the answer to that. "Look, I'm apologizing. Isn't that what you wanted?"

"We're past that now. I want to know why you lied."

"We covered this. To protect myself."

"No," he stated. "You're not getting off that easy. Not after your front row seat to my kick-in-the-teeth past. Now it's your turn. Why?"

"I needed to stay safe."

"Still not buying it. What are you really afraid of?"

"For God's sake," I exploded. "Do I need to keep spelling it out for you? Getting caught, the world finding out, my family hunting me down. You know who I am."

What I am.

He leaned forward and cupped my chin, forcing me to look at him. "No more hiding. No more lies. Tell me why."

I squirmed under the scrutiny of those eyes that saw too much. "You make it sound like I set out to—"

"Deceive me?" His fingers tightened, holding me in place. "Oh, I think that was exactly your intent. To hide your true self from me."

"You mean my true self that you couldn't get away from fast enough? Is that the one you're referring to?"

"What are you talking about?"

"I saw how repulsed you were when you found out who I am. Don't try and deny it."

He released me like I'd burned him. "You think I abandoned you because of who you are?"

"Isn't that what happened?"

"Why would that make me leave?"

I shrugged. "Why would you stay?"

"I hate it when you answer questions with questions."

"Fine, because people leave. It's what they do."

"Only the ones not worth keeping around."

"They leave because *I'm* not worth keeping around."

He frowned. "Why do you think that?"

"Because Jasmine is perfect and put together. She's strong, righteous, and brave. She helps people. But Lily's not worth a damn. She's damaged, flawed, and hurts everyone around her. Suddenly not so appealing anymore, huh?"

"I have news for you, Princess. Jasmine was far from put together. Unless you count paranoid, controlling, and stubborn as positive qualities."

"If she was so messed up, why did you want her?"

"Because she's also smart, funny, and sexy as hell." He shook his head. "Why are we talking about her in the third person when she's sitting right in front of me?"

"Because she's not real. Don't you get it? You spent all that time and energy pursuing something that never existed. In the end, it was always *me*. A worthless, common, white trash criminal. World's worst bait and switch ever."

How could I blame him for leaving me? He deserved better. But knowing that didn't stop me from missing him. A tear rolled down my cheek and I released a disgusted sound. Fucking hell. Jasmine Monroe did not cry.

"Jesus, Princess." Chase's eyes widened. "Is that what you think of yourself? All this time, you hid your identity from me because you were... ashamed of who you are?"

My cheeks flushed with embarrassment. That would explain why I locked Lily away so tight, she lived in a black site of my psyche where no one could reach her. Where no one could find out the things she had done.

Ultimately, my choices were the result of a pathetic woman who could not admit the truth about herself.

But Chase was wrong about one thing. I wasn't hiding my identity from him due to shame. I was hiding it from myself.

"If you knew the real me, you'd understand," I said.

"I do know you and I get it. If you think I hired a hacker to bury my mess just to save my company and that humiliation, shame and ego had nothing to do with it, then *you* don't know *me*. Except I think you do."

Those were only a fraction of Lily's flaws.

Another tear escaped. Dammit. Why did that keep happening? Jasmine Monroe did not cry.

But I wasn't Jasmine Monroe, no matter how much I pretended. She was a construct I'd embraced to fast track myself into thinking I was a better person. Swap out the old with the new and pretend all those horrible things I did belonged to someone else.

The cruelest lies are the ones we tell ourselves, and heaven help us when we believe them.

And I was so tired of pretending to be something I wasn't.

Chase reached out to wipe the tear way. "For the record, I never gave a damn about your past."

"Then you're stupid because the woman you were with doesn't exist. She never did."

"Putting aside your existential crisis for now, are you saying nothing between us was real?"

"Does it matter?"

"Stop answering questions with questions."

"It's irrelevant," I said. "There. That's a statement."

"And I thought I was fucked up," he groaned. "For someone so desperate to distance herself from her inner child, you certainly still think like one. You need to grow up."

"If you're trying to make me feel better, you suck at it."

"I'm telling you the truth. This isn't some split-personality bullshit. Lily is Jasmine and Jasmine is Lily, the grown-up version. Look, I am nothing like my self-destructive younger self, but he still rears his ugly head on occasion because it's *me*. Call yourself whatever you want, but Lily had to grow up at some point and she did. She turned into you. A kind, generous, whip-smart, funny, adorable person who's also stubborn, annoyingly logical, intrusive, and many other pain-in-the ass qualities."

"There are things you don't know about Lily."

"Add terrible listener to that list."

"You don't know what she's done."

"What *you* did," he said simply. "And I don't care. Whatever it is, you had better find a way to reconcile it with who you are now or you're going to give yourself an ulcer. Hell, you're going to give me one. And if it's as bad as you think it is, look harder. You were just a kid."

He made it sound so easy. Like absolution waited at the end of a finger snap. If only the world worked that way. But I was starting to hate myself for hating myself. Another new low. And with it came a desperation for anything to help me cope.

I thought about Lily and all her flaws, and for the first time, I pushed beyond the wall I'd created. The disgust, judgement, and shame were so strong, they nearly crippled me but I kept going... and going... past what she'd done... reaching for who she was.

And then I saw her. All of her. For the first time.

And what I found nearly brought me to my knees.

I felt the pain of an abandoned, scared, and lonely child, lost and hurting, hopeless and sad. She was sweet, kind, caring and compassionate until he took it all away. He stole her innocence and humanity and left her with nothing.

My heart ached for what happened to her. For what happened to *me*.

"Oh my God," I whispered. And this time, when the tears fell, I didn't try to stop them. Lily—no, *I*—deserved them. We deserved to mourn for our childhood so violently ripped from us.

The cushions shifted and strong arms locked around me. I buried my face in Chase's chest and gave in to the sorrow that could only come from years of denial. Now unleashed, the long-suppressed hurt, regret, and guilt threatened to rip me apart.

Ironically, after fighting so hard to protect my lies, it was the truth that undid me.

Eventually, the tears subsided, but the pain remained lodged in my gut. Climbing into the ring with your demons hurt like a bitch. I could almost hear the countdown as I lay sprawled face down on the mat.

"I have to admit," Chase interrupted my pity party, "I didn't think you had that in you."

I pulled away and when I spoke, my voice was hollow. "Would you like a medal for breaking me?"

"While I'm flattered you're giving me credit, that was all you. Do you want to talk about it?"

"About her?" *Us. Me.* This pronoun thing was going to mess me up. "No. I can't. There's too much that she... that *I* did..." *And you would never look at me the same again.*

"People reinvent themselves all the time. Be a better version of yourself and make amends. I know you're a good person."

But finding compassion for my younger self was a far cry from seeking forgiveness. Was there a line that, once crossed, rendered salvation impossible? Or could you restore pieces of your soul?

Who the hell knew?

And while I was asking questions I'd never get the answers to, why did the cosmic universe demand all personal growth hurt like a bitch? Maybe more people would do it if it didn't come at you like a two-by-four to the skull. I rubbed my throbbing temples. I'd endured more than enough for today. I was exhausted. "Don't you have to get back to your retreat?" I asked.

If he was surprised by my abrupt change of subject, he didn't show it. "Not today. The purpose is for employees from both companies to get to know each other. That's easier done without the CEO present. Plus, they're doing trust exercises and I always drop my partner. Not a good look for the CEO."

"If it's Brandon, let him fall. He deserves it for messing with me."

"I'll deal with him later."

"Did he even have a conflict today or was he lying about that too?"

Chase shrugged. "He's been downstairs all day."

Bastard!

I mentally added gullible to my growing list of defects. "If I see him on my way out, I'll deal with him right now."

"I have a better idea." Chase took my hand and drew me close. "Stay with me tonight."

My heart fluttered. How could four words have such an effect on me? Especially when everything was clear. To walk away from this life, I needed a clean break. A clean break meant no complications. No complications meant no *him*.

So why was I entertaining his invitation? And why was I raising my face to accept his kiss. I closed my eyes.

And jumped at the knock on the door.

"Chase?" A woman's voice called out. "Are you there? What's going on? You stood me up."

I grimaced.

Fucking Teresa.

33

S*tupid, stupid, stupid.*

Here I was, one kiss away from spending the night with him and he already had plans with another woman... with *her*. Ugh. What kind of man does that? Oh yeah, a womanizing one. And what kind of woman falls for it? Oh yeah, a stupid one.

Teresa knocked again and Chase directed his eyes upwards as if praying. Or so it seemed until I heard a string of curse words followed by 'crazy' and 'women'. I assumed I was on that list.

"Stay here," he ordered.

Too late. I was already up and on the move.

I reached the door before him, opened it, and had the satisfaction of meeting Teresa's stunned expression. I'd never seen the ice queen flustered. Too bad I couldn't stay and savor the moment, but I had things to do. Number one on that list... not be here.

"He's all yours," I said. "But you're a fool for thinking you'll ever be more than a sure thing."

Her jaw fell while I shoved past her and headed down the hall.

"Princess, wait," Chase called out. "We are not done here."

I continued without looking back. Why couldn't he leave me alone?

Maybe because I'm the one who set this crazy circus in motion by stumbling into his lair. Where I then proceeded to have a breakdown followed by a near sex experience.

Thank goodness Teresa came along when she did.

And if I was thanking that bitch, I knew I'd lost my mind.

The elevator opened and I entered. A man smiled politely. "Where to?"

"Lobby," I responded, though after my round-trip to hell, it sounded anti-climactic.

I had a future to focus on that did not include Chase. No more distractions. No more complications. No more him.

Even as gullible as I was turning out to be, I didn't believe that for a second.

I wasted no time once I got home. With Nicki working the dinner shift, I took advantage of the solitude. After a quick shower, I dressed in Minion pajamas, created a to-do list, then started checking off items. I wrote letters to Sue, Nicki, and Brandon detailing instructions regarding the business, the apartment, Warrior—I couldn't resist— and the royalty checks. I left Nicki money to cover my share of the rent for the rest of the year, though in this city, she'd find a roommate in a minute.

Next came the paperwork to activate Rose's—yes, my new name is also a flower—identity, followed by the physical work. I dragged my suitcase out and started tossing in a few selected items.

New identity. New wardrobe. New me.

At this rate, I could leave tomorrow.

And not a moment too soon. Between the boulder in my stomach, the dread throttling my insides, and the adrenaline shooting through my veins, I was discovering a whole new kind of nausea worthy of a medical journal. I always suspected that one of my names would eventually end up with the word 'syndrome' after it.

I cringed at the lily pin lying at the bottom of a drawer. After Anthony's morbid delivery, I had kept it. Not out of sentiment—hell no! I hated that thing—but as a harsh reminder to never be complacent again. I threw it in the suitcase.

My hand hovered over the remaining item. From the second Chase had given me the jasmine pendant, I knew I couldn't keep it, but after all hell broke loose, jewelry had been the last thing on my mind. I opened the box. It really was beautiful. Beautiful enough to give to another woman... like Teresa. I snapped it shut and slammed it down on the dresser. Nicki would know to return it. After that, Chase could do whatever he damn well pleased with it. Not my business.

I went to my closet and yanked my favorite garments off their hangers with more force than necessary. By the time I moved on to the bathroom, the anger had waned enough for my original nausea to return. I wasn't sure which felt worse.

A knock sounded from the front door and my heart lurched. What are the chances it would be a mistaken pizza delivery? Zero with the way my luck ran. It was him. I dropped my toiletry bag and started for the door. He clearly wanted to say more back at the hotel, but I'd been hoping, just this once, I'd catch a break and be long gone before he came around. The one time I needed Teresa to keep him occupied for a night and she couldn't even get that right.

I sighed dramatically. May as well get it over with, except this time, I decided to try an alternate tactic. I needed him gone and if that meant giving him and his massive ego the last word, then that's exactly what I intended to do. The hell with my pride. I'd left most of it at the hotel anyway.

I opened the door. He had changed into faded jeans and a tight black T-shirt. He looked positively scrumptious. After all this time, I never tired of looking at him.

It was annoying.

I gestured for him to enter then closed the door behind him. "Whatever it is you need to say, go for it. The floor is yours."

The determination in his eyes turned to suspicion.

Followed by silence.

Apparently, he needed more encouragement. "You obviously have something to get out of your system, and if this brings you the closure necessary for us to move on then do it. I can take it. I won't fight back."

Why bother? I had already lost. Besides, at this point, nothing could surprise me.

"I am not fucking Teresa."

Except that. "Say what now?"

"I have not had sex with her since I met you," he clarified.

I shook my head. "You admitted it when I confronted you."

"No. You asked if I was with her that night in the photo and I was. Along with Lyndham, two execs, Derek and Lyndham's attorney. One of many grueling and unnecessary negotiation meetings."

"Don't lie to me," I warned.

"Funny coming from you."

I ignored the jab. I was getting used to them. "Then explain why you invited her."

"I didn't. Prep School did."

"Wayne? Why?"

Chase released a derisive snort. "Because she saw the acquisition as an opportunity to climb up the food chain, and Prep

School was too weak to resist her Jedi mind tricks. He never stood a chance. She's perfected her body as an interrogation technique so potent, the military could learn from her."

I didn't need a reminder of how he knew that. "But she wants *you*."

"That woman would eat her young to get ahead."

Those two conniving backstabbers deserved each other, although I'd put my money on Teresa. She'd devour Wayne and use his bones as toothpicks.

"Are they still together?" I thought about Wayne's kiss.

"Doubtful. Prep School's no longer of use to her."

"And you didn't think to mention this to me?" I snapped. All those tortuous nights envisioning him with Teresa when the entire time... I started to see red. "You purposely let me think you were with her. How could you do that? Do you know what I went through?"

"You deserved it."

"For what?" I yelled.

"For breaking my fucking heart," he shouted back. "And don't put this all on me. When you're dead set on believing the worst, nothing derails you."

I opened my mouth to respond but stopped. I couldn't argue. My survival mechanism consisted of a simple formula—assume the worst and you'll always be prepared. As a kid, letting down my guard resulted in horrific things happening to me. Stay alert, be aware, and prepare for the most messed up thing possible. That mindset saved my life.

It also kept me lonely.

A necessary evil.

Which is why I needed to think with my head. Not with whatever was threatening to leap out of my chest. And certainly not with anything lower.

“If you’re not sleeping with her, why give her Warrior?” I asked.

“Because even when you’re not in my life, you wreak havoc on it.”

“What did I do?”

“Not you. Brandon. He refuses to look at Warrior without you.”

“Oh… that’s kind of sweet.”

“No, it’s not sweet, it’s a colossal pain in my ass.”

“So why not give it to someone else? Or did you choose Teresa to piss me off?”

“I want Brandon on it. Which is why when he witnesses her demolishing your revered legacy, he’ll get his traitorous ass off his high horse and back in the game. Pissing you off was a bonus.”

I silently applauded the manipulation… except the last part. “When Brandon’s back on the job, what happens to her?”

“She’s gone.”

Good answer. “And Wayne?”

His eyes cooled. “Your concern for your new boy-toy is admirable.”

“Boy what? As in sex?” I almost laughed. “Where’d you get that idea?”

“Oh, I don’t know. Maybe when he was sticking his tongue down your throat.”

“You saw that, huh?”

“The entire fucking hotel saw it.”

“Then they would have witnessed the encore where I slapped him.”

His brows shot up. “You did what?”

“I’ve never been with Wayne.”

“Good. You deserve better than him.”

“Funny, that’s what he says about you.”

“Except I’m right. Now my next question is very important. I’m going to need you to think carefully before you answer.”

I groaned. "Now what?"

"Did you hit him hard?"

A laugh escaped me. I couldn't remember the last time that happened. "I wish I'd decked the weasel for what he did to you."

The humor on his face disappeared. "What did he do besides act like his normal prickish self?"

I sighed. I guess none of it mattered anymore. "Sterling stole Warrior from you for Wayne."

"And you know this how?"

"Because I hacked into Lyndham and found the program. Then I hacked into Predator to determine how. Then I went back into Lyndham and destroyed it." How was that for the Cliffs Notes version?

"The rumor about a cyber-attack on Lyndham?"

"Not a rumor." I waited for the lecture on violating his privacy, overstepping my bounds, poking my nose where I shouldn't, and whatever else his hypocritical ass might conjure up. But nothing happened. "Isn't this the part where you reprimand me for digging into your life then start pacing a hole in my floor while spewing colorful curses about Wayne's lineage?"

His lips twitched. "Not if I already knew about the theft."

"What?"

His smirk turned into a full-blown grin. "Did you go through Project Stryker's lines of code while you were in there?"

"Sure, 'cause when I'm *illegally* hacking into a system, I always make a pot of tea and lollygag, waiting to get caught."

He ignored my sarcasm. "If you did, you'd have noticed that version was designed to blow up in his smug little face."

"But how?"

"It's amazing how loose-lipped the threat of prison can make someone. After you identified Sterling as the one who'd messed with Wolfe, I couldn't get him to shut up. He's been a loyal snitch ever since. He notified me when Prep School hired him again and this time, we made sure he succeeded."

"Seriously?" I threw my hands up. Maybe I didn't get punished for this good deed, but it still resulted in an epic waste of time. "Why haven't you fired Wayne yet? You are his boss now, which I'm sure is torture for him and... Never mind. I just answered my own question."

His grin was positively evil. "In good time. In hindsight, I should have made Lyndham can Prep School along with Bryce but since I missed that opportunity, I may as well have some fun with it now."

I shuddered at the memory of that beady-eyed pervert. I should have guessed Chase was responsible for getting him fired. My knight in dangerous armor from day one.

"Why didn't you tell me any of this?"

"Like you did when you went charging in to protect my company?"

"That had nothing to do with you. I was preserving the sanctity of my project."

"Sure you were." He smiled. "And I love you more for it."

Love?

I froze.

The word was almost too foreign to comprehend. Yet it still managed to illicit conflicting emotions: disbelief, hope, fear, sadness, and physical illness.

All at the same time.

Love and I didn't exactly have the healthiest of relationships.

As Lily, love was a kindness I desperately wanted but tragically never experienced.

For Jasmine, love was a weakness I desperately avoided and gratefully never experienced.

Until now.

"Princess." Chase sliced through my thoughts. "I know you heard me, so either say it back or tell me to fuck off, in which case I will leave you alone."

How about option C? Fleeing and never seeing him again. Because that's where this was heading. Feelings had no business weighing in here.

I opened my mouth to tell him he meant nothing to me, just a physical distraction to pass the time. But my words would not cooperate. "I can't do this," I said instead. "Please go. I'm sorry." I ran to my room before the tears started.

I guess there are some things even I can't lie about.

I was sitting on my bed, torn between feeling numb and feeling way too much when I heard him approach. "Please go," I begged.

He stopped in the doorway. "Before I do, you're going to answer one question for me, and I want the truth. Understand?"

Wasn't that my original plan? Give him whatever he wanted to make him leave? It seemed much simpler at the time. "What is it?"

"Was it only sex between us?" he asked.

"If I say 'yes'?" I mumbled.

"Then I'll never touch you again."

There it was. The desired end result. Except instead of satisfaction, my stomach plummeted at the finality of those words.

"And if I say 'no'?"

"Then I'll never stop."

That did it. I dropped my head in my hands to hide the emotion. Christ. Ever since I'd reconciled with Lily, I'd become a blubbery mess. Or was this normal human behavior? Sad that I didn't know.

"Princess, what the fuck are you doing?"

Having a meltdown.

"Answer me," he bellowed.

I looked up and groaned.

He was gesturing to the suitcase, but before I could answer, he noticed the contents and went still. "What the hell is that doing here?"

I followed his gaze and groaned again. The lily pin.

When I didn't answer, his eyes swept the room and landed on the letters. He walked to my desk and reached for them.

"Those are personal," I said.

He grabbed the one to Sue.

"Stop!" I shrieked. "That's none of your business."

He opened it.

"Okay, okay," I relented. "I'll explain. Just put it down." Better to hear it from me than an out-of-context sheet of paper.

He complied but continued to hover.

"Anthony's back."

"Your father? Or the man you thought was? Isn't he in prison?"

I reluctantly explained the meeting and everything Anthony had said to me. When I reached the part about the mugging and lily pin, Chase's eyes turned to shards of ice. "I'll kill that motherfucker," he breathed.

In that moment, I believed him.

I rushed to Anthony's ultimatum and attempted to downplay my leaving as temporary, but Chase knew me too well. He picked up the letter and started reading. When he finished, he did the same with the remaining two then looked at me.

"Nothing for me?" he asked in a cold voice.

My eyes involuntarily darted to the jasmine pendant.

The muscle in his jaw flexed. "Keep it," he said curtly. "I want answers, not a fucking piece of jewelry."

"There's nothing left to say."

"There's plenty left to say, starting with WHAT THE FUCK IS WRONG WITH YOU?"

I cringed. I'd been on the receiving end of his temper before but nothing resembling the inferno raging in him now.

"I have no choice."

He glowered at me. "There's always a choice."

"You don't understand. He's going to use me again. He's going to make me do all sorts of awful things. Just like he did before. I can't. I won't." My voice broke on the last word.

"Then make me understand what happened. Tell me. What was so bad you blocked out an entire childhood to disassociate from it?"

When I didn't speak, he sat down beside me. "Talk to me, Princess." I could tell he was trying to control his anger but between his stony features and rigid posture, he needed to try harder. "This is crazy. I can't believe anything you've done could warrant this—"

"I killed someone," I blurted.

I'd never said those words aloud and hearing them now made me itch with the need to get as far away as possible.

But you couldn't outrun yourself.

"Keep talking," Chase said.

It took me a few minutes to start. After suppressing the memories for years, acknowledging them now felt like flexing an atrophied muscle. Awkward and weak, "After Anthony hit rock bottom, he had nothing in his miserable life. Then he learned what I could do with a computer and forced me to do things for him. At first, I thought it was temporary, and he'd stop when he'd had enough, but he blew everything on his addictions and always needed more. Then I rationalized it by telling myself we were scamming rich people who could afford it. That didn't make it right, but at least it helped me sleep better. Until Jacob Morales."

I paused as if the name should mean something. But it wouldn't. Not to anyone. Except me.

"It was a personal vendetta. Anthony wanted me to not only clean Jacob out but destroy his life. They had run a scam together and Jacob had cheated my dad—I mean Anthony— out of his share. I justified this one by telling myself Jacob was a crook who deserved it. What I didn't know was that Jacob had a daughter with a rare form of cancer and he was struggling to pay for experimental treatments. He had leveraged everything he owned and was working two jobs to make payments to the hospital. I'll never know if he did scam Anthony but if so, it was for his daughter." Shame and self-loathing spread through my body so visceral, I felt the weight of it in my bones. "I took everything from him. He was unable to care for his daughter and she died in the hospital. Jacob committed suicide two weeks later."

Not one. But two deaths by my hand. And at least one of them had been innocent.

Silence enveloped the room while I stared at my lap. What now? It didn't matter. Whatever it was, I deserved it. Jasmine's kangaroo court had already played judge, jury, and executioner.

Finally, Chase spoke. "Did you want to do it?"

My eyes snapped up. "Of course not."

"Why did you then?"

"I tried saying no but he..."

"He beat you."

I nodded. He had seen the scars.

"And if you didn't comply?"

"I wouldn't be here now."

"And what happened after you complied?"

"I couldn't do it anymore. I sent everything illegal he'd ever done to the FBI then took off." Except I'd managed to fuck that up too because he was back.

"You do see that Anthony is responsible for the death, right? You may have been the weapon, but you hardly had a choice. You were exploited."

The words made sense, but my head wasn't winning this battle. "But I feel like—"

"Because you're a good person," Chase interrupted as if he'd made a revelation. "If you weren't, you wouldn't feel a thing, just like that sociopath who made you do it. You left so you'd never be put in that position again. You got him arrested so he couldn't do it to anyone else again. You're not a bad person. You're a good person who was forced to do bad things."

I listened to his words. Words uttered as if they were the simplest thing in the world to comprehend. And while he spoke, he was looking at me with—wait, was that understanding? He took both my hands in his. "I am sorry for what he did to you."

"But how can you—" I didn't get it. I had just exposed the darkest part of myself and he was... apologizing?

"You were just as much a victim."

More neglected memories started to surface. The glee on Anthony's face when he forced me to do awful things. How he relished seeing me struggle with his demands. He delighted in knowing each act killed me a bit more than the last, and the more I suffered, the happier he became. When he figured out that hurting others destroyed me more than any physical beating could, it became his favorite pastime.

"I am so sorry," Chase repeated, "and I forgive you. Even though that doesn't mean a damn thing if you don't forgive yourself. This is not your burden. You need to find a way to let it go."

I continued to watch him, mesmerized. Not by his beautiful face or his rational words but by his eyes. More specifically, the compassion in them. It bathed me in warmth, reaching deep inside with an intensity so strong, it cast my shame and fear out of the shadows and into a place of light where my grisly nightmares couldn't follow.

A lump formed in my throat except this time, instead of terror, a feeling of lightness came over me.

They say there's power in confession and I never believed that. Until today. Whether it was his reaction, confronting what I'd been running from, or sharing the burden with someone willing to shoulder it with me, I didn't know. One thing I did know. None of this would have happened without him.

And when I repaid him by running away, I would hate myself all over again.

34

I woke in my bed, disoriented, exhausted, and in the dark—both literally and figuratively. A glance at my clock confirmed it was either too late or too early, depending on your motivation. Mine was to get more sleep. I yawned and rolled to my side... then jumped at the warm body beside me. Christ, what was he doing here? Then I remembered. After introducing Chase to my demons—who I sadly had a longer relationship with than anyone I knew—I'd succumbed to the emotional toll and fallen asleep mid-discussion. Possibly even mid-sentence. He must have stripped my pajamas, tucked me in, and then done the same.

Wide awake now, I listened to the sound of his breathing. Slow, deep, and steady. With no chance of falling back asleep, my mind started to race. This was exactly what I needed. I'd be crazy to squander this opportunity. Rose was waiting.

I carefully rolled out of bed and grabbed some clothes. After closing the bathroom door behind me, I dressed in jeans and a Muppets T-shirt, slipped on my socks and sneakers, then re-entered the bedroom. Although the room held little light, I navigated carefully from memory. The last thing I needed was to wake him over a stubbed toe. I could envision the outcome. Him springing into action and arranging a security detail so confining, my post-mugging incarceration would feel like spring break. We're talking some next level 'seal me in a tower and grow my hair out' bullshit.

No, thank you.

Due to my earlier manic obsession, it only took a few minutes to get my suitcase in order. I slowly zipped it shut while holding my breath. All good and quiet if you didn't factor in my pounding heart.

When I reached the apartment door, I paused to bid farewell to my first real home, my makeshift family, and the man in my bed I was too chicken to face. I quashed the temptation to return for one last kiss. Stirring the beast would only invite trouble.

This was the best way.

The only way.

Just like that night sixteen years ago. Sneaking out while everyone slept to abandon my former self and start a new life. Years had passed but with the memories so vivid, it could have been mere moments. Had anything changed? Had *I* changed? The answer presented itself in my actions. Same predicament, same solution.

Same Lily.

Annoyed, I blinked back tears. What the hell? After a lifetime of avoiding them, they sprang up with practiced ease now. Was there anything else left for me to fail at?

I reached for the door handle.

And jumped when light filled the room.

Terror gripped me. I was caught. The consequences would be fatal. He was going to kill me.

And then I realized my surroundings.

I am Jasmine. Not Lily. This is not sixteen years ago, and I am not running away from my childhood home to get away from my father.

No. I am running away from my adult home to get away from him.

Somehow, that was worse.

With a resigned sigh, I turned to see Chase standing beside the lamp, wearing nothing but boxer briefs and disappointment. My heart rate sped up. How could I miss someone I hadn't left yet? And why did my mind instantly go to that final goodbye kiss?

But given his strained expression and rigid posture, that seemed unlikely. What a waste. Our last moments shouldn't be spent fighting. Not when I could be using the time to etch that sculpted body into my brain. Some things were too perfect to forget.

I readied myself. Cue the anger, the yelling, the lecture.

Instead, his quiet voice surprised me. "Is this what we've come to, Princess?"

I needed a second to catch up. "It's the only way."

Leaving? Yes.

Slinking away like a coward? Not so much.

"I expected more from you," he said.

Cue the guilt instead. "Maybe you shouldn't have. You want to think I'm a good person but what if you're trying to convince yourself of something that isn't true?"

"I don't believe that and I know you don't either." He sighed, either in dismay or displeasure. Maybe it was denial. Hell, I couldn't tell. I was having a difficult time navigating this uncharted terrain. "What I do know is, you're Jasmine fucking Monroe, genius IQ, world class hacker, and this is the best you can come up with?"

Apparently, we were going with accusation now. "That's not fair." I bristled though unsure if he was questioning my abilities, my commitment, or both.

"Or is this about your fear of getting too close? Of being vulnerable? Heaven forbid anyone discovers the stoic Jasmine Monroe has feelings." He cocked his head. "Or does she?"

She did. Too many. And while that posed a problem, it wasn't the driving force behind my departure. At least, I didn't think so. Could it be related? I shook my head. Now was not the time to descend into a psychotherapy rabbit hole. For Rose's sake, I needed to be on my game. "No hacking solution exists or I would have found it. Feel free to come up with something if you think it's so easy."

"Okay. You and Anthony cannot coexist which means it comes down to you or him. Why not eliminate him? Hack into a cartel or mafia, steal their money, and frame him. He'll be dead before you know it."

His response surprised me. Clearly, he'd given this some thought. But so had I. "Who knows what contacts he's made in prison? They could tip him off. Or the hit could fail. Too many unknown variables."

My reasons sounded rational but truthfully, after receiving my genetic reprieve from the vile blood running through Anthony's veins, the thought of willingly inviting the darkness in by committing any heinous act sickened me. Even one that could save me. Especially after Chase had just helped me reclaim a piece of my soul.

"Fine." He raked his fingers through his hair. "Next idea."

"Leaving. If I don't, he'll out me and take down everyone I care about. It's what he does."

"Then beat him to it," Chase said. "Go public on your own."

I blinked, positive I'd misunderstood.

"Remove the threat entirely," he explained. "Come out of hiding."

"Are you crazy?" I asked, incredulity adding ten octaves to my voice. “If the whole point is to keep me safe, how is throwing me to a hungry pack of wolves the answer?”

“You wanted another solution, here it is. Take the power away from him. From all of them. You control the narrative. No more worrying and hiding.”

“That’s because everything that makes me worry and hide would actually be happening.”

“Just think about it. We bring you into the spotlight, tell everyone the truth—well, maybe leave out a few things—and then you live your life like a normal person, with me. Or as normal as you’re capable of.”

I *was* thinking about it. How else could I explain the cold sweat breaking out along my skin?

He walked towards me. “Look, I’m not stupid enough to think I can keep you from leaving, and a part of me is questioning whether I should even try. If staying results in you getting hurt, or doing something you can’t live with, or living in fear, then I can’t justify keeping you here no matter how I feel.”

My eyes clouded and I quicky focused on something else before I deteriorated into a blubbering mess. His body made an excellent distraction. I fixated on his strong, smooth, and perfectly sculpted muscles, flexing with every step he took.

My Beautiful Dangerous.

And even more so on the inside.

That I had to give this up proved how much life sucked.

A tear spilled down my cheek. Dammit.

But he wasn’t finished lobbying for his terrible idea. “The FBI had nothing solid on you to begin with and, if they did, it’s too late now. And what’s Anthony going to do? Refute your story? Like anyone would line up to believe a known criminal. You can do this. *We* can do this.” He stopped in front of me, his green eyes imploring. “Trust me. I would never let anything happen to you.”

I excelled at many things. Unfortunately, trust was not one of them. "I'm sorry," I said, though the words sounded pathetic. "I can't."

"If coming clean is not an option..."

"Then this is the end," I finished.

I watched the struggle play out in his eyes. Frustration, disbelief, defiance, hurt... like a customized version of the stages of grief. Everything but defeat. That was not in his nature.

Overcome with an urge to console him, I reached up for our goodbye kiss, and he accepted my token by pulling me close. As the kiss deepened, I felt an ache grow inside me like an unfilled chasm. The familiar emptiness was returning. Not again. I clutched at him and my movements grew frenzied. Anything to not feel that void.

This was not about consoling him. This was for me.

And he knew it. He quickly stripped off my clothes and pushed me against the door, his mouth on mine again. Our tongues twisted and danced while his hard body pressed against me, promising the reprieve I knew he'd deliver.

But I couldn't wait.

I cupped him through his boxer briefs and he groaned. So hard, so hot. But when I tugged at his waistband, he pulled away and dropped to his knees. He buried his face between my thighs and his stubbled jaw scraped against my delicate skin. He inhaled deeply. "God, I missed your pussy," he growled. And then his hot mouth was on me, licking, sucking, and devouring like a starving man. My head fell back with a thud, while self-indulgence made me frantically rock against him.

My eyes flew open when his teeth nipped my clit and I yelped. But then his tongue followed, bathing my sensitive swell with a caress that launched me into a tailspin. He bit again and this time, lightning fired, followed by pure bliss when the tip of his tongue darted in tight little circles. Biting pain then waves of pleasure. Again and again, over and over, until I couldn't tell where one sensation ended and the other began. His tongue sharpened and pressed hard against me. "Ohmygod," I moaned and flailed as the pressure grew unbearable. My fingernails dug into his shoulders and my legs started to tremble. Pleasure, pain, fear, ecstasy... the adrenaline from my emotions tightened into a muscle-seizing, mind-jarring orgasm. I bucked and writhed as my head thrashed from side to side, the release too much, but Chase gripped my hips in place, forcing me to experience every relentless stroke of his tongue.

My world was still a blur when he carried me to the couch and hovered above me. I registered the absence of his boxer briefs and grew dizzy at the sight of his jutting cock. This is what I ached for. This would fill the void. I reached for him and parted my legs, expecting him to fuck me hard and fast. No, *needing* him to fuck me hard and fast, but when he pushed inside me, he filled me slowly, gliding against every tightly wound nerve. I whimpered and wrapped my legs around him, urging him to move faster, but when he pulled back, he entered again in a repeat performance, leisurely stretching me wet inch by glorious wet inch.

With every restrained thrust, the prolonged friction teased, increasing along with my desperate cries. Feverish with need, my body pleaded for more, but he maintained his delicious pace, driving me to experience every exquisite sensation. Torture and heaven. Just like our time left together.

And with each deliberate movement, his eyes held mine. Dark green pools of desire. And something else vaguely familiar that made my world tilt.

It took me back to our first night together, when those knowing eyes had latched onto mine and I feared he could strip me bare. And that's exactly what he did, somehow penetrating my defenses to expose the real me.

But now, his eyes held something else. An unspoken request seeking *me* to take down my barriers and allow him in.

Panic reared up. Shedding your clothes was easy but discarding your armor and allowing someone in, that's when you truly became naked. And at your most vulnerable.

Sweat beaded Chase's forehead as he continued to move with excruciating patience, coaxing me to an unrealized level of intimacy, while inundating my senses with slow-burning pleasure. I couldn't look away. I was mesmerized. Unable to separate myself from this moment. Unable to escape him.

And I didn't want to.

And then it happened.

Something akin to a *whoosh* shot through me followed by a wave of longing so intense, it left me queasy. Chase grabbed my chin, forcing my eyes to stay on his, and like a trap springing open, my body felt like it wanted to burst. A rich warmth flowed through me and damn if I didn't feel like I was glowing. Chase's eyes softened with tenderness, and I knew they were a reflection of mine. I had already surrendered—heart, mind, and body.

"I love you, Princess," he said and then with a wicked smile, plunged into me up to the hilt. I gasped and jerked my hips against him, but he grabbed my thighs and pushed my legs up, close to my shoulders. I grimaced. The pose was uncomfortable but… ohmyfuckinggod, his cock went so deep, I screamed.

He drove into me hard and fast, robbing me of my breath, yet somehow leaving just enough to gasp his name over and over. He was reaching places I'd never felt before, the connection so deep, I sensed him vibrating with each pulse of my body. Like sparks of fire, the thrumming started in my fingertips, my toes, and then spread to every cell until I couldn't think, couldn't process. There was only him and my dizzying climb to madness.

He reached down to stroke my clit. Once, twice...

The orgasm hit like a tidal wave, drowning me in ecstasy and yanking me under with wave after wave of pleasure. I clawed at Chase as the spasms took hold, jerking my body and shaking everything loose until there was nothing left to hold onto. Chase's beautiful face blurred beneath my tears as something deep inside shattered and every cell lit up with soul-wrenching joy. Never had I relinquished so much. And he took it all, finding his release with me.

We lay together long after, two souls entwined, two hearts laid bare.

There was no hiding anymore.

"I'll do it," I whispered.

35

I looked at my watch but not much had changed in the last two minutes. One more hour to go. Plenty of time for my jitters to eat me alive. I paced faster. At this rate, I feared for both myself and the hardwood floors in Chase's office.

"Calm down." Chase glanced up from his computer. "What's the worst that can happen?"

Public ridicule, condemnation, banishment, deportation. Okay, that last one was a stretch since I was born here, but I was on a roll.

"You've got that runaway bride look," Chase observed. "You were on board when we made this decision. What's changed?"

Maybe the grapefruit size ball in my gut that my ribcage was attacking like a trespasser. Or how about reality? In theory, this idea sounded smart. Beat Anthony to the punch, control the narrative, take my power back, blah, blah, blah. A desperate decision in a slew of bad options.

And the only one that allowed me to stay with Chase.

But that didn't prevent me from envisioning hordes of people entering the building carrying cameras, microphones, and rotten tomatoes. All weapons for my demise.

I smoothed down a nonexistent crease in my conservative blue dress, chosen for its illusion of credibility. I should have gone with red to mask the tomatoes. Oh no. Just thinking about food made my stomach lurch. I groaned. Upchucking on reporters would not help my cause. Maybe, we should have signs like the ones at SeaWorld designating the first three rows as splash zones.

"Everything will be fine," Chase reassured me.

"You don't know that."

"Sure I do. As long as you don't agree to a reality show."

"Can't you see the risk you're putting yourself in? You shouldn't have anything to do with me."

"It's a little late for that," he observed. "I can hardly disassociate myself from a press conference in my own building."

Why Chase insisted on holding it at Predator flabbergasted me. He represented the American dream while I embodied the product of a nightmare. Once I came clean, his reputation would be tarnished by association even without his giant logo plastered in the background like a product endorsement for poor judgement.

"You should be running away. Not doing this." My mind began to race along with the speed of my pacing. "There's still time. Call it off or toss the press some other news tidbit about your company. I'll reschedule on my own."

He leaned back in his chair. "Like maybe I can announce my new head of software development?"

"Sure. Whatever. Do that."

"She needs to accept first." The corner of his mouth tilted. "What do you say?"

I stopped mid-step. "Me? Why?"

"Because you're the best."

"What about Brandon?"

"Who do you think has been lobbying for this since the day he met you?"

"What about your rules?"

He stood and walked around his desk to take me in his arms. "We're way past that now, don't you agree?"

I thought about Warrior and the potential future projects I could develop, and the programmer inside me bounced like a giddy child. But that didn't negate the problem at hand. I couldn't be that selfish.

"Chase, I love that you think so highly of me, but I won't bring you or your company down." I'd be lucky to keep my own software company afloat.

He brushed back a strand of my hair that had escaped my respectable low bun. "Haven't you figured it out yet? I'm all in. Have been from the day I dropped in on a small start-up company run by a couple of snot-nosed kids."

"Did the company turn out to be worth it?"

"No. But the girl in the elevator did." He smiled down at me with so much tenderness, my insides melted. "I should have known I was in trouble when the ugliest dress on the planet gave me a hard on."

I would have laughed if I wasn't about to be target practice for a bunch of vultures. They were probably congregating outside right now, cackling with glee while plotting my destruction. The damn press loved to prey on the fallen. My chest grew tight, and I struggled to draw in my next breath. Christ, I was having a panic attack.

"I can't deal with this right now," I gasped.

"It's okay. Slow and deep." Chase guided me through a series of inhales and exhales worthy of a Lamaze coach. Much better than Brenda's useless swami technique.

"No hanky-panky," Nicki said as she walked into the office. "Plenty of time for that later." Chase released me and stepped back, allowing Nicki to come in for a hug. Relief had me tightly returning her embrace. After agreeing to this insanity, I had embarked on phase two of my apology tour which meant coming clean to Nicki. Though nerve-wracking, I couldn't reward her friendship by letting her learn about me from a press conference.

I'd love to say she forgave me immediately but instead, she needed time to process her feelings of anger and betrayal. I felt terrible at seeing her so dejected—even her curls were deflated—but mentally, I understood. Emotionally, I worried I'd lost her. Thankfully, her loyalty and compassion persuaded her to grant me a pardon. I knew we were okay when she joked about a reward for finding me.

She took in the expression on my face. "It's okay, Jas. Go out there and own your past. The hell with what everyone else thinks. We know who you are."

"What she said," Chase agreed.

"And what if you're wrong?" I asked them both. "What if this turns into a bloodbath with pitchforks and torches and wild mobs calling for my head?"

"While I applaud your theatrics, you're disseminating information, not going on trial for witchcraft," Chase said.

"But—"

Chase grabbed my shoulders. "If it goes south, choose your favorite island and we'll go into exile together."

"Make it somewhere tropical and I'm in," Nicki added.

"Done," Chase said.

I'm glad they found it easy to joke while I was teetering on the verge of a breakdown.

A knock on the door preceded a short blonde woman entering the room. "Sorry to interrupt. I'm Judy. I'm here to do Miss

Monroe's makeup." She carried a portable mirror and a caddy filled with brushes, bottles, and gadgets that looked like instruments of torture. She tsked at me. "We'd best get started. You're white as a sheet."

Nicki crossed her arms. "Really, Jas? You didn't think I could make you look good?"

"Sorry," I shrugged. "She came with the publicist and you're here for moral support. I didn't want to put you to work."

"I can do both," she scoffed and stormed out of the room, possibly more offended at my makeup artist choice than my lies.

"I need to take care of a few things before it starts," Chase said, peering into my face. "Will you be okay here?"

"I'm fine. I have Judy." I looked down at the tiny lady but she ignored me. Judy was all business.

He eyed the door as if debating whether I'd be here when he returned then must have deemed me trustworthy because he departed, leaving me alone with my destructive thoughts... and Judy.

She worked efficiently yet seemed to take forever. Especially when she told me we were going for the natural look. Huh? How could 'natural' mean slathering my face with a boatload of crap? But I stayed silent, makeup being the least of my concerns today.

Judy was finishing up when Nicki came barreling in, her curls nearly as frantic as her expression. She yanked me from the chair, earning a disapproving cluck from Judy.

Wow. She really was upset about not doing my makeup.

"You have to see this." Nicki searched the couch then moved on to the table and chairs. "Where's the damn remote?"

I frowned. The last time Nicki sounded this panicked, an uptown chef had absconded with her soufflé recipe.

I went to Chase's desk to help search and found the remote in a drawer along with some pens, a notepad, and a familiar small slip of paper with red writing. I picked it up.

Your true love may be right in front of you.

My eyes widened. The fortune from our first Chinese food dinner at my apartment. Wow! Sentimental Dangerous? Who would have guessed? The man continued to surprise me. I placed it back where I found it.

Nicki startled me by yanking the remote from my hand. She turned on the TV to a local news channel. I winced. That would be me up there soon.

A brunette news anchor sat at her desk, a smiling picture of Anthony behind her. They flashed to a video of him leaving the courthouse on one of the best days of my life—the day he was found guilty. "In an unexpected twist," she spoke in a nasally tone, "former convicted embezzler, Anthony Brooks, was found dead in a lower east side alley. Police have yet to release details, but suspect foul play. Brooks was convicted of twelve counts of..."

I plopped down, nearly missing the couch. My father—or the closest thing to one—was dead. Not just dead. Murdered.

"I can take it from here," Nicki spoke to Judy, who looked eager to leave. "Jas, are you okay?"

Yes. And that's what worried me. A man had lost his life and I felt... no, it was what I didn't feel that put me on the fast-track to hell. No remorse, no sympathy, no regret. Just relief and a twinge of satisfaction. Was it wrong to wish the perpetrator a medal for ridding the world of a blight on humanity? Like a knight in shining—

I stopped. *My* knight in shining armor? Could Chase have done this? Maybe he assumed I would bail on the press conference.

"In other breaking news," the newscaster continued, "Jerry and Betty Potts, owners of the national pet supply chain, Pettery Barn, were arrested for smuggling illegal gemstones in their animal collars…"

Nicki turned off the TV.

As gallant as it sounded for a man to avenge his love, this wasn't some duel in a medieval romance novel. If caught, it meant serious consequences. All because I had been selfish and dragged him into my poisonous world.

I located my bag on the floor, pulled out my laptop, and returned to the couch.

"Jas, talk to me," Nicki said. "This is a good thing, right?"

Oops. I forgot about Nicki. "Yes. Everything's good. I just want to learn as much as I can about what happened."

She continued to eye me. "Why?"

I noted the suspicion on her face. "Geez, Nicki. I may be a criminal, but murder is not part of my repertoire."

"No one would fault you."

"I would."

"Okay, what can I do?"

"Find Chase." I needed to know if he was responsible. She nodded and left the room.

I hacked into the police records and cursed at the flimsy information. A storeowner, while taking out the trash in the alley behind his shop, discovered Anthony propped against a dumpster posed like a creepy marionette puppet. Cause of death… the huge slit in his throat. From the scarce tangible evidence and lack of blood, the murder had taken place elsewhere. Most likely a professional hit.

With Chase's means, he could arrange it as easy as ordering Chinese food.

I'll have the sweet and sour pork, mu shu chicken, and a decapitation. Oh, and don't forget the soy sauce.

I thought back to his desk. Was there anything there I might have missed that could help? Should I go back and look?

Seriously? Like a hitman business card? For a solid whacking, call Jimmy at 555-BANG.

I cursed. Sometimes my mind pissed me off with its smart-ass tendencies.

Chase entered a few minutes later.

"Where's Nicki?" I looked behind him.

"She's talking to one of the reporters of a morning show that hosts a cooking segment she's obsessed with. I think she has a shot. I told her we have this under control." He eyed me carefully. "Do we?"

"We will once I make sure nothing can lead back to you. So far, the police have little to go on."

His brows hiked up. "Are you insinuating I had something to do with it?"

"You said you'd do whatever it takes to keep me safe and..." I trailed off as he started to laugh.

"This isn't funny," I lectured him. "No matter how reprehensible the victim."

He laughed harder.

"Chase, there could be dire consequences. We have to—"

"I thought it was you," he said.

"What?"

"I thought you got cold feet and decided to go with the cartel solution or maybe a dark web hitman." The smile remained on his face. "I wouldn't know the first thing about something like this, but you... You can be kind of scary."

"Um, thank you?"

"He probably crossed the wrong people." Chase waved it off. "He had it coming. You realize what this means, right?"

"That we don't know what happened to him."

"And?" Chase waited patiently.

My mouth fell open as it sunk in. With Anthony dead, my mother gone, and Helena neutralized, I was... I hesitated to use the word lest I jinx it. "Am I...?"

"Free," Chase said with a grin. "To live your life any way you see fit as long as it's with me." He leaned down for a quick kiss. "Which means no press conference required. Stay here while I get rid of them. They're more eager to start reporting on Anthony anyway."

"Free," I repeated. I had been dreaming of this day my entire life. When the weight of my family lifted, and I no longer lived in terror. It was finally here. I closed my eyes and waited for the joy to hit me.

But it didn't come.

I frowned. What was happening? I was ready to resume my life now.

You mean the fake life you've trapped yourself in?

And suddenly, I didn't feel very free.

Because I wasn't living a life but more like a series of detours. Hiding and ducking for cover, believing the further I ran, the safer it made me. Hell, I'd been running for so long, I could have been a spokeswoman for Nike, but for all my efforts, it was like trying to stay one step ahead of a fire. No matter how fast or how far, the flames always loomed a hair's breadth behind, breathing down my neck, and licking at my heels.

I felt the heat even now, threatening to engulf me.

Along with an overwhelming sense of fatigue.

I was so damn tired. Tired of trying to control everything. Of denying who I was. Pretending to be something else. And above all, I was tired of pushing away a piece of me that mattered.

Then stop running!

The unexpected voice shocked me and my first reaction was to ignore it.

But the weariness in my bones listened.

Just. Let. Go.

I pushed past the resistance to envision what would happen if for the first time in my life, I stood perfectly still. Would the flames swallow me whole? Could I survive them? The strongest steel is forged in fire, but first, you had to make it out the other side. Did I have what it takes to get through?

"Wait," I called out. "Can you give me a minute?"

Chase paused. "You're running the show. Tell me what you want."

I wish I knew.

Because whatever I was doing had stopped working a long time ago.

Living as Jasmine Monroe had never alleviated my burden, it had only renamed it, while forfeiting the only authentic part of myself that existed. Disassociating from Lily had launched me into an endless spiral of lies and shame, and now that I had acknowledged her, how could I have a shot at a solid future without including her? Until I was whole, I knew I'd never be free.

I rose to my feet and joined him. "If I'm going to move on, I need to do it as me. The real me. No more hiding. No more running." I couldn't believe what I was saying, but I owed it to myself and to the little girl I'd tossed aside. She deserved a shot at a better life. We both did.

"Are you sure?" he asked. "Because if you can't do this, it's okay. I've got your back either way."

I reached up to stroke his cheek. My Dangerous Knight in Shining Armor. The man I feared from the beginning as a threat to everything I held onto had turned out to be just that. He threatened the darkness in me, the past that held me hostage, and the way of life that prevented me from living. By challenging it all, he pulled me out of the shadows and introduced me to a life filled with more than just survival, but with light and love. Go figure. The bad boy I'd been drawn to turned out to be Mister Right all along.

Maybe I wasn't as broken as I thought.

Which meant I could do this. I nodded and gripped his hand.

"Hey." Chase raised my face to look at him again. "I'm here. If anyone tries anything, I'll save you."

I smiled at him and took a step forward. "You already did."

EPILOGUE

Helena pushed open the bedroom window and inhaled the damp, salty night air before letting her robe fall to the floor. Naked, she perched on the edge of her bed and opened a heavy bottle of moisturizer that glistened like water on the beach. Following her nightly routine, the thick perfumed lotion glided across her skin, leaving a shimmer from the tiny flecks of gold infused in the mixture. It was shipped from Europe where their skin care regime far exceeded our inferior products. Rumor had it, English royalty used the same product.

Helena closed the lid and gazed down at her body. She prided herself on keeping in perfect shape. That meant a sparse diet, grueling workouts, and no expense spared on beautification products. So far, she was blessed enough to avoid surgical enhancements.

Always keep the assets preserved. She lived by that motto. If something happened to Phil and she found herself destitute, she and her tight ass would attract another wealthy man in no time.

Pleased with her evaluation, Helena placed her arms in a silk white nightgown and let the fabric cascade down her like a snowy shower. She stretched out on the royal blue duvet and sighed. The empty space beside her indicated Phil had found a low-life floozy willing to spread her legs for a couple of watered-down drinks. Fine by her. The more ass her vapid jackass of a husband scored, the less she had to provide. When he hit a dry patch, Helena was generous enough to service him though she preferred it when other women attended to her husband's sexual proclivities.

A small price to pay for her gold card and bank account. Especially in comparison to what she was accustomed to doing for money.

Money made everything better.

Maybe she would call Gabby tomorrow for a shopping spree. Gabby could afford it since she'd landed a rich old geezer who was too sexually enthralled to demand a prenuptial agreement. Before he'd refilled his first Viagra bottle, Gabby had divorced him and become a wealthy, independent woman. Good for her.

Helena picked up the remote and flicked on the television. She instantly regretted it when the image appeared. With a curse, she launched her jar of cream at the sixty-inch screen. It cracked against the frame, spattering white goop across the picture, but the image of Lily's damn press conference remained. This was a mild reaction compared to the first time it aired.

Poor Lily Brooks. That's what everyone was saying. She ran away from an abusive home to escape the physical violence at the hands of her notorious and alcoholic father who was subsequently sentenced to prison.

As a child, out on the streets with nothing but sheer will and determination, she had struggled to survive. Filled with shame regarding her origins and fear that her father would find her, she realized she'd never have a clean start without removing the stain associated with her family, thus she changed her name to Jasmine Monroe. Armed with a second chance, she worked diligently to put herself through school and persevered by rising above her tragic circumstances to make something of herself.

What a fucking joke. Helena wanted nothing more than to expose that calculating bitch for what she really was.

The press conference droned on with those idiots exalting Lily's will and fortitude. But that wasn't the worst part. Billionaire Chase Hale hired her to work on one of his most famous releases, and like some fucking fairy tale, the infamous playboy fell for our beautiful heroine. After a lifetime of knowing nothing but hatred and fear, he showed her what it felt to be loved.

What a crock.

And that still wasn't the worst part. That came when Chase shocked the world by dropping to one knee in the middle of the press conference and proposing to her with the biggest goddamn diamond Helena had ever seen. The entire press corps went ape-shit. They were painting it as the Cinderella story of the decade. Bigger than the royal couple.

It didn't help that Rita immediately went out to buy that sweet, brave Jasmine an engagement present. The only small consolation was that she assumed Helena had been protecting Jasmine the whole time. Idiot. But nobody seemed to care about Helena. Not one reporter had come around. Helena was torn between being pissed off and relieved. The stress from having to say nice things about Lily would probably cause wrinkles.

Helena wanted to punch something… preferably Lily's face. Lily didn't deserve Chase Hale or his money. There was no way he wanted someone as annoying as her. That manipulative hack was probably blackmailing him with her stupid super-computer skills. As soon as he figured a way out, he'd dump her whiny ass.

Until then, she was going to be richer than Helena.

Helena made a mental note to demand a bigger diamond.

A picture of the happy couple flashed on the screen and she stubbed her finger attacking the off button. They could all rot in hell.

So what if that bitch got slapped around as a kid. Helena may have been the recipient of preferential treatment, but she'd earned it. It wasn't her fault Lily was too dumb to figure that out. Helena understood at a young age that privilege came with a price and as long as you had something to barter, you held the power.

Lily had no concept what real scars felt like.

It always started with a soft knock on the door, somewhere between his first few drinks and passing out. "How's Daddy's little angel?" he'd slur as he stumbled into her room. "You remind me so much of your mother." The words came as he lowered himself on her bed, sometimes louder depending on the amount of whiskey in his system. Helena would close her eyes and pretend he was the captain of the football team or one of the college boys she fooled around with.

It was a simple business arrangement, like her marriage with Phil.

But her recurring nightmares said otherwise. Every night since his temporary release, she'd woken in a sweat, memories pushed to the forefront of her mind. Pills, alcohol, and shopping provided a temporary numbness but no lasting peace. There was only one way to stop the nightmares for good.

Money was truly a beautiful possession capable of removing all obstacles. Even if it meant having the obstacle's throat slit like an animal and dumped in a back alley. The day she received confirmation preceded the first restful night of sleep she'd had since her mother left.

Who said money couldn't buy happiness?

Helena turned off the bedside lamp, slid beneath the covers, and drifted off into a dreamless slumber.

THE END

ACKNOWLEDGMENTS

As MBD was my first book, it took a village. Thank you to my editor, John Hudspith, for guiding a first-time author through the terror of writing her first book. Not only did you polish and tighten my work into a much improved and shiny version, but you taught me much about writing along the way. Thank you, John, for your patience and mentoring.

To Mary, thank you for showing me how important it was to pursue this project. Cindy, thank you for your encouragement. And Maria, one of the first to read the earlier draft, your enthusiasm both surprised and encouraged me to keep going.

Sharon and Barbara, my first beta-readers, you did an amazing job! Your feedback was insightful and relevant, and I appreciate you taking the time to help. I look forward to sending you more books in the future.

To Rosy and Marissa, who are always there for me no matter what crazy idea I come up with. Your unwavering support has given me the confidence to put myself out there and reach for my dream of being an author. I am lucky to have people who have so much faith in me. And Marissa, thank you for reading my novel when I know how much you hate reading in general. Even when I gave you a reprieve, you powered through. That is love...

To the rest of my family, thank you for all the dysfunction and drama. A fucked-up family makes for one hell of a book!

ABOUT THE AUTHOR

High Tech Heat!
Software analyst by day and author by night.

After reaching her fill of logic and data throughout her work life, Laila desperately needed a creative outlet to express her emotional and whimsical (and possibly a little bit crazy) side. And so... an author was born.

She enjoys writing romance novels filled with suspense, heart, wit, spice, and a plot twist or two. Her heroines are intelligent, strong, sarcastic, and perhaps a bit quirky. They may start off misguided, but they always mean well. Of course, the men are hot as hell and worthy of a steamy sex scene or two (or three, or four...) to showcase their talents.

As someone who devours all genres of books, Laila has a soft spot for love and promises her readers a happily ever after.

What about her real life? She lives in the desert where it's almost as hot as the men she likes to write about. She loves her dogs, movies, watching hockey, and someday, she aspires to kick her Cheetos addiction.

Thank you for reading Laila's debut novel. If you enjoyed her book, a hug in the form of a review is greatly appreciated.

Please sign up for my newsletter to find out more at:
http://www.lailaamlani.com/newsletter

www.ingramcontent.com/pod-product-compliance
Lightning Source LLC
Chambersburg PA
CBHW030546260626
47157CB00006B/2213

* 9 7 9 8 9 8 5 3 2 3 3 0 6 *